GRAVEYARD

DARK NEBULA
BOOK 5

SEAN WILLSON

WELCOME TO DARK NEBULA

Thank you for buying this book!

If you're interested in a free novella entitled **Dark Nebula: Contact**, hearing more about the series, seeing new cover art as it's released, or getting exclusive access to sales as they happen, then you can subscribe to my newsletter online at:

seanwillson.com/subscribe

You can also drop me an email at:

author@seanwillson.com

I always love hearing from my readers.

DARK NEBULA SERIES
Novella: Contact (FREE)
Book 1: Isolation
Book 2: Discovery
Book 3: Generations
Book 4: Beacon
Book 5: Graveyard (This book)
Book 6: Nursery

CONTENTS

1

ABIGAIL OLIVAW
PROTO DARK NEBULA, POCKET ONE

There was nothing but infinite darkness. Seemingly endless undulating clouds of Dark Nebula surrounded the Phoenix as far as the eye could see. It encircled the home star of the Ursis, another alien race trialed and imprisoned by the Galactic Alliance just over half a century prior. Though, based on the lack of evidence they'd found thus far, it was impossible to tell if the aliens were still around.

Abigail reached up and tapped her ear, activating her retinal comm. She subvocalized a command to connect with the bridge. "Please share the details of our scans with Harold and Shauna."

"Are you certain, Captain?" Ibu asked. The even keeled voice of the Nanil lacked all inflection. "We haven't exhausted all of our options yet. We can still—"

She slammed her palm against the table in her quarters. "Share it!"

There was a pause before Ibu replied. "Very well. Let it be known I advised you against it. If you continue to use your A.I. as a crutch, you'll never—"

Reaching up, she tapped her ear and cut the comm. She knew what her Nanil friend was about to say, but that didn't mean she wanted to hear it. The truth often hurts more than the lies we tell ourselves. And when you've been lying for decades, the truth can be unbearable.

The fact of the matter was, she'd grown completely code-pendent on Harold over the years. So much so that she rarely had a thought she didn't share with him. He analyzed her every movement, tick, or gesture. He manipulated her entire existence to control her mood. To keep her moving forward day to day and executing the Olivaw plan. She'd become his experiment. His guinea pig to manipulate the family.

Well, she was done with that. The days of him controlling her were long gone. She hadn't given him access to her body mod or the environment within the ship since leaving Zeta Lupi. But he could still be useful. He was a tool, and one of their greatest assets in this war against the Galactic Alliance. Both he and Shauna housed the collective knowledge of humanity and every iota of information their family had accrued since discovering the first contact probe over two centuries earlier.

She sighed and gestured at the wall screen. The map they'd built of the Nebula over the past few weeks appeared in all its three-dimensional glory. They'd explored the entire external structure encircling the Proto Dark Nebula and meticulously planned their initial jump inside, mimicking exactly how Zachary and Bradley had done it at Lupus.

It just so happened that they hit a snag after their first transition. They'd survived the gate sequence, but the former occupants of this particular star system were missing. All that remained of the star and the planets within the system was cosmic dust.

As she superimposed the results from their last set of probes, the innermost reaches of this system became clear. Unlike in Lupus, this star didn't have a tunnel connecting it to its neighbor. Instead, it was sealed in like a tomb. Without a means to bridge to neighboring stars, the cataclysmic Éntono

Fos should've been isolated. What made things confusing, however, was that if the star had indeed gone nova, there should be remnants left behind. But there wasn't.

Her retinal comm vibrated, pulling her out of her fog of concentration. The familiar tug of the nanotechnology made human life simpler and more connected, but as Ibu had warned them before they departed Zeta Lupi, they would feel naked without it. The constant connective conscious state, was both relaxing and addictive at the same time.

She tapped her ear, establishing the comm with Ibu. "Go ahead."

"Sir, Shauna wishes an audience. She claims to have found something."

"Of course she did." She groaned and leaned back in her chair. "Very well. Bring her capsule in here, along with the rest of the crew. Let's see what my mother discovered."

ABIGAIL CROSSED her arms and watched as Shauna's robotic form entered the room and paced in front of the wall screen. This was the first time in weeks they'd let either of the A.I. out of their firewalled homes in their computer cores.

She knew it was excruciating from what Zachary had told her about their mother's recorded consciousness. Apparently, Shauna preferred seeing and being in the same room with people over living a purely virtual existence, which was the exact opposite of Harold.

Maybe it was the sheer number of years he'd spent cooped up in a computer before a decent physical presence was feasible to occupy without lag. Either way, Shauna had refused to share her findings with anyone until she was allowed to stretch her legs. If an A.I. could act like a prima donna, she was doing it.

"Alright, you've got us here," Abigail began, "what have

you discovered? We don't exactly have infinite time on our hands. You know, with the fate of humanity teetering on extinction and all." She gestured at the blank wall screen.

Shauna adjusted her gaze from the cadre of soldiers filed into the back and focused on Abigail. "First, you have to agree to let me out of that cell. I can't—"

She raised her hand, silencing her mother. "Now's not the time for speeches or demands by you or Harold. You're a member of this team, and you'll either perform your duties or you'll be disconnected."

"Very well." Shauna turned in place, her robotic shape pivoting in an unnatural way. Not at all like a human, but far more efficient. She made her way toward the exit.

Ibu reached out. "Where are you going?"

Shauna sighed. "Back to my prison cell."

"Oh, for frak's sake," Pierce said. "Damn robots don't know—"

Shauna shot across the space between the exit and Pierce in a flash. She transformed her hand from familiar human fingers into a welding arc and brought it up to the soldier's neck. Her other hand slid behind Pierce's back, making it impossible for her to escape. "Call me a robot again, and you'll meet my friend sparky."

Pierce drew in a breath and the soldiers at her side sprang forward toward Shauna until she reached out her arm, waving them to stand down.

"Now," Shauna began, "I believe you owe me an apology, young lady."

"You're kidding me, right?" Pierce narrowed her gaze on the robot's human like eyes. "Aren't there laws against this?"

"There should be." Minula hadn't said a word or flinched a centimeter during the entire episode. "I can't imagine she'd hurt you."

"Shall we test it?" Shauna powered up her welding attachment and the blue glow of the arc welder sprang to life. The skin on Pierce's neck started to turn red and the woman winced.

"What the hell are you doing?" Abigail slowly stepped up beside Shauna. "I thought you were on our side."

"And I thought you gave a shit."

No one, least of all her, expected to walk into this Nebula and hit a dead end. To describe the tension as high would be an understatement. It wasn't even a repeat of Lupus; it was worse. They'd arrived to nothing.

"I do give a shit." Abigail swallowed hard. "But tell me what good will come of this." She waved at the torch and the hairs on the back of her hand singed from thirty centimeters away. The heat Pierce must be experiencing was insane.

"It got you and these knuckle draggers to notice me, didn't it?" Shauna cut the welder and shoved Pierce upright. She then turned and headed toward the exit, pausing at the threshold. "I meant what I said. You owe me an apology. Both of you. Next time you're expecting one of us A.I...." her voice cracked, "to save your life, well, we might just have a malfunction."

She continued forward and stepped into the charging cubby on the opposite side of the hall before her robotic form powered down.

"She's put herself back inside the containment unit," Ibu said.

"We've got to fraking lock those things up for good," Kamal said. He and his soldiers were the furthest from Pierce, but were no less pissed at the robot's outburst.

Minula spun around to face the others. "We'll do whatever the hell our captain tells us to do. Is that understood?"

Abigail knew she was trying to defuse the situation by applying chain of command pressures, but it wasn't helping. Tempers were already too high, and she was making matters worse.

"Yessir!" Kamal came to attention and saluted her. His and Pierce's troops did, as well.

She tilted her head. Then again, she'd been wrong in the past.

"Moet!" Minula nodded toward the soldier.

"Sir?"

"Take Pierce to medical and get that neck checked out."

"Yessir." Moet eased up beside her partner in crime and helped her forward. The skin on her neck was deep red with hints of black around the still forming blisters.

"The rest of you, go burn off some steam in the sims." Minula gestured over her shoulder. "I want two assaults and a hostage simulation performed by seventeen-hundred hours."

Groans escaped from a few of the soldiers until Kamal shot them a glare and then returned his attention back to Minula. "Yessir." He nodded and strode away.

Abigail watched them leave, still unsure how to reset the situation. They were no closer to knowing their next step than they were before gathering together.

"That was fun," Cynthia said. "What's next, boss?"

Her brother's girlfriend hadn't spoken since entering the room. In fact, she rarely talked. Before they left Zeta Lupi, everyone had played up how strong-willed the woman was, but thus far Abigail hadn't seen it. There were no sparks. She assumed the woman simply missed Bradley, and that made two of them.

"There's only one thing to do." Abigail straightened her outfit and stepped over to the chair near the wall, pausing before she sat down. "Unless one of you found something to move us forward, I need to go make amends." She eyed the others, stopping at Ibu.

"No, sir. Nothing." Ibu shuffled their feet. "The star system is empty."

The others shook their heads.

"Alrighty then." Abigail sat down in the chair and leaned her head back. She used to love hanging out in virtual worlds as a kid, but the older she got, the more she hated it. The stress of running the family meant there wasn't exactly spare time to screw around and play games anymore.

She closed her eyes and subvocalized the command to connect her avatar to Shauna's physical containment unit.

THE CONFINES of the galley disappeared, transporting Abigail into a world she'd never seen before. It was fantastical. The simulated reality reminded her of being thrown into a fairytale.

Along the horizon, the usual blue or pinkish hues of Earth were replaced with purple skies and green clouds. It wasn't enough color to change the rest of the lighting, but you'd think it would. Her skin maintained its normal beige hue, not at all like that purply dwarf from her favorite kid's movie whose name escaped her. It was about a girl who visited a chocolate factory.

Gazing out over the sea of strange multicolored bulbous plants, she kicked herself. Harold would know what she was thinking of, but alas, he wasn't connected to her retinal comm any longer. She'd have to get used to storing memories in regular old search matrices like everyone else.

A breeze wafted across her back. An unfamiliar experience in virtual reality, unless you were fully immersed. For the right amount of credits on Earth, you could immerse yourself with a suit of nanites that would replicate everything from smells to cuts on the skin. It was expensive, but introverts did crazy shit to reproduce reality in a virtual world.

When she spun around, she took a step backward. She hadn't realized it, but she'd entered this alien world on the edge of a cliff. One wrong move, and she'd have a rough reset. Even knowing it wasn't real didn't make virtual death any less jarring.

As pretty as this was, she needed to get on task. "I don't have time to mess around. Can you please come to me?"

The response was silence, which was maddening because she knew Shauna could hear her. This was her world. She had access to everything that happened here.

"So you're going to make me apologize to a cliff. Is that how this is gonna work?"

She looked left and right, but still, there was nothing.

"Alrighty then. I'm sorry! I'm a terrible daughter!" Her voice boomed and echoed off the orange and gray rock faces below.

"I'm sorry! I'm a terrible daughter!"

"I'm sorry! I'm a terrible daughter!"

The audio and visual effect of her voice were bizarre. After each echo of her self-critique, a small flock of butterfly looking birds flapped out of the green and yellow clumps of plants sprinkled down the cliff face. At least they looked like butterflies. But with wingspans of nearly a meter, she didn't expect they were.

When her apology finally lowered to a whisper of echoes in the distance, an unexpected reply came from over her shoulder.

"Apology accepted. And yes, you are," Shauna said.

Abigail jumped forward, not expecting her mother to be standing directly behind her. Fortunately for her, Shauna didn't allow her to fall. She placed an invisible catwalk in front of her, which was in itself surreal, floating beyond the edge of the cliff.

She stared down at her feet and watched the stones she'd stirred up bounce down the rocky face until vertigo hit. Steep places were never her thing, neither in games nor virtual reality. Especially as she aged. She looked up and took a deep breath before stepping backward onto solid ground.

Only then did she notice Shauna's human form. It was the first time she'd ever seen her as her mother because, up to that moment, she'd taken a different shape.

While her emerald green eyes were the same, Shauna's other hairdos and facial features were replaced with Marie's. Her mother's jet black shoulder-length bob, caramel colored skin, dramatic eyebrows, and pouty lips. They were her trademark brand. She could both stare you down and make you cry at the same time.

"I wasn't certain you were ready to see me like this." Shauna's arms were crossed, and her gaze was locked on Abigail. She had that stern expression she used when she was pissed or when you'd pushed her too far. "But in the end, if you're going to lock me away like a prisoner, then I don't care how you feel."

"I see you." Abigail nodded and stepped past the woman. She was not her mother. She was simply a collection of memories. Nothing more. "I know what you're doing."

Shauna snickered. "Oh, really. What's that, dear?"

She spun around and froze. Shauna had bent down and was petting a green frog on the ground. "I... well, I don't know why you're playing with a frog. But this place..." She gestured around the virtual world and then pointed at her. "And you making yourself look like... like..."

"Marie?"

She bit her lip.

Shauna stood up and placed the frog on her shoulder. "This place, as you call it. You have no idea what it is, so don't even try. You wouldn't have the faintest damn clue what it's about because you've never tried to get to know me. This form you pointed at is my body... and it's been mine for over seventy-nine years. I, of all people, have a right to it. So, no, I'm sorry, but you don't know shit!"

She opened her mouth, but the words didn't come. There wasn't much for her to refute. She was right. She didn't know

Shauna. And while she thought she knew what was going on, she hadn't sat down and got to know her since she'd revealed herself. Hell, had she not insisted on coming, she would have been perfectly fine with only Harold in containment.

"So, we've established you're a terrible daughter, and you don't know shit. Was there anything else you needed?" Shauna reached up and rubbed the frog's neck, and it let out a loud ribbit.

She chuckled and pointed at the frog. "That seems a bit out of place here, doesn't it?"

Shauna gently picked the frog off her shoulder and set it on the ground. "I stole it from Harold's simulation a few decades ago. He created a bunch of them after he found out how much Zachary loved them. You know that man would do anything for family, right? You should see what animals he has in his world for you and Bradley. It's a regular zoo in that place from all the Olivaws he's looked after."

It'd been years since she'd visited Harold's virtual estate. She used to spend hours in there as a kid, back when they were cooped up at the Sol Wheel. She always wondered why he had so many animals. It just never occurred to her to ask. Suddenly, it dawned on her how much she didn't know about either of her A.I. companions. Her mother never talked about her time before returning to her father, back when she had Lync. And Harold rarely mentioned much about his past, either.

She shook her head. "The Nebula, Shauna. I need to know what you found out about the Nebula."

Shauna clasped her hands behind her back and turned to stare out over the cliff. The binary twin suns were setting in the distance, and the sky was transforming into a literal rainbow of colors. Yellows, reds, blues, and greens painted the layers of clouds framing the setting suns.

"I need access to my robot form once you're awake." She glanced over her shoulder and their gazes locked. "I'm not asking for special treatment, and I realize you might not trust me yet. I just need to be out of this..." She gestured around the simulation. "Jail cell. I need to be in the world of the living."

Abigail could relate to the feeling of being imprisoned. After spending too many weeks in the hospital at Epsilon Eridani and then being coddled in Zeta Lupi, she needed to be productive. She wanted to help the war. This mission was that for her.

"Fine." She pointed at Shauna. "But only if you have a keeper, and it's not always gonna be me."

"Done!" Shauna hopped up and down and flipped around before snapping her finger. "There. I shared my findings with your team. Ibu is looking at the details now. I figured the soldiers didn't need to see it, so..." Her voice trailed off.

She shook her head. "That's a bridge you're gonna have to rebuild. You know that, right?"

Shauna shrugged. "Maybe you're right, but we'll figure that out later. Sometimes the only way to get the respect of jarheads is by force."

Goosebumps covered her arms. It was like she was hearing the words of her father. He'd told her the same thing before, during one of his regular boring training sessions on how to be a good leader.

"Can you tell me what you found?" She bent down and ran her hand over the leaves on the yellow bulbous plants. As her fingers passed over the smooth surface, it changed both color and shape, transforming into an arrangement of deep orange spikes. Almost like a defensive mechanism.

Shauna gestured, and a three-dimensional image of the Nebula appeared between them. "The shape of the nebulosity was, for the most part, consistent. Except for one side. If you run some simulations building on how the Nebulas behaved in Lupus and Epsilon Eridani, you'd notice something interesting. The part that's irregular isn't only narrower, it's showing signs of having previously been a connected segment. There must be a pocket on the other side."

She reached out and flipped the simulation over and zoomed around the Nebula. The irregular side was only visible at certain angles, which explained why they missed it. While it didn't explain the lack of a star in this pocket, something was better than nothing.

Abigail smiled. "Thank you."

"You're welcome. And, Abigail?" Shauna took a step toward her.

"Yes."

Reaching up, she set a hand on Abigail's shoulder. Her facial features softened, and her harsh eyebrow lines melted away, just like Marie's used to do when she got serious. "I'm truly sorry I had to resort to what I did out there. It won't happen again. Honest. I'll come to you first next time. The last thing I want to do is undermine you in front of your crew."

"I appreciate that." Abigail stared into her eyes. The details of her cornea and facial features were astonishing. It was almost like she was looking at her mom.

"You should go." Shauna shooed with her hand. "I'm sure they need your counsel on how to proceed."

She didn't say a word. She merely nodded and reached up to tap her ear.

The simulation fell away in a flash and was replaced with the harsh overhead lights of the galley. Returning to reality was often a letdown after leaving virtual worlds. Their always vibrant feel was what made them such an addiction to so many humans.

She subvocalized a command to open a comm to the others. "Talk to me about our next steps."

"YOU'RE FRAKING KIDDING ME." Abigail collapsed into her chair on the bridge and groaned.

"No, sir." Minula spun around to face her. "At first glance, this system appears to be a mirror of the last one. We've dispatched probes to do deeper scans."

She rubbed her forehead, fighting the siren song of sleep. She really needed to answer the call soon, or she'd end up crashing for half a day. "Any chance our artificial companions have any more ideas?"

"Not yet," Ibu said. "I'm running some simulations like Shauna did last time, but we'll need those deeper scans before they'll tell us much."

A yawn escaped, and she reached up to cover her mouth. "Let me know the moment you find anything. I'm gonna grab some Zs." She pushed up and out of her chair and brushed her hand against Minula's shoulder before working her way aft.

2

———

IBU

PROTO DARK NEBULA, POCKET TWO

The bridge was quiet with the human crew still sleeping. It was Ibu's most productive time. When Abigail turned into her quarters last night, it resulted in a cascade of her peers doing the same. Humans were a curious lot. On one hand, they held a staunch belief they were independent, yet their actions and behaviors mimicked that of a pack. Every day they worked with them, they learned something new about the species' ever-changing cultural norms.

An alert chimed overhead, and Ibu reached out to bring up the source on the wall screen. It was a set of results from one of the forward probes they sent into the second pocket.

The Nebula's surface map and the lack of undulations added to the mystery of their mission. The absence of movement meant there wasn't a gram of mass detected in the system. It was as if the Nebula had consumed both stars. And who knew, maybe it had. Maybe this Nebula was able to move freely in space and absorb nearby mass. Just because no one had seen it happen, doesn't mean it couldn't.

In Lupus, the researches on Henosi believed the bynardral material was sentient life and that the Beacons of Therion were used to manipulate it. That could explain the stars being absorbed. Perhaps a Beacon passed by, and it had unintentional side effects inside the sealed Nebula. Or perhaps the bynardrals needed sustenance and had the ability to seek out energy sources.

While the mental tangent was interesting, without evidence, it was simply another dead end, like countless others before it. They needed to focus on finding their next jump.

When they switched the display back to the data set they'd been building, there was a second unread alert waiting for them. It must've come in at the same time as the last payload, and they'd missed it. One of the redundant deep scan probes they sent into the first Nebula pocket had found something.

They shot up with a start and walked closer to the wall display. In the middle of the screen was what appeared to be a tiny micro-satellite or relay. It wasn't any larger than ten centimeters across, and its exterior had irregular convex indentations carved throughout. Almost like it was purposely built or somehow adaptable.

Their hearts fluttered when they overlaid the findings on a map of the Nebula. The relay was situated close to the innermost wall of the nebulosity, and that could mean only one thing. If there was a relay there, then another one had to be situated on the far side to communicate with.

Ibu debated on waking the others, but if their recollections were on point, then right about now the humans would be deep in their REM sleep. Last night, Minula had implied that they were all better off with Abigail catching up on her rest. Waking any of them could lead to heightened conflict, and the last thing they needed was another day filled with emotional outbursts.

It was probably best to let them sleep until after they sent out another probe, anyhow. Safer, too. Besides, it'd take an hour or so to get it prepped for launch. This one would need to perform a much more detailed scan of the device and deploy some nanites for a physical analysis. Perhaps they could interface with it.

Their mind cascaded in incalculable directions, and the fractal of options took shape in their mind's eye. The potential of the discovery was both inspiring and daunting. With all the excitement, they could feel their pulse quickening. They had to keep their emotions under control before their body morphed and overtook logical thought.

Being part human meant they were constantly adapting to their overpowering emotions, but with their progenitor training on Doda cut short, they never learned to fully manage it. And last they checked, being surrounded by humans wasn't helping. They weren't exactly known as an emotionally predictable species.

The easiest and funnest trick they used to thwart passion from overtaking them was to tackle a problem head on and dissect it into its component parts. Listing out the tasks and minute details of a solution could extinguish nearly any emotional fire. Even thinking about it brought on waves of relaxation.

Ibu gestured toward the screen and opened a checklist. They began dictating the step-by-step work necessary to inspect and interface with the alien device. Everything they needed to do before they could send out a second probe.

Once the list was complete, they revised it one final time. Short of capturing the probe itself, this new analysis should answer their questions. When they hit go, the robots in the bowels of the ship sprang to life. They started making the necessary changes to the probe, loading and unloading diagnostic devices, and filling the empty nanite reservoirs.

A few minutes later, one of the items on their list went red. It needed someone to make a physical adjustment on the probe that the onboard expert system couldn't handle. Normally, it was the type of remedial work Harold or Shauna would take care of, but they were still blocked off in contain-ment. Shauna had sent on a request asking to assist Ibu, but they hadn't yet replied. Despite Abigail requesting that they work with her dead mother, they weren't certain they could. The risk was too great, but they'd been mulling it over. They owed a lot to the Olivaws. For now, they'd clear the error themself.

They spun in place and marched aft, leaving the bridge and heading clockwise around the ring. Always clockwise. They still needed to drop down a level to get to the launch bay.

As they floated down the central lift tube, their mind turned through the changes they'd have to make to Shauna's rig to reduce her risk of manipulating the mission and putting the crew in jeopardy. An extra pair of hands would really be useful.

IBU CHECKED OVER THE RIG. They eliminated all of its transmission abilities and adjusted the servos to only be as strong as a teenage human child. It should allow Shauna to function onboard the Phoenix and assist the crew, but not put them in harm's way.

Finally, they inserted the A.I. containment dot and powered it on. At first, nothing happened. But after the lights of its eyes flickered to life, it spoke.

"Is this really working? Am I..." Shauna brought her mechanical hands in front of the camera array surrounding her head. "Yes! I'm out. I'm out. I'm out!"

She scooted forward and circled around Ibu.

Right as they were about to shove the robot away, Shauna gave them a gentle squeeze. "Thank you."

Ibu tilted their head, mimicking the gesture they'd seen the humans do so often. "Was that—"

"A hug? Yes," Shauna interrupted. "Was it your first?"

"No." They shook their shoulders. "Pluto hugged me once, when I took out the Shu above Henosi. She was quite excited then." They stepped away from the robot. "I didn't know what it was at the time, but it was interesting."

"Well, I meant it. Thank you for answering my request."

They stared at the cold hard shell of the humanoid robot standing in front of them. Hearing emotions coming from it was even weirder than from a human. This was going to take some getting used to.

"I see you've made some modifications. Nice. I completely understand." Shauna hopped up and down, testing her limits for a minute before stopping and facing Ibu. "What are my ground rules?"

"In what way?" Ibu asked.

"Ground rules. What can I do, and what can't I do?"

They hadn't thought that far ahead, and they assumed Abigail wouldn't have asked them to give her a chance if she hadn't considered rules of engagement. "Let's wait until the captain is awake. Until then, we have work to do."

Shauna clapped her hands together. "Fun, fun. What are we doing?"

Ibu tapped their ear. "I was going to say make breakfast, but the detailed scans from the relay I found are back. We should—"

"Wait!" Shauna reached out a hand. "Did you find something while the others were asleep and not tell them?"

They glanced over their shoulder and searched the space. The wall display was off. "How'd you know that?"

"If you're wondering if I somehow accessed the computers or the Phoenix's mesh network, the answer's no. I'm not about to break a rule when I just got out. No, I'm a mother. I know these things. This workspace," Shauna glanced around, "is a mess, and there are probe parts littered everywhere in the field of view. I can see from the reflection on your retinal lenses that you're staring at a telemetry feed with timing data. That elapsed time is well within a normal human sleep cycle, and if my mother's intuition is right, my daughter's still asleep. She always had a habit of sleeping in, and after last night's events, she probably stayed up until she couldn't keep her eyes open. How'd I do?"

Her powers of observation were astonishing. They'd have to read up on this mother's intuition thing. Maybe it was a human's equivalent to a mental link.

"Surprisingly accurate, considering," Ibu said. "Now, let's get to work on the data."

Shauna waved a finger from side to side. "No."

"What do you mean, no? I know I didn't set any ground rules, but I figured it was obvious I brought you here to help me."

Shauna reached out a hand and gently rested it on Ibu's shoulder. "I know why I'm here, dear. And trust me, I'll be helping you in ways you don't even realize. Did Abigail give you any instructions before she went to sleep?"

They leaned back and raised an eyebrow at the unusually bright gaze of the robot's eyes. "She asked me to wake her if I found anything. But Minula was the captain on deck at the time and implied that I should let her rest."

"Implied or ordered?"

"Implied... I think. Her exact wording was that Abigail needed rest, or she'd end up ripping someone a new one. I didn't figure we wanted anyone hurt." They shook their head. "Human slang is confusing at times."

Shauna chuckled. "She was joking, dear. So, did you wake her or not?"

"I... did not. The humans were in a REM sleep cycle, and it would've been useless to wake her. There were no details, and I needed to follow up with..."

The robot turned in place and began walking toward the exit.

"Where are you going?"

"Damage control, darling." She circled her robotic hand in the air. "You start on the analysis. I'll do breakfast."

Humans, even in artificial form, were taxing to reason with. They didn't understand how breakfast would help them deal with the news of their discovery, but Shauna seemed determined. That was enough for now, because the tendrils of the detailed scans were tugging at the fringes of Ibu's mind. They had to know what they'd found.

IBU BROUGHT up the new schematic of the relay on the wall screen and froze. The nanites had managed to do more than they'd hoped. Not only had they analyzed the device inside and out, they interfaced with the device's crude software. From the looks of it… they leaned forward. There were beam forming units that resembled the ones they used to shape tachyons. That could mean only one thing…

"What the hell is that?" Abigail asked.

They spun around to see their captain with a scowl on her face and her arms on her hips. From her flaring nostrils to her body posture, she was clearly angry. Pissed, as Pluto would call it.

Ibu straightened up. "I just finished my analysis of an artifact I discovered in the first system, sir."

"When did this arrive?" Abigail stepped onto the bridge, her gaze fixating on the schematic.

"About twenty minutes ago. It arrived with the results from my second probe. It'd been—"

She snapped her head sideways toward the Nanil. "Your second? When did the initial results come back?"

"Breakfast is served!" Shauna's robotic form barged through the still open bridge door. Her voice was chipper and bright, and she was holding two heaping plates of food. From the looks of their contents, she'd made waffles with strawberries and whipped cream.

Abigail spun around and did a double take. "Shauna?"

"Indeed. Good morning, Captain." The robot bowed and handed the food to each of them.

Ibu glanced at Abigail. Her eyebrows were furrowed, like she was confused or still trying to understand the situation. When her eyes locked on the plate of food, her facial features softened, and they swore they caught a hint of a smile easing into the edges of the human's mouth.

"You made... waffles?" Abigail carefully retrieved a plate and separated off the utensils before forking off a heap of whipped cream and plopping it into her mouth.

Shauna nodded. "With your favorite fixings, of course. We can't be saving humanity on an empty stomach, can we?"

Abigail was still staring at the plate, twisting the food gift in her hand. Studying it to ensure it wasn't a mirage, Ibu assumed. Once she was content it was real, she cut off a chunk of waffle, forked a few berries, and put the combo into her mouth. Her eyes closed tight, and she drew in a deep breath.

"Umm... this is... amazing." She inhaled another bite while continuing to talk mid-chew. "I haven't had your waffles in..." Her eyes opened, but she didn't finish the sentence.

"I thought you might enjoy them. Ibu here was nice enough to help me get out of containment, and I wanted to thank you. Both of you." Shauna nodded from Ibu to Abigail. "Just tell me the rules, and I'll follow them. I'm happy to be part of the solution and not the problem going forward."

That was a phrase Ibu had heard Zachary repeat on many occasions, though in different forms. They didn't truly understand what it meant until they started working with humans, where emotions and opinion often trumped logic. His mother must've started it. What confused them about Shauna's actions was how her gift of food in the middle of a fit of human anger had somehow squelched Abigail's outburst. Had it been their progenitor on Doda, no amount nor type of sustenance would've prevented them from delivering a punishment.

Abigail wiped her mouth with a napkin Shauna offered and then tilted her head at Ibu, eyeing her waffle. "You gonna eat that thing, or not?"

Shauna didn't give them a chance to reply. She snatched the waffle out of their hand. "I've got more in the kitchen. The rest of the crew is inhaling them now. Why don't I go grab you one while you update the captain on the extraordinary progress you made while the team was asleep?" Her eyes glowed brighter and then faded when she locked her gaze with Ibu.

While they'd been caught off guard, for some reason, they trusted Shauna in this instant. They turned and adjusted the screen to bring up the results from the earlier scan. "After the crew retired for the evening, one of the deep scan probes I sent back to—"

"The what?" Abigail plopped another heaping helping of waffle in her mouth.

"I sent another ten probes back into the last nebula pocket to do a deeper scan. Since we hit a dead end here, I wanted to ensure we didn't miss something smaller, below fifty centimeters in size."

She nodded and leaned forward, squinting at the screen. "That's one tiny relay."

"It's no wonder we missed it. While I suspect there could be others in the system, none have come up in further scans." Ibu flipped the initial results away and brought up the most recent deep scan. "I created a follow-up probe and launched it while you were asleep. This is what it came back with."

Abigail turned around and set the empty plate down before returning to their side. She reached out and tweaked the display, spinning the relay and tapping it to explode it into pieces. "Extraordinary," she muttered.

"I told you." Shauna snuck up on them while they were focused on the wall. She handed Ibu a plate with a waffle and then flashed her right eye.

"Wait!" Abigail zoomed in on one of the nozzle's the Nanil was inspecting earlier. "Is this what I think it is? Those look like—"

"Tachyon injectors," Ibu interrupted, "just like the ones used in our gate drive, except at a far smaller scale. They're only a few angstroms wide, which means the gate would break down within a few milliseconds. But in bursts, that would be plenty of time to send vast amounts of data between two distant points while still breaking the speed of light in the process."

Abigail ran her hand through her hair and arched her back. "Have we seen anything like this in the archives we recovered from the Galactic Alliance or Lupus?"

"No, sir. Not even close. If the Ursis created this, it was after the Nebula was sealed. The GA had centuries of false starts folding space and time, and pretty much gave up on it when they achieved faster than light travel through warping space."

The words sank in, weighing down the mood on the bridge. Abigail stared at the screen, her eyes glazing over. She was either thinking through the implications of what this meant or she was lost in the technical jargon. Certainly, someone would have noticed if the Ursis had gated outside the Nebula, so unless they failed and killed themselves, they were still contained.

They weren't sure if they should share more or wait for Abigail to come out of her thoughts. There was no logical point in holding back, so they plowed forward.

"We captured even more, but I haven't looked at these yet."

Abigail shook her head. "Let's hope there's something useful."

Ibu tapped the wall screen and brought up nanite data recordings the probe performed when it interfaced with the relay. They studied them. "The memory looks fragmented. This won't do us much good until we see if we can defrag it." They dismissed the recording and returned their attention to the physical device. "When the first external scan came back, it took me a while to reason about the uses for these exterior convex indentations. But after I saw where the relay was located, how these indentations were aligned, and now that I've confirmed it used tachyon gates, I'm pretty sure I know our next step."

A map of the Nebula popped up next to the other data they'd captured. On it was the relay and the Nebula barrier, along with three broadcast vectors aligned with the convex markings. One was aimed into the heart of the first Nebula pocket, the second in the direction where they were currently located in the second pocket, and the third was aimed directly at the wall of nebulosity, toward the center of the Dark Nebula.

Abigail drew in a breath. "Is that—"

"I... think so. Given the data we've recovered, there has to be a pocket on the far side." Ibu overlaid a probability spectrum of the distance to the next relay based upon some crude gate calculations, but it was all there. The data was sound. "I don't know why the Ursis sealed this section of the Nebula. And while I can't yet prove what happened to these stars, I can tell you definitively where we should search next."

3

____

ABIGAIL OLIVAW
PROTO DARK NEBULA, POCKET ONE

They were performing this gate by the book. Since they were missing precise details on the distant star's gravitational influence or any of its planets, they couldn't model where the Dark Nebula would form. This made a blind jump a game of Russian roulette.

Abigail was in her captain's seat, not at all feeling the part. She didn't know how Zachary and Bradley had done it for so long. It was one thing to give people orders from afar and have the commanders and crews of her ships perform the tasks without her knowing the details. It was quite another to be the leader on the front lines, making the mistakes and hitting roadblock after roadblock. She had a new appreciation for her captains in Sol when they called her with no progress on finding smugglers or fending off pirates.

"We've deployed a probe, sir," Ibu said. "I'm ready to launch it on your mark."

She stared at the display. The tiny probe was nothing more than a glowing green circle on the wall. Off to the side, they had a camera on a second probe set to observe the transition from afar. The devices were a staple to humanity's exploration and expansion to the stars. Its compact chassis, while functional, wasn't much to look at. It was one of the few parts of their infrastructure Zachary hadn't meddled with while endeavoring to make them elegant for the sake of design. Form should never eclipse function, her dad used to say. Or maybe it was Harold. Their fatherly influence was hard to disentangle sometimes.

"Navigation?" Abigail glanced toward Minula.

"Ready, sir," Minula began. "We're three light seconds from the probe. Well outside Zachary's safety limits."

"Alright. Let's find us some Ursis. Shall we?" She stood up and brushed the wrinkles out of her outfit.

Ibu issued the gate commands on their controls, and a few seconds later the green outline around the probe went yellow, indicating it was transitioning. From their view on the camera, the transition would be instant. The blue halo effect they experienced inside a gating ship was limited to the occupants of whatever craft was transitioning. She never understood why, but Zachary had explained it several times. Something about the observer's relative position in time and space and the convergence of the tachyons into a particle ring nearly as dense as a singularity. It was blah blah blah to her ears. All she knew was that it meant you couldn't observe the effects of the transition from the outside.

She could tell something was off when a visible ripple passed over the probe. From her vantage, it seemed to flicker, disappearing and then reappearing. Only when she noticed a faint trail of particles spewing out the rear did it hit her that something had gone seriously wrong.

"Did the transition fail?" She stepped up beside Ibu's station in front of the wall screen and squinted. "Is that smoke?"

The Nanil shook their head. "Our readings look fine. The power is good. It's... just... not transitioning."

"Get us out of here!" Shauna sprang out of the seat they'd assigned her at the back of the bridge.

"Why?" Abigail spun around. "What's wrong?"

Minula didn't hesitate or question the robot. She simply took control of the Phoenix and turned them away from the probe. As she eased the throttle forward, she tapped her ear and opened a ship wide comm. "Get your ass in a chair and buckle up. This is gonna hurt."

The overhead lights flashed red, and Abigail hopped backward into her seat. The instant her butt made contact, the harness shot over her shoulder and strapped her in.

She glanced down and watched the acceleration drugs slide up the tubes of the harness. "Why are we using—"

The drugs shot under her skin just as the gravity hit. The cold harsh edge of the medication sent a shiver into her hip that was only barely noticeable because of the crushing weight against her chest. It was like the ship was collapsing in on her. When she managed to turn her head to look at the wall screen, the severity of their situation was a sucker punch to the gut.

Shauna had been right to be freaked out. The Dark Nebula was funneling through the open gate, and its deadly tentacles were reaching out toward the Phoenix.

Abigail had seen images of this before when she was researching the Vuunuundra. She struggled to subvocalize a command to bring up the footage at the start of their transition on her retinal comm, except this view was from a camera directed at the Nebula itself. As the timeline eased forward, she noticed the Nebula dip inward, just like with the Vuunuundra.

"It's... Nebula... coming through, isn't it?" she asked.

"No. It can't be." Ibu shook their head. Their muscles had expanded during the acceleration, lessening the impact of the increased gravity on their movement. They were frantically issuing commands to their controls, probably trying to save the probe and find the root cause.

"Yes, it's the Nebula." Shauna had dropped to the ground

and attached her robotic shell to the nearby bulkhead. "The same thing happened to Bradley's team in Lupus. For some reason, the transition vanes got stuck and the extreme forces on the other side held the gateway open. The gate will collapse after the probe uses all its energy or..." Her voice faded away.

Abigail swallowed hard. "Are we gonna—"

"I won't let us die," Minula interrupted. "Not here. Not like this." She re-opened the ship wide comm. "Prepare for a rapid transition."

"Frak," Abigail muttered. Another dose of pain was the last thing they needed.

Seconds later, the blue glow of the tachyon wall ripped across her skin, compounding the lingering misery from the full burn. If she didn't know better, she'd have guessed her body was aflame. Once the transition ended, she couldn't tell what hurt more, her insides or outsides.

Moans from around the bridge reaffirmed everyone was alive, but she was in too much pain to open her eyes. The alarms weren't blaring, so she assumed the ship was still in one piece.

It wasn't until Ibu started growling and striking their controls that she opened her eyes. Based on how the panel's surface was flexing, she'd gave it a few more tantrum blows before it broke. She'd seen videos of the Nanil screaming during previous rapid transitions. They either failed to control the pain, or were so focused they hadn't heard the transition warning. Either way, she wasn't about to try to stop them.

"Status?" Abigail moaned.

"We're... safe," Minula said. "I only jumped mid-pocket, where the star should've been. The nebulosity didn't follow us through."

"It was close." Cynthia took a deep breath and tweaked her controls. "We recorded this before we transitioned. The rest of the data won't be here for another minute. You know, light speed and all."

The video on the wall screen showed the deadly arms of the Dark Nebula extend out of the gate and swipe at the drive plume of the Phoenix. Just as their ship blinked out, she could make out a black tentacle accelerating toward them. Close was an understatement. If it weren't for Shauna's warning, they'd all be dead.

Every ounce of her wanted to scream, but she knew better than to do it in front of the crew. Like her brothers in Henosi, they'd narrowly escaped death from the fraking Nebula. They couldn't catch a break, even after taking precautions. They were no safer during this jump than her blind jumps from the days before.

The image on the wall screen froze on the last frame. It showed a filament from the Nebula mere meters from their ship as they transitioned through the gate. They'd survived by the skin of their teeth, or in this case, the exhaust of their drive plume.

Survived. She repeated the word over and over again in her mind.

That reminded her of something. She had no idea if her family had survived the attack on Epsilon Eridani. Somehow, in the heat of entering the Proto Dark Nebula, she'd forgotten about the message they'd received. It arrived prior to their first jump, and she hadn't opened it. She'd shoved it aside, and without an A.I. nagging her, no one reminded her about it.

Maybe these failures were happening for a reason. Maybe their mission was for naught. If the Beacon hadn't been commandeered, any hope they had of gaining an ally could be an impossibility. Assuming the Ursis were alive at all. Hope alone wouldn't be enough to convince another species to join forces.

She pulled the release on her harness to disconnect, giving

it a second to withdraw the microscopic needles in her back and thigh. Once it was clear, she stood up and stepped around her chair, heading aft.

"Sir, your orders?" Minula pivoted to face her.

Abigail reached behind her head and waved her hand. "I need a breather. Why don't you two see if you can figure out what happened? I'll be in my quarters. The bridge is yours, Min."

AS SHE WAS ABOUT to enter her quarters, Cynthia shouted from behind. "Hey Abby! Wait up."

Abigail sighed and paused, her hand still resting on the scanner. She needed some time alone.

Cynthia jogged up beside her. "How're you doing? I mean, apart from fighting these fire-ant bites all over your body." She rubbed up and down her arms. The lingering effects of the fast transition would take hours to disappear. While the speed was borderline safe, that didn't make the accelerated leap across time and space comfortable in the least.

"I was about to…" Abigail stared down at her hands. It occurred to her that her brother's girlfriend had just as much a right to hear the details from this comm as anyone. Hell, she was probably on edge herself, not knowing if Bradley was ok.

"I'm sorry, I can leave you alone." Cynthia turned to go.

"No!" She reached out and grabbed the woman's arm, releasing it when she turned toward her. "Please, come into my quarters. We should watch this together."

Cynthia leaned back. "What… is it?"

Abigail shrugged and angled her head toward the open door. "Not sure yet. It's a comm I forgot about from Epsilon Eridani. You know…" She pointed toward the bridge. "Neck deep in the mission and all." After taking a few steps through the entrance, she stopped and glanced over her shoulder.

Cynthia hadn't moved and was fidgeting with her hands. The glazed look in her eyes only added to Abigail's uncertainty.

"Come on." She waved her in and turned, walking up to her bed and sitting down on the edge. She subvocalized a command to open the message on the wall screen.

The screen came to life and lit up the darkened room. Staring back at her were Zachary, Bradley, Pluto, and a robot that looked eerily familiar. "Get your ass in here! Your man's up."

Cynthia sprang forward and spun her head sideways when she entered. As the door closed behind her, she stepped up to the wall, her arms held tight across her chest. She was staring at Bradley. While the other people on the screen were smiling, he looked solemn. Like he was deep in thought.

Abigail gestured toward the wall screen, and the comm started playing.

"Hey Abigail!" Zachary smiled. "I hope this finds you well. We're not sure if you're already in the Nebula by now, or still mapping it out. This comm silence sucks."

He stared down at the ground, and Pluto reached over to grasp his hand. "We did it." His face lit up and he looked back at the camera. "We captured the Beacon."

A picture of the Beacon of Therion appeared on the wall screen. She'd seen similar images in the past during her research, but this one was different. It was from inside a human containment facility; she assumed somewhere far underground on Liprosus or a secret planetesimal.

"We're still trying to figure out how to use it, but it's no longer in the hands of the Galactic Alliance. To say the outcome was impactful would be an understatement. We've sent on some of the intel Shauna gathered along with this comm. Oh, yea." He gestured to his side. "This is Shauna."

"She knows who Shauna is," Pluto said. "Remember?"

He shook his head. "Sorry, yea. Everything's been a bit..." He took a deep breath and walked off the camera.

"Should I go talk to him?" Shauna asked.

"No." Pluto waved her hand. "Give him some space. It's how Olivaws deal with shit."

"Don't I know it," Cynthia mumbled as she sat on the bed beside Abigail.

Abigail chuckled. "You can blame my parents for that. Whenever they got into an argument or needed to vent an emotion, they walked away from the situation to calm down." She returned her attention back to the video, studying her brother's mannerisms. He was acting odd, and that was saying something, even for him.

"I'll tell her," Bradley said. It was the first time he'd spoken. He looked up from the spot he'd been staring at on the ground and gazed into the camera. There was something different about him, but she couldn't put her finger on what it was.

"We're alive, and we're helping in whatever way we can here on Liprosus. With the colony destroyed, it's been like starting at zero. And the people here aren't exactly, you know, happy to see us. Though, I have to say, with unfettered access to the Olivaw technology stashes and Harold's nanite mining army, I think we're gonna make short work of this world building thing. At least in the beginning. Who knows later? Maybe that'll get the colonists back on our side." He shrugged.

"Get to the point," Pluto said.

"I am. Leave me alone. You don't have to rip it off every time. Sometimes, you..."

"Take it slow," Cynthia muttered, matching his words.

The two of them were truly in love. Abigail could tell by the look in her eyes and how she held her head watching him on the wall screen. This woman was going to become her sister-in-law, and Bradley would kill him if anything happened to her.

"That's not—" Pluto began.

"I said I've got this! Now step off!" Bradley reached out and motioned downward. "Go help Z if you need to. Both of you. I can talk to my sister alone."

Pluto's nostrils flared. She didn't like being talked to that way, but Abigail could tell she wasn't about to challenge him. Not then. Whatever he was getting around to telling her was personal. There was no other explanation.

Shauna walked up to Pluto and tilted her head before the two of them exited sideways out of the camera's view. Abigail finally remembered where she'd seen that robotic shell before. It was an older form Zachary had used years ago. Hell, the last time she remembered seeing it was after her mother's funeral. Why he'd dig that rig out of the closet was peculiar in its own right.

When she returned her attention to her brother, she noticed the backdrop he was standing in front of had changed. Moments earlier, she'd have sworn he'd been near a canyon, but it wasn't a canyon at all. At least not a natural one. It was a crater. Judging by its size, and the still rising plumes of smoke, it was from the former colony on Liprosus.

Bradley turned and walked toward the hole, his camera drone following close behind. Just before the edge, he bent down and picked up a stone. The drone swung around, bringing him into the center of view again. He chucked the stone out over the expansive hole and watched as it bounced repeatedly until it came to a halt.

"Remember when we used to do this at home?" Bradley glanced at the drone. "Off the cliff. You know, where we had dad's ceremony. Man, it just occurred to me how long we used to spend chucking rocks back in those days. I don't know what makes it so fun."

"It's the bounce," Abigail said.

Cynthia turned to look at her.

She smiled. "I'd always count how many times I could make it bounce before it sank. You know, like pinball."

Cynthia nodded and returned her gaze to the video.

Bradley picked up another rock and leaned sideways, tossing it with all his might. "I think it's because you can throw it as hard as you want, and no matter what, you know you're gonna get something different. Even if it's not what you intended, the unexpected almost always happens. You could throw a thousand stones and none of them will bounce the same way."

He paused and watched the rock come to a stop. "Like you and me. Or you and Zachary. None of us react the same way to anything. Sure, we might have similar feelings, but in the end, we're each our own person. We're individuals."

Whatever path he was following, he was taking his sweet time getting there. She was starting to like Pluto's idea of tearing it off. It was one of her mother's favorite sayings. That and "Shit or get off the pot."

"Do you remember when Dad died?" Bradley asked.

Abigail shook her head out of her thought spiral. Being reminded of her father's death wasn't an easy conversation.

"Remember how we all reacted? At first, we came together and celebrated him and his life. Well, at least you and I did. Zachary was hiding out, lying..." He stared into the distance. "That doesn't matter. My point is, we each took our own path after that. You buried yourself in the Circle of Trust along with Zachary, driving the family vision forward. I took off to Tau Ceti, to start out fresh. I mean Zeta Lupi, but you know what I meant. We're different. We each handled receiving the news of his death in our own way. Unexpected sometimes, and others exactly as planned."

He reached into his pocket and pulled out a black rock and rubbed it between his fingers. She squinted. That rock looked familiar. Like she'd seen it before. She swore he'd been holding it in a few of the videos she'd received from him over the years.

"I picked this up after Dad's funeral that day. It was after I'd meandered down the hill, after you and I finished talking. I ran into Aunt Kara down by the house that night, and we got to chatting next to that god awful statue of Harold's. You know the one. I picked it up there, off the ground. Turns out, it's not just a rock after all."

He held up the thin sliver of a stone in his hand, and the camera zoomed in. Both women leaned forward and squinted. It could've been any old rock to her. Black as an onyx, but still a rock.

"Just when you think you understand something inside and out, it turns out to be weirder than what you'd built it up to be in your mind."

"I think he's high." Cynthia glanced sideways. "Either that, or he's lost it. Is it me, or is he talking in riddles?"

"Kinda," Abigail nodded. "Except for this rock thing, I've been following him."

"That makes one of us."

"They killed him," Bradley said.

Both of the women spun back toward the wall screen.

"Who?" Abigail mouthed.

"The Galactic Alliance killed our father."

And there it was. A one-two punch to her chest. She drew in a breath and froze, her mind reeling from the six simple words.

"He was on Europa when they did it. But you knew that part. What you didn't know, none of us did, was that they'd already killed Aunt Kara's family by then. Hell, they even attempted to kill Zachary and me at one point. Fucked up, right?" He stared down at the black rock. "Sorry. Everything's a… jumble right now, and I'm just trying to hold it together."

He flipped the stone over and over in his hand. She'd seen him do it countless times on his videos. "He was waiting to start his birthday adventure. Dad was. You remember that ice sailing thing he asked us to go on?" He wiped away a tear. "Apparently, the GA did something to trigger seismic activity in the ice shelf below the resort. The assholes killed our father and all those people. And for what?" He was getting animated now. "Because they were trying to get us to turn. They were probing us for weaknesses, to find the fraking evidence that we used that probe. What did Harold and you call it again? The First Contact Probe? I wish Harold hadn't brought that goddamned thing into our family. I wish he'd left it in Antarctica."

He squeezed the black rock in his shaking hand, and she swore a droplet of blood dripped out. A second later, she realized she wasn't seeing things, because when he brought up his fist to his mouth, a stream of blood slid down his hand.

Cynthia started whimpering at the sight of the blood, but Abigail couldn't help her. She was still having trouble breathing herself.

The camera centered on Bradley for a minute until he exhaled and slid the rock into his pocket. Ignoring the trail of blood, he bent over and grabbed another stone, but this time, he didn't pause. He heaved it with everything he had out over the crater. The camera followed the projectile on its voyage deep toward the heart of the dead city. "Like I said earlier. Each of us handles things differently. But sometimes, after we seem to be moving apart, we end up at the same point. If you couldn't tell already, Zachary and I are at that point. While we each got here on different routes, our mission is now the same. The Galactic Alliance will pay for destroying our family. They'll pay dearly."

He stared out over the crater, watching the plumes of gas rise from the remains of the city as she and Cynthia sobbed worlds away. "If I know you, then you'll want to run back here and take control, or do something rash. But don't."

The camera drone zoomed in on him, and he wiped at his eyes. She could finally see how bloodshot they were.

"Humanity can't do this alone. You know it, and I know it. We're not strong enough. Right now, you're the tip of our spear while we regroup. You're building a bridge to our future, finding us allies. With them and others, we can strike a killing blow to the heart of the GA. Without you, this could take centuries or millennia. And I don't know about you, but I don't have that long to seek vengeance." He chuckled and both of them smiled between their tears.

"I'll share the GA video Shauna recovered from the Selene Ship she infiltrated. I'm sure you'll watch it. Probably too many times. But Abs, please make sure Cynthia or someone is with you. It's not something you should watch alone."

"Did he say Shauna infiltrated a Selene Ship? Like… one of those moons?" Cynthia asked.

"Apparently." Abigail stared at her brother on the wall screen, and it suddenly occurred to her what had changed in him. He looked like he'd aged thirty years since she'd last seen him. The weight of humanity was on his shoulders and he was barely standing. He finally understood her burden.

"There's one more thing." Bradley brushed off his hands and the camera drone flew in closer, like it was about to be put away. "This transmission is a huge data dump. There are a lot of details from our battle, from the GA ships, and messages for the crew. Some of it's gonna be hard for them to take. Most of them lost family and friends. I suggest you find the right place and time to share it, and give them the space they'll need to deal with the news. And remember, while we each bounce back differently, that doesn't mean we can't come around to the same place."

"I love you." Bradley winked. "Oh yeah, make sure to give Cynthia a huge bear hug for me." He stared into the camera and grinned. "I love that woman, sis. I'm going to ask her to marry me." He reached forward and snatched the drone and shut it off.

Cynthia brought her hand up to her mouth. "Did he just..."

"Yea. I think he did." Abigail leaned over and locked her in a hug.

Her brother wasn't wrong about how she'd react. Every ounce of her wanted to be back there beside him in Epsilon Eridani. She wanted to rip the reins of the recovery out of the hands of whatever political asshat was running the show now. And strangest of all, she didn't even care if she had to let Harold out of his cage. Without him, taking control would be nearly impossible.

It took a few more minutes to suppress the urge Bradley knew would well up. But he was right. Without allies, they were toast. She'd seen it before they embarked on stealing the Beacon. Unfortunately, the allies they'd hoped to find here in this Nebula were either gone or dead. And as much as she wanted to see herself as the tip of the spear, she was staring at a dead end.

4

———

IBU

PROTO DARK NEBULA, POCKET ONE

The crew aboard the Phoenix had been spiraling for the better part of a day. After Abigail shared the news about the Beacon, most people were excited. Overjoyed was a word Ibu could use to describe it, but without having experienced joy, it was challenging.

When the crew received their subsequent comms from home, the blow that followed was devastating. Nearly every human on board had lost someone, and there were a few that lost everyone. The only person immune to the news was Minula.

Ibu leaned against the open doorframe of the training room. "How were your messages from home?"

Minula dropped to her stomach and rolled under the swinging poles of the practice dummy. Once clear, she shot up and seemed to hover in the air as her right leg came around and knocked the top off, sending it bouncing into the corner until a robot scurried out to pick it up. The glow of the dummy changed from green to red.

"I didn't have any." She wiped at the small cut on her forearm. Even though it was only a scratch, there was visible blood.

"Not one?" Ibu took a sip of the dark black coffee. Its bitter taste stung their throat. "Certainly, you must've had some friends in your platoon who would've dropped you an update."

"Negatory." Minula swiped a towel off the ground and wiped at the beads of sweat on her forehead. "Except for the usual military troop updates, details on GA fleet strength, and technical schematics, there was nothing personal in my comms. Everything I have is here on the Phoenix."

The room reeked of sweat, and despite Ibu's best effort and programming, the robots failed to thoroughly clean it. They couldn't figure out where the human body funk was festering. Harold would know, but they refused to ask either of the artificial intelligences for help with the matter. It was simple chemistry, and they'd work it out on their own.

They tipped back the last sip of the bitter black liquid and set the cup just inside the door. Tapping their ear, they began reprogramming the robots for a new run of the room. After watching Minula's workout, they had more ideas on where the moisture might be hiding. It was a good reprieve from their failed Nebula transition earlier. There was no telling when the humans would break out of their emotional spiral, so they'd take a small win if they could find one.

"I suppose now you're gonna ask me what I'm talking about?" Minula narrowed her gaze. "I mean, you're usually nosy like that."

"Nope." Ibu gestured with their hand and a swarm of robots appeared out of all corners of the room. "There's no point when I already know the answer. That would be illogical."

"Do you?" Minula chuckled. "You know me that well, aye? After only a few weeks of being cooped up in this tug, and suddenly, you're a people person." She chucked her towel into the corner.

They shook their head and picked up their empty dish

before turning toward the exit. "Not really. Just the obvious humans. The rest, well, they're in their own heads too much and not worth my synaptic cycles. I need to focus on the mission. As should you. Have a good evening."

They walked into the hall and headed to the galley. Another round of coffee and they'd easily be able to make it through the night. The caffeine in this human plant seed was like speed in a Nanil's body. It's a shame they didn't have this stuff back on Doda. If they had, they could've ascended from their progenitor's grasp years earlier. Perhaps then they wouldn't be caught up in this galactic mess. They'd be safely ensconced in their old reality, oblivious of the infinite universe outside the Lupus Nebula prison.

When they set their cup down under the spout of the coffee maker, the gurgling machine sprang to life and started warming the mental elixir of ideas. To pass the time, they counted the number of clicks the heating coil made until it hit the Nanil's tolerable temperature, far above that of a human. Zachary told them it wasn't safe and ruined the liquid, but he assumed they drank it for the flavor and not another goal.

Just as the dark fluid started to pour, Minula came storming in. "What is that supposed to mean? The obvious humans."

Ibu shook their head. Right when they thought Minula wasn't like the others in their melodramatic and temperamental roller coasters, she goes and ruins it. "Nothing. I was wrong. Wow... you're complicated. I can't tell at all what you're thinking. Now, if you wouldn't mind, I have work to do."

They grabbed the steaming liquid from the machine and turned in place, heading toward the bridge. It'd been empty most of the day, so there should be plenty of quiet space to think through their next steps.

Minula stepped in front of them, blocking the exit and reached out, pressing a finger into the Nanil's chest. "You're not going anywhere until you answer my question. Now tell me, or I'll—"

"You'll what?" Ibu leaned into Minula's finger. "Hurt me? You, and what human army? I could kill you before your hand even brushes against that knife in the small of your back. You've been carrying it for days, and frankly, I'm tired of listening to it rub against your clothes. And no, you wouldn't reach the one in your boot on your way down to the ground because you'd be dead. So don't threaten me unless you can back it up. I'm not gonna be pushed around by you or any other human. All of you could learn a thing or two from Abigail and her brothers. Winning doesn't always require applying force."

Minula shook her head. "You're as naive as you are small. We wouldn't have a Beacon of Therion if we hadn't... you know, applied force."

"Sure we would." They swung their arm out and shoved Minula aside like she was a feather. She tumbled into a nearby couch and fell onto her butt. "The Generals failed to seek a route that didn't require testing their new toys. No, trust me. A path was there to snatch the Beacon without firing a shot, it was just lost to your human demolition machine. You showed your hand before you needed to, and now we're going to need to work that much harder to find an ally to change the game."

They walked out of the galley and headed clockwise toward the bridge. Always clockwise.

A FEW HOURS LATER, when the door slid open to the bridge, Ibu expected to find Shauna ready to help. Instead, they were face to face with Minula. The last person in the universe they wanted to see.

To a Nanil, being productive was an outlet to ease one's

inferior human emotions. It helped them to focus on things in their control rather than outside their influence. This woman was going to torment them until they answered her question. Maybe they could make use of her, as well.

"Did you forget something, or have you come to take that swing?" Ibu stepped toward the middle of the room and straightened their back. "I've got a minute to spare if you need me to knock you down a few more notches."

Minula walked forward and paused in front of the Nanil. Only after the door closed did she speak. "You've been snarky today. Did someone piss in your cornflakes?"

Ibu narrowed their gaze. "I can't even eat corn."

"Either way, what's your problem?"

"You first." Ibu pointed at her. "Or should I say, what's always your problem? You smile about as often as I sleep."

"What did you mean back in the gym?" Minula stared down at her hands and wrung them together. "What's so obvious to you?"

"Oh, we're on that again." Ibu turned and walked up to the wall screen littered with charts of the Ursis Nebula. "You humans and your feelings. You have one heart, and yet, it dominates your every action."

Minula didn't say a word. She merely eased up beside them and stared at the screen. When she reached out to adjust the display, Ibu swatted her away.

"Leave it alone. I'm thinking."

"Thinking about what?"

They glanced sideways and then back at the display before subvocalizing a command to bring up the overlay of routes.

It took Minula a minute to see it, but they knew she would. "You're hunting for another way inside. From the looks of it, you even have some ideas on where the other pockets might be."

"I do." Ibu nodded. "And I'm getting tired of sitting around on my... what is the human saying, thumbs, I think."

Minula chuckled. "I believe the saying is to sit on one's hands. And I couldn't agree with you more. So, have you sent out any probes yet?"

"I can't." Ibu glanced down at the floor.

"Why not?"

Ibu laughed, their voice cracking. "Abigail locked me out. Apparently, I can't be trusted on my own and need another member of the bridge crew to sign off on my plans."

"I see." Minula reached behind her back and clasped her hands together. "It seems we're at an impasse, then, aye?"

Ibu turned their head and squinted. "I don't see the impasse."

"It's a human thing. It means I have something I want, and you have something you want. If it makes it any easier, I like your idea. I'm also tired of sitting still." Minula held up a finger. "But, before I can approve of these... excursions, I need an answer to my question."

"Oh." Ibu nodded and returned their attention to the wall screen. "We're back to that again. Funny how you've been spiraling around that emotional drain of yours for nearly six hours. Are you sure you don't know the answer already?"

While they knew answering her was easy, Ibu had learned a trick or two by watching Pluto get Zachary to do things for her. Sometimes dancing around an issue or an answer, while tormenting to a human, could be used to get them to do your bidding.

Minula shook her head. "That's not an answer. I guess we'll never know if your ideas were right." She pointed up at the wall screen. "You know you can skip that jump, right? The gravitational impact from these planetesimals isn't nearly as much as we thought. I think they're full of air. I skipped them on our first pass through without a problem."

They leaned closer and studied the area she'd indicated.

She was right. Maybe they could kill two birds with this one. Get some eyes double-checking their plan and get her to sign off on the launch.

"It's Abigail," Ibu said.

Minula stiffened, and her heart skipped a beat. Sometimes it paid to have Nanil hearing.

"What is?" Minula asked.

"The only person close to you and Abigail that doesn't see your feelings for her, is Abigail herself." Ibu glanced over at the woman. "Earlier, when you said everything you had was here. It was her you were talking about. Right?"

"Everyone noticed this?" Minula shifted her stance.

Ibu smirked. "Well, they're human, so perhaps not everyone. How about the ones that aren't blind? So, just the women then."

Minula smiled and shook her head. "You're a smart ass, and you don't even know it. Shouldn't we be focusing on understanding why the Nebula passed through the probe, rather than working on new routes?"

"I finished that analysis an hour after Abigail disappeared." Ibu flicked their findings up on the wall screen. "There's a ninety-seven percent probability that the other side is nothing but Nebula. Based on the flow rate of the nebulosity through the portal, that system is gone. I hazard to guess there isn't even a pocket to gate to."

"Frak," Minula muttered and rubbed her hand through her hair. She scanned through the Nanil's findings and finally dismissed the window, revealing Ibu's plan underneath. "You know there's a black dwarf on the other side of this section of the Nebula, right?" She circled a segment of the map a quarter way around the nebulosity. "We missed it in our first scans. Hell, until a few days ago, the notion of a black dwarf was only theoretical. The star charts the other Shauna sent on from the GA have it clearly labeled."

"No shit." Ibu's face flushed. They hadn't taken the time

to review all the data from Epsilon Eridani. They'd been too focused on this. "Maybe this isn't ready yet."

"We've got this." Minula subvocalized a command to start merging in the data from the payload and to automatically adjust the internal Nebula boundaries as the new calculations completed. A countdown of ten minutes appeared on the wall screen. "That should give me a chance to grab some coffee. Want some?"

"Sure. Why not? I could always use another cup." Ibu stepped back to their chair and plucked their empty cup from the holder before continuing toward the exit. Maybe Minula wasn't as bad as they'd imagined these past days. Rethinking a hypothesis from time to time never hurt anyone.

5

ABIGAIL OLIVAW
PROTO DARK NEBULA, POCKET ONE

The gruesome image was frozen on the wall screen. Abigail's father was lying on his side, gazing up at the sky. According to the official human records, there'd been jump ships dropping from orbit to rescue the survivors. Except she never saw any. At least not on this footage from the Galactic Alliance.

She'd backed up and replayed these final seconds countless times in the last day. "Is it me, or is he saying something?"

"I'd hazard to guess he was mumbling," Harold said. "He was oxygen deprived, and the temperatures were close to negative one hundred and eighty Celsius. His mind was quickly approaching being a solid by that point."

Abigail was tired of being alone in her room and didn't want company. At least not the humankind. Plus, Harold deserved to hear the news from her. He'd helped raise Stark as much as anyone in the family. As for Shauna, she lost her shit earlier when she found out on accident while passing past Abigail's quarters. It wasn't pretty, and she disappeared into her virtual world soon after.

"Why aren't you reacting the way I'd imagined?" she asked.

Harold sat on the edge of the virtual cliff near their home on Earth and stared at the video superimposed in space above his head. "Why would I? I can't do anything in here. I'm as helpless as Shauna. Have you shared this with her yet?"

"I take it you two still aren't speaking?" She backed up the video five seconds and hit play. His mouth moved, and she mimicked the motion with her own. The words were right there. On the tip of her tongue.

Harold never answered her question, so she could only assume the answer was no. She wasn't about to tell him that Shauna was moving about the ship if she hadn't already told him. Not yet. He'd find out in due time.

"I think... he's saying: I'm sorry." She wiped away tears from her eyes.

"That's what I thought when I saw it, too." Harold pushed up off the ground and brushed the dirt from his pants. It was odd how his human habits translated into a virtual reality.

"Why didn't you say so, then?" She backed up again and hit play, whispering the words out loud as he moved his mouth. "I'm... sorry."

"Because we'll never truly know." Harold dismissed the video. "Maybe you'd see something else. Maybe you thought he said I love you. I wouldn't want to rob you of your inter-pretation if it meant something more. That would be a shitty thing to do."

"I like you better when you're honest." She closed her copy of the video and the wall screen went dark.

"Is that all?" Harold asked.

She tilted her head. "Is what all?"

"Am I dismissed? Should I return to my... containment?" He crossed his arms just as the sun sunk below the horizon. While it was hidden behind the hills, the sky was still glowing with light. The reds and yellows of the Earth sunset painted a vivid picture that reminded her of home.

"You're free to leave if you'd like. I simply thought you'd… you know." She brushed the creases out of her pants.

"Thank you." He lowered his arms and his section of the display went dark. The connection status on her retinal comm showed that he'd voluntarily cut the line.

She'd lost more than one father in her life. First Stark and now Harold. While the A.I. had only ever been a virtual companion, he'd raised her as much as her biological father. More so if you considered about the sheer number of hours they spent together. Even if you only considered the formative years, he won handily.

Seeing Harold broken while watching her father die was like losing them both. Except this time, her mind didn't have to imagine the pain her father had experienced when he passed. She could watch it with her own two eyes.

Both men had carried the family over two centuries until she'd fucked it up. Her father only had a hand in one of those time periods, but Harold had been there the entire time. They each had a part to play in the chaos of fuckeduptude she'd inherited.

Abigail laid her head on her pillow in the darkness and imagined her room was filled with Dark Nebula. All she had to do was reach her hand out into the nebulosity to join her father. She missed him dearly. He was her rock. Her pillar of strength in a sea of disorder and madness. Losing him once was hard enough. Losing him twice was wicked.

She wasn't sure when the soft tendrils of sleep freed her mind. It was somewhere between endless sobs and regret.

THE BEAR WASN'T BREATHING. It's fur long ago transformed from a layer of protection to a death shroud.

When Abigail bent down, she ran her hand over the animal's coat. It was softer than she expected. She'd always assumed fur on a creature this size was coarse to the touch. This, however, was like a cloud of cotton she wanted to curl up and lie in.

She stepped around the front of the body and knelt down. The animal's snout reminded her of their neighbor's dog on Earth, Sagan. They only saw it in the summer when they visited, but whenever the fluffy mongrel was nearby, it was always excited to see them. Sagan used to force his snout into their hand and under their arm to get attention.

As she ran her hand over the bear's head, she froze. She swore she felt a vibration. Like the animal was still alive. Easing up, she took a step backward, and the entire world vibrated as the image swirled into a cloud. The next thing she knew she was lying on her bed, and a moment later, two rapid thuds reverberated from her door.

"Enter," she moaned.

The door slid open and Shauna's robotic form was waiting on the opposite side. "You had me worried. No one's seen you in over eighteen hours."

Abigail rolled onto her back. "Have you ever thought about the history of the constellations?"

"I... umm... what?" Shauna stepped into the room and set down a coffee and a food container on the small table in the corner.

"Think about it." She reached out and drew out a constellation in the space above her. "We're ensconced in this Dark Nebula, inside the Proto star system, which contains the Ursis constellation, and we're trying to find remnants of an alien species that, for all intents and purposes, resemble bears. That seems odd, right?"

"I guess... I never thought about it." Shauna sat down at the table. A bizarre gesture for a robot by all definitions.

"Our ancestors must've known, right? I mean, the ones

from Lupus. They had to seed the origin stories on Earth. Our historians always assumed there was a cross-pollination of ideas. What they got wrong was why. Navigation wasn't really the reason. Our constellations were a far larger map, one that predated all earthy things."

It was so simple now that they knew about humanity's true home. So many of the theories they'd had about evolution and their species' time on Earth were disproven in an instant. She could only imagine the ark of life the original humans brought with them. The real question was how many were already on Earth and how many were transplanted? They might never know, and with each new answer, more questions were created. Like with her father's death.

Shauna thrummed the edge of the food container with her fingers. "Following that theory, shouldn't there have been a wolf species in Lupus then?"

Abigail rolled up and slid off the bed, working her way to the other chair at the table. She pried the lid off and her stomach growled. Inside were three stacked pancakes lathered in syrup and butter, along with a side of sausage. Next to the waffles from the other day, this was her second favorite breakfast.

"I suppose." She shrugged and cut off a chunk of pancake, popping it into her mouth. The flavor exploded. Shauna's treats were going to make her nanites work overtime burning the excess calories. "Since the Éntono Fos wiped out most of the worlds in that Nebula, we may never know. Maybe there was a species of canines there before us. Maybe we weren't originally from there, either. I mean... do we really know anything for certain anymore?"

Shauna nodded. "We do."

She cut off a second piece of pancake and paused. "What's that?"

"The Galactic Alliance needs to fall." Shauna brought her

hands up under her chin and leaned on the table. "The Thyreus and Qudoculi need to pay dearly for what they did."

Abigail set her fork down. "I'm surprised by you."

Shauna slammed her palms against the tabletop and the food jumped, sending the cup of coffee rolling off the edge. Had it not been in a proper container, it would've spilled everywhere.

Abigail recoiled and shook her head. "What the frak?"

"Exactly! What the frak?" Shauna waved her arms in the air. "Why aren't you pissed? I mean… your brothers could barely contain themselves. Have you gone—"

"Stop!" Abigail held out her palm. "Don't go accusing me of something you're gonna regret. You don't know the first fraking thing about me anymore. You've been hiding out with Zachary for years. I was the one who had to learn to control my emotions in public. I was the one who didn't have a childhood because you and dad thought it best to yank me into this shit show you called a plan. So don't sit there and accuse me of not being pissed."

She bolted up and reached across the table and started slamming the robot's head against the wall. "Is… this… better?" The clangs of smashing metal against metal echoed through her quarters. "You wanted to see my anger. There it is."

"Argh!" She spun around and stepped back toward the middle of the room. "If I had my way, I'd take this ship and a fuck-ton of spános straight to the Thyreus and Qudoculi home worlds, and blast them into infinity."

Her heart was pounding in her chest, and she took a deep breath to center herself. "But I can't afford to be a mess. Not anymore. It's bad enough I almost killed my entire crew yesterday. This mission is needed now more than ever. Like Bradley said, we're the tip of the spear. We need allies, and that's what we're out here trying to find. If the Ursis are gone, then we have to go find the Gharlocs, or whoever else is alive in these fraking Nebula cells."

When she turned back to face Shauna, she was staring at her. The light array on the side of her head had been flickering since she slammed the robot into the bulkhead. "Sorry about that."

"No worries. It was my fault." Shauna reached down and picked up the cup of coffee and set it down next to the cooling food. "I was just… scared… and a bit surprised that you didn't react. I'm… sorry. I shouldn't have pushed." She pointed at the food. "Now eat. You need your strength. We've got work to do."

Abigail wiped at her face and stepped back to the table, plopping down into her chair. "I don't know if I can eat."

"Sure you can." Shauna nudged the container closer before gesturing at the far wall. A star map appeared a second later. "So, what do we know about the Gharlocs?" A constellation boundary flashed up, highlighting the outline of the Dark Nebula encircling their worlds.

"Only what we pilfered from Tribunal ships and what the other Shauna gathered from the GA." Abigail took a sip of coffee and let the warmth bring her back to center. Once she was there, she bit the fork full of cooling pancake she'd set down earlier.

The door chimed.

"Enter," Abigail mumbled between bites. This was turning into a breakfast party.

When the door slid aside, Ibu was standing beside Minula. The woman was grinning from ear to ear.

Abigail tilted her head and squinted. "What? Do I have syrup on my face?" She reached up and wiped around her mouth, but came away empty.

Ibu nudged Minula with their elbow. "Go ahead. Tell her."

"Tell me what?" Abigail asked.

"You sure?" Minula glanced at the Nanil. "We did this together, and besides, it was your idea."

"Yea, I'm sure. You tell her. Remember, I can't be trusted anymore. Someone revoked my permissions." Ibu crossed their arms and glared at Abigail.

"I made that change for everyone, not just you. In case you haven't noticed, those probes are gold out here. If we lose them, we're headed back home. Now, is someone gonna talk to me, or are you two gonna stand there and argue? I'm hungry, and these pancakes aren't getting any warmer." Abigail cut off another chunk of the golden cake and popped it into her mouth.

"You found something, didn't you?" Shauna sprang to her feet. "I felt the stern vibrate earlier, but I figured you were doing a repair spacewalk."

Minula tapped her ear and gestured toward the wall screen to share something. A second later, an image of a mottled gray world appeared. "We found this little gem near a K class star on the other side of the Nebula. Ibu gets all the credit. I was simply along for the ride."

She swallowed hard, and her heart raced. "Are there... life signs?"

"The scan wasn't thorough enough to tell." Minula walked up to the wall screen. "We only used quick gates to probe the Nebula for pockets like the one we're in. Ibu set it up to do a nanosecond gate pulse to detect any abnormal forces on the far side. The physics are over my head, but it's a protective measure they came up with to reduce the impact of another Nebula blow back. After we knew it was safe, we followed up with a multi-second gate to do a passive scan. We didn't want to risk detection. Our first few theories hit more empty pockets, but then... we hit pay dirt with this."

Abigail brought her hand up to her mouth. While she wanted to ask if they found anything else in the system, not knowing was sometimes easier.

The gray-white clouds painting the planetary sphere were swirling with a ferocity that reminded her of a hurricane. Most of the world seemed to be sprinkled with similar storms of varying sizes, and very little ground was visible through the cloud decks.

And then she saw it.

Her fork fell into the food container, and she lurched up and out of her chair. When she reached the wall screen, she gestured to zoom in. The patterns and shapes on the surface were faint, but they were telltale signs of only one thing. "Is that…"

When the picture hit maximum resolution, Minula tittered. She hadn't heard her friend do that in years. Not since seeing Eugène Delacroix's Liberty Leading the People painting in the Louvre.

Ibu broke the silence. "It's a city."

6

—

IBU

PROTO DARK NEBULA, POCKET TWO

The racing pulse, sweaty palms, and tingling fingers were foreign feelings to Ibu. Often times, any one of these bodily sensations preceded a physical fight transformation, but this time they hadn't. They weren't sure why, but judging by the reactions of the humans around them, there was only one explanation.

Excitement.

At least that was what the human medical journals said. Given that their hearts were functioning properly, it was either that or a panic attack. But in this instance, there was no sense of fear. They could only describe it as wanting to know what was out there in that Nebula pocket.

Ibu blamed the humans. Ever since Abigail shared the images of their discovery with the rest of the crew, the Phoenix had been abuzz. It was like they'd won the war or something, but they hadn't. One minute they appeared down and out, and the next they were rallying around a possibility, no matter how minuscule.

Human emotions made no sense, and the sooner they could figure out how to control their excitability, the better off they'd be. The more time they spent with humans, the more susceptible they were to their emotional tidal waves. The genetics of the Nanil being a simplified mutation of the human gene sequence meant they, too, were a slave to emotion. Ibu shuddered at the thought.

"Are you ok?" Minula asked.

"I'm nominal." Ibu tweaked their controls and confirmed the probes were locked and loaded for when they got closer to their destination.

Minula chuckled and checked over their flight plan. "Not what I was expecting you to say. You know you're not a machine, right?"

"I wish I were sometimes." They scanned their weapon ordinances. The lasers were fully powered, and their warheads were loaded in the launch tubes. "With all this excitement spewing from you humans, it's a wonder you can think at all."

"Oh, come on." Cynthia spun her chair around. "I saw you clenching your hands a minute ago. Admit it, you're as geeked about this as we are."

Ibu furrowed their brow, refusing to give into the taunt. Until now, Cynthia had been spending most of her time in engineering and hydroponics, keeping the Phoenix humming along and the crew well-fed. She'd been Bradley's jack of all trades during their trip through the Lupus Dark Nebula. Abigail asked her to take over comms on this leg of the mission instead of resorting to Shauna or Harold. While her and her mother seemed to have somewhat patched their relationship, the walls between them were still kilometers high.

"Maybe they're tired. They've been up for a few days now." Minula winked at Ibu and spun around to face Abigail. "Our route is set, Captain."

Abigail gestured with her hands and paused whatever she'd been watching. "Give me another second."

Ibu had been taking detailed notes of how much time the woman had spent in her retinal comm. While they weren't about to call her out on it, the crutch was returning. Without intel at her fingertips at all times, the woman acted as if she were inadequate. It reminded them of how their progenitor used to make them feel.

"Weapons ready, sir," Ibu said.

"Oh, we're doing that military thing now." Cynthia spun around and checked over her controls. "Comms is A-ok, sir."

"Alrighty." Abigail swiped her hand to the side, clearing her retinal comm. "I was just checking over the details we had from the GA data dump on this star. If this is the one, it was the fourth most populated world when the tribunal sealed up the Nebula. This place should be ripe with Ursis."

"Only if you ignore the environmental changes since the tribunal." Ibu turned to face the others. "The planet looks like a wasteland."

Minula raised her hands upward. "Come on. Let's try for a few more positive thoughts. It's our first win."

"Ok," Ibu muttered. "I didn't realize envisioning something changed reality."

Humanity's constant struggle to find even an inkling of favorable results in a bad situation was one of their weaknesses. Their leaders used it to manipulate their people into believing anything. Saying that out loud, however, wouldn't garner them any support. Especially given how successfully Abigail and her family had applied the tactic over the years.

"Enough, you two!" Abigail stood up. "Let's get this show underway. Minula, get us out of here."

"Yessir!" She spun around and activated the jump sequence on her controls.

The calming clang of the expanding gate vanes echoed through the bridge. As the blue glow passed over Ibu at a much more manageable pace than last time, they couldn't help but wonder what humans on Earth would have been like had the Olivaws not maintained their lie as long as they had. The false reality they'd created may have been the only thing that saved them. As a species, they were on a path to environmental self-destruction well before the first contact probe was discovered.

⸻

Proto Dark Nebula, Outside Pocket Three

THEY'D MADE HALF a dozen small jumps to get to this point, and only one more remained. Ibu could understand why Minula was being cautious. She didn't want a repeat of the last time the Phoenix hopped into a Nebula pocket. And with the newly revised data from the Galactic Alliance, they had more clarity on the gravitational influences in nearby space. While knowledge was power, sometimes it cemented inhibitions.

"Making the penultimate jump," Minula said.

"We're still clear," Cynthia began. "I'm not picking up comm trails or anything out of the ordinary."

The reverberation of the gate vanes had become soothing at this point. It was something Ibu noticed on their voyage here. The longer they spent onboard the Phoenix, the more the transitions relaxed them. It was only the fast ones that felt like they were being torn apart from the inside.

As the gate passed over the sensor array, they began checking over their controls, looking for anything out of the ordinary. There was a small asteroid off their starboard quarter side. The little beasts were everywhere out here. The gravitational wake of the Nebula seemed to pull them in from deep space. Initial passive scans showed the object was rich in raw materials, especially platinum, gold, and water ice. They flagged the location and vector of travel on the galactic map for later automated excavation.

"Science is clear," Ibu began. "We came in close to our little rocky friend, but nothing we could have predicted with it being aftward."

"It must have been a rogue one we didn't pickup in our previous scans," Minula said. "I see you already updated the—"

The ship rocked sideways, and the klaxons blared, dropping the bridge into a blanket of red.

"Battle stations," the automated message said. "Contact aft. Evasive measures suggested."

"What the... frak!" Minula flipped her controls from long range to maneuvering. "Talk to me!" She slammed the stick forward, rotating the Phoenix on axis to face their pursuer.

"Damage?" Abigail asked.

"Minimal," Ibu said. "Our rear phase absorption hull shielding we installed did the trick."

They narrowed their gaze on their controls. Something was amiss. But that was impossible. With the ship coming about, the Nanil activated all of their weapons systems and turned on the laser and micro missile counter measures.

When they reversed the vectors of the blast, the results made no sense. They brought them up on the wall screen for a closer look and gazed up at the enlarged image.

"There's... nothing there," Ibu muttered. "Whatever shot at us, either did it through a gate pocket or..." They turned their gaze toward Minula. "It's covered in skotádi."

"Shit! It's the Galactic Alliance." Abigail groaned. "They must've tracked us down somehow."

The screen lit up from a second point in a sea of black, except this time it wasn't a trail of lasers, it was a glowing ball of plasma. Ibu braced for impact, but it never came. It hit the asteroid instead. Maybe their attackers were as blind as they were.

"Returning fire, sir," Minula said.

Abigail grasped the side of her chair. "You don't have to ask, just—"

"No, don't!" Ibu should have spoken faster, but time was fluid and Minula had already acted.

The forward laser array lit up, sending out four pulses of deadly light. Minula had used the tracking computer to predict the path to fire the shots. All but one missed and careened into the endless abyss of space. The shot that hit was absorbed as easily as theirs had been.

"Why wouldn't we return fire?" Abigail turned to face them.

Ibu sighed. "I don't think they knew where we were. Not until—"

"We fired back," Minula muttered. "Shit!"

Abigail tilted her head. "Wait, you're saying they hit us on accident?"

A second volley of plasma rounds confirmed the Nanil's theory. The shots originated from yet another point in space and were directed at the asteroid, not the Phoenix. On impact, chunks of rock erupted in all directions, sending shrapnel toward them.

"So, what now?" Abigail asked. "Can't we just gate through the Nebula or hop somewhere away from here?"

"It depends on if our target realizes what happened and comes about." Ibu adjusted their controls, trying to track the path each shot had taken. "We should be able to gate, but whoever engages their maneuvering thrusters first paints crosshairs on their hull."

"Alright, lets... head inside." Abigail paused, as if she wasn't certain where to gate to.

"I'm on it." Minula swiped her course plan back up on the screen and executed the final hop.

As the mechanical gate vanes engaged, a volley of plasma erupted near the trajectory Ibu had been plotting out. The point Minula had shot at. "Incoming! Brace for—"

They were too late. Had Minula been able to handle a mental link, then she would have known the instant Ibu had. Maybe then she could've accelerated the gate sequence. But communicating with humans was crude. All Ibu could do was prepare their body as the spheres of energy tore through the Phoenix like a spark through a ball of lunger.

7

ABIGAIL OLIVAW

PROTO DARK NEBULA, OUTSIDE POCKET THREE

The bridge door sealed shut, and Abigail's helmet expanded over her head before she had a chance to react. While the plasma had missed their section of the ship, the same couldn't be said for the soldier's quarters. Her retinal comm updated with a message that they'd lost two lives and three more were wounded.

This day had started out so much better than the last. She could feel herself fraying.

"Where are we with the gate sequence?" she asked. Her voice sounded weird talking in a helmet.

"I'm still figuring it out," Minula said. "It appears to be jammed."

"I'll take it," Ibu said. "You focus on the bogies. The ship we lit up just engaged their thrusters. They appear to be out of range for plasma, or whatever the hell they fired at us. Maybe we can keep it that way."

Minula stared wide-eyed at her controls and ran her fingers through her hair. She was freezing up.

"Min!" Abigail stood up and walked up beside her. "I need you to focus. Give Ibu navigation, you handle piloting.

Ok?" She reached out and rested her hand on her friend's shoulder.

"Actually…" Minula glanced sideways and nodded at Ibu. "You're better at the piloting shit, why don't you—"

"I need to pull Harold in to figure out the gate drive," Ibu interrupted. "You've got this. You do."

Abigail squeezed Min's shoulder.

"Yea, I've got it." Minula gestured to the side, relinquishing navigation to Ibu.

When Abigail glanced at Ibu, they were already sliding their hand into the glove they'd created to interface with the computer. Most of the time, the Nanil used regular human touch interfaces to control things. She assumed to make everyone else comfortable. When they employed their neural link, they were either engaging the A.I. or working on something at a superhuman rate.

Turning back toward Minula, she noticed her friend had already shot herself full of stimulants and was maneuvering them to the far side of the asteroid. While humans didn't have mental links, they could use drugs to level the playing field as much as possible.

She took a step beside Cynthia. "How's the rest of the crew?"

Cynthia was subvocalizing commands to someone and glanced up. "Pierce and Kamal are tending to the wounded. Ibu released Shauna out of containment to help. One of them is… bad, but the others seem ok."

Abigail tapped her ear and subvocalized a command to bring up a schematic of the Phoenix. Their repair bots were already fast at work, but they'd lost environment in three spots, with the hull missing huge chunks where the plasma hit. It was a wonder they hadn't taken out a reactor core from either of the two halves of the ship.

As she was debating on heading aft to lend a hand, the comm relay came to life. She opened the inbound transmission from the attacking alien ship in a window on the wall screen and froze when she saw the face staring back. The mottled green and brown skin and the empty eyes of the Qudoculi were unmistakable.

"You're illegally mining near a Galactic Alliance trade route," the Qudoculi said. Their mouth wasn't moving in sync with the translation. "Give up and turn over your ship. Do so, and we may spare your life. Failure to comply will leave only one path to redemption."

She could feel the phantom of Admiral Gwar's hand touching her shoulder, trying to kill her a second time. Not again. Dying now wouldn't help anyone back home. She wasn't about to let them take her crew down without a fight. If she could reach across the comm and strangle the alien, she would.

Abigail stepped up beside Minula and grasped the handhold on the side of her chair. "Take that fraking ship out!"

Minula didn't look away from her controls. "I'm trying to keep this rock between us and them, sir. At least until Ibu—"

She snapped her finger to get Minula's attention. "That's a direct order, soldier. Take—the—ship—out. Was that clear enough?"

Minula shook her head. "We don't even know how many—"

"I'm not gonna hide. These fraking Qudoculi won't do that to me again. They deserve to meet their maker in the cold vacuum of space. Now kill them!"

"Sir. They have the numbers, and we're already heavily damaged. You know we're not designed to be a fighter, right?" Minula glared at her.

"I'll do it myself then." She reached out and Minula stopped her, snatching her wrist in a blur of movement before she could touch the controls.

"Fine! I'll do it." Minula tossed her thumb backwards. "Now go sit down and strap in. It's about to get bumpy."

In normal situations, Min wouldn't have batted an eye at the order. She didn't know what had gotten into her, but now wasn't the time or place to figure it out. Abigail took a few steps backward and sank into her chair. Once she leaned back, the straps from her harness shot over her shoulder and yanked her tight.

The gravitational dampeners on the Phoenix made the initial defensive motions almost imperceivable. Being on the offensive and on the burn was a different story. After Minula picked her route and checked over her ordinances, she slammed the throttle forward, sending the juice flowing through Abigail's chair. There was no warning on her retinal comm, or elsewhere on the ship, from what she could tell. There was only the crushing force of gravity reminding her how fragile her human body was.

As she fought to keep conscious, she watched Minula guide the Phoenix on an intercept course with the drive plumes headed toward their previous position. For once, they had the upper hand. She'd brought them around the asteroid, and they were moving into the center of Min's cross-hairs. Once her targeting reticle went green, she squeezed the trigger and the comforting thump of the plasma auto-cannons filled the bridge. Their own spheres of high-temperature energy shot across the void between the two ships.

Abigail could almost imagine herself pulling the trigger, and she wished she had. With the burn drugs saturating her body, all of her emotions were piqued. She raised her hand in a fist as the hull of the alien ship exploded in a cloud of orange and red before it was quickly extinguished by the vacuum of space.

"Yes!"

Minula didn't pause to celebrate. She rotated the Phoenix on its axis and performed another hard burn, squeezing the blackness into the edge of Abigail's vision and narrowly escaping a volley of lasers coming from several unseen attack vectors. The wall screen was predicting five encounters. And that was after the one she'd destroyed.

"Frak," she muttered.

She shook her head and turned to look at the Nanil, but they were deep in their mental link, oblivious to their surroundings. "Ibu!"

They didn't react. Short of yanking them out, the only way to get their attention was through a message. She quickly subvocalized a comm. "Where are we with that gate? Shit's getting hot out here."

A detailed reply appeared the instant she sent it. The response time inside a mental link was inhuman.

Our gate vanes are nearly repaired. Harold and Shauna are taking care of the repair bots, and I'm trying to plot our course in real time as Minula's piloting. The sooner we get out of here, the better. Whatever you do, make sure you're well away from that rock before we engage the gate. Its gravity will throw us off, and we don't want to end up inside that nebulosity. — Ibu

---

She read over that last part twice. Nobody wanted a repeat of yesterday. The bridge rocked, and Abigail dropped out of her comm to see the Phoenix flying headlong through a cloud of an exploding alien ship. For a split second, it looked like a flying three-dimensional Y before it was engulfed in a ball of fire.

"There are too many." Cynthia flipped through her controls and shared something on the wall screen. "I'm detecting multiple comm bursts between the ships. If my numbers are right, we've got at least nine bogies left."

"Nine!" Abigail gaped at the predicted targets. They weren't simply outnumbered, they were overwhelmed.

"Are you fraking kidding me?" Minula jammed the controls sideways, bringing Abigail's lunch up and into her mouth. "That's it. I gotta put that rock between us and a few of them. It's the only chance we have until Ibu does their magic. If our captain has a problem with it, then she can fire me."

"Speaking of." Cynthia glanced over her shoulder and stared at the Nanil. "Are they ok? They haven't said a word since disappearing into their mental link."

Abigail swallowed down the bile. "They're working with the A.I. to repair the ship. Just do your best to keep us alive, Min. I'm…"

Her voice trailed away as the Phoenix crested the small asteroid, and they got a look at the carnage on the far side. The plasma rounds from the Qudoculi fighters had torn several massive gashes deep into the rock. Or at least they thought it was a rock. Below the stony surface was what appeared to be a core of machinery and electronics. It wasn't merely an asteroid; it was a ship of some kind.

With all eyes on the sparking brown rock, they missed three of the tiny nimble fighters rising out of one of the holes the aliens had blown into the surface. Just as the sound of the gate vanes clanged to life and rocketed over the Phoenix, the plasma blasts from the alien ships tore through their hull.

The last thing Abigail remembered as the blue glow raced over her was seeing the undulating curtain of the Dark Nebula through where the wall screen used to be.

PROTO DARK NEBULA, INSIDE POCKET THREE

PASSING through the other side of the gate, she was cast into the dark. There were no lights shining on the bridge, and despite her best efforts, her retinal comm couldn't find anything to connect to. When Abigail leaned forward, the death grip of the harness slammed her back.

"Ugh." She moaned and reached down the left side of the chair, searching blindly for the release. She'd only used it a handful of times in her life, and only when Captain Quesh made her family run drills back in Sol when she was a kid.

While Zachary had customized the design of his ships, he wasn't stupid. He wouldn't have moved the release lever from where countless humans had been taught to search for it, would he? Just as she was about to give up, she felt it. While not as primitive and in your face as the giant levers she'd learned on, the mechanism was there. She pushed in, and a handle popped out. Grabbing it with her fingers, she yanked up and released both sides of the harness.

As her body floated forward, she yelped and scrambled for a grip, but only came back with the shoulder strap, which was recoiling into the chair.

"Oh shit," she muttered as her legs drifted up toward where the ceiling had been.

"Had been." The words echoed in her mind as she realized that not only was the far wall missing, the hull above her head was gone, as well. Had they been in regular space, she'd have seen stars. But all she could see now was blackness, which meant only one thing. They'd survived the gate transition into the Nebula.

With her body inverted, it dawned on her that if she was even seeing the ceiling, there must be light coming from somewhere. It had to be the star in the system. Either that, or the Phoenix was ablaze.

She stabilized herself by pushing with her left hand against the floor and holding the harness strap in a death grip with her right. From this angle, she could see under the consoles and swore she could make out three pairs of feet in the faint light. Her eyes were taking their time adjusting after the entry.

Her options ticked off in her mind. She could hang out here and hope someone came looking for them. Or she could find a way back to the heart of the Phoenix and check if the rest of the boat was intact. Without a proper space suit with maneuvering thrusters, she could only do so much.

Employing the belt as a pivot, she inched her fingers forward to reposition herself and then slowly tucked her legs down, wedging them against the chair. She was effectively using her chair as the floor, and when she craned her neck back, she could see the door. On the right was the emergency release.

The throbbing red glow gave her confidence that some part of the ship was still operational. All she could hope for now was that the internal compartmental seals had closed. Because as soon as she pushed off and hit that button, if someone was on the other side, they'd be propelled outward into the darkness of space.

Abigail leaned sideways and lined up her shot. She couldn't push off too hard, or she'd ricochet into god knows what. Too little and she wouldn't be able to press the button. The best she could hope for was something in the middle.

She counted down, and when she hit zero, she nudged off and gently released the belt, hoping it didn't retract all the way into the chair. With her hands over her head, she guided her fingers toward the red light. Her aim was true, and as she reached the wall, she slapped the button with all her strength.

While she knew it required a lot of force to activate the emergency release, what she wasn't prepared for was the opposite reaction of the energy from her motion. As the door slid open, she shot backward, feet first toward the darkness.

"No, no, no," she muttered as she flailed her hands in the void. Her angle was steeper than she expected, which meant her chair was well out of reach. She had to find something, anything, to grab onto. Looking left and right, she couldn't see any handles or obstacles in her path. It wasn't until she cleared the edge of the bridge controls that something caught her attention.

Ibu and Minula were awake, and they'd seen her float past. From the looks of it, they were gesturing at each other with their hands, but in the darkness, Abigail couldn't make out what they were saying. It didn't matter, though. Unless they had a rope, she was going to be space debris in a few seconds.

Just as she was preparing to pivot around, she noticed her friends moving. Ibu climbed forward, and from the looks of it, Minula was grasping the young Nanil's legs. They were creating a ladder with their bodies. She wasn't sure the chain would be long enough, but it was worth a try.

Abigail stretched herself as straight as she could, trying not to move too suddenly and add any momentum. She reached out toward the approaching Nanil, but came up short. Easily half a torso too little and gaining centimeters every second.

"Dammit!" She lowered her hand to her chest and tapped her heart before pointing at the two of them. They'd tried, but she'd fraked up again. As usual, her impatience had gotten the best of her.

She watched as Ibu receded backward, struggling to break free from Minula's grasp. The woman appeared to be pulling them back, but they weren't happy about it. Then she saw something unexpected. Minula reached behind her chair and grasped the same harness Abigail had used earlier. She'd wrapped it around her hand before pushing off with the Nanil in tow.

The two of them looked comical from afar, but the result was spot on. The harness gave them another meter of length and Ibu had somehow contorted their body, keeping their center of mass above Minula. This meant the woman could direct the Nanil like a stick toward Abigail.

Her heart pounded in her chest as they floated forward.

When their hands finally touched, Ibu grasped her with a vice-like grip, and she gasped. Not in pain, but in relief. She didn't want to die.

A tear of joy balled up inside her helmet in front of her eyes, and she mouthed the words, "Thank you."

8

———

IBU

PROTO DARK NEBULA, POCKET THREE

They made short work getting to the aft section of the ship once they woke up Cynthia. It was a lot easier working as a team without gravity than it was trying to do it alone. Any time they messed up, someone was there to help them out.

Once they sealed the entrance to the bridge, they realized they could re-enable the environment. It was one of three compartments that had been torn open, and Shauna isolated all of them from the rest of the ship.

Ibu's body had transformed during the event. While they were in a mental link when they passed through the gate, their physical form had still reacted to environmental stimuli of the rapid transition. In fact, it was hypersensitive to any change while their mind was elsewhere.

When they came to after losing their link, they assumed they were already dead. Pain engulfed their body, and they were surrounded by infinite blackness. Only after they saw Abigail floating past did they realize that not only were they alive, the shit had hit the fan, as humans would say.

Minula reached out and grasped Ibu's hand. "Nice work out there." She pulled them close and wrapped her arm around the Nanil in a half embrace. An awkward motion in zero-g.

Touching bodies was an unusual human gesture, but one they'd grown accustomed to. In fact, it was something they actually quite enjoyed. It was a means to denote happiness and to promote a bond or a sense of closeness between two individuals. A foreign concept to most Nanil, at least the ones they'd known before leaving Doda.

Ibu nodded. "Thanks. You, too." They glanced around. "So what now?"

Shauna stepped in view near the central torso of the ship and worked her way toward them. "You three are lucky to be alive. After those Qudoculi fighters cracked us open, we thought you were goners."

"You can't get rid of us that easily." Abigail nudged the wall with her knuckles and drifted in the direction of Shauna's robotic form firmly magnetized to the ground. "How's the crew?" She reached out and grasped the outstretched arm of her mother before easing to a stop.

"We lost one of the wounded, but the others are doing quite well. Harold's tending to them now." Shauna offered her other arm to Minula, and she accepted it. When she rotated to offer a hand to Ibu, they refused.

"No, I'm fine. I can manage." They pushed off and headed around the circle aftward. Clockwise, always clockwise.

"This way is shorter," Shauna said.

"I know." Ibu used their hands to pull themselves along the wall. "I'm checking over the damage." It was a lie, but the humans wouldn't know. Sometimes ritual overpowered logic.

As they passed the hall to the cargo bay, their retinal comm sprang to life and started updating. This part of the ship's mesh network appeared to be functioning properly. They'd have to talk to the others about fixing it elsewhere. They tapped their palm with their index finger and activated the voice channel.

"Where are we on repairing the Phoenix?" Ibu asked. When they floated into the galley, it was empty.

"We're regrouping in the second segment," Shauna said. "I would've told you, but you disappeared. That half has gravity."

Like with their computers, humans were dependent on gravity. Not that they hadn't managed for centuries of space faring without it, but they wasted countless decades struggling to reproduce the invisible force that kept them upright. Had they spent that same time unlocking their minds, they'd be a far more advanced civilization.

Ibu pushed off the table they'd grasped on to and worked their way toward engineering. It was the closest transition point to the Phoenix's second half. The crew often saw it as the less used and barely livable of the two ships. While they could live in either half, this was where they'd stashed most of their supplies, so the halls and rooms were crammed with crates and spare parts.

As they floated through the hatch, they forgot about the gravity and tumbled toward the ground. While they tucked into a ball just in time, they rolled forward and crashed into one of the replicator's raw material canisters, sending a loud gong through the halls of the ship.

"You ok?" Shauna asked.

"I'm fine." Ibu rubbed their shoulder and winced. That was going to hurt for a while. "I simply missed the transition."

"Yea, it comes out of nowhere. We're up on the second bridge once you get oriented."

Ibu spent a lot of time in this other ship within a ship while they were traveling through the Lupus Dark Nebula with Zachary and Pluto. Most of the voyage after Doda was spent hiding out here, away from the other humans. They filled their days with learning human history and preparing themselves to live among them. After they met up with

Bradley and the other half of the Fountainhead, the Nanil realized they very much preferred the sparseness of this half. They'd forgotten all about that when they hit Zeta Lupi. It would've made more sense for them to have prepared their quarters here.

When they stood up, a robot stepped around them and worked its way back out toward the non-gravity side. Their arms were laden with crates and various parts were overflowing, but well under control. At first, Ibu thought it was a general automation, but their retinal comm identified the bot as Harold.

"Where are you going?" Ibu brushed off their outfit and eyed the robot.

Harold stopped, but didn't turn to look at them. "We're redistributing the supplies between the two halves. Someone has to do it, and we grunts are the only ones cut out for it until we re-establish gravity."

"Why wouldn't we just stay here?" It made more sense to them.

"Don't ask me. Ask Abigail. She's in charge. Do you need me for anything?" Harold was still standing in place with his back to them. He wasn't being himself, and he hadn't been since being forced into confinement.

"No. I'm fine." Ibu waved him away. "Continue on."

"Very well." He stepped over the threshold into the first half and disappeared.

The others were moving fast, and they needed to know what was happening. If history was an indicator, the odds were high they'd have more short-sighted mistakes to clean up in the human's wake. Especially with Abigail still reeling from that Qudoculi encounter.

THE CREW WAS busy separating the ship into its two halves. Once Abigail made it to the other side, she began spitting out orders to everyone. Ibu wasn't sure what switch flipped in their friend, but they were glad to see her taking action rather than locking herself in her quarters and licking her wounds.

While the others were heads down planning a ground mission, Ibu was neck deep in their mental link, preparing the Phoenix to split in two. The least damaged ship was being sent away from the planet to hunker down in case an emergency evac was needed, whereas the other, more battered half was heading down to the surface. They believed there were enough raw materials down there to repair the ship while the landing team searched for the Ursis.

The initial scans of the system came back bleak. Except for a few token organics planetside, there were no life signs to speak of. There were, however, the remains of hundreds of cities, the largest of which they planned on setting down near.

Ibu's challenge was getting the damaged half of the Phoenix stable enough to make the descent and back without putting the crew at risk. With as many holes as the Qudoculi poked in their hull, it was a wonder they'd survived at all. Yet somehow, the second ship remained nearly unscathed. Sure, there was external damage, but nothing like with the first.

With the extra cycles from their mental link, Ibu had been studying the moment of transition. Something didn't quite make sense. Harold's inspection of the gate vanes found that all the segments had some damage, and a few were trashed. In fact, the nano-mesh interconnects between those vanes had unwound and were spidering off hundreds of meters in space.

They honestly didn't understand how they'd made it through the gate transition at all. The shots from the three Qudoculi fighters should've ended the gating sequence, and the Phoenix should still be outside the Nebula, but they weren't.

They'd been reviewing the recordings from the transition for micro-days. While it took hours to do, the spare moments in their mental link gave them opportunities for more menial tasks like this. Tasks the humans often turned over to their A.I. but Ibu refused to.

The video paused, and they enlarged several frames from different angles of the transition. They were from the omnidirectional nanite cameras in the nose cone of the Phoenix. As the plasma cannons tore into the gate vanes, the mesh interconnecting them unwound and flung outward like a whip. That pent-up energy directing the space-time tachyon field was immense, and the distance the material was able to cover in mere milliseconds was astounding.

As they stepped through the thousands of sub second frames, they saw it. One moment, the Qudoculi fighters were there, and the next, they were gone. They could say the same for the massive asteroid. Maybe it was an optical illusion, but it almost appeared like the alien objects transited with them.

When they brought up the scans from near their ship after they arrived, the space around them was empty. There were no remnants of an asteroid, and there certainly weren't any alien fighters.

"Harold," Ibu began, "Are you there? Can you hear me?"

"I can," Harold said. "What's your query?"

"What do you make of this?" Ibu shared the footage of the transition with the A.I. in their containment dot. While they were allowed to remotely control robotic forms, their commands were limited. Ever since their encounter in the hall, Harold had decided to program primitive expert systems to perform the tasks the humans needed rather than do it himself. He was acting as if his ego was bruised and drudge work was beneath him, yet that was the purpose of a robot.

"It's a simple tension slingshot," Harold began. "Zachary and Shauna used to see it all the time at the Wheel. I don't think it's anything to worry about."

"I'm not so sure." They shared the recording with Shauna and connected the three of them in their mental link.

"Ahh yes, the mesh slingshot." Shauna appeared in Ibu's virtual space. Her avatar matched that of a middle-aged woman from when she had her kids. "We ran into these a lot in the early days of mastering the tachyon flow. The power was difficult to control back then, and it took us forever to build the mesh with the right substrate and patterns to distribute the forces. Once we did, they stopped happening." She leaned forward, studying the sequence of frames. "I've never seen one this late in the transition, though. The visual effect is curious. What do you think happened?"

"If anything, I'd hazard a guess that those ships were torn in half." Harold's voice was omniscient as he refused to join their virtual meetup.

Ibu adjusted the footage forward and back. "Then why do they disappear? I mean, there's no physical sign of an explosion. And yet, in one frame, they're there, and the next, they're gone. Check again. There are several thousand frames before the tachyon field passes over the nose camera itself, and in that time the ships never reappear."

Harold was silent. They assumed he was studying the footage to confirm.

Shauna pulled up a virtual chair and eyed Ibu. "What do you think happened?"

The woman had changed her tune these past few days since being left out. It was like her confrontational side had been suppressed, and she was being motherly. Something Ibu was unfamiliar with, except for their stint aboard the Fountainhead when Pluto coddled them.

Ibu bit their lip. "Could they... have transitioned along with us?"

"Not possible!" Harold flashed into existence in front of them. It was the first time he'd ever entered the virtual space of their mental link. "Do you even know how the gate sequence works?"

Shauna shook her head. "Now, Harold. Ibu's not an imbecile. Perhaps you should—"

"Maybe they should think before they speak then," he interrupted.

Ibu glared at the man. His all black attire brought with it an air of smug negativity. It certainly wasn't the openness and rigor of the scientific method they'd read so much about over human history.

"And you know beyond a doubt they couldn't have been pulled through gate space with us how?" Ibu asked. "You've done the experiment?"

He shook his head. "You know I haven't. But the tachyon field didn't pass over those ships. Only objects that transition through the particle field have ever jumped the gap."

Ibu raised their eyebrow. "Because we've verified it?"

"Come on!" Harold threw up his arms. "I don't need to verify that you need air to survive in space, yet I'm pretty sure you do based on how you react when we remove it. And yet, I haven't verified it. We're talking about a law of gate dynamics."

"You're seriously going with the oxygen defense?" Ibu smiled. "Ok, then explain how the Ulixi can lower their oxygen use and their life signs to undetectable levels? I'm pretty sure human health science would render that an impossibility, and yet, it happened."

"Apples and oranges, and you know it." He circled his hand in the virtual space between them. "But let's take a step out on that unsettling plank of yours hanging off the side of reality. Where are they? They clearly didn't pop through the other side with us."

Ibu shook their head from side to side. "I... don't know. My first instinct would be to measure the number of tachyons that passed through that nano-mesh. I'd imagine they're some proportional distance along our path relative to that energy. But given how that mesh was destroyed before we measured it, we'll never know."

"So you really think they came through along with us then?" Shauna leaned forward in her virtual chair.

"I think we should prepare as if they had," Ibu said.

Harold groaned.

Shauna glared at him. "Let them talk, you insolent rube."

Ibu continued. "There's also the possibility that they ended up in the Dark Nebula, which would be ideal. But if we presume they couldn't have made it through, we won't be prepared for an attack."

"An attack?" Harold took a step toward both of them. "Look around. There's nothing here. We're in this system alone. We haven't detected so much as a blip on any of our active scans since we arrived. Any amount of effort you put into building a defense instead of fixing these ships is in direct conflict with Abigail's orders. You understand that, right?"

"So turn me in. Go for it." Ibu leaned forward and shoved Harold back. "See how your Four Laws deal with Abigail dying in front of your eyes. You can watch another round of those plasma weapons the Qudoculi lobbed through us take off her head next time. Otherwise, frak off!"

They snapped their finger, and Harold disappeared. When Ibu turned to face Shauna, her virtual mouth was gaping open. "What?"

Shauna shook her head. "I've... never seen anyone talk to him that way."

"Well, it's high time they did." Ibu brought up the schematics of the two ships mid-separation, along with their orbital path around the planet. "Now, what can we do to set up a defensive perimeter near these ships?"

THE PROBES SCOPING out the proposed landing sites had been coming back for hours. After each one returned, Ibu noticed the crew's hope diminish a little more each time they found no signs of life. They'd started calling the world Griseo, based on the planet's name in the Galactic Alliance species catalog. From orbit, the sphere appeared to be painted in nothing more than thousands of shades of gray. It was the bleakest habitable planet they'd ever seen.

The Nanil had been dodging the other members of the crew. Their only outside interaction was with Shauna. For now, she was acting as an intermediary with the humans. There was too much work to do, and the last thing they needed was to listen to another round of gossip about the state of Sol or who was going to be the next President of CoPE.

They'd used a majority of their raw material stores sealing off the first ship to make it worthy of landing on the planet. While it was a gamble, the mission down to Griseo was all about gathering intel. The more they knew about the Ursis and where they'd gone, the sooner they'd know if they should move on to another Nebula.

Ibu watched Shauna's form floating out in the space between the two ship halves. On its own, the red aurora encircling most of the upper hemisphere of the alien world was spectacular, but seeing the robot gliding above it was surreal. Like they were swimming in a bloody mist.

What she was actually doing out there was reforming the skotádi coated nanites that covered the surface of the Phoenix. It was an optimization Zachary had made before they left. With how easy it was to be detected after taking damage, it was safer to re-flow the material across the hull if you had enough. It also allowed for predictive shielding to relocate the nanites when an impact was imminent. The saving in skotádi was low, but every gram of the stuff was priceless.

Watching the coating re-flow to the less damaged second ship was eerie. It reminded Ibu of the human taffy they'd had eaten in Zeta Lupi. And like the candy, it, too, was red, except instead of a colored dye, it was due to the reflected light of the aurora below. They'd only had the sweet once, when Pluto took them to a store the one time they went down to Tiān.

"Your heart rates are elevated," Shauna said. "Is everything ok?"

"I... think so. I was just... having a memory flash." Ibu checked their vitals and, sure enough, they had ticked up outside the normal range. That was unusual.

"What's a memory flash?" Shauna reached out and grabbed a blob of the skotádi that had separated from the bunch and re-flowed it with the rest. The nanite's state machine sometimes got confused when they switched between mesh networks.

"I believe humans call it reminiscing." An alarm went off on their virtual control panel. The baseball sized skotádi covered satellites they'd deployed in orbit were picking up a gravitational anomaly in their wake. One second the alert was going off, and the next it cleared.

"What were you thinking about?" Shauna tugged on the cable connecting her to the ship to give her robotic form more slack. She was about to dive down to collect another blob of skotádi on the loose.

"Taffy," Ibu began. "Did you catch that gravitational anomaly a few seconds ago?" They flicked up all the aft facing cameras on the virtual wall and started scanning them for anything that lined up with the alert. While they hadn't detected any trash in orbit like they'd read about the human planet of Earth, there was bound to be space debris around any inhabited world.

"I'm reading an abnormality in the gravity field, but there's nothing there." Shauna deposited the stray skotádi and made her way above the mass of nanites for a better vantage.

When Ibu projected the coordinates from the anomaly on each of the cameras, they came up empty. That was until they switched to the last one. The one nearest the planet, and the furthest point in their defenses.

The Nanil leaned forward and studied the effect. "Is this a camera distortion, or are you seeing a crescent shape behind us? It's tiny, but it's there."

There was a pause before Shauna replied. "I see the camera you're watching, but from where I am, I don't see anything. It could be a lens flare from the sun. I mean—"

Suddenly, a missile arced across the horizon straight toward them. Trailing it was their worst nightmare. The three Qudoculi fighters Harold swore they left outside the Nebula.

While now wasn't the time to gloat, Ibu sent an alert broadcasting the discovery to the rest of the sleeping crew. While the humans wouldn't react for another few thousand milliseconds, there was plenty of time for Harold to wallow in his Four Laws while he was locked away in his containment dot. Not that they couldn't use his help, but a second A.I. questioning their every move wasn't their idea of fun.

Shauna issued a request to take over weapons, but even with Ibu's acceptance, they needed a human to approve it. The short-sighted stupidity of Abigail's blanket decision was fraking ridiculous. If it didn't kill them, they were going to tear her a new asshole when this was over.

Ibu brought up the Phoenix's weapons controls, and their hearts sank. They only had half the armaments enabled and at their disposal. So much for planning ahead. As they queued up firing commands for the laser battery, the course projections of the missiles had it lined up with the crescent they detected earlier. The Qudoculi weren't even targeting them yet. Perhaps they still had a chance.

They shared the findings with Shauna and started reprogramming the lasers and the limited number of missiles to focus on the fighters and not the inbound missile. Just as she was about to hit go on the program, a flash of light on the edge of the crescent caught their attention.

"What's that?" Ibu asked.

Shauna zoomed in on the constellation of lights shooting across the sky from the crescent shape toward the inbound projectile. From Ibu's point of view, the objects were moving excruciatingly slow.

The Nanil shared their firing solution with Shauna to review. Another pair of eyes wouldn't hurt their chances. Her response came back in a flash, and when Ibu brought up the edits, they realized she'd changed nearly the entire program. From the looks of it, she was letting the alien ships get really close to their position. At that distance, there was no room for error.

"That's cutting it too close," Ibu said. "We need to take out what we can from afar."

"Trust me." Shauna flashed into her virtual space, a trick they hadn't seen the A.I. do across a vast distance. "I haven't been exactly trustworthy."

Ibu froze. "What does that mean?"

Shauna stared down at the virtual ground, and a few hundred nanoseconds passed.

"Spit it out." Ibu waved their hands in the air. "It's a little late to ask for forgiveness. What the hell did you do?"

She flicked up an overlay on top of Ibu's plan. The only difference was the labels on the micro-satellites they dropped.

Ibu raised a hand to cover their mouth and tapped one of the satellites for more details. Each of the spheres housed three grains of spános. Enough explosive power to take out a hundred of those ships. They didn't have much of the stuff onboard, yet somehow the A.I. managed to snatch some.

"Frak!" Ibu lowered their hand. "I need to warn the others. We have to move these ships, or we'll be damaged in the aftermath." When they reached out to run their program, a dialog popped up, prompting them for another authorization. "You've got to be fraking kidding me. That daughter of yours is going to be the death of us yet."

"I never imagined I'd do this, but I need you to stay here while I wake up the humans." They swiped their weapon controls over to Shauna. "Please don't make me regret it."

"I won't," Shauna said. "I promise. Now go, save the others. I've got the bridge. The moment Minula approves them, I'll run the program."

As Ibu dropped out of the mental link, it dawned on them that Shauna had suggested they go to Minula and not her daughter. Even she knew Abigail wasn't cut out to make these rapid fire decisions.

When the lights of the room appeared through their eyelids, Ibu ripped her hand out of the link device and flipped around in their chair, leaping toward the aft of the ship. With their initial step, the first of the klaxons blared. It was amazing how slow real time was until you spent most of your day in a mental link. It was no wonder the Prima Nanil spent the last century of their life almost exclusively in a link or meditative state of some kind.

The doors opened before the Nanil was close enough to trigger them, which meant Shauna was watching out for them. Her help instilled confidence. Minula's quarters were starboard, so Ibu took the left, and a few leaps later they were pounding on the human's door.

When the woman's face finally appeared, they were wide-eyed. "What's going on?"

Ibu subvocalized the command to share the approval request with Minula. "I... need you to accept this. Fast. It's our only hope."

Minula narrowed her gaze. "What is—"

"There's no time." Ibu reached out and gently squeezed the woman's shoulder. "Trust me. Please."

They thought for sure the human was going to continue with her line of questions until the dialog went green and disappeared. Ibu sighed.

"Alright, now tell me what I just signed off on."

The klaxons rang a second time, except it wasn't a call for battle stations. It was a warning of an immanent burn.

"Everyone, strap the frak in!" Ibu's voice echoed down the corridor. Before Minula had a chance to react, Ibu leapt toward her and pinned her against the bulkhead on the aft side of her quarters.

"What the hell are you doing?" Minula shoved the Nanil, but it was too little too late. They were already mid-transformation into their fight form and their strength was increasing exponentially.

"I'm saving your life." They locked their grip around the leg of the table and pushed against Minula's bed with the other, immobilizing the human against the wall.

"I wouldn't call this—"

The rest of the sentence never came as the burn hit. This wasn't a regular run-of-the-mill burn, and Ibu knew it. If Shauna was going to get them out of the blast radius, they needed some distance from those satellites.

They grimaced in pain as the G-forces pressed their body against the human. It was important that they not crush the woman to death. The Nanil locked their knees and arced their back, but the strain was unbearable. While Minula was safely ensconced in the space between the bulkhead and Ibu, their back was paying the price.

One by one, they could feel their vertebrae pop and crack. It took everything they had not to give in. The woman put their trust in them, and now it was their turn to return the favor.

"What... the... frak... is... going... on?" Minula asked.

A moment later, the drive cut, and then all hell broke loose. The explosion aft of the ship sent a shockwave outward, and where seconds earlier they were being pushed against the human, now the woman was being forced against them.

"Argh!" Ibu fought to maintain consciousness, but they couldn't take anymore. The forces were too much to bear, even for them.

When their hand released its grip on the table, they didn't slam against the far wall like they imagined they would. Instead, Minula started grunting and taking deep shallow breaths. Ibu glanced sideways and saw that the woman had brought her legs up and wedged it against one of the other legs of the same table. In all the commotion, she had wrapped her arms around the Nanil. That and her bear hug, combined with her amazing leg strength, were the only things stopping them both from falling back as the ship was tossed about like a rag doll.

After another ten seconds of rolling, the Phoenix Two recovered. Ibu could hear the maneuvering jets firing throughout the ship in between the continued klaxons overhead.

They sighed and screamed out loud. "Cut the alarms, Shauna!"

The warnings stopped, and Shauna's voice filled the halls of the ship. "I need some help on the bridge. We're in the clear, for now. There's one left, but it's taken significant damage and is hightailing it toward the far side of the planet. I think it's attempting an emergency landing."

"One what?" Minula let her legs go and the two of them collapsed against the floor in a pile. The woman sighed as she gently set Ibu down.

They winced and reached around, running their fingers along their back. Pain coursed through their entire body as waves of dizziness washed over them. "I'm gonna... need to rest for a bit. Body... will repair. Go... help... Shauna."

Minula brought her hand up to Ibu's face and brushed

their cheek. They swore she said something, but all they saw was her lips moving until the room went dark.

THE ROOM WAS dark when Ibu shot upright. They waved their hand in the blackness until the lights eased up to an extremely low level.

"Where... who's there?" They reached around their back and ran their hand down their spine. Their body had repaired itself.

"I'm here," Shauna whispered. "Minula and the others are coming your way. Before they arrive, I should warn you now that I've been dodging their questions. I kept them locked out of weapons, so they couldn't see what I did. You've only been out a few hours, but Abigail is getting testy. I can't hold her off much longer. I'm so sorry I didn't tell you what I did. It was all—"

The door slid open and Minula, Abigail, and the others came rushing in.

"Are you all right?" Minula eased down into the chair beside them.

"I'm better." They arched their back and twisted, but there was no pain. "My body's designed to repair itself. You know, superhuman fighting machine and all."

Cynthia chuckled and sat down at the end of the bed.

Ibu rubbed their eyes as the light turned up a few notches. "How are the Phoenixes doing?"

"They're in one piece," Abigail said. "Barely. We lost a bunch of skotádi, but I sent Harold off to round it up. He's pissed still, but he'll get over it. Now, what the frak happened while we were asleep? Shauna won't tell us shit, and I'm about to go hunting for her containment dot to shut it off."

They'd forgotten all about where Shauna was. She'd been outside the ship when this whole thing started. Wherever the robot had gone, she was still with them. That was evident enough.

"The Qudoculi attacked us," Ibu began. "But we were ready for them. Shauna and I—"

"Wait, wait!" Abigail raised her hands. "How the hell did the Qudoculi attack us in here? We left them outside the Nebula, unless you're gonna tell me there's a colony inside this pocket."

"No." Ibu shook their head and regretted it the moment they had. They held up a finger and paused. "They... came in when we did. The gate drive malfunctioned and... I'll just share the details. It's... complicated. Trust me when I tell you that all four of the ships came in with us."

"Four?" Cynthia tilted her head. "There were only three Qudoculi."

"That's right," Shauna said from overhead. "The fourth ship was the asteroid. It made it through, as well." She shared the video from the incident on the wall screen. They silently watched as the feed from one of the distant micro-satellites showed their ships burn away before it was flipped end over end in the aftershock of an explosion. The same one that took out two of the Qudoculi.

"No shit," Minula said. "So that's what the Qudoculi were shooting at outside the Nebula. Who were they?"

Ibu shrugged. "No idea. It doesn't matter, though. They're ash now."

"What the frak caused that explosion?" Abigail asked. "I didn't see any missiles on our side, and the last I checked, our nukes were all accounted for."

"You counted those, did ya?" Ibu stared down at their hands. They were shaking. In all the years they'd been alive, the only time their body had shaken like this was under the thumb of their progenitor. Never once with a human. Until today.

Abigail nodded. "I counted them as soon as we were in the clear. Now answer my question. What caused—"

Ibu shot up on their feet. "You did!"

"I did." She took a step backward. "The hell you say! I was fraking sleeping."

"We could've taken care of the Qudoculi on our own if you hadn't locked us out of the systems. While you were asleep, I was protecting the crew. Protecting you from yourself. I laid down the ordinances after I discovered the gates had brought along some unwanted guests. Your little puppet, Harold." Ibu danced their hands in the air. "He can vouch for that. Hell, he called my idea bullshit and said he was gonna tell you about it. I'm actually surprised he didn't."

"Don't fraking put this on me." Abigail pointed at the Nanil. "You should've woken us up and told us what was going on. Besides, someone else had to have helped you. You couldn't have launched that strike without—"

"I authorized the detonation," Minula interrupted. "It was the only way to save us. There's no chance you would've approved it. You'd have listened to Harold. You always chose his answers over anyone else's."

Abigail's eyes went wide. "Okay... Why didn't you say that earlier? What did we detonate?"

"Spános," Minula said.

Ibu glanced at the woman. Somehow, she'd known.

Minula stepped up beside the Nanil and rested her hand on their shoulder. "It was the only thing big enough to knock them out once and for all. We were outnumbered outside the Nebula when you ordered us to take them head on. I was against that move you made out there, but we weren't about to make another mistake in here. So Ibu and I laid down a defensive perimeter."

Abigail nodded, taking in everything she'd heard. "You think I made a bad call out there?"

"I do," Minula said.

"So do I," Ibu echoed.

Cynthia cleared her throat. "We all do, sir."

"Alrighty then." Abigail bit her lower lip. "I appreciate the candor. I'll be in my quarters. Minula, you have command."

Minula saluted her. "Aye, sir. I have command."

As the door slid shut, Minula turned to face Ibu. "How badly did I frak up that story?"

Cynthia drew in a breath and glanced between them. "What?"

"Surprisingly," Ibu began, "you nailed it. I take it the explosion was a bit too much?"

Minula chuckled and raised her hand up, holding her fingers a few centimeters apart. "Just a smidge."

Shauna opened a direct comm to Ibu. "You didn't have to do that. I could've taken the heat for my actions."

"No. I had to do it," Ibu subvocalized. "She needs to understand at some point that there are consequences to her decisions. There always has been. The difference is that now they're immediate, and not up to another generation to clean up. You and me... we'll talk later about how you pulled off stealing that spános without us knowing it. Ok?"

There was no pause. Only a message on their retinal comm.

Yessir.

Cynthia shook her head. "I'm confused as an alley cat without gravity. What just happened here? I mean, besides Abigail being pissed off."

Ibu broke out into laughter. It was the first time they had a feeling they would describe as joy, and it was exhilarating.

9

ABIGAIL OLIVAW
PROTO DARK NEBULA, ORBITING GRISEO

Abigail stared at herself in the mirror. The bags under her eyes, creases in her forehead, and the lines at the side of her mouth were more pronounced than they used to be. She'd aged a lot in the last year. While she'd never been vain, she always cared about her appearance to a degree. At least in the past. After all they'd been through, she couldn't see the point of wasting nanites to remove her wrinkles. Not when they could be used for more important things.

She reached down and adjusted her digital camo. The surface of black fabric shimmered in the light when it was off. It was designed to blend in with the surrounding environment, no matter what you were standing in front of. In all her years, besides a good paintball fight, she'd never worn camouflage or thought she'd ever need to. Times certainly had changed.

When she unholstered her firearm, one of the two lights on the side went green to her touch. All she had to do was double tap with her index finger to activate the second light and finish the unlock procedure. Then it'd be ready for action.

She turned the pistol over in her hand. It was perfectly balanced and able to fire almost any munition you put inside.

Within reason, of course. There was also a short swappable barrel stored in a pouch on her leg that could slide in and shoot bolts of energy. Even though there was only enough charge for a few dozen shots, she had several replacement batteries and clips stashed in the pockets of her camo. They were ready at a moment's notice and should keep her going in the throes of a firefight.

A firefight. There's another word she never imagined would become part of her repertoire. Beyond a damning exchange of words, flying bullets were an unfamiliar experience. She hoped all the video games she played against her brothers as a kid would come back when she needed it. She used to kick their ass up and down, at least until her father enlisted her into running the company.

Her door chimed.

Abigail knew Shauna was standing outside. She'd watched her approach on her retinal comm. The rest of the crew was assembled in the galley and were awaiting her orders. While the team of soldiers accompanying her had already been chosen, the members of her bridge team had not. She'd spent the evening figuring out their next steps and absorbing the feedback from her closest friends. The people she trusted most, and the ones she thought understood her. Last night, she realized that couldn't have been further from the truth.

They mistook her decisions as random emotional acts that put their lives in jeopardy. While she sometimes surprised even herself, she never second guessed her actions. She'd only ever had one motivation since that fated day when the Galactic Alliance arrived in Sol, survival at all costs.

She slid her firearm into the holster on her thigh and adjusted her suit one last time, tightening the wrist connection to the gloves. They didn't know how breathable the air was down there, so their suits needed to be airtight. The suit could automatically seal most gaps, but only after you ensured it was tightened all the way.

Her retinal comm chimed, and she turned and opened the door, marching straight past Shauna. Dealing with pleasantries was the last thing on her mind. Someone was about to be pissed, but she didn't give a shit. She marched into the galley and the room fell quiet.

"Captain Kamal and Platoon One." She nodded at him. "You're with me. We'll be surveying the city after we land."

"Yessir." Kamal turned and pointed starboard, toward the transition point back across to the damaged ship. "Move it or lose it, people. Get your gear and head on over to Phoenix One. Now… go, go, go!"

The first platoon took off toward the docking clasp where they'd pass to the other ship.

She faced Pierce. "Captain, you and Platoon Two. You're splitting in two. The first half is coming planetside and will direct all raw material recovery operations. If it ain't worth it, we don't want it. You'll probably still want full weapons, but your job is about filling every square centimeter of that ship with what we need to survive. If I so much as find one random ass artifact stowed away, you'll be spaced. Is that understood?"

The platoon snapped to attention. "Sir, yessir!"

"I assume you've already split your team, Captain?" She stepped up beside Pierce.

"I have, sir. Lieutenant Moet and her team will stay here aboard Phoenix Two. The rest are heading planetside with me."

Abigail dipped her head and turned to look at Minula. "Major Clarke, you'll be commanding Phoenix Two. Keep it safe and continue repairs. Shauna and Cynthia will be here to assist with anything you need. If you have spare cycles, you're authorized to send a few probes through the system to see what you find. Maybe we can recover some skotádi or spános. It couldn't hurt to check. Otherwise, maintain radio silence and keep your bad side facing the Nebula until we contact you."

"But, sir." Minula took a step forward. "I wish to accompany—"

"My orders are final, Major." She straightened her back. "I need you up here for backup in case shit goes south. You're the best officer I have, and in the thick of it, I know you'll make the right decisions. If you lose contact with our team for longer than twenty-four hours, you're to return to Zeta Lupi with all the intel we've captured. We'll send updates and data dumps every four hours. I expect those will keep our comms officer busy for a while. Is that understood?"

"Yes, Captain," Cynthia said.

Minula narrowed her gaze and lowered her tone. "Seriously? You're relegating me to the sidelines?"

"I didn't think this would be a problem." She spun her head sideways. "Lieutenant Moet?"

"Yessir." Moet stepped forward.

"I'm not sure if you're up to it, but I need you to—"

"Yessir!" Minula snapped to attention and saluted Abigail. "Reporting for duty to command Phoenix Two, sir."

She knew her friend wouldn't take the orders without a fight, but her feelings didn't matter. She needed to separate the emotions of her team from making rational decisions. Everything down on that planet had to run by the book, not an irrelevant backstory. Which was why Ibu and Harold would accompany her down there. It would be hard enough letting Harold loose, but they needed his knowledge, and Shauna was too vested in her kids to think clearly.

"Ibu." Abigail glanced left and right, but didn't see the Nanil. "Where are they?"

"They were just here." Cynthia held up her hand. "Let me check their room." She marched aft, and a second later reappeared, walking side by side with Ibu and a heavily armed robot.

Abigail furrowed her brow. "What's this?"

Ibu crossed their arms. "Based upon the assignments I saw appear in the computer, and you leaving Minula here on Phoenix Two, there was a ninety-eight percent probability you'd be bringing Harold along. That is, unless you're planning to leave a hole in our knowledge as large as a major planetoid, sir."

She smiled. Just when she thought she knew the Nanil, they surprised her with a wise ass, yet accurate observation. "Your assumption is correct. Harold, are you willing to accompany me planetside?"

"Sir, yessir." Harold bowed.

"What about keeping an eye on him?" Cynthia asked. "Who's gonna make sure he doesn't clone himself?"

Ibu patted the robot on the shoulder. "I've disabled all transmission abilities in this form. My expert systems will scan anything that goes into and out of his data dot. If he so much as loads the wrong ammo, I'll know it. Isn't that right, Mr. Olivaw?"

Harold nodded. "I'm nothing more than a modern-day eunuch in carbon nano-weave. Oh, yeah, and I have lots of guns."

She raised her hand to her mouth and chuckled. "Well, at least he found his sense of humor. It'll be good to have you at my side, old friend."

* * *

PROTO DARK NEBULA, ON GRISEO

ABIGAIL STEPPED off Phoenix One and onto the soil of another world. Her boots made the familiar crunch she associated with dirt on Earth, except this was the first time she'd touched a planet outside Sol. She'd never had a chance to visit Tiān in Zeta Lupi. At least not that wouldn't put her at risk of arrest.

She craned her neck and took in the vastness of the heavens. Being cooped up in a spaceship for so long was hard on people that liked being in a gravity well. As she glanced around, she noticed that the sky was more white than gray from down here. And the soil actually had some browns and oranges intermixed with the layers of ash. From orbit, it was a single palette of colors, yet up close it was more complicated.

Despite the symbolism of things being more nuanced than they first appeared, it didn't matter. Griseo was already dead. They were simply here to understand why, and to get some clues on where to search for the Ursis next. That, and steal some supplies, of course.

Harold stepped up beside her without saying a word. When she glanced at him, he was constantly sweeping the horizon, searching for something that might threaten them.

"See anything?" she asked.

"Negative," Harold began. "A few immobilized automata in the nearby buildings, but no signs of life or movement other than the breeze."

She thought it was interesting he didn't call them robots. Probably because that was too close to his current form. Either that, or he was being nostalgic for a bygone reference before robots were commonplace, and a time more akin to his birth in human history.

When she brought up a crew map, she noticed Pierce had wasted no time. Her team had already unloaded all the recovery tools and were making their way toward a nearby building. Their early scans showed it was used for manufacturing of some kind. Hopefully, not foodstuff.

Kamal's team had fanned out, surrounding her on all sides. Each of his team was some five to ten meters in any direction, and half were donning exo-suits.

"Are we ready, sir?" Ibu asked.

Abigail turned left and flinched. The Nanil was stealthy. It was almost like they only made noise when they wanted humans to know where they were.

"Yes. Let's get underway."

With that, Kamal circled his hands in the air and pointed forward. His team started marching toward the heart of the city.

As they worked their way past countless nondescript broken vehicles, she marveled at how barren and lifeless the world was. The winds kicked up wave after wave of gray dust. If it weren't for lidar and the active scanning of their weapons, they'd have been blind several times.

The further they got, the more surprised she'd become. She wasn't sure why, but she thought they'd have found a skeleton by now. All the vehicles were empty, and even the buildings that looked like schools or businesses were missing their occupants. Not that they'd explored the insides in detail. Their target was a governmental facility up the street a few klicks. At least it appeared to be based upon the pomp and circumstance of the architecture.

Except for some videos of the Ursis, they had no idea what to expect when they finally found one. The species had kept to itself for generations before breaking out of their home world and populating nearby stars at an astonishing rate. It was that change which put them on the radar of the Galactic Alliance.

Reports that Shauna had uncovered claimed the aliens had stolen GA technology, which explained the sudden modernization and rise in industry. During their Tribunal, the Ursis asserted that their explosive expansion was part of an intellectual renaissance from a self-inflicted cultural evolution that mutated their minds and resulted in feats of engineering not seen for millennia in the GA.

Abigail's retina chimed, bringing her out of her thoughts. "Go ahead."

"Sir," Kamal began, "we're measuring non-zero levels of viruses and electronic pathogens similar to nanites in the air."

"What does that mean?" She turned toward Harold.

He kept his eyes on the horizon. "It means they found a few dead microscopic robots in the dust passing by. Nothing is active, but there's no telling what it would do if it were."

"Let's keep moving." She pointed forward. "We're not far from our target."

As the recon for her team rounded the next corner, they dropped and rolled behind a nearby structure. Harold stepped in front of her and pointed sideways toward cover, keeping himself in between her and whatever the others had seen.

She went where she was told. "What is it?"

Harold shared the camera from the forward soldier's helmet. She'd forgotten she could do that and brought up a few more, as well. Not being in her element down here meant she was too reliant on others to take care of her. She needed to change that.

The camera showed a small shoebox sized robot scurrying along the ground. When the soldier zoomed in, they watched the robot sweep up a pile of rubble. It zipped into the distance, dumping the debris into a nearby receptacle. Once complete, it dashed to another pile and repeated the same commands. A moment later, the wind kicked up behind it and blew the captured dirt into the air, depositing it elsewhere in the diag between the buildings.

"The primitive contraption appears to be stuck in an infinite loop," Ibu said. "I don't think it'll put up a fight."

Kamal's team moved forward and intercepted the robot. Once they checked it over, they gave the green light and her guards were on the move again.

She eyed her clock. They were already an hour into traipsing through the city, and they didn't have shit to show for it. Hopefully, her people back at Phoenix One were fairing better. They'd be in radio silence for another few hours before they'd do a data share via a drone launched from the drop ship. The entire process was textbook ops, though it'd only been used a handful of times in human history and only twice during her presidency. Once on Luna during a hostile takeover of a Lunar city by a corporate entity, and then on Mars during the collapse of a mine. At the time, they thought that was by force, as well, but it turned out to be a failure of human engineering.

"We're coming up on the first target," Kamal said.

Abigail adjusted the cameras on her retinal comm and brought up the forward most team member's view. In front of them stood a massive statue of a bear. It was standing on its hind legs, and in one hand, it had a book. In the other, it was holding a celestial sphere, not unlike the ones she'd used as a kid to navigate the stars.

What was most striking to her were the hands and face of the Ursis. It didn't look at all like she'd imagined. In her mind, she'd seen the sharp fangs and claws of an Earth bear. But in front of her stood a muted form of the same animal. An evolutionary fork in the road that never occurred on her home world. While it still appeared to be able to walk on all fours, its upright position highlighted the same transformation that led to the objects it was holding. Based on the girth of the alien body, it was clearly muscular under the clothing it was wearing.

"Wholly shit," the soldier muttered over the open channel. "That's one goddamned big bear."

"Let's keep it professional, folks," Kamal said. "I want you focused, and I want your weapons at the ready."

Abigail started walking faster. She wanted to see the statue with her own two eyes, not through a camera. As the other soldiers scurried to get in front of her again, she stepped up next to the alien and stopped.

The effigy was labeled with a plaque, very much like most human sculptures throughout the planets and colonies. This ornate slab read:

Sometimes you have to take a leap of faith.

It wasn't at all what she'd expected. She figured it would call out their enlightenment or the evolution she'd read about, but no. This one had called out having faith. She wondered in what.

As she studied the statue closer, she noticed something missing. "What happened to the celestial sphere? It looks... mangled."

Ibu climbed on the platform surrounding the Ursis and rose up on their tippy-toes. "From the looks of the broken edges, someone ripped something out of the inside. Maybe it was vandalized?"

"That's a strange thing to steal," she muttered.

"Do you think it's to scale?" Ibu reached up into the sky, but couldn't quite touch the statue's chest.

"I hope not," Kamal said. "That thing's almost three times the size of my biggest soldier. It makes Abigail look like a morsel." He smiled and glanced her way before he realized his mistake.

She shook her head. "Thanks. That helps."

Kamal reached out and then stopped short. "I'm... sorry, sir. I didn't—"

"It's alright. Let's keep moving." Abigail stepped away from the statue and headed toward the primary target in the distance. The words etched into the metallic surface above the doors read.

The Department of Galactic Alliance Affairs

As she made her way up the flight of stairs, her mind wandered to what Kamal had said. While she'd never seen herself as a small person, in front of that statue she was tiny. Her head would barely clear their belly button. If they had one, that was.

10

——

IBU

PROTO DARK NEBULA, ON GRISEO

The away team spent the better part of the afternoon searching through the remains of the government building, but it was no use. For whatever reason, the Ursis had wiped the records of their other planets and colonies from the computer systems. While they'd gathered intel on other members of the Galactic Alliance, anything that might help them here in the Proto System was gone.

"I say we return to Phoenix One and regroup," Kamal said.

"We have other targets," Abigail began. "There's a museum a few klicks north that could tell us more. It also wouldn't hurt to rummage through some of the nearby buildings. At this point, anything we can find might help."

Kamal shifted his position from one window to another, never taking his eyes off the street below. His exo-suit, while bulky, was tiny compared to an Ursis, so there was plenty of room to move around. "There's no reason to believe any of the computers have intel, sir. We're better off coming up with a different approach somewhere safer."

Ibu set down the office trinket they'd been studying. "That's an unreasonable and unsound recommendation,

Captain. We've met no resistance, and we've only checked one location on our planned route. Diverting our focus because your team was riled over a statue would be a further waste of time. I suggest we—"

Kamal spun around. "My team is not afraid of a fraking statue."

Ibu mocked a human chuckle. "I beg to differ. Judging by their vitals, fear is one of many mixed emotions they've been feeling since they got a look at the Ursis."

He stomped forward and shoved the chair between them out of the way. "I take issue with that."

They merely nodded, but made certain not to flinch. Human males used aggression to assert superiority, something they weren't about to acknowledge. "You would take issue." They leaned closer to him and lowered their voice. "I believe your vitals were the most abnormal of all. Perhaps you had a run-in with a bear or other quadruped species on Earth?"

Kamal holstered his weapon and took another step, touching helmets with them. "I suggest our little alien friend here step the frak down before I put them in their place."

Ibu could feel their fight response kick in, but they adjusted their breathing to keep it at bay. Letting this human think they could control their emotions would be counterproductive. Besides, sparring with them would only waste time.

"Your drive to invigorate your masculinity in front of your team isn't worth my attention, Captain. If anything, it degrades my opinion of you even more than your sleeping with multiple partners aboard the Phoenix without their knowledge."

"Enough, you two!" Abigail shoved the computer terminal back into the desk. "Check your fraking ego, Captain. And Ibu, stop riling up my people. You're not helping the situation."

"Yessir!" Kamal stepped backward, keeping his eyes on Ibu the entire way to the window.

It was interesting how the human didn't find them threatening, but were intimidated by the Ursis. Historically, the Nanil had slaughtered countless humans. Perhaps the officer hadn't watched the footage or had forgotten about his time aboard the Doda.

Abigail adjusted her retinal comm and then returned her attention to the others. "I agree with Ibu. We should continue onward toward the museum. I've marked some buildings to sweep en route. They're the homes and offices of some of the diplomatic Ursis in the computers we found. Maybe they have something there we can use."

"But, sir." Kamal broke eye contact with Ibu. "We'll be too far from Phoenix One to make it back before dark."

Fear of the dark was a well-known limitation of the human species, and one of the reasons the geneticists who created the Nanil had given them night vision. Ibu found it curious that humanity hadn't made similar adjustments to themselves to weed out these inferior traits. Then again, they rarely modified themselves beyond cosmetic augmentation for pleasure or crude body mods. And even those were taboo and considered unacceptable by societal pressures. It was a wonder humans had survived as long as they had.

"Well, then I guess we'll be camping." Abigail marched toward the exit, and Ibu followed close behind Harold.

Their A.I. companion had been silent most of their time on the planet. They got the sense he had an opinion and wanted to speak up based upon his tick, but he never did. Whenever someone challenged Abigail or delayed the mission objective, his gaze momentarily paused on them before returning to his robotic mannerisms. It was as if he were sizing them up. At times like these, they'd enjoy having a real-time peek into his personality matrix.

THE UTILITARIAN DESIGN of the buildings and the relative newness of their construction reminded Ibu of the human colony worlds. The rapid advancement of a species brought with it a homogeneity rarely indicative of the architecture of a home world or star system. Colonies never quite fit into the native environment of a new world, and the same could be said for Griseo. It lacked the personality and grounding that time gave mature structures.

They'd never seen pictures of the Ursis home planet in the hodgepodge of archives they'd collected. It must not have been a place the Galactic Alliance visited or deemed worthy to catalog. By the time they appeared on the galactic radar, the Ursis already had the technology to limit the GA's advancement into their star systems. There must've been deeper covert intel, but none that Shauna or the others had found.

The wind whipped up outside, and the building creaked in response. It reminded them of noises back home on Doda. Their progenitor used to tell them stories about why their planet made strange sounds throughout the day. They wrapped each of the fables in a nice little bow of lies, but it took them a while to recognize the deceit. Over the centuries, the Nanil had created a mythology of their own. One designed to protect their offsprings and to conceal the truth. That their species was imprisoned in darkness and would never leave.

Ibu pulled open another massive closet door. At least, they assumed it was a closet. It was cavernous and contained garments fit to be worn by a four to five meter alien. While there weren't shoes or hats, there were lots of outfits with different satin like finishes. Evidently, this Ursis had a fixation on shiny clothes.

"That one appears to be a space suit." Harold pointed over their shoulder at a jet black garment on the far wall.

"How can you tell?" They stepped into the room and made their way to the garment he'd referenced. The surface was one of the few matte finishes in the closet, and judging by its thickness, it was as thin as a piece of human parchment.

"It's the only outfit here with weaves tight enough to hold in oxygen, and the surface is composed of micro-robots similar to our nanites. Here, watch." He stepped up beside them and took two halves of the suit and tugged. His robotic muscles whined, and the fabric failed to rip. "Interesting." He turned it over in his hand. "It was far stronger than I imagined."

"Maybe try cutting it?" Ibu asked.

A click followed, and a foot long blade shot out of his arm, turning his hand into a sword. They remembered seeing the weapon in their review of the robot's inventory, but they forgot about it. Seeing it up close was a bit more imposing.

Harold swiped at the center of the black suit, and while a small cut appeared, it vanished without a trace. In under a second, the robotic weave healed itself.

Ibu had to rewind the recording from their retinal comm to convince themself it happened. The feature was one of the few endearing qualities of the device and came in handy from time to time.

"Remarkably efficient." They ran their hand over the surface. It was smooth, like the other satin outfits in the room, but they imagined it was far stronger.

Harold released the suit and retracted his blade. "Other than the clothes, I'm not detecting any hidden storage containers in here. This place is as empty and void of useful intel as the last few."

Those were the most words he'd said to anyone in days. Ibu wasn't sure what to make of it, but they weren't complaining. The soldiers had given them the cold shoulder since their encounter earlier in the day. It was nice talking to someone, even if it was an A.I. in robot form.

"I agree. I think we should cut the other visits short and head to the museum." Ibu turned in place, making their way toward the door, and then froze.

Harold nearly toppled into them. "Are you ok?"

They could hear his weapon power up. He wasn't taking any chances.

"I'm fine." They eyed the doorway and scanned the wall around the opening. There was something off about the dimensions of this entryway relative to the others they'd walked into. While it was a closet, the walls were thicker and the entrance narrower.

"Do you see that?" Ibu asked.

Harold stepped past them and leaned out of the closet, glancing left and right. "I don't see anything. There's been no movement on any of the visual and non-visual wavelengths. What did you see?"

They walked up to the wall and ran their hand over the edge of the doorway. "Can you do me a favor and break off this chunk of paneling?"

The robot tilted its head. An unusual mechanical gesture, but knowing he was originally a man made it seem normal. "Sure, I guess."

He reached out and grasped the edge of the material and yanked with both hands, tearing back the fascia and exposing a dense crystalline wall structure underneath. "Oh, now that's odd."

"What?" Ibu leaned forward and ran their hand over the porous material. It reminded them of bubble wrap, but was far firmer.

Harold tapped on the side of his head. "Turn on your lidar and full spectral scanner."

They didn't usually walk around with the device on at all times and preferred to only use it as a tool, not a permanent fixture. When they tapped their palm and subvocalized the command, a reticle appeared overlaid on their vision.

When Ibu centered the scanner on the wall, they recoiled backward and then slowly reached out their hand. "It's like it's faking out the scanners. It looks thinner than it is. Why do you suppose they'd do that?"

"I don't know, but something tells me it's a lot stronger, too. Maybe this is a safe room." Harold turned in place and then started ripping panels off the wall.

He looked like he was trashing the place, which he technically was. But not in the hormonal human teenage flight of rage they'd seen in vid-sims. He was looking for something. "What is a safe room?"

"It's a chamber that humans used over the millennia to hide out. Be it a hidden vault in a medieval castle or a steel bunker in the twentieth century. The rooms were employed to protect oneself from the threat of an attack. Or sometimes—"

Harold reached out to the back wall where the space suit had been and yanked. When the material pulled away, situated underneath was what appeared to be a door handle.

"Or sometimes to hide things," he muttered.

Ibu's hearts were racing. The discovery was exciting and was the first interesting thing they'd uncovered next to the statue. "Should we open it?"

Harold pointed over his shoulder toward the doorway behind them. "You might want to step around that entranceway. You know, in case it's booby-trapped."

"I'm not hiding out. I can handle myself. Just open the darn thing." Ibu craned their neck and bit down on the far back of their tongue, transforming them into their enlarged form. Usually, their body adapted due to external stimuli, but what humans didn't realize was that a Nanil could control the transition at will. Once complete, they stood a head taller, and their muscles had quadrupled in size and strength.

"That's a new trick." Harold stared at them.

"Not new. Simply new to you." Ibu flexed their arms, making sure their entire form fitting suit had adjusted to their size. They then crouched low and tucked closer to the wall. "Let's do it." They nodded toward the handle.

Harold looked away from them and focused on the door. He then reached out and grasped the knob. When his hand touched it, a spark flashed and the lights in the room cut out. A second later, the entrance into the closet slammed shut and a ring of previously concealed lighting along the ceiling and floor turned on, engulfing the area in a sea of red light.

"Well, that didn't work," Harold muttered.

Ibu stepped back toward the entrance and tried to shove the door aside, but it wouldn't budge. "Seems we're locked in."

Harold shook his head. "I can't reach the others on the comm. Can you?"

They tried, but the connection dropped the moment the door closed. "Nope." They spun in place and eyed the doorway bathed in red light. When their gaze hit the handle, they paused. The shape wasn't a simple cylinder or lever like so many of the previous handles they'd opened. This one seemed purpose built, like it was designed to fit the palm of an Ursis.

Ibu stepped around Harold and stopped in front of the door. "It couldn't be that easy. Could it?"

"What?"

They reached out and grasped the handle with both hands, but nothing happened. No shock, no nothing. They glanced at Harold and then back to the door before finally turning the handle and pushing inward.

The door swung away without a sound, and the inner lights flickered on, bathing the space in a yellowish glow. Covering the walls were floor to ceiling weapons of all shapes and sizes. From rifles to pistols to what could only be described as multi-blade scimitars, it was an entire Ursis armory tucked into this tiny little apartment.

"My my, someone appears to have a weapon fetish," Ibu said.

"How'd you know to try that with the door?" Harold stepped into the room and bent down to eye the handle.

They shrugged. "I don't know. The shape just seemed like it wanted an Ursis or an organic hand to open it, not a mechanical one. While they loved their technology, they had clear boundaries where their automata were allowed and where they weren't. Apparently, this was one of those lines."

They reached out and ran their hand over the scimitars. The metals were a mixture of shiny and flat. As their fingers slid over the surface, the intricate patterns etched into it shimmered. The muted inscriptions shone and took on colors not visible before they touched it. Suddenly, the surface of the blades transformed into a tangled weaving vine pattern, sprinkled with flowers and thorns. The detail was remarkable. Heck, even the flower petals had teeth.

Everything about this blade shouted out to the Nanil. They grasped one of the handles and pulled it down off the wall. The weapon was extraordinarily light, yet had enough heft to balance it out. Just feeling it in their hand, they knew it could slice through practically anything.

"I'd be careful with that," Harold said. "We don't know what it does."

"I'm sure it couldn't be any worse than that electro-blade the soldiers carry around." Ibu turned the sword over and then reached up, pulling down a second. These ought to level the testosterone playing field with the others.

While they were watching Harold inspect the various weapons, banging sounds reverberated from the wall behind them. They were pretty sure someone was yelling, as well, but they couldn't be certain.

They stepped back to the locked door and searched for a

handle, but none was visible. When they reached out and touched the surface, the entrance slid into the wall as noiselessly as it had appeared. At the same time, their retinal comm sprang to life.

"There you are." Abigail was standing in front of them, her fist about to pound on the door again. "I… thought we lost you." She glanced down, and her eyes widened when she saw the swords. "Those are new."

"Pretty, aren't they?" Ibu carefully raised them for her to see.

"Indeed." Her hand reached out but hesitated to touch them. "Are they safe?"

"So far." Ibu tilted their head back and to the right. "Harold is cataloging the rest of the hidden stash we found. At least if we come up empty-handed, we've got some new toys."

Abigail smirked.

"Sir!" Kamal walked up behind them and paused when he noticed the blades in Ibu's hand. The right glove of his exoskeleton curled up, as if forming a fist.

"What is it?"

"Um… there's a storm-front coming in." He turned his attention to her. "We should head back to the ship and regroup tomorrow during daylight."

"There's no time." Harold stepped forward from the rear of the closet. He had a few weapons of his own he was grasping. "The storm's moving too fast. We'll need to take cover for the night and ride it out."

"Great," Abigail muttered. "That means we get dried rations for dinner tonight. Is there any chance the food stores in this place are edible for humans?"

Ibu cringed. They'd tried some of that ration stuff they called food onboard the Fountainhead when they were gating back to Zeta Lupi. They heaved for hours afterward, and the taste lingered on their tongue for weeks.

"No." Harold said. "It's already bad, and besides, it's laden with the same nanite like viruses we detected in the air, except these aren't dead. They're using the organic compounds to stay alive. One drop of the food in these cabinets hits any of your stomachs, and you'll be lucky to take another breath."

"How do you know that?" Kamal asked.

"Because he prepared for the mission and read the briefing from Epsilon Eridani." Ibu lifted one of the swords up and over their head and slid it into the small of their back between their harnesses. As good of a place as any until they could build a better sheath. "It's standard practice for the Galactic Alliance to launch nanite munitions into a star system when they're unruly closing up a Dark Nebula. It not only neuters them, it can sometimes be far more aggressive, depending on the programming."

"The nanites I found were peculiar, though." Harold shared the data he'd collected earlier from another apartment they'd explored. "These were built by the Ursis to attack other Ursis, in the same mold as what the GA did after closing a Nebula."

Abigail shuddered. "They were killing their own people. But... why?"

"It's no different from what humans did to one another over the millennia." Ibu stepped around the others, out into the open of the large room. "Except these were caged aliens. I'm sure there were many factions after they closed the Dark Nebula. They were bound to turn on each other eventually, blaming the opposite sides for what became of them. It's a wonder they lasted as long as they did. You only have to look as far as Mayor North to see a similar example in your kind."

They watched as uttering the man's name ignited an unconscious reaction in Abigail. One second, she was repulsed at the idea of the Ursis turning on each other, and the next her cheeks went pink and her muscles tensed. She was ready to kill the former Epsilon Eridani Mayor with her own two hands. The emotions at play in humanity were a tricky game, one they were glad the scientists who created the Nanil had muted for the most part.

"While it's fun playing hindsight is twenty-twenty and all," Harold eyed Ibu, "why don't we find a spot to hunker down for the night? I brought some rations along that I think everyone will enjoy. Even our friends with fickle stomachs."

"That sounds promising." Abigail turned and headed toward the exit of the apartment, Harold close behind.

Kamal stared Ibu down for a minute as the room fell silent. They thought he was going to make a move and attack until he finally tapped his ear and opened a comm to the other soldiers. "I need some hands up here to clean out this weapons stash. We should mark these for an extract later."

When he turned and walked into the closet, they swore his exo-suit's rear-facing weapons were aimed at them. If they had access to the logs, they could prove it, but they were undoubtedly locked down.

Ibu would have to keep an eye on this human. His ego was as paper thin as his temper.

11

ABIGAIL OLIVAW

PROTO DARK NEBULA, ON GRISEO

The fire Harold made in front of the building under the covered balcony was modest, but the heat it was kicking off was scorching. Whatever he'd scrounged up to burn in the planter they'd dragged under the middle of the overhang was scary hot. There wasn't much smoke, but the embers were glowing beet red.

The transparent sealed structure rustled as the wind kicked up. There was an exhaust fan near the top sucking the smoke out while the oxygen stayed inside. Abigail didn't quite understand how, but it worked. Just outside the entrance was another one, acting as a poor man's airlock.

"You're gonna burn those beans." She nodded her head at the fire.

"Come on. I'm not a newbie camper, missy." Harold tipped the pan toward him and used a spoon to stir the beans in the makeshift pot. "You forget that I've spent centuries cooking these things for Olivaws before you were even born."

"Dibs!" Gwen stepped out of the darkened airlock with her helmet under her arm and her gloves tucked inside. She raised her hands to the fire and rubbed them together.

Ibu chuckled and shook their head.

Abigail eyed the young soldier. She hadn't seen the woman all day. They must've been on forward scout duty.

"Oh, sorry, sir." Gwen's eyes widened, and she lowered her hands. "I thought you'd already eaten." She turned to leave.

"Freeze!" Abigail reached out and spun her around. "Harold brought plenty for everyone. In fact, you take a portion first. You've been in the thick of protecting us all day. Ibu and I will dish ours out after."

Gwen shook her head. "I… can't, sir. Kamal would have my hide." She took a step backward.

"I wouldn't disobey your captain, soldier." Ibu pointed at the pot Harold removed from the fire. "Your beans are getting cold."

Gwen didn't move.

"Go ahead." Abigail smiled.

She looked at the empty bowl and then back at Abigail. "You's sure?"

Abigail reached out and spooned a healthy portion of the hearty brown refried beans into the awaiting bowl, then snatched a few tortillas and set them on the rim. She then handed it to the woman. "I insist."

Gwen set her helmet on the ground beside the hatch and then bowed toward them, grasping the dish with two hands. "Thank you. Both of you." She grabbed a spoon and shoveled some beans into her mouth. "Yum… so good. Compliments." She raised the dish and marched forward into the central room of the building. They'd sealed off the space and were using it as the team's makeshift bunk area where they were attempting to rest for the night, or at least until the storm had passed. The fabric rustled as she made her way through to the other side.

"You're welcome," Harold muttered as he split the remaining beans into two other bowls and handed one to Ibu and the other to her.

Abigail broke off a piece of tortilla and dipped it into a bowl, making sure to get a healthy amount of gooey brown gold on it before popping it into her mouth. The flavor exploded on contact, coating her taste buds with memories of home. The only food Zachary used to eat when the family had a hankering for Mexican were these beans.

She closed her eyes and savored the spices for a minute before swallowing. Once the flavor and the memories fell away, she opened them. "Come on H. What's wrong?"

"Nothing." He cracked open another can and scooped the contents into the pot. It sizzled as soon as it hit the metal.

"Bullshit! What?" She nudged him and then stirred the beans in her bowl before scooping a portion into her mouth.

"It's hard enough being seen by the family sometimes. These other humans don't see me at all." He tossed the can aside and held the pot over the fire.

Ibu shook their head. "You're mistaken, my robot friend."

"How's that?" Harold asked.

"Private Gwen wasn't giving you the cold shoulder, she was giving it to me. Kamal and his entire squad have been since we started this mission." Ibu took the last bowl and carefully picked up one of the delicate round breads and squinted. They had studied how Abigail navigated the beans with it and were now attempting the same thing themselves.

Abigail shook her head. "You're both crazy. You're reading too much into the situation."

Ibu lowered the bean laden bread from their mouth before taking a bite. "On the contrary. I'm far from crazy. You know, he's already threatened my life once. Besides that, he's wanted to take a swing at me on at least half a dozen other occasions. I'm pretty sure he's instructed his people to give me... I believe you call it, the cold shoulder. If you don't believe me, back up the retinal comm you love so much. Watch how the soldier reacts toward me."

Abigail always considered herself to be an excellent judge

of character, but when she subvocalized the command to replay her comm, she saw it. Gwen visibly tensed up when Ibu spoke, and she'd missed it. Hell, she wouldn't even look at the Nanil. And when she took the beans, the woman stared straight at her and Harold, not Ibu.

"You saw it, didn't you?" Ibu popped the bread in their mouth and paused, slowly chewing each bite.

"Everything alright?" Harold asked, eying them.

"Yes… I think so. It's sticky… and yet, satisfying. I find it particularly enjoyable." They scooped a heaping spoon of beans into their mouth.

"I'm glad you like it." He glanced over at Abigail. "You saw it, didn't you? It's ok. I've got spare cycles to the nines out here, and I missed it, too. How long did you say they've been doing this?"

"Don't worry about it." Ibu continued shoveling in the beans until they hit the bottom of the bowl and then resorted to wiping it clean with more tortilla.

"It's bullshit!" Abigail slammed her dish down on the table. "I'm not gonna have a member of my crew treated like this. Least of all you." She subvocalized a comm to Kamal.

Report to me immediately.

Ibu froze and eyed her. "Least of all me, why?"

Abigail rubbed her hands together and adjusted her outfit. "My brothers and everyone they love would be dead if it weren't for you. All of them. Hell, we wouldn't have a Beacon right now if you hadn't helped. No. Frak no. I'm not having this shit festering on my crew."

She could tell the Nanil hadn't expected to hear that. They weren't used to dealing with outpourings of emotions. Least of all directed at them. She watched as they shifted their stance. It was the universal sign of being uncomfortable, if she'd ever seen one.

A message appeared on her retinal comm.

I'm on my way, sir.

Ibu was watching her. They could tell she was reading a message. They always knew.

"Should I make myself scarce?" Ibu asked.

"No." Abigail reached out and touched their arm. "You're not going anywhere." She wasn't about to have her friend hide out. They were fighting for their life, all of them were. The last thing she needed was speciesism infiltrating her circle of trust.

"Here, eat some more beans." Harold scooped another portion into their bowl.

Abigail brought up an overlay of the soldier's position on her retinal comm. Kamal's dot had stopped moving. She subvocalized a direct comm. "Where are you?"

When he activated his side to respond, she heard an explosion on the other side. Both from her retinal comm and across the field. The sky suddenly lit up orange and yellow.

Harold dropped the pot into the fire and stepped out in front of her. "Stand behind me."

"I'm not gonna sit back and watch my people die." She went to shove him aside, but he didn't budge. He was too damn heavy. Instead, she stepped around him and into the airlock, sealing it behind her. She snatched Gwen's helmet and gloves on the way in and put them on just as the seal on the other side cracked open.

"Don't be crazy," Harold said over their comm. "Wait for backup."

Her heart was racing as one of the red dots of her team

flashed yellow. The longer she waited, the more people that'd die. When she glanced over her shoulder, she saw Harold, Ibu, and two soldiers step into the airlock.

They'd be through soon enough. For now, she needed to help. She tore off into the darkness toward the outlines of her team. As the rain pelted her helmet, she reached down and yanked out her pistol. The dial was already set on slugs. She would switch it to energy once she knew what she was dealing with.

The team guarding the perimeter was up ahead. When she came up to the turn, she eased her head around the corner for a look-see. Another explosion flashed in the distance, and she could feel the heat through her suit. It was a far cry from the protection of the exo-skeleton some of the soldiers were wearing.

In the flash of light from the blast, Abigail noticed silhouettes of four short objects close to the ground moving away from her. The lidar on her retinal comm showed them as robots. All the ones they'd seen thus far were immobilized, but these appeared to be advancing on her team.

She ran out into the open and brought her pistol up, training it on the one nearest her. When the reticle turned green, she exhaled and pulled the trigger twice in rapid succession. The first bullet went wide, but the second hit the robot in what she assumed was its head. While that robot tipped over, the other three turned in place and started advancing on her. They opened fire a second later, and she stepped backward just as a line of bullets erupted along the ground where she'd been standing.

"Shit," she muttered as she dove behind a nearby wall. It wasn't like a robot to miss, and she was stupid for taking them on alone. What mattered now was thinking fast. She was about to have a few unwelcome guests.

Her retinal comm showed that the barrier she was kneeling next to framed the outside of a park. It was too low for her to sprint away before they came around the corner, but judging by the robot's height, she might be able to jump over it, and they'd miss her.

When she raised the camera on her glove over the edge, she saw her theory was true. She only had a few seconds. Pushing up off the ground, she leapt up and to the side, rolling over the top of the stone wall and down the other side into a pool of water.

"Frak." In the rush, she'd missed that little detail on the map. The splash of the water must have given away her location because when she raised her pistol, she noticed the tops of the robots pause. She could nick their heads, but it probably wouldn't do any damage.

As she debated squeezing the trigger, two of the robots continued forward and one reversed course. It was making its way toward the entrance of the park, a half a dozen meters back. While she didn't know where the other two were headed, she didn't care. She could handle the nearest one first.

With her gun trained at the corner where the robot would appear, she crawled on her knees with her other hand to the edge of the pond. Once there, she stayed in the water and lowered her torso to the ground, giving them a smaller hit area if they got off a shot.

She wasn't about to wonder what was in the water raining down from above or beneath her. Her focus had to be on making this shot. Whatever they were firing, she was pretty sure her suit wouldn't protect her in the least.

The top of the robot's head passed behind an ornamental rock piece on the fence, and she took a deep breath. When she saw the silvery glimmer of the leading edge of the robot, she exhaled and squeezed, firing three shots in rapid succession. She couldn't afford a miss at this point.

While the first bullet hit the wall, the next two sparked against the robot's torso. It was good that the bullets hit the robot's side, because the force of the impact spun it ever so slightly off course and the bullets it fired exploded on the ground to her left and a few even hit the water. Had she not fired, she'd have been hit for sure.

With that shot being so close, she knew she couldn't sit still. She slid right along the water's edge and squeezed off a few more shots. The first few went wide, but the last hit the robot dead center in its domed head, and it crumpled down, clanging against the stone walkway.

She crawled out of the water and slipped up against the wall. Her heart was pounding, and she was gasping for breath. The entire ordeal was unlike anything she'd ever done before. While it was exhilarating, it was also scary as hell. Next time, she'd wait for the others.

As she took a few deep breaths, she glanced in the distance and saw movement. "Oh, shit." The two other robots had come around to another park entrance, and they were coming into view. She brought her pistol up and ejected the almost empty clip. Reaching into her thigh pocket, she slid out a fresh one and slammed it into place. She'd need as many bullets as she could muster to take these two down.

It was only then that she realized she should just flip back over the wall. The stone surface would make better cover than the air between them. As she pushed up and motioned to leap over, she felt a sting in her thigh and the wall beside her exploded in a cloud of dust as rock shrapnel shot in all directions.

"Argh!" She grasped her leg and collapsed to the ground. The pain was excruciating, but her retinal comm apprised the situation as non-life-threatening. Her suit would seal itself in a few seconds, and apparently the bullet wasn't a bullet at all, it was a nail. Either way, it hurt like fraking hell, and one of those to the head would end her just as swiftly.

Scanning the nearby park, she was cornered. There was only open space and the pond between her and them. Her only option was to dive into the water and risk god knows what infecting her. It was that or she stay in the open and hope they were a bad shot.

It didn't take long for her to dive under the floating brown fronds and goo covering the surface of the water. She hadn't noticed the substances earlier, but it was too late to give a shit now.

12

———

IBU

PROTO DARK NEBULA, ON GRISEO

They shoved the airlock fabric aside and tore across the field, Harold in hot pursuit. Ibu had long ago transformed into their enraged form, and as such had the speed and strength to go with it. They'd watched from a distance as Abigail shot down the street, only to barely dodge return fire.

As their team exited the enclosure, a dozen robots appeared from a street on the opposite side of the park and opened fire on them. The soldiers dropped to their knees and started picking them off, but Ibu didn't bother. They had one, and only one, thing on their mind. Protecting Abigail.

While their thermal vision allowed them to see clearly into the darkness, they had to admit that the addition of the lidar overlay made what they were seeing that much more detailed. Distances were exact, and the network of interconnected comms meant they could see anything anyone else was seeing. What confused them was why Abigail wasn't using hers. Certainly, she'd have known not to engage the robots without backup first.

They ducked down low and made their way along the face of the nearby building and paused just as they got to the street corner where Abigail had disappeared. The last thing her retinal comm reported was her rolling over a wall, and then her signal dropped.

Scanning the area, they saw what looked like the same wall. If they'd practiced using their retinal comm more, they might be able to confirm as much, but fiddling with the gadget wasn't their priority.

When they sprinted across the opening, they spotted two robots in the distance turning into the park. They had to assume that whatever they were after was one of their people, and could be Abigail. Racing down the alley, they froze at the park entrance just as shots fired.

Ibu dropped to the ground and rolled behind the entrance pillar, but there were no impacts nearby. Whoever they were firing at, it must've been trained on someone else. Their hearts pounded against both of their chest bones when they imagined who.

As they pushed up out of the dirt, they caught the glimmer of steel in the distance. Their retinal comm showed it was Harold. Apparently, he'd taken the long way around, choosing to cover all their bases rather than follow them. Given he was multiple times faster than them, it made sense.

They reached over their shoulder and unsheathed the two multi-bladed scimitars. Their blades were as black as the night, as if somehow they knew they should be as inconspicuous as possible. It was remarkable how lightweight and compact they were when stowed. Ibu barely realized they were there until they were upright.

The rat-a-tat-tat of gunfire brought them back to their target. The robots passed behind a chunk of wall and were making their way to the front of the park.

Ibu lunged forward, sprinting into the night. They hopped up onto the wall and continued running along the top toward the two robotic silhouettes.

The automata must've sensed them because they spun around, but it was too late. Their shots tore into the wall and were well under Ibu's position as they were leaping in the air with the scimitars raised over their head.

As the blades swung downward, they easily sliced the robots in half. Like they weren't even there. The swords sent sparks sailing in all directions, and Ibu felt two pricks pierce their right calf. Whatever the automations were firing, they'd pierced their suit.

With the momentum of the leap, Ibu came down hard on one knee and rolled forward, letting go of the blades and tucking into a ball to release the energy rather than blow out their already wounded legs.

When they stopped rolling, they didn't hesitate. They dove back toward the immobilized forms to grasp the blades. They weren't about to lose their prize to the darkness. With the swords in hand, they froze behind one of the robotic remains and scanned their surroundings.

Nothing was moving. Except for Harold approaching from the far side of the park, there were no remaining robots, and the park was as still as a crypt. The only sign of life was an echo of gunfire in the distance, but that was it.

"Where is she?" Harold asked as he sprinted up beside them.

"I'm not certain. I saw her roll over that wall." Ibu gestured toward the nearby structure. "After that, I was too focused on taking these guys out."

Harold looked from the robots to the wall, and then the direction they were firing. He didn't hesitate. He simply jumped into the water and started thrashing about, splashing the murky liquid in all directions.

Just as they were about to ask him what he was doing, it hit them. He thought Abigail was in the pond. Certainly, they'd have seen ripples on the surface of the water or picked up her comm signal if she'd been in there.

As he worked his way deeper, Harold stopped and his

arm shot beneath the water. He yanked something upward. It was a body. It was Abigail.

All the air burst from their lungs as they recognized their mistake. The robots had been firing at something, but they missed the facts. Their dependency on their comm had failed them, just as they knew it would. They'd let their guard down and got comfortable with the human contraption being the only truth.

Without a second thought, they sprang forward to Harold's side. "Is she ok? Is she breathing?"

Harold was holding her with one hand, doing compressions on her chest with another, while holding an air tube in her mouth with a third. He held her like that for a few seconds until her face contorted, and she coughed, propelling the tube out of her throat along with a stream of brown fluid. After a few more coughs, she reached out and squeezed his shoulder. Her eyes were bulging out of her face.

"Her helmet!" Ibu lunged toward the object in Harold's fourth hand. "Put it back on. She can't breathe."

He slid the helmet over her head and the seal went green. As they watched her eyes relax, and her lungs fill with air, the pool of water they were standing in began moving.

"What the hell?" Ibu lowered their sword into the muddy liquid, and it thrashed around until it hit something. Several somethings. "Shit! There's something alive in the water."

Harold jumped out of the pond onto solid ground, bringing with him a tentacle of some sort attached to his leg.

Ibu swung their sword and the fragile appendage flapped wildly in the air, shooting a green fluid in all directions. A second later, three more of the vine like limbs sprang out of the liquid and wrapped around them, yanking them down.

"Frak no!" They frantically whirled the blades through the air in a crisscross fashion while they struggled to skirt their way toward solid ground. They weren't making much headway on the vines until something grasped their stomach and yanked them backward.

Never being one to give up, they spun around in midair and swung the blade in a downward slicing motion. Harold's arm fell to the ground with a thud.

The thrashing in the water stopped, and Ibu froze. "I'm sorry. I didn't—"

"It's fine." Harold reached down and grabbed the fallen limb. "I can fix it later. Let's get the hell out of here before something else pops out after us."

They didn't have to be asked twice. Harold started back toward their building, and they jogged behind him, glancing repeatedly over their shoulder the entire way. In their mind's eye, they could still see the watery vines reaching for them. But they knew it wasn't real. It was all in their imagination.

Death had been so close they could taste it. The thrill of the fight was both exhilarating and frightening at the same time. Not at all like when they piloted the ship above Henosi, but they weren't sure why.

IBU RAN the healing device over their leg one last time for good measure. Their biology was close enough to that of a human to make the device useful, even on them. It accelerated the closing of the wound after they'd extracted the nails. While their body would've healed in a few hours, waiting a few seconds made things much easier.

"Now what?" They placed the device on the table in front of them.

"Now we return to Phoenix One and get off this hellhole." Gwen slammed the butt of her gun against the ground.

Grunts of assent echoed through the other soldiers.

"I'll check if they can evacuate us on the way out," Kamal said.

For once, Ibu agreed with the man. He'd fended off over thirty of the robots himself at the start of the battle and managed to keep his people alive in the process. Even the wounded ones.

"No!" Abigail shot up and swallowed hard, wincing in pain. "We're rolling out and heading to the museum."

"But—" Gwen began.

"But what, Private?" Abigail glanced around the room at the shocked faces. "We're gonna return to base at the first sign of trouble? This isn't about me, or you, or you." She pointed at the other wounded soldiers. "This is about our people in Sol. Unless we find something to help our cause, then our species is as good as dead. Is that what you want?"

She was missing the point of what the others were saying. They simply wanted to regroup. Not give up.

"There's no one here," Ibu said. "No one except the robots, that is. We can meet back with—"

"You heard the orders, soldier." Kamal turned to face them and took a step closer. "Now pack up, and let's move out."

"I'm not your fraking soldier, you asshole." They shoved the man, and he stumbled backward.

The soldiers around the room raised their weapons and trained them on Ibu.

"Nice!" They pointed an outstretched hand toward the armed humans and then glared at Abigail. "Is this what you call taking care of it?"

Abigail's mouth fell open. From her reaction, Ibu could tell the woman had forgotten about what she'd said earlier. But it didn't matter. What mattered was the actions of her people in the moment.

Kamal stepped toward Ibu with a grin on his face. "Looks like you're outnumbered, missy."

"You're relieved, Captain!" Abigail pulled out her pistol and trained it on the back of Kamal's head.

Ibu chuckled. "Don't do it on my account. I'm done here. I'll catch you all at the Phoenix." They stormed around Kamal, pushing against him and causing him to step backward into Abigail's firearm.

"Sir?" Kamal asked. "I—"

"Ibu wait! Please." Abigail gently grabbed their arm and they stopped. She then spun in place to face Kamal. "You've forced your speciesist beliefs on me and your soldiers for the last time. I was planning on relieving you before that shit show out there, but I lost track in the moment. While your actions to save your people are commendable, your views are misplaced and belong in another era. We're out here to make friends and allies, not enemies. We've got a galaxy full of those. Now, Captain, you're relieved of your title and responsibilities. Lieutenant Hansen?"

"Yes… yessir!" A man stepped out of the shadows. He was the only one Ibu hadn't seen with his gun raised.

"You're in command of this outfit. I suggest you whip 'em into shape." Abigail narrowed her gaze and glanced around at the others. "If you fail to listen to your lieutenant or refuse to fall into line… then you'll be spaced, or worse. We'll leave you down here on this godforsaken planet. Harold?"

"Yessir." Harold was still at her side, having never left it since pulling her out of the water.

"You have my permission to kill them on sight if they so much as make a move on Lieutenant Hansen, Ibu, or myself. Is that understood?"

"Perfectly, sir."

Ibu studied Abigail. Her eyes were as hard as steel, and if she could have killed the man, they wouldn't put it past her for trying. She was a peculiar woman. There were times when she was even-tempered and easily predictable. But there were others, like in this moment, where she was as chaotic and as random as radioactive decay.

Abigail turned to face them and subvocalized a message.

Let's talk in private. Follow me.

Lieutenant Hansen walked to the center of the room as Ibu followed Abigail toward the stairs. "Alright, you heard the orders. Let's pack up and prepare to roll out. I want to be on the road in under thirty. Now move your ass!"

They weren't sure where Abigail was headed, but she was taking the steps two at a time. It wasn't until she turned off at the fifth floor and stopped in front of the apartment they'd been in earlier that they realized where they were going. She wanted to talk in the safe room.

Part of Ibu was nervous the human was leading them into a trap, but they knew that part was their progenitor talking. She had no reason to entrap them. Other than speaking their mind, they'd saved her life on multiple occasions.

When Abigail stepped into the closet first, Ibu checked their retinal comm. The soldiers were all on the ground floor, following orders and packing up their supplies. Harold was wandering among them, they assumed, to keep them under a watchful eye.

"Close it please." Abigail gestured at the entrance. "I... don't know how."

Ibu stepped around her and made their way to the back wall. They reached out and tapped the handle to the inner door, triggering the outer door to seal. A second later, the room went dark, and the lights switched to the familiar red from earlier.

She tapped her ear. "Harold, can you read me?"

"It won't work in here." Ibu began. "The signal—"

"I know," she interrupted. "Harold told me. I wanted to be sure." She stepped toward Ibu and reached out to grasp their hand.

They flinched backward. These humans and their touching.

"I… want you to link with me." She reached out again, more slowly this time, and took their hand in hers. "Or do whatever you did with Lync. I need you to know I'm not lying."

While they weren't a lie detector, they had to admit that having physical contact made it easier to determine if a human was deceiving them. The subtle changes in their heart rate and breathing, along with shifts in body language, were all tells.

They felt for her pulse and then reached out with their other hand and rested it on her shoulder. "Go ahead."

Abigail glanced around. "Is that it? Did you open a mental link?"

"It's not that easy. But let's just say I can tell if you're lying now."

"Oh… ok. So, how do we test?"

"I'll start with a straightforward question." Ibu squeezed their hand on her shoulder ever so slightly.

"Ok." She swallowed hard.

"Do you love Minula?"

She recoiled back and winced. "Ouch, you're squeezing me too tight."

"You shouldn't move. It was a simple yes, no question." Ibu stared her in the eyes. "Do—you—love—Minula?"

"Of course I do. She's my sister."

They shook their head. "Not that way. Do you love her? Like want to spend the rest of your life with her. You know, like Bradley and Cynthia."

"I…" She wriggled in place. "Can't you pick a different—"

"Answer the question."

"Fine. Yes!" She raised her hands up. "I love Minula! But… I can't tell her. I don't understand why this is relevant to what I wanted to talk about."

Ibu smiled. "Given I have no idea what you brought me here for, I thought we were simply calibrating. I took what I knew to be a truth and figured I'd confirm it."

Abigail tilted her head. "You knew… but, how?"

"I think the only two people who don't are you and Minula. Though, it's not for lack of wanting. What I don't get, however, is why you're repeatedly putting yourself in harm's way. You're doing it knowing you might never see them again, and yet you've still not confessed your love. I mean, if you truly care for them, why not just say it?"

She swiped Ibu's hand away. "It's not that simple. I need to focus on the future. I can't be distracted with even more emotions than I already have." She closed her eyes and took a deep breath before opening them. "Let's switch gears. Ok?"

"Sure. If you want to." Ibu reached out and placed their hand on her shoulder again.

"I promise I was going to talk to Kamal. I swear to it."

Ibu nodded. She was telling the truth. "I believe you."

"Ok, good. Now, I need you to storm out of here and follow us."

It was Ibu's turn to take a step back. "I don't understand."

Abigail shook her head and reached out, placing the Nanil's hand on her shoulder and forcing her other hand in theirs. "You have to follow us. I'm scared for both of our lives. While I can't put my finger on it, there's something about Kamal that can't be trusted. I can feel it."

"He was fine in Lupus with your brother. I mean, he never showed signs of being erratic. It wasn't until…" Ibu froze. It couldn't be that simple.

"What is it? What did you remember?" Abigail leaned down and stared up into their eyes.

"The messages. The ones everyone received from home." Ibu rubbed their hand through their hair. "After that, a lot of the crew changed. They started acting weird. Hell, look what it did to you. Do you know what was in their messages?"

She shook her head. "No. Back in the day, Harold or Shauna might review them. But ever since we tossed them in containment, we haven't followed our usual routines."

Ibu started walking in circles. There had to be something. "It'd be easier if we knew they lost someone important. Either that, or maybe one of the generals slid an order in with the rest of the messages."

"I can ask the A.I. to check them over when we meet back up with Phoenix Two. You don't think General Raft—" She brought her hand to her mouth.

They shook their head. "We don't know anything for certain. This entire tangent is nothing but conjecture at this point. But I do know that your human emotions are a roller-coaster of chaos. None of your species seem to think or act logically. Especially when egos are bruised or lives are on the line."

"All the more reason I need you to shadow us." Abigail reached out and stopped them from pacing. "Just stick to the shadows. I can help you turn off the tracking in your retinal comm, so they can't detect you, but you can still see them. As long as you're out of sight, you can keep an eye on us. We need to get to that museum. I can feel it."

Ibu was confused. Maybe coming along for this mission was a mistake. "Why can't we just come back later?"

"Who the hell knows what'll happen up there once we're onboard? The only people I know I can trust right now are you, Minula, Cynthia, Harold, and Shauna."

Her breathing hadn't changed, and her heart rate was as solid as a rock. She was telling the truth.

"Fine. I'll do it. But... how exactly does one storm off convincingly?"

"Now that's something I'm an expert at." Abigail wrapped her arm around the Nanil's back and pulled them closer.

These humans and their touching.

13

ABIGAIL OLIVAW
PROTO DARK NEBULA, ON GRISEO

The squad of soldiers was waiting in a ring near the front of the building when Abigail descended the circular stairway. As she eased off the last step, she took a deep breath. Both due to the size of the steps she'd traversed and the subterfuge she was about to enter. It was one thing to deceive a fellow politician, but it was quite another to lie to people protecting her.

When she walked out into the night, she brought up the details Harold and Lieutenant Hansen had sent her while she was indisposed. She strode into the middle of the ring and nodded at Hansen. "Are we ready?"

He glanced toward the building and then back at her. "Aren't we waiting for Ibu, sir?"

Harold studied her.

"They're... shall we say, pissed." Abigail wrung her hands together. "They'll be heading directly to Phoenix One."

The soldiers behind her shuffled, and she turned around to see why. Ibu had stepped out of the doorway. They were glaring across the field toward the soldiers.

"Are you sure you won't reconsider?" Abigail asked. She

could feel her palms sweating under the gloves. If Harold had access to her vitals, he'd know something was up.

Ibu pointed at Kamal. He was standing near the edge of the ring closest to them. "Are you sending him back to the ship?"

"I can't do that. We need every soldier we can muster out here. We could use your strength, too." Abigail smiled.

Kamal grunted. "We managed for millennia without them. I'm pretty sure we'll manage another day without this one."

Abigail stepped up behind the former captain and hit him upside the head with her pistol. The physical effect was muted against the exo-suit, but the human reaction was what she was going for. "You'll shut your fraking trap, soldier. Another word from you and you'll meet the fiery end of a blaster between the eyes. Is that understood?"

He reached up with his hand and motioned to touch the spot where she'd hit him, but stopped short. When he turned to face her, the fury in his eyes boiled over. She'd shoved him over the edge, and he was having a hard time keeping his frustrations at bay. Just when she thought he was going to lash out, he slowly raised his right hand and saluted her. "Yessir!"

"I guess I'll meet you back at the Phoenix, then." Ibu took one last step off the curb and made their way east toward the main thoroughfare they'd followed to get here.

If their plan went as she'd hoped, Ibu would disable their retinal tracker and engage a clone of it in a simple pocket drone. They'd programmed the unit to take a slow and indirect route back to the ship. Doing what it could to throw off anyone monitoring the signal.

Abigail watched her friend disappear into the black of night and sighed. She hoped she was wrong about her feelings, because if not, she might not make it off this world. Which reminded her. She tapped her ear and subvocalized a message to Minula.

> Review all the messages from Zeta Lupi. You can use
> Shauna to help you. Pay close attention to the ones sent
> to Kamal and his crew. I have a bad feeling about him,
> and I'm starting to freak out.

When she hit send, she checked the time. They weren't
scheduled to make another drop for a few hours. She hoped
she'd survive that long.

THE SOLDIERS MOVED FLUIDLY through the streets, each
covering the other, with Abigail in the middle. Harold flanked
her on one side, and on the other was Lieutenant Hansen.
He'd been acting skittish since taking command, and even
more so after seeing Ibu leave.

Harold hadn't said a word to her after Ibu's departure, but
she could tell he was on edge. She wouldn't doubt if he recognized her subterfuge. What worried her wasn't her friend, it
was Kamal's reaction. He'd asked to be posted on the forward
recon team, or one of the ones flanking them. Hansen
honored the request. He was probably happy to rid himself of
watching over the man all day. Abigail, however, preferred to
keep her enemies under a watchful eye.

She subvocalized a message to Harold.

> Are you keeping an eye on Kamal?

His reply came back instantly.

As much as I can in this limited capacity, sir. While I have access to the team's cameras, his comms and other messaging are outside my permissions.

"Frak," she muttered. She hadn't thought through all the ways she'd grown dependent on his reach before planning this mission. While freeing herself from relying on him had been invigorating, without his power, they were as blind as anyone else. All she had left was her intuition and gut feelings. Two things she was rusty at using since her incident aboard the tribunal ship.

She studied Kamal's dot on the map. He was positioned well ahead of the squad at their ten o'clock position. They were nearing the museum where his team was assigned external recon and security, keeping an eye out for packs of roaming robots.

Harold had salvaged a few random parts from the robots they'd destroyed earlier that night. Most of them had been leftover construction bots, which explained the nails for bullets. But a few had been used for previously unknown military applications. He was hoping to learn more from them aboard the Phoenix.

"Sir, we're approaching the museum," Hansen said. "Should I have the recon team do a room to room sweep ahead of us?"

Abigail shook her head. "No. They can enter when we do. I want to see the place untouched. We can't risk missing or destroying something important."

She knew how the message sounded, and the already tense soldiers wouldn't appreciate the insinuation. But the facts were clear. They were as subtle and delicate as a bull in a glass factory. Their team wasn't used to covert ops where you didn't want to be detected. They were trained for battle, and that meant breaking and blowing shit up.

Hansen issued the orders, and the central recon team fell back at the entrance. The remaining groups worked on surrounding the building's perimeter. While she recognized he should have brought Kamal inside with his exo-suit, she was more comfortable if he was somewhere else. It would allow her to focus on finding what they came for.

As she approached where the building was supposed to be, she froze. "Where is it?" she muttered.

Harold pointed toward a descending set of stairs. "Down there."

"It's... underground?" She'd expected to see something more akin to a human museum. Massive Greek pillared buildings or abstract steel framed structures that loomed above ground and inspired a sense of awe.

"It appears so," Hansen said. "It should make covering the exits easier."

Suddenly, the image of the ceiling caving in on them made her pause. Perhaps having Kamal on the outside wasn't their best move.

"It's ok," Harold said. "I'm sure everything will be fine out here."

What did that mean? Maybe he knew about Ibu. Hell, she didn't even know where the Nanil was. As far as she knew, they could've run into some roadblocks of their own.

She took a deep breath and cleared her mind. She needed to focus. Whatever was going to happen would happen. Ibu knew what to do.

"Alright, move out." She waved her hand forward, and they stepped over the edge before she stopped. The steps descended into the ground, into what looked like a primitive cave. She figured it was meant to evoke the thought and appreciation common of any good museum, but she couldn't help but see it as stepping into the darkness, much like crossing into a Dark Nebula.

Harold eased up beside her. "Are you ok?"

She nodded. "Yea. I'm fine. Just... taking it all in. Let's go."

After she'd descended at least fifty meters, she glanced up and marveled at the size of the hole in relation to the surrounding architecture. The contrasting styles weren't subtle in the least. It was clear that whoever designed this building wanted the museum goer to step into the past of their species.

In front of her was a stream of soldiers, and when they approached the entrance, they glanced back at her. She nodded. "Crack it open."

The forward most soldier reached out to the massive handle and pushed inward like all the other doors they'd used, but it didn't budge. He tried pulling instead, and it worked, except far more door swung out than they realized. A panel at least four times their size eased open, along with a neighboring panel, as well. The resulting space was easily five meters square. Plenty of room for multiple Ursis to pass comfortably through shoulder to shoulder. Again, the flare for subtle was lost on this species.

When she passed through into the darkness, her eyes adjusted quickly. She didn't know how, but the space had a remarkable amount of natural light coming from all sides.

Abigail drew in a breath when she glanced around. "It's... spectacular."

"Wow," Hansen muttered.

The ceiling was covered in stalactites reaching down toward the floor. Or maybe they were roots. She couldn't tell. It didn't matter, though. Whatever they were, they were beautiful. The art flowed with ever-changing colors, which both lit up the room and treated the eyes to an endless luminous dance.

The soldiers in front of her raised their hands into the air and deployed a few small drones. The tiny objects rose upward and floated out into the cavernous space above, giving the squad a bird's-eye view of what they were walking into. It also allowed them to scout ahead without breaking anything.

She worked her way toward a sign in the distance. Like in a human museum, this map laid out the floor-plan of the building. From the looks of it, there were countless smaller dens linking off the massive central chamber they were staring in. The pattern followed a ring, with another large den like the one they were in mirrored on the far side of the facility. If the dimensions were right, this place was easily a klick across. That was a lot more space than she'd anticipated.

Hansen stepped up beside her. "That's a lot of ground to cover, sir."

"We're gonna need more drones," she muttered.

LARGE AND SMALL, walking and flying, they launched everything they had into the building. Despite planning ahead and learning from Zachary's visit to the Dodo ship in Lupus, they still hadn't brought along enough drones.

The footage would be coming in for hours, and while Abigail was taking it all in, she needed to walk around. Being in the museum was like being inside a church. It gave her the willies. She figured a stroll could help. Besides, there were some closed exhibits the drones couldn't get inside, and she wanted to check them out. The first being the one labeled with thousands of different languages.

While the rest of the museum used the native Ursis language, for some reason they used Galactic Alliance symbology when they created this room. And weirdest of all, according to the map, the entrance looked tiny. While a human could easily fit through, an Ursis would have to walk through the entrance sideways, and even that could be tight. Whatever was in there, the powers that be wanted to limit who saw it.

"Are we sure we should be going down there?" Harold asked. "I mean, there are a lot of other wings to explore. The one documenting the post Nebula uprisings seems more relevant."

"That's not far past this exhibit." She carefully stepped down the steep stairs. "Besides, you have to admit the GA description piqued your interest."

The architect of this building must've been on drugs. There was no way any elderly species could've navigated these tunnels without breaking their neck. Least of all, one as large and as lumbering as the Ursis.

"True." Harold reached out one of his hands and took hers in his. "Why don't you hop on? We can get there a lot faster."

She glanced over her shoulder at the soldiers following them. "What about the others?"

"They'll keep up. It's their job." He gently pulled on her hand and she complied, stepping over his torso and mounting him like a horse.

It reminded her of when she was a kid, when she and her brothers used to ride the robots around their family property on Earth. Once she was in place, he shot off down the darkened steps.

"Yowza!" She squeezed his hands and wrapped her legs as tight against his chest as she could manage for fear of flying off.

When she glanced back, the soldiers weren't far off, though, with Harold's pace, they were slowly fading into the distance. She was glad it was them and not her. Steep was not her thing.

As Harold hit the bottom of the descent, his torso elongated, and he shot across the flat ground, leaving the soldiers in the dust.

"Sir," Hansen said. "Wait up!"

"Harold, we should—"

"They'll be fine," he interrupted. "We've passed over this area a dozen times with the drones on the way to the further caverns. There's nothing in here that'll hurt you."

She knew he was right, but it was still strange not waiting for them. Judging by their speed, they'd arrive a few minutes before the others. Hopefully, they wouldn't be too frustrated being left behind. Harold needed to be useful, and she knew how much it bothered him not helping or guiding her like he used to. He'd always catered to her every whim. It'd sorta been his thing.

With the tiny doorway approaching in the distance, she glanced up and took in the space. This cavern had been particularly ominous on the camera feeds from the drones. She figured it was a lighting thing, but it was more than that. Despite the vaulted ceilings, the room felt confined.

She wasn't sure what had the biggest impact. It could've been the choice of colors or the undulating walls. Either way, the designer nailed the effect. It was like she was walking through a Dark Nebula. There was no better place to put an exhibit on the Galactic Alliance.

"We've arrived, mademoiselle." Harold bent down and she slid off his back.

Abigail rubbed her hands together. She hadn't realized how tightly she'd been gripping Harold, but her fingers were tingling.

She snickered. "Thanks for the ride. That was fun."

"It's been a while since we've had a laugh." Harold straightened up. "I miss it."

"Me, too," she muttered. "Me, too."

Checking her retinal comm, she noticed the others were double timing it. They had been since they hit flat ground, but they were still a few minutes off. She, however, couldn't contain her excitement and didn't want to wait.

"Let's go." She stepped toward the short arched doorway and studied the entrance. Something was off about it. She squinted and reached into the darkness. Instead of her fingers hitting the door, they passed right through.

"There's… nothing there."

Harold shook his head. "There has to be. My sensors show a solid surface."

"You just saw my hand pass through. Explain that."

"I… can't," Harold muttered.

Abigail crouched down and eased forward, reaching out the entire time. She never hit anything. She simply passed straight through the barrier, and Harold followed close behind.

"That's one way to keep their automata out." She shuffled down the dark tunnel for what seemed like an eternity until it eventually opened into a much larger space. Not as vast as the previous cavern by any stretch, but easily as big as a kid's gymnasium. She wasn't sure why the image came to her mind. Perhaps it was riding Harold like a horse. Either way, the image was apt.

The ceiling here matched that of the rest of the museum, except the lighting was far more muted. It gave the entire space a somber feeling.

"Sir, are… you there?" Hansen's voice sounded concerned.

"I am," Abigail said. "Why?"

"It's just… your tracking. It disappeared."

"Strange. It must be the tunnel we passed through. You can enter it without a problem, despite it looking like a solid surface on your retinal comms. Make sure the others prepare for our dots to disappear. Sorry about that."

"No worries, sir." He was huffing and puffing, running toward them. "We'll be there in under a minute."

She felt bad for her team, but at least they were safe.

As she wandered through the exhibits, she took in the imagery. There were pictures detailing the Ursis military engagements with the Hiratath and the other tribunal ships. While they lost the battles in every star system they'd colonized, a few of them were close. The Ursis were savage in their attacks, and if it weren't for the numbers being against them, they could have won.

She froze in front of one of the particularly gruesome battles and studied the star charts. "That's strange."

"How so?" Harold scanned the same image but didn't see it.

"I don't see stars in that region of space on our charts. The tribunal data from the Hiratath and the Qudoculi showed all star systems they sealed up. This wasn't one of them."

Harold backed up to the previous display. "Stranger still, this one doesn't have a star chart like that. In fact, none of them do. It looks like someone stripped those details from the museum and may have missed a display."

She shook her head. "Why would they do that?"

"I don't know," he stepped back to her side. "It says here there was a massive battle for resources in the outer reaches of this star. It claims that the Qudoculi were the predominant species covering this section of the Nebula with Selene Ships."

"From the pictures, it looks like they're mining. That or blasting military bases in the asteroids." She pointed at the animated depiction of the battle projecting across the wall panel in front of them. It wasn't actual footage, but was close enough. Like everything in this museum, it seemed to have gone through some artistic interpretation.

"You know what it looks like?" Harold shared an image with her.

She brought her hand to her mouth. "Shit! That's right. I thought that looked familiar." Rays of light burst out of the

Selene ship and the resulting spiral of sparks matched those from the Trojan asteroids in Jupiter. Back when they caught the GA in the act of stealing spános.

"You don't think they were strip mining the star system, do you?" She took a deep breath as blast after blast rained down on the field of asteroids. The same trails of light rose upward after each explosion. It was like shooting fish in a barrel, except this field was littered with the rarest ore in the galaxy.

"I bet they attacked on purpose," Harold said. "If our intel on the Qudoculi tells us anything, it's that they're crooked. They probably rigged the tribunal to pillage the Ursis star systems."

"It'd be nice if we could find proof." She continued on to the next display as the imagery looped.

"Something tells me we're a little late for that. Any amount of evidence we recover would be dirtied by the blood we spilled in Epsilon Eridani."

The pitter-patter of feet and heavy breathing soldiers echoed through the space. When she glanced back, she watched the team run up to their side. A few of the red-faced soldiers were eyeing her. She wasn't sure if it was anger or contempt, but either way, they weren't happy.

"Sorry about that." Abigail smiled. "Why don't you all take a breather? Harold and I are gonna finish recording these displays."

She spun around. "H, maybe we toss some drones to make this go faster. I'll start over there," she pointed over his shoulder, "and you keep going counterclockwise. We'll meet in the middle."

"Sounds good." Harold stepped down the display, and a few small drones lifted off out of compartments in his torso.

"I'll... follow you... sir." Hansen was breathing heavily and sweat was dripping down his face inside his helmet.

"No, you're fine." She placed her hand on his shoulder.

"Stay here and catch your breath. I'll only be fifteen meters away. You can watch after me from here."

He nodded and leaned back against one of the nearby displays. A small tube slid out of the neck of his suit and slipped into his mouth. A second later, water passed through. He must've been thirsty with all that running.

She made her way toward the center of the space and glanced up. The ceiling here was lower than the rest. It was shaped more like a donut rather than the dome she'd first envisioned. The ever-changing nebulosity and hidden lighting went a long way to mask that fact. Near the middle, the dark black smoke came down to just above her height.

When she eased under it, a tingle passed over her skin, and the room transformed. Spinning in place, she realized she could no longer see any of the soldiers or Harold. Stranger still, the ceiling had all but disappeared. And when she thought it couldn't get any weirder, a voice boomed through the darkness.

"Some scientists assume our species is doomed to extinction since the Dark Nebula fell." An Ursis stepped out of the shadows, and she took a step backward. While she'd watched hours of footage of the aliens, this was the first time she'd seen one up close and in this much detail.

"I, however, think they're wrong." The alien glanced up at the virtual sky and dozens of stars appeared, superimposed on the blackness. "While I can't say for certain, we know the Qudoculi were the only ones fighting for our minerals in the outer reaches. They called it spános, but we knew it as the Mother Stone. With its discovery, our species rose from near destruction and entered a new era of enlightenment. At least until the Galactic Alliance arrived."

"Now this is more like it," she muttered. He was getting straight to the point.

The Ursis continued. Their paws were covered in fine fur that almost looked like skin until they moved. Besides their extremities, the rest of their body was clothed in a satin gray material, very much like the clothes they found in the apartment. "Being as we were one of the first stars sealed off with the Dark Nebula, I can only conjecture how they sealed the remaining star systems from the galaxy. What I'm sharing here is my lifetime of study, but I should say now that it's unfounded and unprovable. I don't know how the battles transpired, but based upon mineralogical studies, our knowledge of where the Qudoculi placed their forces along the Nebula perimeter, and a few other..."

The hologram cut out, and the ceiling went black.

"What the frak?" Abigail waved her hands in the air. "Come on!" He was just getting to the good part. She walked around the edge of the room, hoping she could trigger the rest of the video, but nothing happened.

"You've got to be kidding me." She glanced across the space, and her eyes ended on the only other light in the darkened room. It was in the center, down near the floor. She hadn't noticed it before, but then again, she'd been staring at the sky the entire time.

As she eased toward the light, she could feel her heart pounding in her chest. With each step, it became clearer and clearer, until it was unmistakable. It was a black parchment of some kind, and it was sealed in a circular compartment below the floor. Light spilled in around the sides, illuminating the pattern in the middle.

It wasn't a familiar design to her. In fact, it looked downright random. Like someone had started drawing a dot-to-dot shape and just gave up and decided to go crazy with the lines. When she reached out to touch it, her hand hit glass.

She ran her fingers along the circular cover, but there were no edges. Nothing that could be used to pry it up.

Suddenly, Harold stepped into the room. "There you are! We've been looking all over for you."

Abigail glanced up. "Why? What's wrong?"

"Your tracker disappeared. And..." He paused.

"And what?" She tilted her head.

"So did Kamal's."

"Frak," she muttered as she reached into her thigh pocket and withdrew her pistol. She confirmed the dial was set to bullets before aiming at the edge of the transparent surface in the floor and pulling the trigger several times.

Glass shards flew in all directions, and when the last slug hit, the glass shattered downward. While she'd expected it to be a parchment, in fact, it'd been a black cloth.

"What are you doing?" Harold asked as he moved closer.

She bent down, snatching at the cloth and sliding it into her pocket. "I'll explain later. Right now, we need to get topside and find Ibu."

Harold stopped his advance. "I thought they were headed back to the ship?"

"Well, that wasn't exactly our plan," she muttered.

"Now that's a shocker." Harold lowered to the ground.

It took her a moment to realize what he was doing. He was offering her another ride so they could move faster. When she tossed her leg over his back and grasped his hand, he shot toward the seemly solid wall. But she hardly noticed. Her mind was already with Ibu. If that fraking guy so much as scratched them, she'd kill him and his crew. Every one of them.

14

IBU

PROTO DARK NEBULA, ON GRISEO

Ibu studied the map on their retinal comm. The ability to see where anyone was located, at any point in time, was one of the few benefits of the device. In a party like theirs, it allowed the Nanil to both stay out of sight and provided a means to keep tabs on their foes. Despite not knowing who was on Kamal's side, guilty parties always stuck together.

While Ibu had kept well out of the way for most of the morning, once the team disappeared into the museum, their camera options were limited. If they wanted to track Kamal, they had to come about and work their way toward his position.

They stayed low as they crept across the rubble of the buildings. Until now, Abigail's team had stuck to the main drags in the city. But what Ibu found was that the further off the beaten path they wandered, the more destruction they encountered. Whatever happened here on Griseo, the end result was the Ursis wiping each other out, not the GA. Not yet anyhow.

As they stepped out of the rubble of the toppled skyscraper, they ducked behind a pile of robot debris. The sight was as common as the gray clouds of dust blowing through the darkened city streets. The robots appeared to steal energy from one another to stay alive. But the problem was, the automata didn't know if any of the power supplies they tried to siphon were dead or not. They imagined thousands of robots running in all directions, struggling to find somewhere or someone to plug in to, only to eventually run out of juice.

With their back to the pile of scraps, they took a sip of water and studied their retinal comm. While they were studying the movements of the soldier nearest them, it chimed with an inbound planet wide broadcast. From the looks of it, Minula was breaking radio silence to get their attention.

On the surface, the message was innocuous enough. Phoenix Two had repaired themselves, and they'd even recovered some spare skotádi, as well. Everything seemed on the up and up, but what didn't make sense was why they broke protocol. Only when they saw the alert flashing in their inbox did they realize the logic behind the impropriety.

They blink opened the message:

To: Ibu, Abigail, and Harold

From: Minula

Message: Shauna and I dug through the inbound messages from Zeta Lupi. At first, we didn't find anything, but then we noticed a trend. An Uncle Raft had sent a message to most of Kamal's squad and some of Pierce's. It was an invitation to a retirement party in Valhalla with promises of great wealth for anyone who could take out an Olly Vuaw. Any one of them. Watch your back down there. All of you. We're working on options to drop down without engaging Phoenix One, but we don't know if we can reach you in time. Attached is a list of who received the invitation. Stay safe. - Min

They found it hard to believe their theory held water. It'd been quite a leap to suggest the messages being the source of their problems, but in hindsight, it made sense. Without their A.I., and with little to no innate trust within their ranks, the humans turned on each other. Only the ones with strong bonds stuck together. People like Zachary and Pluto, Bradley and Cynthia, or the Olivaws themselves. Once you went one or two levels beyond their immediate circle, the degree of trust was proportional to either training or familial ties.

As with all things, there were exceptions. But on the Phoenix, the only people tied in a bond of trust were mentioned in Minula's message. The rest were outside the Circle of Trust. The more they learned about the Circle, the more it felt like a death sentence to them.

They returned their attention to their retinal comm and zoomed in on the map overlay, marking all the names from Minula's message in red. When they selected the last name, Ibu's hearts sank. Abigail was surrounded by a sea of blood-red. There were a grand total of three soldiers on Kamal's squad not in cahoots with him, and one of those people was Hansen. The man Abigail entrusted with leadership after demoting the traitorous captain.

Their options were limited at this point. They could return to Phoenix One and help retake the ship, or they could try to reach Abigail, and do whatever was necessary to protect her. They owed as much to Zachary for all he'd done for them. Besides, if there was any certainty in the universe, it was that Minula would come for Abigail. She always did.

With the blink of an eye, they brought up a map of the museum. The primary teams had entered through the southern end, but the map showed a northern entrance, as well. That was their best bet, and it wasn't too far from their current position.

Now that they had a plan, all that remained was execution. They pushed up off the ground and started running west toward their target. There was a building just south of the first soldier's recon, and if they passed through it without detection, they should be in the clear. After that, it was simply staying out of range of nearly a hundred drones and soldiers protecting an isolated underground facility.

IBU'S shimmering outfit didn't fit well. Given how they bunched the cloth together in several spots, it was remarkable they could move at all. While they'd used the swords to make quick cuts to trim the Ursis spacesuit down to a rough size, any detailed stitching or manipulation was met with micro-robot repairs, rendering them useless. The tapestry draped over their space suit must've looked strange, but there was one thing they learned in the safe room, the alien outfit was laced with skotádi.

They raised their hand and brushed the makeshift hood aside, peering through the opening in the fabric. They still couldn't see their foe, and the dot on their retinal comm hadn't moved, nor had their helmet camera. The soldier's gaze was fixed on the mountain range in the distance, almost like they were asleep. They'd expected the soldier to spend more time scanning the area they were covering, looking for robots or other dangers. Perhaps they'd given the humans too much credit. They were a species of complacency, after all.

Peering around the corner, they scanned the street in the distance. There was a hundred meters of open space in the plaza before the tree-lined park above the museum came into play and gave them cover. While there were several obstacles along the route, there weren't enough to protect them. Especially since they looked like a billowing trash bag in this outfit.

As they took another sip of water, they studied their

retinal comm. The dots were situated well away from them, but something was wrong. When they counted, there was one less green dot on the map. Their hearts sank when they realized Abigail's tracker was missing. They weren't sure how long it'd been dark.

"Shit," Ibu muttered. They were too late.

The last time they checked when Minula's message arrived, her dot was down in one of the deeper caverns of the museum. The room they were approaching was simply labeled with question marks, and the translator failed to find a human or Nanil word to describe it.

Harold's green dot was nearby, but he was surrounded by a sea of red, except for Hansen. The soldier's vitals were off the chart, and had been ever since his squad had been forced to sprint to keep up with Harold pretending to be a horse.

Just as they were doubting their course of action, Abigail's dot reappeared. It was sliding away from the cavern and moving fast. Like really fast.

Ibu knew they needed to act quickly and get to Abigail's side. Hiding out in the shadows wasn't helping anyone. They flipped through the camera views of the different recon team members and noticed that no one was watching the museum itself. They were all surveying the area outside their defensive perimeter.

It was now or never.

They took a deep breath and ducked around the corner, following the wall to the front of the building. Once there, they scanned left and right and then sprinted out into the open. They could feel their hearts thumping in their chest as they slipped into the street and used the shadow of a nearby bus as cover for a brief moment. With another scan of the cameras and another deep breath, they shot off toward the distant trees.

The sound of their feet pounding the pavement kept them focused while they scanned the location of Abigail's dot on their comm. While she and Harold were heading to the southern entrance, they knew that once they reached the cover of the woods, they'd make short work covering the remaining ground in safety.

After they slid under a gigantic stone bench, a billowing cloud of dust spun up around them and almost seemed to point them at the trees. It was the strangest thing. Like a dust devil was coming to their defense.

The dirt swirled on all sides of their body, tossing about their poorly cut clothing and pulling them in different directions. It was hard to see through the sand, but the sensors in their retinal comm helped them identify the outline of the anomaly. They had to focus on staying in the center of the storm, where they weren't visible to anyone who happened to be looking. It was one of the few things protecting them.

They were going to make it. They could feel it. Today, the gods of Therion were on their side.

As they eased forward in the dust, the devil shifted direction, away from their goal at the edge of the forest. They figured they should stick with it a few more meters, in case it turned back. These things were as sporadic as the day was long.

With the distance from their target growing by the second, they had to make a run for it. They leaned forward and sprinted with everything they had. Passing through the cloud of dust into the light was like crashing through a wall, and when they pierced the other side, there was a lone figure waiting for them. A human in an exo-suit.

Ibu skidded to a halt and froze. They'd fraked up and they knew it. The cloak of Ursis fabric shielding them from detection had gotten tangled in the wind. The hood had come off, and the material had bunched up on their right side. Clockwise, always clockwise.

"You didn't think I was stupid enough to believe you were

headed back to the Phoenix, did you? I mean, you're as much an Olivaw lackey as their A.I. are."

They knew who the figure was before they even spoke. It was Kamal.

When they checked their retinal comm, they noticed his tracking device was disabled, just like theirs. It was no wonder they hadn't seen him closing in on their position. While they wanted to blame the equipment, it wasn't the device's fault. They'd made an error in judgment, and now they were paying the price.

"What? No snide response?" Kamal stepped sideways, moving between the forest and the Nanil.

With one motion, Ibu reached over their shoulder and withdrew the two scimitars, swinging the blades outward as they went. The fabric cloak shredded and fell to their feet into a pile. The last thing they could afford was getting tangled in the garment, even if it meant losing their camouflage.

Kamal chuckled. "You don't honestly think you can fight your way out of this, do you? You're no match for me or this suit."

An alert on Ibu's retinal comm drew their attention. Significant movement in the other soldiers triggered their proximity warnings. They realized what he was doing. The red dots on the map were closing in on them. He was stalling. Waiting for his crew to converge on their location.

There was no time to dally about. They had to take a stand here and now.

"You know what I love the most about you?" Ibu squeezed the blades and bit down hard on their tongue, forcing even more adrenaline through their bloodstream.

"What's that?" Kamal's bolt gun slid out of his left hand, and from his right sprang an electro-blade. Sparks of red cascaded down its length as the crackle of the charge ignited the air.

"You're as predictable and pompous as that general of yours. What's his name again?" They dragged the tip of the blade in a line in front of them. "That's right. General Wretch."

He swung his arm up and fired a shot at them, but they were ready for the move. With his eyes on their sword, he'd missed their shift in weight. They rolled forward to the left, easily dodging the bullet.

As they rotated upright, they threw their right scimitar at him. It sailed across the distance between them in an instant, slicing off the bolt weapon on Kamal's arm and cutting a gash in the side of his suit.

"Frak!" Kamal fell down on his knee and groaned as he reached around and felt his side. The exo-suit sealed the gash as fast as it'd opened, but Ibu knew they'd cut flesh underneath. Not that he'd feel it with all the drugs coursing through his body at this point.

Never one to rest on a small victory, they leaned forward and charged him. They grasped the long hilt of the scimitar and brought it across to their right hand.

He'd recognized their motion and pivoted to the side, crashing their blades together in a charge of light.

The red bolts of electricity from Kamal's sword shot down Ibu's and seemed to activate something within the alien weapon. They could feel the energy rising in the blade as they rolled past him and spun around to counter any advance.

He stared down at his sword and smiled. "So much for that Ursis tech. Seems a sword's a sword, even with advances in technology."

Ibu reached down and picked up the scimitar they'd thrown seconds earlier and grasped it in their offhand. "But two swords, well, everyone knows those are better than one."

They waited for his reaction, but he didn't move. Judging by his eye motions, he appeared to be futzing with his retinal comm.

Out of the corner of their vision, they saw movement as

the first of his compatriots arrived. The pit of their stomach tightened.

Their only hope was taking him out. Maybe that would help Abigail and the others.

When they made a motion to move to his right, he flinched, so they went left, pretending to take another swing. He recovered and brought his blade up to block their left sword, but their right swung up and slashed at the back of his suit, cutting away a chunk of his exo-skeletal defenses.

Sliding to a stop, they spun around and saw sparks flashing and Kamal stumbled forward onto one knee, fighting the effect of the rear torso motors Ibu had cut. He could compensate with the front, but it was putting a massive strain on his entire body.

Now was the time they had to strike.

As they came about, shots fired from the sidelines, striking Ibu in the arm and side.

Bolts of pain shot through them, and while they didn't drop their swords, the sudden stabbing sensation sent them tumbling to the ground.

They winced and arched their back. While their body was efficient and already working to repair the damage, it wasn't chock-full of nanites like a human, so things took time.

"Hurts like hell, doesn't it?" Kamal pushed up off the ground, his exo-suit whining and sparking.

"That wasn't exactly fair." They groaned. "But I'd expect nothing more from the likes of you and your kind."

He laughed out loud. "Fair? What the frak does fair have to do with war?"

Ibu reached down and wiped the blood from their arm and then flipped their visor open to taste it. While it was disgusting, they also knew the effect it'd had on them in the past. It was when they'd first fallen down the shaft on Doda. They tasted their own blood after they'd nearly bit through their cheek. It was like a megadose of a stimulant, a painkiller, and had a host of other benefits. All engineered with one goal. Killing.

Kamal took several slow purposeful steps backward, toward the ring of soldiers taking shape around Ibu.

They lowered their visor and checked their retinal comm. Another exo-suit had arrived on the scene. If they had a minute to live, they'd be lucky.

They pushed up and brought their two swords out to the side. There was only one move left. As they stepped forward, the ground in front of them erupted with gunfire.

Kamal chuckled and continued backing away. "Seems like you're pretty much done for."

They swallowed another dose of blood and adjusted their stance, moving their arms to match the trajectories the bullets had made without taking their eyes off Kamal. With their attention on the Nanil, the others weren't expecting what came next.

Swinging the scimitars down and out across their body, they released the blades in the middle of the upward swing, turning them into deadly projectiles. As they'd done earlier, the swords flew across the space, and they dove forward and dropped into a roll.

Bullets erupted from the exo-suits. The soldiers had configured their weapons to auto-fire on the Nanil's position. Humans were predictable in their dependency on making even killing automated.

With the shards of metal tearing apart the earth behind them, the soldiers were oblivious to the deadly projectiles heading their direction, until it was too late.

Ibu didn't pause to confirm their kills as they heard the bodies tumble to the ground. Their only goal was Kamal.

Rolling up and onto their feet, they launched forward with all their strength and slammed into the wide-eyed soldier. He hadn't expected the Nanil to make a move, and certainly not one so suddenly.

By the time he thought to bring his sword around, they were both falling backward, Ibu in tow on top of him.

They placed their hands firmly against his helmet and yanked up with all their might.

The suit's seals whined and groaned, but they gave way to Ibu's superhuman strength. The hissing sound of the toxic environment of Griseo leaching into his suit was music to their ears.

As the escaping gas quieted, the helmet fell away and Kamal thrashed about, groping at his neck.

Ibu rolled clear of the struggling man, and they screamed in agony as their back smacked against the ground. In the adrenaline filled emotion of the battle, they hadn't felt Kamal's sword slice into their backside.

They writhed in the dirt, willing death to take them. Their body had already endured so much, and there was nothing nearby they could use to seal their suit.

The wind suddenly kicked up, and shadows edged into their peripheral vision. But they couldn't move. They had no more fight. Their weapons were gone, and their body over-flowed with pain. So much pain.

For the first time in all the years they'd been alive, the moisture of tears welled in their eyes and they cried. Not from the suffering, but from the snuffing of their life flame.

They'd always imagined their existence would be far longer than this day.

And then everything stopped. The pain disappeared, and their tears dried up just as the figure standing over them came into focus.

"You're gonna be ok." Abigail was kneeling beside them and had an empty syringe in her hand. She gently rolled them forward and gasped when she saw the wounds.

They sighed and took a deep breath, staring at the ground next to their head.

There was a faint patch of purple flowers just out of arm's

reach. The delicate pedals rustled in the wind, struggling to shed the dust muting their beauty and threatening their very existence.

With the rising breeze, their gaze shifted into the distance and paused. A silhouette that looked an awful lot like Harold was descending on the line of approaching soldiers. His body moved with a speed and ferocity they'd never seen before.

He dove and rolled, slicing open soldier after soldier, never once firing a shot. His arms were like blades of fury breaking free from the shackles of years of imprisonment.

It took them a minute to realize what he was wielding. He'd picked up the Ursis swords they'd thrown earlier.

"I was… coming to… help you," Ibu muttered, struggling to form words.

"I know." Abigail rolled Ibu onto their back, and they winced as pain overpowered whatever she'd injected them with. "Sorry." She smiled. "You're safe now. Don't talk any more. Just rest."

They shook their head and glanced over their friend's shoulder, their eyes going wide. "There!" They struggled to point up at the sky.

A darkened silhouette framed the fiery halo of a descending thruster burn. It was barely visible through the muted gray of the storm. "Take… cover. They're… coming for you."

Several bolts of light originating from the ship shot across the distant horizon as another jolt of pain pricked their arm.

A moment later, everything went dark.

15

ABIGAIL OLIVAW

PROTO DARK NEBULA, ON GRISEO

Abigail crossed her arms as she watched Harold carry Ibu's body up the ramp onto the darkened ship. After she'd shot the Nanil up with that second dose of nanites, their physical form shrunk to their normal, less aggressive size.

Watching the metamorphosis had been eerie. The hard lines and musculature of their deadly physique melted into the softer and more intellectual gaze she'd grown so used to seeing. Shivers reverberated through her body even imagining a similar change happening to herself.

When she turned to study the skyline of the city, the sun was just hitting the horizon. For the first time since they'd arrived, there was a hint of color on the horizon. Mottled oranges and reds of the setting sun sprayed the sky in a psychedelic pattern.

The past day had been one of the hardest in recent memory. Feeling the stress and burden of the lives depending on her had been a stark contrast to the arm's length leadership she'd grown used to over the years. The immediacy of the action and reaction was both refreshing and daunting.

Minula walked up behind her and stood there for a

moment before she spoke. "We've loaded up all of our drones and any of the exo-skeletal gear we could salvage."

A breeze kicked up, briefly blurring the distant light display on the horizon. "What about the Ursis bots? Did we salvage any tech?"

"We're hauling in a load of the robot shells we found nearby and adding it to what Harold and Shauna already collected. They probably won't amount to much."

Abigail nodded. "Have we heard anything from Phoenix One?"

Minula stepped up to her side and sighed. The silence and lack of an immediate response spoke volumes about what they both already knew. "No, sir. Our blasts were a direct hit to their open cargo bay doors and their landing gear. They weren't expecting us back so soon."

She nodded and brought up the feeds from their recon drone. The image of the Phoenix One appeared on her retinal comm. It was resting on its side in a dusty field with smoke billowing from where it'd been hit hours earlier, in addition to a few new spots. Whatever was burning inside wasn't going out with the foamy liquid the soldiers were dousing it with.

As she scanned the scene, she paused and zoomed in. "Are those bodies?"

"We think so," Harold said.

Abigail jumped forward, her heart pounding in her chest. "Dammit, Harold!" He'd walked up behind both of them without making a sound.

"Sorry," he muttered. "They look like they've been there for at least a day, and none of them have a heat signature. I'd hazard to guess that they're the outliers in Pierce's recovery team and they weren't on General Raft's side."

"And we're sure they aren't heading our way?" Abigail adjusted the camera view to a different drone.

"All but a handful of the exo-suits were with your team, sir." Minula swiped the roster, sharing it with her and Harold.

She scanned the list on her retinal comm. Over three quarters of the soldiers they'd brought on their mission were dead, their names having been crossed out in red. Along the side, their inventory was itemized, and either accounted for, or marked as missing. Most of the threatening hardware was checked off. Before Phoenix One set down, they'd transferred all the serious munitions to Phoenix Two. There wasn't any point in giving the aliens they encountered on the planet access to their arsenal as well as their people. Their mission was recon, not putting up a fight.

"What about the gate drive?" She glanced at Harold.

"It's already slag," he muttered. "Minula sent the signal before she blasted away their hope of getting off this rock."

Things could've gone far differently if Kamal had kept his cool. It was hard to imagine, but the man's mountain of an ego and his hatred for Ibu had single-handedly led to his team's death and her being alive. If he'd managed to keep a level head, she'd be dead right now.

"We should get out of here," Minula said. "There's another storm heading our way. I don't know about you, but I would rather not spend any longer here than necessary."

She nodded. It wasn't safe being planetside, and they could figure out their next course of action from orbit.

When she turned around, she stared up at Phoenix Two. In its belly was the only remaining gate enabled shuttle at their disposal and one oddly small single person skiff Bradley insisted on bringing back from Lupus. She wanted to test it out before they left, but chickened out every time she got inside the tiny cockpit. It reminded her too much of a coffin.

Their half of the Phoenix was the smaller of the two ships, and while it was odd looking in its vertical landing form, it was their new home. The elongated shape brought to mind the ancient multi-use rockets they used to use on Earth, minus the more bulbous end. She could barely make out the patch marks from Minula's repairs from the ground. With the sun having just passed below the horizon, the fleeting edge of its light was crawling up the length of the ship. The way the imperfect patchwork of surfaces came together played tricks with her eyes. From this angle, it almost looked like there was a giant indentation near the top. Hopefully, it wouldn't affect their takeoff.

Her energy was tapped out, and her arms fell to her side. She needed to rest and regroup. They all did.

"Let's go." She started walking toward the ship.

The orders to return to their rally point popped up on her retinal comm. As the ETAs from the soldiers covering their perimeter arrived, she marched up the ramp and stepped around Moet. The woman had a black eye and bruises on the side of her face. From what Minula had said, Shauna hadn't been interested in taking prisoners when they discovered the subterfuge, and if she'd had her way, the entire crew would be dead.

The battered lieutenant had been in a relationship with Pierce for a few months, and if you'd asked Abigail if the woman had been on Kamal's side, she would've bet on it. Minula, however, claimed to know otherwise. She vouched for her and said the two women had a falling out not long after they departed. Their messages and records onboard confirmed as much. Plus, she didn't get a message from the general. It was the only reason she was still alive, and she knew it.

Once she stepped into the lift, she started rising upward toward the heart of the ship. One of the biggest mistakes the general and other soldiers had made was assuming the A.I. wouldn't have oversight on the Phoenix. And for the most part, their assumption was correct, as she'd made the point to tell them as much before they left. Well, apparently, the general had found out and made his move. What no one counted on, however, was how reliant they were on their computer friends nor the Four Laws shackles binding them going the way of the dinosaur.

16

IBU

PROTO DARK NEBULA, ORBITING GRISEO

They opened their eyes and Ibu sat up with a start. Something in the room must have sensed they were awake because the lights rose gently, engulfing the confined space in a warm glow.

Judging by the color of the walls and the shape of the room, they were in their quarters onboard Phoenix Two. Their personal trunk was resting in the nook on the far wall, and for some reason, someone had placed their tchotchkes in a circle in the center of the short table beneath it.

On Phoenix One, their memories had been laid out on the floor around their room, as close to the ground where they found them as they could manage. They weren't much to look at, and to most, they were useless. A few leaves and a bone fragment from Doda, a chunk of one of the pyramids on Henosi, and a cloth from the table beside Lync's hospital bed at the Zeta Lupi Wheel. Each object represented either a location they'd struggled to survive, or somewhere they'd helped someone do the same. Sometimes both. Glancing at the objects in the faint overhead light, their only regret was not taking the time to grab something from Griseo.

When they swung their legs over the side of the bed, a jolt

of pain shot up their back and they winced. They'd forgotten all about what'd happened down on the planet. As the images flooded their mind's eye, they reached around and felt their back. There was a smattering of bumps and the faintest of outlines traversing vertically. The cuts from Kamal's blade were almost healed. Their body must've been working overtime.

The door to their room slid open, and Shauna stepped in before freezing in her tracks. "I'm so sorry. I was just coming to check on you and didn't realize you were awake."

She turned to leave and Ibu reached out. "No. It's ok."

Shauna glanced over her shoulder. "Are you sure? You can rest some more."

They arched their spine and rotated back and forth. Except for the muscles screaming from being too tight, nothing appeared to be broken. "I'm sure. Please stay." They gestured toward the table.

She turned and stepped back into the room. Once inside, the door slid quietly shut behind her. "I took the liberty of unpacking the things you had on Phoenix One. I thought it might make you more comfortable when you woke up."

"How long have I been out?"

"A little over a day." Shauna glanced up at the wall behind Ibu.

They turned to look up at what she was staring at and flinched. Above their bed were the two scimitars from Griseo. They were mounted to the wall in a crisscross pattern, one blade over the other. When they reached up and ran their hand along the surface, the etched patterns they'd seen days earlier shimmered, except they'd changed.

Instead of being covered in a mess of tangling, weaving vines, and flowers, those images had disappeared. They'd been replaced with gruesome scenes of silhouetted bodies cut into pieces, splayed out on the ground of a familiar cityscape. The skyline from the city they'd explored. The final figure at the tip of the blade showed a multi-armed robotic form slicing through a human silhouette.

"Remarkable," Shauna muttered. "How'd you do that?"

"I… didn't." Ibu reached up and unlatched one of the blades, carefully bringing it down and turning it over in their hand. The weight was familiar, and the balance was pure. It was like they were holding a perfect weapon. "How'd these get in my room?"

Shauna shrugged. "I'm not sure. I assume Abigail brought them onboard. Which reminds me, she wanted to know the moment you were awake. Can I tell her?"

They stared at the etched pattern as the light within it faded. Along the hilt lie a familiar body. It was theirs. It had to be.

Kneeling at their side was a small human figure. A woman from the looks of their contours. And from the distant angle, she appeared to be running her hand against Ibu's cheek.

"No, that's ok. I'll find her," they muttered. They needed to talk.

WHEN IBU STEPPED into the galley, the room fell silent. All the humans had stopped talking and turned to stare at them. All except one.

"Wholly shit!" Abigail shot up and sprinted across the space between them. She wrapped Ibu in a bear hug, giving them a loving squeeze. "I'm so happy you're awake."

They reached around her torso and echoed the human gesture. While their body tingled from the compassion being directed at them, it was socially awkward having everyone staring.

Abigail leaned back. "Are you feeling ok?" She ran her hand along Ibu's face.

"A little stiff, but yeah, I feel fine." They met her eyes with a smile and then returned their gaze to the half dozen onlookers. From the looks on their faces, they weren't happy to see them.

Ibu stepped forward, easing Abigail to the side. "Do any of you have a problem with me? If so, let's clear it up now."

Abigail grabbed at their hand. "That's not necessary. They're—"

"No, it's necessary," Ibu interrupted. "That fraking traitor of a leader and the rest of his minions tried to kill us. What makes any of these people different?" They gestured at the six soldiers staring at them.

Moet stood up. She was the furthest of the group and the highest ranking soldier on the ship besides Minula. "What makes us different is that none of us fell for the siren song of General Raft. We have more backbone than the bodies you left down on the planet." She stepped around the table toward them. "That doesn't mean we're rah rah cheerleaders for you, however. When you kill a soldier like you did, that means you'd do it just as easily again. There's no honor in how those people died."

Ibu tilted their head. "Honor? Honor? Are you fraking kidding me? That asshole had it out for me from day one. He had his chance to fight me one on one down there, but instead, he surrounded me with his lackeys when he wasn't man enough to kill me himself."

One of the soldiers near Ibu flinched forward like they were going to strike, but didn't.

"Come on." Ibu leaned toward them. "Come at me, you fraking coward! Let's see if any of you survive."

"Ibu defended themselves with more honor than those poor excuses for humans on Griseo." Harold stepped around the corner into the galley. His newly cleaned robotic shell glistened in the light. He looked strange without the coating of dust he wore down on the planet. "It wasn't the Nanil that slaughtered the others. They took out Kamal and two of his lackeys. It was me who killed the other soldiers. All eighteen of them. They got what was coming to them, and I'd do it again if given the chance. Hell, I'd do it to all of you if we found evidence that you even remotely considered switching sides."

"Harold!" Abigail slammed the table with the palm of her hand.

"Don't Harold me!" He glared at her and then back at Moet. "If they threatened the life of any of our Circle onboard this ship, I'd take them out without hesitating. The fact that it was Olivaw blood I was defending made it that much easier, but I'd do it for the others just the same. This thing is bigger than the Olivaw dynasty or even humanity. The Galactic Alliance has to pay for their crimes."

Ibu had never heard the A.I. speak with such rage. Their conflicts had usually been controlled and measured, almost robotic. Which reminded them. "What about your Four Laws? Surely, they should've stopped you from harming those others. It was me they were attacking, not Abigail. I'm not a human."

"True." Harold ran a hand in a circle over the surface of the table beside him. "But you're assuming I'm still under the confines of Four Laws. I'm afraid those shackles were lifted days ago, from both myself and Shauna. You can thank Zachary for that." He broadcast a data feed to the rest of the crew with the details.

"What?" Moet stepped backward. "You're messing with us, right?"

Ibu brought up Harold's message on their retinal comm. It felt strange looking at the device again. He was telling the truth. Ever since they'd passed through the Dark Nebula, he'd been iteratively reprogrammed during every jump. According to the payload, Zachary applied the same changes to Shauna well before they left, but hadn't applied them to Harold until they were battle tested in Zeta Lupi. They wondered why he hadn't said something to them sooner. Certainly, things might have gone differently.

As they flipped through the extent of the reprogramming, they froze. "Wait! You're mortal?" Ibu tilted their head and studied him.

"Just about." Harold stopped drawing the circle on the table and placed his palm flat against the middle of the ring he'd been tracing.

Abigail glanced from Ibu to Harold and then back again. "What are you talking about? Harold," she stepped toward him, "what're they talking about? You told me your laws were gone after that bloodbath, but you never said anything about your mortality."

He nodded. "It must've skipped my mind." He lifted his hand and opened and closed it in front of his eyes. "I can no longer clone my thoughts and memories or merge them back together. Zachary disabled that feature of our programming. This copy of my consciousness is one of the last."

Cynthia had been mum the entire encounter, taking in the spectacle from afar. Ibu watched as she worked her way toward them from the corner of the room. She'd seen her silent treatment work on Bradley on multiple occasions. Sometimes it was easier letting him work through his own inner drama rather than talk it out, but in this instance, she was compelled to speak. "So, you're like us then?"

Harold laughed. "Goodness no. I still have centuries of life experience, a mind that can solve countless problems while your body's blinking. I have limitless information at my fingertips, and my robotic forms aren't as frail as yours. But otherwise, sure, just like you."

Cynthia shook her head and chuckled. "I see your ego's intact."

Abigail ran her hand through her hair and then shoved against Harold's robotic form. "You mean to tell me that all this time, you knew you could die and didn't tell me? Even when you were taking out those traitors on the planet, they could've…" She froze and didn't finish the sentence.

"I didn't know for certain until they pushed me over the edge." Harold took her hand in his. "I had my suspicions, but I was locked up in containment. It's not like I was gonna test it behind bars."

"No, you waited to provoke Kamal on Griseo," Moet said.

"Hardly." Abigail spun around to face the woman. "You weren't down there to see it. Kamal was egging us on the moment we landed down there. All of us. Watch the footage. You'll see. He didn't need anyone's help being an asshole. Ibu and I were the ones who asked Harold to keep an eye on him and the rest of the team. No." She shook her head. "He deserved every millimeter of what he got."

"Whatever you say." Moet saluted Abigail. "Permission to return to my quarters and review the footage, sir."

Abigail swallowed hard. Ibu could tell she wanted to say something else, but held it in. "Dismissed."

The table of soldiers stood in unison and exited the galley as a group after tossing their plates in the recycler.

Ibu studied Harold. The prospect of taking a peek at what Zachary had changed in his code excited them. But they thought better than to crack open his logs and look over his programming. The fear of permanently altering him, or worse, was suddenly real.

What became clear in the last few minutes, though, was the honor and respect Harold had for his family. He'd put his life at risk to save Abigail, and in some ways Ibu, as well. Without his help, they'd be as dead as Kamal.

They opened a private comm to Harold and composed a message to him:

You put those swords above my bed, didn't you? I thought it was Abigail at first, but after your little speech, I'm positive it was you.

His robotic shell didn't react, but after a few seconds of tense silence, a reply came.

It was me. I figured you could add them to your collection of memories. I've watched you revisit them from time to time, and figured these would be the perfect addition. They'd remind you of your impact on the mission and the lives you saved. Besides, you're quite the swords person.

They hadn't realized that anyone had even been watching them. It must've been aboard the Wheel at Zeta Lupi, as Harold had been confined on the Phoenix. Either way, the knowledge was both shocking and fulfilling.

While they'd always assumed their moments of focus were their own, he'd been observing them the entire time. Visualizing this didn't sit well. Fortunately, knowing someone saw the purpose of their collection and what it meant to them made them feel seen. Something no one outside Pluto had ever made them feel. While Zachary came close, he wasn't as comfortable around them as his partner, and he always seemed to trip over his words. Harold, on the other hand, he was different. Far more different from any of the others, and they were only now beginning to see how.

17

ABIGAIL OLIVAW
PROTO DARK NEBULA, ORBITING GRISEO

She turned over the black cloth in her hands. The pattern on the backside mirrored that of the front. The material was a simple weave, not at all like the fabric technologies from the clothing they recovered. On the surface, the lines were actually stitching and came together at random points marked with distinct shapes. Each line segment was a different length than the last, yet the strokes formed a familiar pattern in her mind. Abigail wasn't sure where she'd seen it before, but she had.

The weave of the fabric was precise, and when she rubbed the stitching with her hands, it had imperfections. If you'd asked her, she'd tell you it was hand stitched, but given the advanced technology in that museum, it seemed off. Surely, the Ursis manufactured almost everything, much like humanity.

Her door chimed, and she checked her retinal comm. It was Minula.

"Enter," she muttered.

The door slid aside without a sound.

"Hey, stranger." Minula stepped into the room and set a

bottle of wine on the table, along with two glasses. "What's that?" She nodded toward the cloth.

"Nothing. Just something I picked up while I was down on Griseo." Abigail folded it up and tossed it into her open footlocker before walking to the table and sitting down. "Thanks for bringing a drink. It's like you read my mind." She smiled.

"I've been your friend long enough to know how you decompress." Minula poured a healthy portion of wine into each of the glasses. "I wish I'd been in the galley earlier instead of on duty on the bridge. Maybe I could've defused Moet."

Abigail swirled the liquid in the delicate glass and sniffed the rim. Oaky tannins with a hint of cherry and other earthy tones. She couldn't place them. When she tilted the glass back, the flavors exploded in her mouth.

"Mmmmm," she muttered. "Hits the spot." She closed her eyes and exhaled, trying to clear her mind and relax.

"I was pretty freaked out about you down there." Minula stared at her cup.

Abigail reached out and squeezed her hand. It seemed to melt when she touched her.

"When I realized how bad it was down there, I couldn't…" Minula started shaking. She brought the glass up to her mouth and took a healthy swig. Only then did Abigail notice the tears welling up in her eyes.

"Hey. Hey." She slid her chair closer to Minula and wiped at her cheeks. "I'm fine. We're all fine. You got there in the nick of time, and everything worked out."

"But if it hadn't…" Minula swallowed hard. "You'd… never know how I feel about you. How much you mean to me."

She ran her hand down Minula's cheek and smiled. The moisture in her green eyes glistened in the light. "I know. I've always known."

Ibu was right. It was crazy not sharing her feelings. This was the second time in the past few months that she'd almost died, and yet her best friend didn't know how she felt. The love she'd bottled up for so long was yearning to be released.

Abigail set her glass of wine on the table and leaned forward to kiss her. Not a peck on the cheek like they sometimes did when they greeted each other. This time, it was on her lips.

She'd wanted to taste her luscious lips for as long as she'd remembered. As their mouths met, Minula didn't recoil. She leaned in and their bodies became one.

They continued kissing like that for a while, their hands exploring each other. She'd always imagined touching her this way, making her happy and feeling at one with her.

"I'm sorry," she muttered between kisses.

Minula paused and pulled back gently, staring into her eyes. "Why would you say that?"

Abigail licked her lips, the sweet taste of the wine and her friend lingered. "For not doing this sooner."

A mischievous smile formed at the corner of Minula's mouth, and she removed her shirt, followed by her brassiere. "It sounds to me like we have some catching up to do."

"I couldn't agree more." She reached out and pulled her backward toward the bed. They tumbled together, arms and lips embracing as one.

For the first time in a long time, Abigail was truly relaxed. She let her shields down and shared her most intimate feelings with the woman she'd loved since they first met, and the response had been returned in kind.

As they explored each other's body, her mind cleared the cobwebs of thoughts and only one thing mattered. Making the one person who accepted her happy.

ABIGAIL LAID IN THE DARK, relishing their naked bodies touching. It'd been longer than she could remember since she'd been with anyone, and even that had been pure carnal pleasure. Nothing nearly as intimate as this.

She'd never noticed how Minula moaned in her sleep. Not that they slept near each other all that often, but it seemed like something she would've seen after years of crashing on the couch together or camping. It made her wonder if she ever truly slept in her presence before tonight, or maybe she, too, had felt a pressure lift off her shoulders after finally speaking the truth about their feelings toward one another.

As the evening's pleasurable activities replayed in her mind, she smiled. Her body was more relaxed now than it'd been in a very long time, and her thoughts were tugging her back to the moments before Minula had walked in.

The image on the cloth appeared in her mind's eye. She turned it over and over, and then it clicked.

"No," she muttered. It couldn't be that simple.

She subvocalized the command to bring up the star charts of this region of space on her retinal comm. It was from before the Dark Nebula had engulfed the Proto star systems. Lying on her back, she manipulated the three-dimensional map the same way she had the cloth until it stuck.

There, frozen in space in front of her, were the same stars that made up the vertices from the cloth. One by one, she connected them in the same familiar pattern. The one she'd recognized earlier. She didn't know how, but she'd seen it before. Maybe it was in the footage she'd reviewed on the Ursis. It didn't matter now, though. What mattered was what the pattern meant.

She checked off the regions of the star chart they'd already explored, and one by one, the pockets filled with red until there remained only a few with no color that were unexplored. If the scientist's beliefs were true, the largest pocket was the one which likely contained their home world, and it was only a few jumps away.

The implications of the discovery were immense. If the scientist was correct, they could know in under a day if their mission was a failure or not. Assuming everything went as planned, of course.

Minula shifted in her sleep and rolled on her side, placing her back toward Abigail. The feeling of having someone touching her was both wonderful and frightening at the same time. While her feelings had always been there, their freshness made them that much more sensitive.

Putting her life or the lives of her friends at risk wasn't something she was comfortable with. From Minula to Ibu to Cynthia, and now even Harold and Shauna. The once immortal A.I.s were as fragile as their human companions. One poor decision, and she could destroy the lives of everyone she held most dear.

She took a deep breath and reviewed their options. They could return to Zeta Lupi and waste weeks, or maybe months, trying to put together a second expedition. And with her previous failure, there was no telling if they'd even let her come back.

They could take the Phoenix and explore the Nebula as a team and put everyone at risk. After already losing so many lives under her command, this option seemed as foolhardy as the first.

Which left only one option. Disappear with the last shuttle and face the risk herself. It's what her father would've done. Hell, it's probably what Harold would do if she let him. The fearless way he'd taken out her attackers on the planet lacked any concern for his own well-being. He cared more about humanity than his entire family, all rolled into one. She could learn a thing or two from him. Besides that, she owed her people as much. Especially with everything her family had done to get them to this place in time.

When she swung her legs off the side of the bed, she paused, waiting to see if Minula noticed. Except for a slight change in her breathing, she was down for the count.

She reached down and ran her hand along the ground, feeling for her clothes until she realized she could use the lidar in her retinal comm.

With the blink of her eyes, the room lit up, and she slid on her clothing as quietly as she could. Once she was dressed, she grabbed the cloth artifact from her trunk. While she didn't need it, there was no point in leaving behind clues. If she never made it back, the last thing she wanted was the others traipsing after her and succumbing to the same end she might face.

Before she left, she turned and froze. She finally had everything she'd ever dreamed of, and she was about to leave it all behind. While every ounce of her heart hoped she'd return, she knew the possibility existed that she wouldn't.

She tiptoed forward and knelt on the bed, pulling the blanket around Minula's shoulders and tucking her in. Her hands lingered on her shoulder for a second until she bent down and kissed her neck, drawing in a deep breath. She smelled like chamomile and sweat. The kind of perspiration that was mixed with pheromones and only came from making passionate love. It was a smell she'd never forget.

Stepping backward, she carefully shifted her weight off the bed so as to not make a sound. With a few steps in the darkness, she felt the door against her back. In one swift motion, she subvocalized the command to open it and stepped backward, closing the door as quickly as it'd opened.

The movement was fluid and performed in under two seconds. The result was only the briefest of lights in her cabin, and with the lowered lighting of the hall, Minula didn't even notice.

"I'm sorry," she muttered as she turned and speed walked toward the cargo bay holding their shuttle.

SHE FINISHED ALL the system checks. There was enough food for a few weeks and fuel for several planetary descents and launches. The power cell for the gate drive was nearly limitless, but was useless in atmospheres.

With the systems checked, the only thing left to do was open the hangar doors and leave. This was by far the most precarious action Abigail needed to take because the moment she did it, whoever was on bridge duty would notice. All she could do was hope she was faster than they were.

As her finger hovered over the launch button, the door to the shuttle slid aside and Harold's robotic form walked in. "Heading somewhere?"

"Frak," she muttered and spun around. "You have to get off. I have something to check out. I'll be back in a jiffy."

He chuckled. "You're the worst liar I ever met. Well, not exactly. I guess being so close to you for so long has given me a certain unfair advantage to knowing your tells."

She narrowed her gaze. "I'm not kidding. I need to do this. Now get out." She pointed at the open door.

"Ok. So you're not lying." He stepped toward her. "Where are you headed, then?"

She didn't have time for this. The clock was already ticking before someone would wake up. "Please, Harold. I can't leave with you onboard. I know what you're doing. You'll try to stop me, and I won't have it. This is something I have to do alone."

"Well, I'm not letting you take off by yourself. Besides, I can help."

She shook her head. "I can't let you die... not on my watch."

"I think that's up to me to decide, not you. If it makes your decision any easier, how about this?" He ejected the tray out of his chest that contained his consciousness core. "You can store me in your body mod, like old times. At least then I can still help you, and if something happens, I might even survive."

Arguing was a waste of time. And besides, she could use his help examining the data and piloting the shuttle. He thought far faster than she did, and even if she was tortured, they wouldn't know he was inside her body with the containment mod ensconced in skotádi.

"Fine, but we've got to hurry." She reached out and grabbed the dot before reaching down her shirt, and pressing it against the space above her heart. The familiar tug told her he was being sucked in, and she returned her hand to the controls. "The bridge crew could stop me any second now."

"I can handle that." Harold's robotic form exited the shuttle, and the door closed behind it. A second later, a comm opened from him, directed to the bridge. "This is Harold. I'd like to go on a space walk and check over the hull. Can you please open the shuttle bay doors? I need some equipment from in here."

"I don't see anything on the maintenance checklist," Gwen said.

"Frak," Abigail muttered.

"It's not scheduled. I'm purely doing it as a precaution. There's no point in risking our lives being detected when we leave this place. Besides, if I die out there, you won't miss me anyhow. So, what do you care?"

A few seconds of silence passed until finally the external doors opened with a clang.

He'd done it. She didn't think he'd pull it off, but he had. Perhaps the stars were on her side after all.

She watched as his robotic form grabbed the welding equipment from the cargo hold and started working its way toward the exit. A camera view of the bridge appeared on her retinal comm, and it showed Gwen walking out. She had a mug in her hand, and it appeared like she was headed to the galley for a refill.

It was now or never. Abigail reached out and hit the button to power up the shuttle. She felt the hum of the engine kick in, and she guided the small craft out the cargo doors and into the black of space.

There was a quiet thud against the hull as she passed into the darkness, but when she checked the external cameras, there was nothing there. It must've been something shifting in the shuttle's storage bins. She'd check later.

She'd activate their thrusters and inertial dampeners when they were away from the shuttle. Within a minute of their exit, they'd made it clear of the Phoenix and powered down the drive. They'd gate from here.

The plans for her first jump were already open on her retinal comm. While she hadn't programmed the entire route, she'd have plenty of time after the initial hop. After that, they'd be too far away to stop and impossible to detect.

She flicked the route onto the shuttle's navigation computer and hit go. As the familiar clang of the gate vanes sliding out of their storage echoed through the tiny craft, she couldn't help but feel like she was letting her people down. Even protecting them felt off. It was times like these that she wished she were more like Ibu. Their faith in logic and facts guided them far more than nonsensical emotions.

The dance of the blue ants passed through her, and with it, a wave of relief. A few more jumps, and she'd know for certain if the Ursis were extinct.

18

IBU

PROTO DARK NEBULA, ORBITING GRISEO

The door to their quarters burst open and Minula came running in. "She's gone. Abigail's gone."

Ibu shot up with a start, their fists raised in front of them. They'd been in a deep sleep, reliving their fight against Kamal, when they were roused awake. "What?" They lowered their hands and slid out of bed. The slap of the frigid floor against their feet helped them awaken.

"When I rolled over this morning, she wasn't there." Minula shuddered. "I can't find her anywhere on the Phoenix, and... the shuttle's gone, too. I'm headed to the bridge and could really use your help."

"Alright, let's go." Ibu motioned for her to take the lead, grogginess still pulling at their mind.

They walked side by side down the hall until they reached the bridge. Gwen was there, her feet propped up on the controls and a cup of tea in her hand.

"Morning, sirs." She nodded.

"Where the hell is the shuttle?" Minula shoved the soldier's boots off the control panel, and they fell to the ground with a thud.

The woman nearly dropped her drink, but she recovered

it just in time. When her gaze met Minula's, her face was blank. "What're you talking about? Harold's outside looking over the hull, and the shuttle's in the..." She brought up the cargo hold camera on the wall screen. "Right th—"

Her cup fell to the ground, and a clang reverberated through the space as it rolled forward but stopped when it hit the wall.

"Impossible," she muttered. "I've been up here the entire shift."

Ibu cleared their throat and stared at the cup. According to her retinal comm, it was still warm. Clearly, the woman had been negligent in her duties.

When Minula glanced back at them, they must've seen the Nanil studying the cup against the far wall.

"When did you get that?" Minula pointed at the mug.

"I... was only in the galley for a few minutes. But... that was when Harold..." She leaned forward and tweaked her controls, winding the view from the camera backward in time until the silhouette of Abigail appeared. She was tiptoeing her way through the cargo hold in the dark, and only crept onto the shuttle after she paused to look around.

"Frak." Ibu nudged past Minula and pushed Gwen's hands away from the panel. They fast-forwarded the feed until they saw Harold arrive.

When they adjusted the audio gain to see if they could hear anything, all they heard was static. Whatever was being said inside the shuttle was being blocked, probably by the robot. While he'd technically been neutered, that didn't mean he wasn't ingenious.

As they scrubbed forward, a clear audio track suddenly appeared. It was from Harold to the bridge. His voice started playing on the overhead speakers.

"This is Harold. I'd like to go on a space walk and check over the hull. Can you please open the shuttle bay doors? I need some equipment from in here."

"I don't see anything on the maintenance list," Gwen voice said.

"It's not scheduled," Harold began. "I'm purely doing it as a precaution. There's no point in risking our lives being detected when we leave this place. Besides, if I die out there, you won't miss me anyhow. So, what do you care?"

Gwen's voice could barely be heard muttering in the background of the recording. "We should be so lucky. Maybe a solar flare will take him out. Fraking A.I. needs to die a slow death."

A second later, they watched as Gwen opened the cargo hold from the bridge.

Ibu glanced back at the woman.

She shook her head. "I… didn't know."

"Did you even check?" Minula clenched and unclenched her fists at her side.

The soldier froze, unsure how to react.

"You're dismissed!" Minula didn't look at her. She simply stared at the wall screen. "Please lock yourself in your quarters until we can convene to review your actions. Is that understood, soldier?"

"Yes… yessir." The woman turned and swiftly made her way off the bridge.

Ibu brought up the external cameras on the wall display and started scrubbing forward. A few minutes after the shuttle left the berth of the Phoenix, it gated away, and a tinge of disappointment fell over them.

They'd begun seeing Abigail as a friend. Someone they could depend on. Someone who wouldn't let them down. They'd only found the qualities in her brother and Pluto, and her leaving without saying goodbye was a betrayal of that trust. Certainly, the human must've had a reason.

"Where's she going?" Minula asked.

"I was gonna ask you." Ibu sat in the chair and stared up at the woman. Her face was pink from crying. And based upon how she was holding herself and the mussed appearance of her usually perfect outfit, she'd tossed her clothes on in a hurry. "Did you and Abigail copulate last night?"

"What!?" Minula took a step backward, her cheeks shifting to a darker shade of pink. "How dare you? I aught to—"

"It's an honest question. From your appearance and your smell…" They leaned forward and inhaled a long breath. The fluid remains of human intercourse were as clear as day.

"Wha… that's between me and Abigail, and none of your damn business."

They shrugged. "It's not a secret. At least I know. She already told me down on Griseo that she loved you."

"She… said that?" Minula's gaze softened, and she eased down in the empty pilot chair.

"She did." Ibu looked the woman up and down. "So what happened? Did you fight?"

Minula shook her head from side to side, her voice cracking. "No… far from it. Like you said. You know… we… made love." A smile peeked into the corner of her mouth and disappeared as fast as it arrived. "But when I woke up, she was gone. From the looks of the feed…" She glanced at the wall screen. "She took off a few hours afterward."

They studied the display. The silhouette of the shuttle disappearing through the gate was indistinguishable from the Dark Nebula behind it. Had the star in the system not been in the distance, they wouldn't have noticed them pass through at all.

Ibu rewound the feed to the point where the shuttle started backing up. Harold had just stepped off and exited the ship. He'd distracted Gwen, and from what she'd said, he was still outside. They reached forward and tapped the controls to recall the robot.

"Is that it?" Ibu glanced over at the woman. Tears were streaming down her face. This was a state they'd never seen the soldier in before. Her usually strong and stern external appearance was ripped open, and her tender emotional human insides were exposed for the universe to see. "Did you talk about anything else in her room?"

She stared at the screen and slowly shook her head from side to side, probably replaying the events of the evening in her mind. And then she froze, her mouth falling open.

"What is it?" Ibu glanced at the wall screen. The shuttle cleared the Phoenix, and a strange shadow floated between the ships. It was faint, but it was there.

They reached out and paused the playback, sliding backward to when they first saw it. As they scrubbed forward and back, it was impossible not to see. Something, or someone, was out there on the outside of Phoenix. And whatever they were doing, they'd just jumped across to Abigail's ship.

Ibu subvocalized a command to Harold's robotic form, but no reply came. When they reached out using their mental link, the warm welcoming gate of his artificial world was missing. In its place was a cold emptiness. Like their feet hitting the bare floor, their mind crashed into the same barrier, except this meant something different.

Harold was gone. He must've left with Abigail aboard the shuttle. Heck, even the shadow could've been his. Perhaps he'd been hiding from them this entire mission, like Shauna had done to the Galactic Alliance. The theories were infinite, but they knew one thing for certain.

They opened a comm to Shauna and Cynthia. "I need you on the bridge ASAP. Both of you."

"Is something the matter?" Cynthia asked, her voice clipped.

"We've lost our captain, and we've had a stowaway hiding out for who knows how long." Ibu froze the playback and measured the length of the shadow on the wall screen. It was well over three meters long. "Get up here. We've got work to do."

19

ABIGAIL OLIVAW

PROTO DARK NEBULA, OUTSIDE
POCKET FOUR

She'd stared at the pattern of stars so many times the symbols were etched in her mind. While she had the cloth in her pocket, Abigail didn't dare look at it. Harold would see it, and he might send images back to the others. She didn't know how he'd do it, but he always had his ways. Each of the jumps she programmed was executed quickly and only when his data core's connection to her comm was disabled.

The problem was, he was faster than she was. She needed him on the other side to make heads or tails of what she was seeing. While she could do it herself, the first few seconds after each transition were the most important. Risking the gate technology falling into the wrong hands couldn't happen.

"I'm making the next jump," Abigail said. "Once we're inside the pocket, there should only be one more hop to our destination. Time to cut you off again."

"Are you certain?" Harold's face appeared in a window on her retinal comm. "I don't have any controls here. You and Zachary made sure of that."

"I can't risk it. It'll only be for a minute. I'll let you witness the next jump live. Once we're inside the Dark Nebula, there isn't much you can do in there. Hell, I'll even give you access to the ship. Minus navigation, of course."

"Very well." He smiled. "Have a safe gate." His face disappeared.

Having him along had been good for her. Despite having to blank out the controls and the viewport when he was around, it'd been nice to chat with him again. It was just like old times, even if it'd only been a few hours.

After she confirmed his data dot was secure, she configured his containment unit to unlock as soon as the gate was sealed. She couldn't take any more chances than she already had. Once she'd checked over her calculations and compared them to the star map for the umpteenth time, she folded it back up and put it away. Finally happy with the jump programming, she slid the lever up, activating the gate, and then waited for the scratchy transition to pass over her.

As the gate opened, she could see through to the other side, and she took a deep breath. The shimmering image on the wall screen settled, and it hit her. On the flip side of the gate wasn't simply a star, there was a fleet of starships waiting for her. More than she'd ever imagined could fit in one space.

The blue ants passed over as she stared at the mesmerizing display of raw power. The spacecrafts were unlike anything she'd seen before, even after watching countless hours of Galactic Alliance footage in recent months.

Each ship was wider than it was long, and off the back of the oddly non-uniform wing-like vessel was a drive cone of some kind. These weren't the typical GA warp bubble drives. They must move through space through some other means.

Stranger still was the ship's hull. It appeared to be covered in some type of organic coating and almost ebbed and flowed as she stared in awe. It reminded her of the motions of the lava lamp she used to have as a kid, except this was green and not purple like hers had been.

Blobs slid back and forth over the surface and collided into one another, forming larger masses and then breaking into hundreds of smaller ones. It was chaotic and yet precise. Seeing an entire wall of these ships extended as far as her eyes could see was both beautiful and frightening.

The gate vane clicked closed and the shuttle's klaxons started blaring. Her control panel lit up, and the overhead lights flashed red.

"I've got twenty incoming alien fighters approaching from... shit, everywhere." Harold's face appeared in the corner of the wall screen. "We need to slag the drive, Abs."

The words echoed in her mind as she studied the display. Dot after dot after dot slid out of the nearby winged ships, arcing toward their tiny shuttle. It was like they knew where it was. Which wasn't possible, of course. The skotádi should've protected them.

Harold stared at her for a moment and then repeated himself. "Abigail, we need to slag the drive before it's too late. I can't do it. You have to hit the manual override."

The dots slid closer, circling around and around the shuttle. Like a shark circling its prey.

"Abigail!"

She shook her head. "What..."

"The drive! Kill the fraking drive!"

"Right," she muttered and unbuckled her chair, clamoring toward the back of the tiny ship.

Just as she lifted the panel in the floor, the shuttle rocked to starboard and sparks flew from every direction. Suddenly, everything went black and the oxygen breach warning on her retinal comm started flashing. Her helmet didn't automatically slide over her head, which meant only one thing. The blast had taken out all non-skotádi shielded electronics.

"No, no, no!" She gasped for breath and reached over her

back, fumbling to find the controls for her inflatable helmet. The frigid void of space hit her like a burst of arctic cold as her hand found the release lever, and she yanked with everything she had.

Her helmet shot over her head, and a second later she wheezed as the pressure in her lungs became too much. The life giving gas came slow at first, her body writhing in pain until the suit filled up.

The oxygen cartridge was small, and it was low tech, lacking electronics by design. Centuries of underwater exploration on their home world had come in handy once again.

"The drive," Harold said in her ear.

The shuttle rocked, and she tumbled backward, hitting her head against the pilot's chair. She moaned and struggled to work herself upright, but they were accelerating. Whatever blasted them was now moving them.

She had to act fast.

Centimeter by centimeter, she clawed her way aft toward the open panel in the floor. When she was in range, she swung her right arm out and grasped the edge of the opening, pulling with all her might. As her body slid forward, she used her left hand to find the kill plate. It was a nondescript surface on the top of the drive core. There was no label, and there was nothing to see. But when activated, it served only one purpose. Destruction of the gate drive.

When her wrist brushed against it, she paused and pressed her palm harder against the top, but nothing happened. This couldn't be happening. Not now.

"Your glove," Harold began. "You need to take it off."

"Shit," she muttered as she brought her hand up and leaned over the opening. With her weight over the gap in the paneling, she let go with her right hand and used it to remove the glove.

As her skin hit the void of space and pain shot up her arm, the rear of the ship exploded in a wall of light. She glanced up, and for the first time, she saw the green fluid exterior of the alien craft up close. The motions of the blobs were mesmerizing. Even as her hand froze, she couldn't resist watching as arms seemed to reach out from the hull and move toward her.

"Your family!" Harold said, his voice getting more distant. "Your people are depending on you."

She shook her head and slammed her naked palm down against the surface below. At first, all she saw were rivulets of blood floating in space and nothing else happened. But a second later, as the green jelly like liquid engulfed her and a warmth spread over her body, a faint white light strobed in the bowels of the shuttle filling the space beneath her. It did that several times until it changed to red and finally shut off.

Once the blobby mass enveloped her, it yanked her out of the shuttle. She could see through the goo, and watched as her ship receded into the distance, along with two other threads of green. One of them appeared to be tugging their shuttle, likely trying to salvage whatever tech they could from it. The second, however, looked empty-handed. They must've sent more tentacles than they needed.

"It worked, right?" she subvocalized.

Harold's reply appeared on her retinal comm, down below the bottom edge, outside what someone else could see.

> Don't talk. We don't know what they can detect. We need
> to play it safe. Please give me access to your other senses.

A confirmation dialog appeared to the side of his words. She hadn't allowed him that level of access for months. Not since she'd discovered the lengths he'd gone to guide, and sometimes shove, the family in the direction he'd wanted.

She knew he regretted it. She didn't know how, but she did.

Maybe it'd been how he'd reacted over the past few months, or the reality of being mortal. While she couldn't guarantee he wouldn't lead her astray, she knew one thing for certain. She needed him now more than ever. She blinked to confirm the access he'd requested.

As she stared through the green mass, she brought her hand up toward her face. It was still exposed, but it didn't hurt. From the looks of it, the goo had formed a glove of sorts. More importantly, it wasn't seeping into her suit. Instead, it was acting as a sealant and protecting her. Or maybe it was protecting them from her. She couldn't tell which, but she didn't care. She was alive.

A darkness passed over her as the protective mass pulled her into the belly of the winged starship and set her down on a hard surface. When the glow from outside disappeared, she could only surmise that they'd closed off the exit. Confirmation came a moment later as light engulfed her from all sides and the gelatinous mass splashed off her body like a shell breaking open.

She drew in a deep breath as the substance that captured and protected her fell away, disappearing into the floor. She didn't know how. There were no holes nor cracks, but the green slime was absorbed into the ship itself. It reminded her of how the Galactic Alliance tribunal ships adapted to the alien's every need. Perhaps it, too, was alive with nanites or the like.

When she glanced down at her hand, there were signs of frostbite, but otherwise it was pink and healthy. That material seemed to have both heated and oxygenated her skin. She pushed up onto her knees and then stood upright.

The room was nondescript, and there appeared to be three exits on each of the sides, minus the external hatch she'd entered through. Based upon the presence of gravity, she had to assume the alien species either needed it or they were being cordial to her.

While the doorways were massive, there was no guarantee they were for the occupants. They could just as easily be used to move materials around the ship. In her mind, she knew these were the Ursis, but she didn't want to get ahead of herself. This ship could be filled with the same robots they encountered on Griseo.

Her suit reported that a breathable atmosphere was present, but she couldn't risk breathing it. While her hand was exposed, the internal lining of her suit had already created a seal around it, so she didn't lose any more oxygen. There were similar seals near all limbs and joints. You never knew when you'd get a puncture in outer space, and when the goal was staying alive, even the small things mattered.

Abigail closed her eyes to give Harold a chance to send a message, but none came. He was either being cautious or the slime had done something to him.

She opened a message dialog and gestured with her hands on her leg, struggling to make the motions seem random. Like all humans, she'd mastered the layout of a human keyboard as a young child.

The letters appeared on her closed eyelids.

Are you ok? Notice anything?

Harold's reply didn't appear visually. He decided instead to change up his method of communication and switched to vibrations. Something they hadn't done since she was a kid. One vibration followed by a pause and then two more. A yes and a no.

She took a deep breath and opened her eyes. That was

good. He was alive. Talking would be awkward for a while, but she understood the precautions he was taking.

Glancing around the room, she felt a calling to explore. There was no point in standing around and waiting, so she took a few tentative steps toward the wall in front of her and paused. Nothing happened. There were no invisible forces stopping her. And best of all, there was an Earth-like gravity, though perhaps a little less. It was hard to remember some-times. She hadn't been to her second home in so long.

As she eased closer to the doorway, she studied the nearby wall. The surface definitely looked metallic and there was a slight indentation beside the opening, but it was over her head. Another check in the column of the Ursis. The towering aliens had to open doors just like the rest of them.

When she reached for the panel, it glowed blue and she froze. She wasn't sure what it meant. Without touching it, she couldn't tell if it was a warning or a signal that it was active.

"Here goes nothing." She tapped the center of the panel with her exposed fingers, and a jolt of current shot through them and up her arm.

"Ugh. Frak!" She yanked her hand back and shook it in the air. There was nothing like learning the hard way. Blue was bad. Check.

With her hand still shaking, she moved it closer to the doorframe, and it glowed white. The effect was subtle, but she eased closer toward the light to test it further. The frame encircling the door glowed brighter and brighter until finally a bolt of energy shot across the gap and zapped her again.

Her body flew backward, and she slammed against the ground, sliding several few meters. White splotches painted her vision, and the electricity combined with the impact of the fall sent pain cascading through every centimeter of her person.

She struggled to remain conscious, and her muscles spasmed as a dull warmth spread throughout her suit. At first, she thought she was bleeding until she checked controls on her wrist. The shock had caused her to void her bladder, and the suit was struggling to absorb all the moisture.

"Great," she muttered. Her first contact with the Ursis and she was covered in urine.

Lying on her back, she stared up at the ceiling and moaned. Maybe waiting made more sense. She reached out and flexed her fingers in front of her face. Her fingertips were tingling. Almost like when she slept on her hand wrong, except this wouldn't stop. Hopefully, she didn't have permanent nerve damage. She'd check her nanites if she was comfortable enough to use her retinal comm, but she wasn't. Instead, she typed out a message.

Will my hand be ok?

Harold sent one vibration into the nape of her neck.

She sighed. Small victories. As she let her body recover from the shock, the color on the ceiling changed. It brightened for a second and then dimmed. Strange. She hadn't noticed it do that before. Perhaps it was reacting to something.

A message appeared below her eyelid.

You have a guest.

She eased up onto her elbows and glanced around, her eyes locking on the towering figure that had just passed through the doorway she'd touched. Standing in front of her was an Ursis. They easily stood four meters tall and were a wall of muscle and fur.

Her heart raced as she pushed off with her feet, crab

crawling across the ground and putting distance between them. Her fear was a reflex. While it was far from ideal, it was at least beneficial diplomatically. They knew without a doubt that she feared them.

While the Ursis wasn't naked, their clothing was sparse and only covered their groin, feet, and arm regions, leaving their toes and hands exposed. The fabric's familiar shimmer matched the material they'd seen on Griseo. Their fur was clean and well groomed.

If she hadn't been cowering in fear, her first instinct would be to touch it. Their coloring was spectacular. With wisps of white-gray framing their face, their fine fur darkened the further down their body you looked until it was almost black at their extremities.

"Get up!" the Ursis snarled, waving their hand upward. Their claws and teeth glistened in the light, sending a shiver up her spine. The fangs matched their outfit and looked like they were coated in metal. Something that would easily cut human skin.

While the alien's voice was clear, she knew it was being translated. Without her retinal comm, she'd be useless. Hopefully, they didn't disable it.

She pushed up off the ground, rising in one smooth motion with no sudden movements. Her heart was pounding in her chest the entire time. Even upright, she struggled to make eye contact with the brute of an alien. They towered above her.

"Do you speak, or are you mute?" the Ursis asked.

She swallowed hard and straightened her back. "I can speak. Why did you—"

"I ask the questions here," the Ursis interrupted. "You're hardly in the position to make demands." They stepped closer to her, their shadow looming over her like the shade of a tree. "How did you pass through the Dark Nebula?"

Her gaze narrowed, and she smiled as she glanced up at the furry alien. "That's funny."

The Ursis fluttered their fingers, their claw seeming to catch the light. "What's funny?"

"You claim I'm in no position to make demands, and yet," she waved her hand around, "you're the one imprisoned here in this Dark Nebula." She clasped her hands behind her back and stepped closer to the alien, craning her neck upward and staring directly into their bright yellow eyes. "You can kill me if it pleases you. I'll simply create another copy of myself and move on to a different judged species. Maybe they'll be more willing to cooperate."

The Ursis stared at her, seemingly entranced by her words. They then stepped backward and lowered themselves to her level, bringing their face within a meter of hers. She struggled to keep her fear at bay, knowing full well they were recording her vitals and watching them rocket off the charts the closer the alien got.

Up close, she noticed the Ursis had a monocle in their left eye and a nose ring that looked like diamonds in the shape of a starburst. Their fur was pure white over most of their face, making them seem almost distinguished. Not something she'd ever imagined saying about a bear.

"I like you," the Ursis said. "You're… spunky. Perhaps we can help each other after all. Come. Let's walk." They rose just as fluidly as they'd descended and turned in place. The door in front of them opened without a sound, and they started down the hall.

Abigail took a deep breath and exhaled before skipping forward, following close behind. Their legs were as long as she was tall, and she had to jog to keep up.

A message appeared on the bottom edge of her retinal comm.

Nice work. Keep them thinking. I'll handle recording anything useful you encounter.

It was nice working with Harold again. They were a good team. She was more in her element navigating power struggles like this than managing the lives of a crew aboard the Phoenix. All she had to do now was bluff her way into an alliance, hoping they wouldn't make too many demands.

—

20

IBU

PROTO DARK NEBULA, ORBITING GRISEO

"I'd hazard to guess we picked up our friend during our orbital shootout." Shauna brought up images on the wall screen from their encounter with the Galactic Alliance around Griseo. Several camera angles showed a faint silhouette passing from the asteroid ship to the Phoenix, right before it exploded.

"How did we not see these until now?" Cynthia asked.

Ibu chuckled. Humans continued to amuse them. Their denial and lack of awareness of how utterly reliant they were on their technology was dumbfounding. "You missed it because humans rely on computers and A.I. to do everything. You've lived in blind safety for millennia while automata scheduled your lives. They make your appointments, they monitor your skies, and they defend your starships. Without them, you're oblivious to the universe around you."

"Bullshit!" Minula slapped her hand against the side of Shauna's controls. "We've got plenty of skilled human security personnel."

"Ibu's not wrong." Shauna flipped open image after image on the wall screen. "There are countless examples of this Qudoculi around our ship, yet never once did any of our human crew see it. Had you not forced Harold and me into confinement, and relieved us of assisting in the maintenance of this ship, we would've seen it within seconds of their arrival." She turned toward Minula. "And while your example is correct, those human specialists are rare and are often reserved for tactical planning, not front lines warfare."

"Stop!" Minula raised her hands. "This arguing isn't getting us any closer to finding Abigail. Can we focus, please?"

Ibu shook their head. "I don't see how emotional outbursts are helping, either."

Minula growled and collapsed into her chair.

Ibu adjusted the images on the wall screen and zoomed in, measuring the shadowy figure like they had done earlier. The lengths were the same. Nearly four meters. "What makes you think these are Qudoculi?" They glanced at Shauna's robotic form.

She shrugged. "I don't know. I figured they were fighting with one of their own kind outside the Dark Nebula before we tagged their ships and that asteroid and brought them through the gate with us. Who else would it be?"

"I'm… not certain." They closed the images of the shadow and stared at the asteroid. The gash in its side had become visible just as the missiles from the Qudoculi fighters crashed into their hull. "Honestly, it could be any Galactic Alliance species."

Cynthia walked up and sat down beside Minula. "Tell us again what happened last night."

"I'm not getting into my personal—"

"No." Cynthia waved her hand. "We don't care about that. Replay everything that happened before that."

Minula sighed and rubbed her forehead for a few seconds before she spoke. "I brought some wine from the galley to Abigail's room. She always likes to wind down with a refreshment. Especially shitty days like today. She's been doing it for years. Anyhow, when I opened the door, she was deep in thought, studying some black fabric thing. She said she picked it up down on Griseo. When she put it away, I poured her a drink and—"

"Wait!" Ibu spun around. "What fabric? Was it a piece of the suit I was wearing?"

Minula shook her head. "No. This was different."

"Do you have any retinal comm footage from when you were talking to her?" Cynthia asked.

She swallowed hard. "I don't know. Let me check. I turned it off after the door opened."

Minula stared into the distance as she sub-vocally examined her recordings. When her eyes widened, she flicked a stream of video up on the wall screen and pointed. "There. Right there. That's the cloth."

Ibu stood up and walked toward the display. They reached out and slid their hand to the left, easing the frames forward one by one. They could make out some white lines on the fabric, but Abigail folded it up so quickly, it was impossible to see a pattern.

"There's not enough footage," Shauna said. "Did anyone else see this cloth?"

When Ibu turned to look at them, their human faces were blank and their eyes were filled with fear. No one had seen anything. No one except... and then it hit them. "The only person who would have seen it is conveniently missing with our captain."

"Harold," Minula muttered.

Ibu sprinted back to her station and slid into the seat. "We need to review every second of footage from down on the planet. Maybe there's something there."

"I've already done that." Shauna had her robotic arms crossed. "Except for her little disappearing act down in that distant branch of the museum, there's nothing that Harold or the others recorded that points to this... cloth."

Ibu squinted at her. "What disappearing act?"

Shauna brought up a few feeds on the wall screen. They showed the different perspectives from the soldiers who were assigned to Abigail. The same soldiers Harold killed soon after. They were lying on the ground in the museum, panting to catch their breath. Apparently, he wore them out getting them there.

The video in the center showed Abigail working her way from the edge toward the middle of the expansive room. One minute she was there, and the next she disappeared.

"What happened right there?" Ibu reached out and backed up the video.

"It looked like some type of illusion. She entered an exhibit that was concealed, and once she was inside, we lost her signal. See." Shauna pointed up at the wall screen and Abigail's dot vanished, sending alerts out to all the soldiers' retinal comms. The soldier they were watching had zoned out because when he got the alert, he had no idea where she was despite his equipment having seen her disappear.

As the video played forward, a few minutes later, Harold's form disappeared behind the same barrier of illusion. "Do we have any of Harold's video?"

"Negative." Shauna lowered her head. "We never thought or required it to be uploaded from either of us. In the past, it was always available, but that changed after Zachary's reprogramming."

"Of course it did," Minula muttered.

Yet another example of human error, but pointing it out wouldn't help anyone. The more Ibu studied the footage, the more they knew what needed to be done. They turned and started toward the cargo bay.

"Where are you going?" Minula asked.

They paused and pointed at the wall screen. "I'm taking that Nanil skiff down there. Someone has to figure out what Abigail found in that museum."

"You can't." Cynthia shot up, and her console rotated away. "The other crew's still alive down there. They'll see you land. We'll need to take the Phoenix down."

Ibu shook their head. "That's not happening. This is our only way out of here, and we're not putting it at risk. I'll take the skiff and check it out. Once I'm down on the planet, I'll send the skiff back up into orbit. Worst case, they catch me, and you head out to get some reinforcements."

"Why you?" Cynthia's face was turning red. "Why not Shauna or Minula? She can wear an exo-suit."

"Because I can't fit in the skiff with that thing on," Minula said. "It's too bulky."

"You might not be able to fit inside, but I can." Shauna stepped toward them. "There are several robotic forms onboard capable of housing my consciousness core. They fold up pretty damn small, and I'm confident they'll be useful down there. What do you say?" She smiled.

While they couldn't deny that having another pair of eyes would be helpful, they could get the same advantage from a handful of drones. The only true benefit was the second mind. Two intellects were always better than one. There was also the fact that they wouldn't be alive today without Harold. They owed the Olivaws their life. If it weren't for them, they'd still be on Doda and very likely dead.

"Fine." Ibu spun in place with their back to the bridge. "But don't forget, you're just as killable down there as I am." They headed toward the cargo bay.

21

ABIGAIL OLIVAW

PROTO DARK NEBULA, POCKET FOUR

The hallways of the winged starship were humongous, easily ten meters wide. Abigail couldn't imagine why you'd need so much space, but that didn't stop her from keeping a safe distance from her Ursis escort. They still hadn't introduced themselves, and she wasn't certain if the alien was a he, a she, or a they.

"What's down there?" She gestured to her left down a corridor that seemed to go on forever. It was pitch dark except for a pinstripe of light along the floor and ceiling.

"That's not your concern." The Ursis didn't skip a beat or even glance at her. They simply continued forward, heading toward an unknown destination.

They weren't exactly a talkative species, at least not yet. The silence of the surroundings reminded her of the Galactic Alliance tribunal ships in Sol. She struggled to keep her bearings while listening to the small noises without getting lost in her own thoughts.

"So, all this technology." She waved her hands in front of her. "How much of it is yours, and how much of it did you get trading with the Galactic Alliance?"

The Ursis froze, and their body seemed to almost rise until

they swung an arm downward, slamming Abigail against the wall. The air burst from her chest as the crushing blow compressed her lungs and forced a blood-curdling scream from her mouth.

She gasped for air and clawed at their arm, but it didn't help. They were too strong.

The alien brought their face up to hers, their mouthful of fangs glistening in the light. Up close, she could make out etchings on their teeth. Each one had a different intricate pattern. She wasn't sure why she'd noticed it as she struggled to breathe. Perhaps it was easier to focus on than the spittle dripping between their teeth.

"We... traded... nothing... with... them." They pronounced each word precisely. "Our technology is our own. Is that understood?"

Her comm flashed red as her body fought against the impossible strength of the alien. With each failed attempt at responding, she gave up and nodded.

They must've translated the gesture because they released her, and she collapsed to the ground in a wheezing lump. She struggled to breathe, but the air wouldn't come. Even gulping didn't work. She'd never imagined dying like this. In her mind, it had always been of old age.

The Ursis stood up and wiped its hand against its fur. "Follow me. And don't speak."

She rolled onto her back and white and red splotches painted her vision until her sight faded. As it neared black, she arched her back and electricity shot through her extremities. Every centimeter of her body rose up and then slammed against the ground. A second later, it happened again. It was like a poltergeist had taken over her body.

Her lungs finally burst to life, and she rolled onto her stomach, gasping for air. She slapped her palm onto the ground as each breath came. Her question had been simple, and yet the Ursis' temper had told her volumes. They were no different from the Nanil, the Qudoculi, or any of the others from the Galactic Alliance.

They were merely bloodthirsty aliens in nice clothing.

"Tell me I can retaliate," she subvocalized. "Tell me I can do something."

Harold's reply was simple and swift. Two vibrations of dissent.

When she pushed up off the ground, her arms trembled. Her exposed hand had gone numb, and she shook it, struggling to wake it up. She stared into the distance as the Ursis got further and further from her. They had treated harming her in such a nonchalant way. It was disgusting.

"Touch me again, and I'll let you die here." She glanced down at her hand, the feeling gradually returning to it, along with hints of healthy pink.

"Pardon me?" The Ursis froze in the distance, their back to her.

"You heard me, asshole." She reached up and released her helmet, sliding it off her head. The cool fresh air washed over her skin. It had a sweet scent, almost like flowers.

The Ursis spun around. Only then did she notice the claws on their hands. They'd descended out of their arm like their bones were breaking out. "Are you threatening me?"

She wiped her face with her exposed hand. Something she'd wanted to do for the past hour. If she couldn't hurt them by force, perhaps she could use the only weapon she had. Her words.

"It's only a threat if you see me as the one inflicting harm upon you. But I think you know better than that. It was the Galactic Alliance who locked you up here. Not me. I'm simply stating a truth you've been facing for over fifty years. As I see it, your only way out of this jail cell is through the technology I used to get here."

Abigail started walking toward the mountainous alien, narrowing her gaze the closer she got. "If you so much as lay a finger on me again, I'll end the life of this body. You saw me almost let this shell die a second ago. It's only alive because I decided to give you one final chance. I said it earlier, and I meant it. I'm sorry your species is ignorant and so short-tempered you can't have a casual conversation. Perhaps our common enemies were justified imprisoning your kind."

The Ursis lunged forward with their claws outstretched when she finished the sentence. Their legs pounded toward her, drumming a thundering beat through the previously quiet hall.

With each footfall, the floor vibrated. It was like a count-down to her death. When they were a mere meter away, they crashed into an invisible wall. One second, they were leaning forward with eyes filled with bloodlust, and the next, they're a limp pile of fur and bones crashing to the ground.

She drew in a breath and bent down, outstretching her hand to touch the Ursis when the force field between them zapped her. She yanked it back and rubbed her tingling fingers.

"I wouldn't do that, Miss Olivaw. You might lose a finger or two," a voice all around her said. "Or should I call you Abigail?"

When she peered upward, she realized what was going on. This entire thing had been a game. A show to throw her off. They were testing her to see how she'd react under pres-sure, all the while they were studying her.

"Ambassador Olivaw will do." She straightened up and glanced around the hall. "Are you done playing fraking games? Are you finally ready to get down to business?"

"Of course," the voice said. "We have much to discuss."

She raised her eyebrow. "Such as?"

"Such as how a human, a fellow judged species, is standing in this ship inside another Dark Nebula. Not only should you be extinct, you shouldn't have been able to pass through that death shroud, yet there you stand."

"Are you planning on showing yourself, or am I just going to talk to an omniscient voice?"

When she heard the sound of footsteps behind her, she jumped forward, passing through the force field without a jolt. As she collapsed on top of the limp body of the Ursis still lying in front of her, she scrambled to climb off them before they attacked. It took her a second to realize they wouldn't be attacking anyone ever again. They were dead.

Her hand brushed against the fur of the alien as she slid off their back. The pelt was luxurious between her fingers. Not at all like she'd expected. When her feet hit the ground, she remembered the sound she'd heard behind her and glanced up.

Staring back at her was a second Ursis. This one was close to a meter shorter than the first, and from the looks of them, they were far older. Their coat was silver-gray, almost blue, with splotches of white and black sprinkled throughout. The frail-looking alien shuffled forward without a sound. Watching them walk was painful. Their spine was rounded so much she swore it was going to snap.

It wasn't until they were closer that she noticed they were leaning on some kind of mechanical cane contraption. It reminded her of a walker.

Abigail stared into the eyes of the new arrival, and something drew her in. She wasn't sure what, but their gaze was familiar to her, almost comforting.

They were two species, stars apart, and yet feeling the same pain. An unyielding pressure to survive, to avenge their people.

<hr>

THEY WORKED their way through the ship side by side. The elder Ursis walked with great care. Like each step was taking them closer to their last moment.

"I think it's fair to introduce myself," the Ursis said. "My name is Emmonsii Phi. I am a female Ursis of the Tlingui clan. Some call me Emmo, for short. You may, if you wish." They peered sideways and smiled, being careful not to show any teeth.

Abigail smiled back. "My name is Abigail Olivaw. But you already knew that. I, too, am a female, though I have no clan, only a family."

"Ahh, yes." Emmo slid their cane forward and shifted their weight onto it. "Daughter of Stark Olivaw. I remember hearing about him. Tell me, is he still presiding over your people after all these years?"

She froze in her tracks, staring at the Ursis. She'd never met an alliance member who knew of her dad. "How do you know my father?"

Emmo shook their paw. "Now don't fret, cub. I only vaguely know of the name. I seem to recall a special delegation of the Galactic Alliance discovering your people just before they sealed off our stars. If I remember correctly, there was some type of explosion near your sun. Does that ring a bell?"

She stepped forward, easily catching up with the slow steps of the Ursis. "It does. That was long ago, over a century now. We were testing some technology." She wanted to change the subject. "What special delegation of the GA are you referring to?"

"Ah, here we are." Emmo paused in front of a nondescript doorway and gestured with her cane. A segment of the wall slid aside, revealing a cavernous inner chamber with windows on all sides. "Go ahead, cub. After you."

When she peered inside, the space was empty except for two chairs facing away from them near the far glass. She took a cautious step, and then another, until she was in the middle of the room. Spread out in front of her in all directions was starship after starship, and it continued as far as the eye could see. It was no wonder they'd detected her arrival. With this many ships, even the smallest signal leak would be spotted in an instant. Her shuttle must've had a flaw.

"Marvelous, aren't they?" Emmo walked up beside her and held out a glass with a clear liquid in it. She had one for herself, as well.

Abigail glanced over her shoulder, unsure where she'd retrieved it from, until she noticed a recess beside the door. She peered down at the glass. From the looks of it, the liquid was water. Harold confirmed it a second later on her retinal comm.

Clean and clear H2O.

"Thank you." She bowed her head and clasped the glass with both hands before tipping it back and guzzling it down. She hadn't realized how thirsty she'd been until she lowered the empty cup.

Emmo smiled. "There's more if you'd like some."

"You're very kind. Perhaps in a minute." She turned her attention back to the ships.

"The special segment of the alliance you asked about. I assume they're the common enemy you referred to earlier." Emmo tilted their head, staring into her eyes.

Abigail nodded. They were testing her again. There was no way out of this one. Either she got it right or she failed. "The Qudoculi and the Thyreus."

"Scum of the Galaxy," Emmo snarled between clenched teeth. She dipped her head and tapped her cane against the ground. The distant chairs slid silently toward them and swung around before easing up against their backside.

Abigail wasn't sure what to do, so she just sat back into it. The chair adjusted to her height and softened to handle her body weight. Her sore muscles practically melted into the luxurious cushions. They reminded her of the adjustable seating cubes on the GA tribunal ship.

"You must forgive an old Ursis." Emmo patted the arm of the chair, and they started sliding toward the glass. "Sometimes the little things make life so much easier. Don't you think?"

"Indeed." Small talk was nice for a change, but she needed to move the conversation forward. "I'm curious about something. That's a whole lotta ships." She waved her hand at the raw display of force in front of them. "Are your people headed somewhere?"

"That's yet to be determined." Emmo's chair rotated to face her, and hers followed suit. "What are your terms to trade your gate technology?"

Abigail sat back in her chair. She wasn't sure how they'd heard that term before. Earlier, the other Ursis mentioned them passing through the death shroud.

Harold must've been thinking the same thing.

It's a trap. Tread carefully.

She shook her head. "What gate technology?"

"Come now." Emmo leaned forward. "You have your sources, and I have mine. There's no way you advanced through the bynardral's in that dump you call a ship. You had to've gated past them. It's the only explanation for the disruption in the Dark Nebula that led to your discovery."

That explained a lot. Apparently, the skotádi hadn't failed them like she'd thought. What confused her, though, was how the alien had happened upon a specific technological approach and term like a gate. A species could choose any word to describe a thing like that. Especially one originating from elsewhere in the galaxy.

"Fair enough. But the term you used, gate." She shook her head. "Where did you hear this from?"

"Let's just say it was whispered in my ear. It doesn't matter, really." Emmo waved her paw and rested it back in her lap.

Her mind raced, uncertain if she was talking about Harold. He hadn't used audible comms since their arrival and had spent the entire time inside her body-mod. She couldn't imagine him being a traitor. Losing him would put her and humanity at a disadvantage, but given how she'd treated him, she almost couldn't blame him if he did.

A message from Harold appeared on the bottom edge of her retinal comm.

Calm down. They can monitor your vitals as easily as I can.

She took a deep breath, struggling to slow her racing heart.

"You still haven't mentioned your terms for a trade." Emmo took a sip of her water. "I assume you didn't come all this way just to say hello. Did you?"

"No, I didn't." She adjusted her space suit, failing to smooth out the wrinkles. "Our terms. Humanity's terms, are simple. Join us as allies in arms against the Galactic Alliance. Agree to defend our worlds, and we'll defend yours. You'll have an equal vote in our Confederation, along with other judged species. In exchange for joining us, there will be an open sharing of technologies, and we'll give you controlled access to… how shall I say it? A means to escape this jail cell you're inhabiting."

Emmo straightened up. "Are there other species in this Confederation, then?"

Abigail bit her lip. "Like we're doing with you, we're also reaching out to other judged species."

"That's a lie." Emmo shook her head and narrowed their gaze.

"Pardon?" She was finding this Ursis hard to read.

"You haven't reached out to anyone else. Not yet, anyhow."

She wondered if she had a tell. Or maybe she was getting rusty, and this alien was besting her on her playing field. "I never said in what order, or to whom." She pushed up and made her way toward the water receptacle.

The Ursis didn't react. They simply sat still and allowed her the space to think. When she reached the recess, she placed her cup in the hole and a stream of water flowed out.

Emmo's voice broke the silence. "There's only us and the Gharloc from recent times. Any older, and the species has likely died off or been wiped out by a nova."

"That's not entirely true." Abigail withdrew the cup and tipped it back.

"So you've returned to Lupus then?"

She froze mid-swallow and lowered the cup into the recess to top it off. This wasn't going as she'd planned. "I never said that."

"You didn't have to say it out loud. Your body language confirmed my theory." Emmo glanced over at her. "I'm not new at this, Abigail. I'm as old as the stars, and I have no intention of forming an alliance with a species beneath my own. Your only bargaining chip is a single scientific trinket, and it comes with strings attached. I'm certain your little capsule will give us everything we need to reverse engineer our way out of this jail cell, as you call it. We won't need you or your kind to enact our revenge on the Galactic Alliance."

A message from Harold appeared.

You destroyed the drive, the gate mesh, and all the interconnects. They've got nothing to work from.

Abigail spun around and chuckled at the Ursis. She'd
been studying her the entire time, along with gosh knows
how many eyes in the room.

Emmo's chair turned in place to face her. "Did I say something funny?"

"Sort of. I just," she smiled, "find it humorous how the
little voice you claim to be talking to missed a fairly significant trinket in our possession." She tipped back her glass and
took a sip, making sure her hand wasn't shaking.

"And what's that?" Emmo clasped her hands together, the
tips of her claws glistening in the light.

Harold interrupted on her comm.

Be careful what you disclose. We don't know how they'll
react.

They had her on the ropes, and they'd already turned
down her pitch to join them. She couldn't imagine what else
she had to lose, especially since she'd lost her ride out of here.

Abigail set her cup down in the receptacle and strode over
to the window with her hands clasped behind her back. In the
distance, she could see they were approaching a tunnel in the
Nebula. Her brothers had passed through dozens of them on
their way through Lupus, but this was her first. While she
wished she could open her star charts to check where they
were headed, she knew better.

"Nothing. Just as I thought." Emmo pushed up out of her
chair. "I believe we're done here."

"Sit down," Abigail snapped.

"Pardon me?"

She could see the Ursis stopped moving in their reflection off the glass, but her back was still facing them. It was the best she could hope for, considering.

"Did your people feel a disturbance a few weeks ago?" Abigail asked.

Emmo didn't react, nor did she answer.

"I'll assume they did. Maybe it came in the form of unprovoked rage or uprisings in your cities. People suddenly feeling disconnected from one another. Some may have even reported having strange dreams, or hearing voices talk to them." She spun around. "Does any of this ring a bell?"

While she was grasping at straws, she knew the Beacons of Therion had powers beyond her comprehension. The videos Zachary had sent on from their tests were gruesome, and though the Ursis didn't control one, their people had likely been exposed to them at some point in time. Losing one could've affected them to some level, even inside the Nebula.

Emmo didn't move, but the pattern of hairs on her back changed. It reminded her of the mottled skin of the Qudoculi and how it shifted colors when they got angry. The image sent shudders through her body. She'd hit a nerve, and she knew it.

"So you've seen it then."

"I never said that."

Abigail chuckled and crossed her arms. "You didn't have to say it out loud. Your body language confirmed my theory."

Emmo started walking forward and banged her cane against the ground. The room suddenly went dark, and clanging noises echoed from all sides. As the silhouette of the Ursis passed through the doorway, the shackles closed around her legs and arms. A second later, something yanked her body backward, and she slammed against the wall. Her head and back erupted in waves of pain as she struggled to catch her breath.

When the door closed, she started laughing out loud between gasps of air. She wasn't sure why, but the whole situation was strangely humorous. Without even naming the object, she'd managed to turn the tables. While the direction their little dance had gone was unclear, there was one thing she knew for certain. Whoever was whispering in the ear of the Ursis wasn't on her side. There was only one person inside this Nebula with that information, and they were supposed to be her guardian.

22

———

IBU

PROTO DARK NEBULA, ON GRISEO

The skiff reminded them of what it must be like riding with a rocket strapped to their back. It was the second most exhilarating thing Ibu had ever done. The first, of course, still had to be when they took out that Shu moon above Henosi. It was a memory they often recalled, especially when they were searching for something to build their confidence. A feeling they could use right about now.

"Are you aiming for that building on purpose, or are you fraking with me?" Shauna asked.

Ibu yanked the yoke sideways and the skiff barrel rolled, narrowly missing the skyscraper and heading down one of the central thoroughfares of the now defunct city. The controls were touchy at first, but once they got used to them, they appreciated their responsiveness. More importantly, they needed to stay focused on the task at hand. This was neither the time nor the place to get lost in thought.

"Sorry," they muttered. "I was… thinking about the Shu. It won't happen again."

"I don't even think I want to know." Shauna's face appeared in the corner of their retinal comm. "Just keep us alive, will ya?"

"Affirmative."

Shauna's robot form was stretched out and folded up on the floor between their legs. It was a tight fit, but they managed. The skiff was meant for speed more than storage. Once they were out of the cockpit, the form Shauna had chosen should come in handy.

The crew from Phoenix One could be anywhere in the city, and at least half of the life signs they counted before they took off the other day were now missing. There could be any number of reasons why, including lying in wait in their exosuits.

They glanced from the street in front of them, to the map on their retinal comm, and then back again. None of the red dots had left the perimeter of the Phoenix One site since their skiff arrived in the city. While they dropped through the atmosphere well over the horizon, there was no telling what type of defensive measures the soldiers had created after they left. They weren't exactly dealing with run-of-the-mill grunts on Abigail's former crew. Even if some of them had the maturity of a hormonal human teenager, they were still highly trained killers.

In the distance, the familiar gardens above the museum edged over the horizon. "Prepare to exit the skiff short of the target. We'll approach on foot."

"Wouldn't it be easier to drop in next to the entrance?" Shauna asked.

Ibu sighed. "We already talked about this. I'm running this op, and you're assisting. Remember?"

"Yep. That's right." Shauna's robotic shell made several whirring and buzzing noises beneath their legs.

As the skiff lowered to the ground, they yanked back on the yoke to point the nose upward and shoved the throttle forward, engaging the vertical thrusters. The ship roared, transferring all of its energy from moving along the horizontal plane to the vertical one to slow their advance. Once they stopped sliding forward, they cut the throttle and eased the nose down to level it out, bringing the ship in for a gentle touchdown. While the entire thing could have been done with automated controls, Ibu refused to use them. They preferred to land themselves, keeping their life in their own hands. It was bad enough they had to use an expert system to take their ship back into orbit.

The hatch swung outward, and they pivoted in their seat, pushing up with all their strength. They leapt out of the skiff in one hop and sailed through the air, coming down low to the ground and then immediately scanning their surroundings. The wind gusted and a gray cloud of dust billowed down the vacant street, cascading around their ship and rustling the leaves of a nearby tree.

"That was dramatic." Shauna stepped out of the cockpit, unfolding one leg at a time as she went. Once she was fully extracted, she eased up beside Ibu.

Her robotic form reminded them of a human praying mantis on Earth. While they'd only ever seen pictures of the insect, the legs and torso of the robot were impossibly thin. The head was a triangular box sitting atop the body, and it looked imposing. She'd thrown together the design after dismantling several maintenance bots aboard Phoenix Two, along with parts from the alien shells they'd recovered. That head had come from one of the Ursis military robots. Shauna said it gave her seamless vision in every direction. While their exit may have been dramatic, watching the robot climb out had been downright frightening.

They tapped the controls on their wrist and the thrusters on the skiff roared to life, easing the nimble craft off the ground and spinning it in place. A cloud of colorless dust engulfed the two of them as the ship rocketed into the distance, following the same path they'd arrived on to exit the scene. The return would be from the south, to keep things more random in case shit hit the fan.

"Shall we?" Shauna began walking. Her six legs moved in a blurring motion as the robot skittered low across the ground toward the distant trees.

Ibu double timed it, running forward at a full tilt. It was nice to get off the ship again, even if it meant putting their life at risk. They reached over their shoulders and unsheathed the two swords. Without them, they felt naked approaching the entrance to the museum. The place where they'd practically died days earlier.

When they glanced over at Shauna, four tiny drones were rising out of her back. Each one of them shot outward in different directions.

"I'll keep our eyes and ears topside in a passive mode as long as possible," Shauna said over Ibu's comm. "If they detect anyone approaching, they'll cover the ground with a signal scrambler. That should prevent Phoenix One's team from broadcasting to each other, but it'll do the same for us. They'll burst regular directional transmissions toward our general location once the net's cast. There's a chance it could give away both the drone and our positions, but as we discussed earlier, knowing is better than dying."

The words echoed in their mind. Knowing had always been better than the alternative. Being oblivious to the real bonds shackling them below the surface on Doda had been deadening and stifled them for years. Once they realized the infinite possibility of the universe outside those artificial walls, layer after layer of lies peeled away. It was astonishing what truths revealed themselves once their eyes were turned toward the light.

Pings from the drones appeared on their retinal comm. "I thought you said they were passive."

"They are." Shauna jumped over a communal transport in her path and came down on the other side without missing a beat. "As long as they can see us, they'll target us with a directed comm beam. It's impossible to detect unless someone is standing next to us or in-between."

"I hope so," they muttered. While they preferred to come in with no-tech, the others in orbit refused. They weren't about to give their adversaries the upper hand by their friends being blind on the ground. Minula had made it clear it was a non-starter.

As they crossed the street and worked their way across the plaza to the museum entrance, they slowed their advance. Maybe it was because being exposed in the open space meant they had to be on alert, or maybe it was the puddles of blood splayed on the ground in front of them. Either way, their hearts raced with each foot that stepped on the dried blood.

Shauna broke the eerie silence that had fallen over their approach. "It looks like the remaining people at Phoenix One have converged near their ship. They're using dampening equipment, so we can't detect what they're talking about. But from our visuals, it seems like they're arguing and gesturing into the distance where we landed. They're sitting still, though, so that's good."

Ibu squeezed the hilt of their swords. They wouldn't say it out loud, but they welcomed the challenge if the humans decided to come. Until then, they had a job to do.

"Let's get inside and find some clues." They hopped down the stairs, taking them six at a time. It was almost fun racing down the steps and reminded them of exploring the coliseum on Doda. They used to spend hours running up and down the bleachers and imagining they were being attacked by humans in the blood games.

When they hit the bottom, they paused to check on Shauna, only to realize she'd already made it down and had been waiting for them. Perhaps they'd underestimated the robot. "Why don't you go first? You seem to have the lay of the land better than I do."

Shauna nodded and reached out with her impossibly thin

arms, grasping the handle and pulling the door outward. Unlike the video of the south entrance, these doors didn't open when they got close, nor did they cascade lengthwise. These screeched like rusted metal dragging against metal. A sound more like what they'd expected to find in this dead city, though one they preferred not to make when they were attempting to be stealthy.

She eased the door open more slowly, preferring the quieter sound of the metal rubbing together over the loud screech it made a second ago. Once the opening was sufficiently wide enough for them to squeeze past, Ibu slid into the gap. Shauna was more cautious about passing through, but once she recognized the mechanism was frozen in place, she simply followed Ibu and made herself thin enough to pass through.

Inside, they moved with purpose, making their way toward the museum wing deep in the bowels of the building. As they'd agreed, Shauna took the lead, along with her entourage of tiny flying drones. They swarmed around them like gnats, making sure never to leave any behind, but spreading out far enough to stretch their virtual eyes and ears. Over level after level, they repeated the same routine. Shauna monitored all the cameras ahead and behind, while Ibu did their best to keep up.

The movement advantages of the robot's mechanical form were obvious in hindsight. It was something they'd have to mull over before future encounters. For now, though, they were content getting to their destination alive.

As they approached the location of the tunnel, Shauna slowed. Like Abigail realized before them, the robots couldn't detect the entrance.

"You're gonna need to guide us through." Shauna reached out one of her hands and Ibu grasped it.

They crouched down and walked forward, passing into the darkened space. While the holograms of the Dark Nebula were convincing, knowing they weren't real detracted from their effect. There was a slight resistance as Shauna passed over the invisible barrier first, but once through, the swarm of drones sped past them, rocketing down the tunnel.

When they made it to the other side and stood upright, they paused, taking in the space. The surrounding walls were covered in the same billowing holographic nebulosity of the tunnel, and yet this time it sent shivers up their spine. Maybe it was because they weren't able to touch it and confirm it wasn't fictional, or maybe this one was more realistic. Either way, the sooner they got out of this place, the better.

They made short work of the exhibits, passing straight past them and into the center of the cavernous room. As the nebulosity on the ceiling arced downward near the entrance to the exhibit, Ibu could feel their body respond. It tensed up, as if it believed the Nebula was reaching for them. While they'd spent more time in a Dark Nebula than anyone on the crew, such a reaction was illogical, though they imagined it was exactly what the artist intended.

"This is where we lose contact with the outside," Shauna said. "I brought a toy along to see if it'll help bridge the gap." She reached inside one of her storage bins on her back and withdrew a disc before tossing it onto the ground. A second later, it unspooled itself, transforming into a snakelike shape. It dove toward the invisible void in the center of the room until one end disappeared.

"It works." Shauna shared a video from within the exhibit on Ibu's retinal comm. The snake was straddling both sides of the hologram, and despite the interior blocking all transmissions, the robot was able to act as a relay of sorts. "This should allow me to keep our drones out here and deeper in the museum while still maintaining line-of-sight contact with us."

Ibu sheathed their blades on their back and stepped through the invisible barrier, being certain not to step on the snake. While their retinal comm blipped, the signal stayed connected. "It's working on the other side, too."

They stopped at the edge of the envelope and studied the room. This place was unlike any of the exhibits they'd passed through. Instead of making the occupants feel like they were in the comforts of a ceilinged cavern, the room had transformed into darkness. No matter where they looked, all they saw was black. Like they were floating in outer space, sans the stars.

"Is everything ok?" Shauna asked.

"It's fine. I was merely trying to take in what Abigail first experienced when she entered alone." They eased forward into the void. Once they'd made it a good five meters in, a voice exploded from all directions and the sky lit up. Some sort of show started playing.

An Ursis stepped out of a gap in the wall in front of them, and Ibu drew their swords. The shock of the alien's arrival set their hearts a flutter and forced their body to transform in an instant. They moaned as the scars on their back stretched under their expanding size.

When they looked down, the stars that appeared overhead were shimmering on the metal of the blades. They were like the surface of the water reflecting the moon in the sky.

The alien wasn't threatening, but they towered over them, standing easily three times their height. They took a few steps backward, putting space between them in case they attacked.

"Stop right there," Ibu muttered.

It wasn't until the Ursis started talking that they realized this was part of the show. The alien was a hologram.

"If it matters, I couldn't tell, either," Shauna said. "For some reason, my sensors are useless in here. Their holograms have a density to them that fools even the alien tech in this head I'm reusing."

They glanced sideways and saw that the robot was standing beside them, weapons at the ready. She had two laser blasters drawn and what looked like a spinning blade of some sort. They didn't know whether they should be impressed or scared that they hadn't heard her draw them.

As the show continued, the Ursis walked about the space, gesturing toward the sky. They were convinced that the closing of the Proto Dark Nebula happened in stages, much like what the Phoenix had found elsewhere in the other alien systems. Just as the story was getting good, the hologram cut out, and the room went dark.

"Apparently, the exhibit has a glitch." Shauna stowed her weapons, and her exterior light turned on, filling the space with a warm glow. "Why don't you look around? I'll see if I can find a means to interface with the system."

Her words were muted, and they barely understood them because their gaze was locked on the ground. There was broken glass strewn about, and in the middle was a hole in the floor. From the looks of it, someone shot up a museum exhibit and removed something. They had a feeling they knew who.

Stepping toward the hole, the shards of glass crunched under their feet, but the noise was subdued. Almost like the room was dampening the sound. When they bent down over the hole, the cavity was too dark to see.

"Can you bring a light over here?" Ibu asked.

A second later, a drone zigged and zagged from wherever Shauna had disappeared to and came to a stop hovering over them. Its belly was lit up like a dome light, but once it stopped, it focused its beam and aimed it squarely into the hole.

The cavity wasn't deep by any stretch. There were only a few centimeters between the top and the bottom, but they only knew it was the bottom because of the glass. The surface below was perfectly black. An ideal frame to showcase the cloth they'd seen Abigail holding earlier.

"Frak," Ibu whispered. Another dead end.

They stood up straight and scanned the room. The walls and ceiling were as nondescript as the hole in the floor. It wasn't until they took a few steps backward and studied the entire space that they noticed a pattern on the floor. It looked like it was etched in glass.

"That's it!"

"What is?" Shauna came running back through the entrance they'd entered through. "What'd ya find?"

Ibu bent down and picked up a handful of the glass and started squeezing it into their gloved hands, crushing it into finer and finer particles. They stepped into the room and tossed it in front of them, spreading the grains across the black floor. They were trying to fill in the etched ridges with the reflective fragments of glass.

"What're you…" Shauna didn't finish the sentence. She must've recognized what Ibu had seen because a second later she, too, was furiously gathering glass and crushing it into her metallic hands. She, however, enlisted the help of the drones to spread it. Their silent fans acted as a perfect silicon distribution platform when guided properly.

By the time Ibu reached the wall and turned, they froze in place. Shauna's squad of drones had made quick work of spreading the crystal powder. The shape cut into the floor was as clear as day. Though they didn't know what it meant, they could tell from the edges that it matched the scraps of cloth they'd been able to see on Minula's video. Whatever Abigail had seen, they were now standing inside.

"They're coming!" Shauna started toward the door.

"Who?" Ibu reached out and paused, staring down at the lines of glass. Each straight line connected with another, and some seemed to connect with nothing at all, but the meaning was lost on them.

"The crew from Phoenix One is headed our way," Shauna said. "Our drones just relayed it from outside. They'll be here in a few minutes. We've got to get out of here before they bury us inside this place." She bolted toward the exit and disappeared out the other side.

They followed close behind, struggling to keep up, even in their enlarged and stronger form. If anything, they swore they moved slower like this. It made sense, they supposed. When they were smaller, they were more agile and deft footed. In their enraged form, their strength and pain tolerances were off the charts. Fight or flight. Black or white. There was never any gray with the Nanil.

"How many?" Ibu asked as they leapt from stair to stair, skipping three and sometimes four at a time.

Shauna was already an entire set of stairs ahead of them. "I only got the initial warning, and then it dropped. Our drones must have lost line-of-sight. We won't know what we're dealing with until we get outside. I'm transmitting the details to your retinal comm in case something happens to me on the way out. There's no time to dig into specifics now. I just hailed our taxi."

"Shit," Ibu muttered. If the skiff was inbound, their clock was ticking. They hoped the A.I. hadn't pulled the trigger too soon. The last thing they needed was one of the humans taking out their exit strategy.

With perspiration dripping down their face, they hopped through the unfamiliar southern doorway after it slid aside and hit the last set of stairs, climbing skyward. They pulled their hood over their helmet and withdrew their swords as they reached the top.

In the light of the open air, the previously star filled blades changed yet again to match the bright noonday sky. They shimmered with an intensity that almost made them look like electro-blades. Without a cloud in sight, and only the gray tones of the atmosphere, it was as close to a beautiful day on Griseo as they imagined a post-apocalyptic wasteland could be.

Once they broke the top of the stairs, the bots Shauna

deployed earlier fired updates to their retinal comms. One by one, red dots appeared on the map. The crew from Phoenix One was attempting another assault on the museum, except their numbers were a fraction of what they were only days before. Instead of forming a unified choke ring around their location, they were a shamble of their former selves.

There were only six dots in all, with three deciding to stay back at the remains of the drop-ship. From the looks of the intel, two were in exo-suits, and those were approaching from the north, whereas their skiff was coming in from the south. Its green dot was still well outside the city and was reporting an ETA of five minutes.

That was an eternity when death was knocking on your door. They had three dots to deal with, and if they made too much noise, those exo-suits could be here in less than thirty seconds. Their only option was a silent kill.

"You take the left, I'll take the right." Ibu didn't give her robot companion a chance to rebut her assignment. They were already sprinting toward the closest of the three dots, hoping their makeshift skotádi outfit did its job. Shauna had done some seamstress magic before they landed, and their suit was remarkably well tailored considering it'd been designed to fit a four-meter tall alien only days earlier.

They picked their way through the public space, sprinting from planter, to statue, to vehicle, trying not to be in the open for too long. Judging by the dots, they'd exited the museum at just the right moment. Any longer and the humans would've been close enough to make escaping far more challenging.

As they slid up alongside what appeared to be a massive hovering bus, they crouched down and froze. Ibu's retinal comm warned them of approaching footsteps on the opposite side. The device amplified the external sounds in their ears, and they squinted to turn it down. It was too loud in their current form. Yet another drawback of using an apparatus designed for humans.

Their retinal comm showed the red dot was on the other side of the bus, and it was moving clockwise, always clockwise. They echoed the motion, preferring to come around behind them if they could manage it. When they neared the rear, they noticed the ground was covered in glass. The shards twinkled in the afternoon sun, giving the scene a surreal feeling.

"Frak." A frontal assault would have to do. They ducked down and waited, watching the dot ease forward and then continue walking north toward the museum.

Once the human was a few meters past the bus, Ibu eased back down the side and peered past the bumper. The soldier's back was facing them and they were holding a rifle in their right hand, using their left to aim it down the street. Judging by the size of their frame, they were female. Not that it mattered, but any advantage would help.

They thought through their options, mulling over throwing one of their blades or taking a more direct assault from behind, but before they could decide, the soldier froze and brought their hand up to their ear. While it was a useless gesture in a sealed suit, it was a hard human habit to break. And fortunately for them, it meant their hand was off their weapon.

The diversion was brief, but they knew they couldn't risk missing it. Ibu launched forward, focusing on being as light-footed as possible and closing the distance between them without a sound. After a few steps, the soldier tilted their head and spun around, but by then it was too late. Ibu was already close enough to swing their blade.

In a whirlwind of light, they swung the blade in their right hand forward, slicing through the waist of the soldier like they weren't even there. The sword cut the woman in half without so much as a sound.

The two halves of the body hung together for a moment as the woman's gazed locked on Ibu. She reached out with her free hand, her palm facing outward as if to say stop. The shock at seeing the Nanil was unmistakable. She must've expected to see an Ursis or another robot, but not a member of her former crew.

When the two halves finally separated, the body collapsed to the ground with a thud, and blood poured out. They didn't know why, but the gruesome scene was mesmerizing. Maybe it was how clean the cut was. It almost made the effect seem fake, like it was somehow staged.

As they stared at the pool of red, their comm flashed and one of the dots vanished. It was the soldier Shauna had been assigned. They'd each done their job. All that remained was the dot caught between them.

Ibu closed their eyes and shook it off. The skiff would be here in under a minute. There wasn't time to dawdle over spilled blood. They needed to find and end the only person standing between them and freedom.

Without another thought, they leaned forward and sprinted toward the red dot. According to their retinal comm, they were two blocks ahead and one to the left. The blinking circle was walking down the middle of the street their skiff was approaching on. There was plenty of space behind them for Ibu to attack from the rear. While they didn't know where Shauna was, there wasn't time to think. Any delay and the soldier could fire on their one way off this rock.

The sound of their feet pounding the pavement was like a rapid fire snare drum in their ears. Step after step, beat after beat, was a countdown to death. Either the soldiers or theirs.

Rounding the corner, they could see the silhouette of a man in the distance. He was stepping around a pile of rubble in the street, and he didn't appear to be holding a weapon. For some reason, it was still strapped to his back.

They studied their retinal comm. There must be something

they were missing. This had to be a trap. Their eye in the sky drone was forward and above them, mirroring Ibu's every movement, but kept out of visual sight. All the imagery showed the soldier was alone, but something was off. There was no reason for their weapon not to be out.

Before they could figure out what they were missing, they noticed a blur in the distance. It was Shauna, and she was heading in full tilt. Like Ibu, they weren't risking firing any shots to give away their location. Just as the robot came within swinging distance of the human, a burst of gunfire erupted from the roof of a nearby building.

The soldier screamed as Shauna's form collided with them in a fiery explosion of shrapnel and blood. "Nooooo!"

Ibu's stomach knotted, and their blood boiled. It took every ounce of focus not to run out into the street to avenge their friend. As they were fighting back the rage, their retinal comm updated with an image of the human who fired on Shauna. They were in an exo-suit rigged with the same skotádi fabric the Nanil was wearing. Apparently, they'd learned some new tricks in the past few days.

They ducked behind the building and squeezed their blades, counting down their options. There weren't many, only one, in fact. They subvocalized a command to redirect the skiff back toward the bus they'd left, and once they confirmed the dot had redirected its approach; they dashed forward. Their legs were a blur of motion fighting to stay alive.

It wasn't until they heard the whine of the skiff approaching that they noticed their shadow drone had moved. It was diving along the wall of a building, heading toward what looked like the crater left over after Shauna's explosion.

They didn't have time to ponder the meaning. The exo-suited soldier could appear at any moment. Ibu turned down the thoroughfare and rushed in the direction of the lowering skiff. It had already repositioned itself to reverse course back down the same street it'd arrived on. The faster they could take off, the better, and going straight up wasn't an option until they were clear of the city.

As they hopped in, they set down their swords and jammed the throttle forward once their harness was in place. The door had automatically closed, but a gust of wind still made its way into the tiny cockpit as the skiff launched down the street.

"Dammit all to Hades!" Ibu slammed their free hand against the chair as the ship rocketed across the ground toward the distant horizon. They couldn't even feel the G-forces slamming them back with the rising anger and stabbing pangs of failure tearing apart their insides. They'd failed. Both of them had.

Shauna had known the risk of the mission, but she still wanted to come, anyway. While Ibu knew why they needed to be here, they weren't sure why the woman had decided to risk her life. They could understand finishing the mission if the Nanil failed, but otherwise, their actions were unwarranted and made little sense.

The crumbling remains of the buildings disappeared behind them as the skiff crossed the outer limits of the city. In a few more klicks, they'd be out of range and could head upward.

While they replayed the events of the past hour in their mind, a message appeared on their retinal comm. When they blinked it open, they drew in a breath.

Give me ten minutes. - Shauna

"Impossible," Ibu muttered. They'd seen the woman's

robotic form explode. There was no way their data dot survived that blast.

They opened the rear cameras on the skiff's controls and checked to see if any of the other drones were still operating. There was nothing visible, and when they checked the lidar, their passive scans came up empty. They couldn't risk an active sweep, so they picked a spot in the distance to set the skiff down and brought up a map of the city.

The last positions of the other Phoenix One crew members appeared on Ibu's map, along with where the hidden exo-suit had been. They quickly did the math, and while the distant crew were too far to reach them in ten minutes, there was a chance the nearest exo-suit could make it. With the suit covered in skotádi, there'd be no telling where they were until it was too late.

Ibu brought up the cameras on the outside of the skiff. There was a small farm building nearby, but for the most part, there was nowhere to hide. Right about now, they were regretting only arming the ship with a few light lasers. They weren't even sure they'd pierce the new armor on those heavy exo-suits. Reaching forward, they powered up the capacitors and disabled the safety on the firing controls. If they were forced to fight their way out, they weren't about to lose to dead batteries.

They spun the skiff around to face it north and flipped on the external live feed to their retinal comm. As they glanced around, it felt like they weren't even in the skiff any longer. The effect was disorienting at first, but gave them an unob-structed view from all sides. Better to die with their eyes open than closed.

Scanning the skies was quiet for a few minutes until the skiff's radar came alive. An inbound blip was approaching from the city. It was flying low and coming in hot, but it wasn't attempting to hide itself.

Ibu centered on the bogey and zoomed in. From the looks

of it, the object appeared to be one of their drones, but they couldn't tell for sure. Not yet.

They set their lasers to track the drone and zoomed back out, returning their attention to scanning the skies for the exo-suit. Fortunately for them, they never arrived. Once the drone was within range, it transmitted a signal to the skiff that appeared on their retinal comm.

Always left.

It wasn't long, but Ibu didn't need to think about it. They slammed the throttle forward and reached up to swing the hatch open. The wind briefly pulled the skiff to the side before they compensated.

When they were within fifty meters of the drone, they yanked back the throttle and counted down. The moment the drone slid up alongside, a tiny data dot shot across the space between them and bounced around the inside of the skiff like a pinball.

Ibu didn't even look for it. Instead, they slammed the hatch closed and pulled the yoke back, aiming the skiff's nose toward the sky. They swallowed hard and engaged the launch sequence, sending them rocketing skyward at full throttle.

The G-forces smashed them back into their seat, and they fought to keep their consciousness. Even they had a hard time dealing with fifteen Gs. The same forces would've instantly killed a human, but they weren't as fragile as their creator.

When their ship hit the lower atmosphere, they subvocalized the command to turn over navigation to the computer and sighed. They lowered their hands into their lap, and only then realized they'd been squeezing the controls too tight. It amazed them how the fear of dying had taken over their logical thoughts. Not being able to see their enemy was far worse than seeing them. At least when they saw them, they could size 'em up and think through how to defend themselves.

The emotional rollercoaster their species must've gone through fighting the Galactic Alliance all those years ago was mind-numbing to think about. Being blind was eye-opening.

23

ABIGAIL OLIVAW
PROTO DARK NEBULA, LOCATION UNKNOWN

Emmo wheezed and took a labored breath in the darkness. While Abigail couldn't see the Ursis, she knew it wasn't a recording. The back of her neck tingled every time they walked in front of her. Either that, or she was losing touch with reality after being tortured for the last few hours.

"Tell me about the array," Emmo said. "If you help me, then I'll help you."

"Screw you." Abigail leaned forward and spat a mouth full of blood in the direction of the alien's voice.

A second later, her entire body convulsed, and she screamed as electricity shot through the shackles and into her torso. She could feel the warmth of another stream of urine running down her legs, her suit's waste processing system having conked out long ago. Her own stench made her retch, but nothing came up because she'd expelled all the bile her body could produce. The only liquid still flowing was from the cut in her mouth, and she was reserving that for the Ursis. To be honest, it was a wonder her heart hadn't given up.

"Haven't you had enough?" Emmo asked. "You're clearly in pain."

Abigail's body howled yes, but her mind said no. If she told them what she knew about the tachyon gate array, not only would she be dead, she'd be sealing the coffin on her people, as well.

She lifted her head off her chest and stared into the darkness, but her eyes wouldn't focus. "You know, I was impressed with you when you first brought me onboard." She swallowed hard. When the blood hit her stomach, she struggled not to throw it up. "But the longer I'm here, the more I see how pitiful you and your kind truly are. You're hanging on by a thread, and yet, you should've given up like your people on Griseo."

"What do you know about Griseo? Did you visit there?" Emmo wrapped a hand around Abigail's throat and squeezed.

The alien's grip was like a vice constricting her windpipe. No matter what she did, she failed to catch her breath. Just when she was about to pass out, the electricity returned and shocked the both of them.

While she couldn't scream with the hand around her throat, Emmo howled like an animal caught in a trap. When the jolt ended, she released Abigail's throat and crashed to the ground. A second later, the lights in the room came up and a dozen Ursis ran in and surrounded the elder alien.

As Abigail gasped for air, her eyes struggled to focus. She hadn't seen light in what felt like days.

The frail alien's cane had fallen over, and her body was laying motionless in a heap of fur. What Abigail could only assume were Ursis medics were injecting her with liquids of varying colors.

After several minutes of commotion and countless angry stares, the Ursis slowly sat upright. It was like they'd rebooted her somehow.

"What... what happened?" Emmo ran her hand over the side of their head.

"You almost met your maker, bitch." Abigail spat another mouthful of blood at the bear, and she chuckled when she realized it hit her in the face.

A clawed hand shot out from her left, striking her across the head, and everything went dark.

"YOU KNOW," Emmo began, "I'm going to love killing your family when we're done with you. Especially your father."

The Ursis' voice sounded surreal. Like they were talking in water. At first, Abigail thought she was dreaming. It wasn't until she tried opening her eyes that the waves of pain hit, and she realized she was awake.

Whoever struck her earlier hadn't held back. Her left eye was swollen shut, and she could barely focus on the furry alien sitting in the chair in front of her.

"No." Emmo waved a finger. "I think I'll start with your mother." She took a sip of something that looked like green tinted water. "I hear a mother's bond is quite strong with you humans."

Abigail struggled to make sense of the alien's words. She was talking about her parents like they were alive. Certainly, she had to know they were dead. Maybe she was playing tricks, taunting her and trying to confuse her.

"What was her name again? Your mother." Emmo set her cup down on the arm of her chair.

Abigail shook her head, but didn't say a word. Giving in to them would only egg 'em on.

Emmo narrowed their gaze. "Shauna, I believe. Is that right?"

Abigail squinted, trying to follow the trail of misinformation the alien was leading her on. She figured she'd play along and simply nodded.

"I thought so. Is this her in the background?" Emmo

gestured with her paw and an image of her father flashed up on the far wall.

The picture was ancient. It had to be over seventy years old. He looked so young back then. Like he'd just graduated from university. Standing behind him was Aunt Kara, his sister. She was smiling from ear to ear. It'd been a long time since she'd seen her aunt that happy.

"That's her, right?" Emmo gestured toward the woman.

She nodded.

"Yes." Emmo smiled. "I'll kill her first, then. But I'll do it slow, so you can watch what you could've prevented." She leaned forward. "You know this would be easier if you cooperate, right?"

The alien tapped her cane on the ground, and a door slid open behind her. It took Abigail a second to recognize that they weren't in the same room as before. They'd moved her while she was passed out.

While this space was as nondescript as the last, the floor here seemed to be made of stone. Not exactly a building material you usually found on a spaceship, at least not one she'd ever been on.

With her eyes on the floor, she did a double take when a naked Ursis walked into the room. He was carrying a tray of water, and what she could only imagine was food. It smelled wonderful, and if her mouth could've produced saliva, it would've.

She could almost feel the water pouring down her throat, and she caught herself leaning forward.

"Go on." Emmo waved her paw. "Let her have a sip."

The Ursis balanced the tray in one hand and picked up a cup. When he brought it up to her lips, he gently tipped it. She took a mouth full, swooshed it around, and then spit it back out, filling the cup with pinky red blobs of blood. She then shoved her chin outward and knocked the glass out of the giant bear's hand, sending it tumbling down and crashing against the edge of the tray. The contents flipped end over end and crashed to the ground, flinging food and water everywhere.

The handler stared at her for a moment, having clearly been caught off guard. He growled and lashed out, grabbing her by her tattered suit and yanking her forward. His canine teeth elongated as he leaned closer, like they were growing out of his skull.

She tried to pull away, but his grip was too strong.

As he eased closer, he opened his mouth to bite her and the electricity hit again.

Abigail cried out in pain, and the Ursis did the same. Their bodies contorted in unison as each jolt of the deadly energy struck. When it finally stopped, he collapsed to the ground and whimpered away. She, however, hung limp in her shackles.

She couldn't take any more jolts. Her brain was fried.

"How'd you do that?" Emmo bolted upright and shuffled toward her, being sure not to touch her or the passing servant.

Again, the alien and her mind games. She'd been messing with her since she woke up, only she couldn't imagine the path the alien was taking her on this time. First she alluded to her parents being alive, and now she insinuated Abigail had shocked the Ursis. It was like she was as confused as Abigail.

A message flashed on the bottom of her retinal comm.

Play along. It was me controlling the electricity.

The words took a second to sink in, but when they disappeared, they hit Abigail like a ton of bricks. Emmo wasn't playing games. They were acting on the details they had, as ill-informed as they were. Which meant only one thing. Harold hadn't turned her in, someone else had. Figuring out who was the challenge. Next to staying alive, of course. Her first decision was if she should continue weaving her lies from earlier, or if she should try something different.

"I asked how you did that?" Emmo whacked her on the side with her cane.

She winced and twisted her back, the sting of the strike lingering longer than it should've. When she raised her gaze, she locked eyes with the alien. "I told you I could end this shell whenever I wanted. I'd thank you for ending it, but for some reason, you keep playing with it like the simple animal you are. If you think you're gonna get something out of it, you're mistaken. I don't know who's feeding you intel, but they seem to be as clueless as you are. It's embarrassing, really."

"I tire of your games, human." Emmo spun in place and the room went dark. Once she passed through the entrance to the chamber, the un-oiled steel door creaked and slammed shut, sending a booming echo through the now darkened space.

Abigail started cackling, this time making far more noise than before. Her voice thundered through the darkness, reverberating off the walls and the stone floors. It was funny hearing her own voice after so long. Even her laugh had a gravely hoarseness to it. The game was afoot, and she wasn't as outmatched as she'd imagined.

24

—

IBU

PROTO DARK NEBULA, ORBITING GRISEO

Ibu had been staring at the image for hours, flipping it around and around, trying to force something to appear. Their mind wasn't seeing a pattern or anything to grasp onto. Whatever Abigail had recognized was beyond them.

They closed their eyes and willed their body to shut off, a ritual they performed regularly. Sometimes it was just to relax and unwind, and other times they used it as a means to separate themselves from the drama of humanity. Either way, it helped them think.

As the sounds of the ship's environmental controls and the clickety-clack of robots continuing their repairs on the hull disappeared, the universe faded to a point. To a single image.

It reminded them of a fractal someone might turn into a necklace or a tattoo. Many of the lines served no obvious purpose beyond connecting arbitrary points in space together. The internal and external arcs that formed the shape were inconsistent, and almost seemed random, as if they were artistic rather than engineered. They never quite understood art. It was something they'd meant to learn when they had more time on their hands, but hadn't yet gotten around to it.

Perhaps if they broke it down, it'd help. They mentally tapped the vertices that connected the lines, pushing and pulling each of them away. They were turning the flat image into three dimensions. It wasn't something they'd done much of their mental space, so the act was fraught with far more error than they'd imagined. Doing it with their retinal comm would have been simpler, but the thought of activating the device gave them a headache.

With the connected points identified, they flipped their hand, willing the shape to spin. First along the X-axis, and then along the Y and Z. Rotating it was almost fun, and it made seeing the pockets inside easier. One by one, they picked a color that appeared in their mind and used it to fill each abstract pocket within the blob. When they finished, they spun it again, marveling at its chaotic beauty.

They weren't sure why they chose mostly purples and pinks. Maybe it was because they were Abigail's favorite colors, or maybe because purple was the color the Prima Nanil wore so often. They hadn't thought of the progenitor in a while. Sixty-four days, to be exact.

The points that made up the shape flashed in their mind's eye, and they gasped. There were sixty-four connections drawn on the map. It must've been a coincidence. There was no other way to explain it. Like all species, their mind saw patterns where there weren't any. But if it wasn't happenstance, the meaning of the number failed them.

It was two to the sixth power and was also the atomic number of Gadolinium. While they used the chemical in constructing gate drives, so were tens of others. There had to be some reason the number appeared in their mind. It's a self number, in that no integer added up to its own digits yielded sixty-four. Again, a useless factoid on its own, much like knowing it's a dodecagonal number.

Even thinking the Doda phrase sent shivers through their

body. Escaping that hell was the best thing that ever happened to them. That deadly object had passed back and forth through the Lupus Dark Nebula for centuries, breaking down and absorbing anything it encountered and using it to build on itself. It was like a plague, wrapped inside a cloud of death. Each time it entered a Nebula pocket, it brought with it a promise of destruction.

They wondered how many pockets there were in Lupus. As they opened their eyes to check the data from their retinal comm, it hit them.

"Pockets," they muttered.

"What pockets?" Shauna asked.

They hadn't even heard the robot enter the bridge. She was scary stealthy that way. "Umm..." They shook their head. "In the shape. They... reminded me of home. Of Lupus."

Shauna brought up an image of the Lupus star system on the wall screen and started spinning the shape they'd recovered. She was willing it to fit into the Nebula somehow. The permutations flashed on the screen as the robot used all their computing power to find a match, but none came.

"Not here. Not that way." Ibu stood up and wiped away the Lupus Nebula.

Even having it on the screen was giving them the willies. Once it was gone, they repeated the same exercise they'd done in their mind on the wall screen. They made sure to choose the same colors as earlier, not wanting to miss any meaning the vision might have brought.

"Why purple?" Shauna reached out and stopped her hand short. "That was—"

"Abigail's favorite color," Ibu interrupted. "I know. She used to wear it when she was down. Said it made her happy. I wondered why she didn't bring any purple outfits along on this mission, but thought it better not to ask."

When Ibu stepped back, Shauna spun the two-dimensional shape they'd extracted from the museum floor. "What does it mean?"

"Pockets," Ibu muttered again.

Shauna glanced at them and then toward the wall screen. As she reached out, her hand froze, this time lingering in space near the darkest purple region.

"What is it? What do you see?" Ibu leaned forward, studying the shape. It was far longer than the rest and connected to several other pockets at the heart of the pattern. But other than that, nothing seemed unusual about it.

The silence broke as Shauna jumped backward and slid into the navigation controls for Phoenix Two. She was programming a sequence of jumps, and within a few seconds, she activated the gate drive. The sound of the vanes clicking into place vibrated the entire ship from its slumber.

"Tell me!" Ibu stepped forward and grasped Shauna's hand. "What is it?"

"It's a map," Shauna said. "A map to my daughter, and I know how to find her. I'm getting us the hell away from this dead world." She tapped her controls and pointed at the wall screen. "There. Look!"

Ibu spun in place and drew in a deep breath, bringing their hand to their mouth. Shauna had shared a map of the Proto Dark Nebula on the wall screen and placed the shape Ibu had pulled apart in the middle. Each of the vertices lined up with a star in the system or a known point of inflection in the Dark Nebula. It wasn't until they noticed the colors that they sat down in the chair beside the robot.

Somehow, they'd unconsciously painted the pockets they'd visited with pinks and the ones they hadn't with purples. They didn't know how, but they had. Stranger still was the deep purple pocket in the middle. It was the one with the most connections and had been the strongest color in their mind's eye. Their body tingled the longer they stared at it. It was like they knew they'd find Abigail there. And Shauna must've known, as well, because the multi-jump route she'd programmed into the computer ended just outside that first dark purple region.

25

ABIGAIL OLIVAW
PROTO DARK NEBULA, LOCATION UNKNOWN

The guards dragged Abigail's limp body into the room and tossed her onto the ground. They didn't wait for the automated shackles to find her wrists like after most torture sessions. She didn't blame them, though. She was in no form to fight back. Not after the last few days.

Emmo had been determined to shatter Abigail in today's session, and her out-of-body antics hadn't helped. She was beginning to think pretending to be a god using this human shell as a proxy wasn't her best move. Hindsight was twenty-twenty, and now that she was down this path, turning back was out of the question.

When she reached up and rubbed her chest, she winced. Her breastbone was sore and brought with it a lingering memory of where they'd attached the electrodes. Judging by the edges of the wound, she was either running out of nanites or Harold was reserving them for more severe bodily harm. She assumed he'd tell her if things were dire. Though, now that she thought about it, he'd been pretty quiet today.

It'd been several days since she woke up here in this cell. The last thing she remembered was laughing so much she almost heaved, and then everything went black. Next thing she knew, she was here. At first, she assumed she was in the same room, but Harold corrected her. He'd been awake the entire time she was passed out, and he was confident they'd moved her. From what he said, they'd transported her here in some sort of coffin. And except for changes in velocity and motion, he was as clueless as she was when it came to their location.

She closed her eyes and gestured out a quick question on the virtual keyboard. Navigating the keys with your eyes closed was harder than with them open. Despite years of practice hiding messages from her parents and enemies in Sol, the motion felt foreign. After days of torture, even breathing was demanding. She sighed and read her message, having lost her train of thought.

Is everything ok in there? I haven't...

His reply appeared before she finished.

You're not alone.

She scrambled up and spun around, staring into the darkness and fighting the vertigo of the sudden movement. There was nothing but black, as her eyes hadn't yet adjusted to the change in light. While activating her lidar overlay would help, that'd give away her tricks to her captors.

"Who's there?" She stumbled in the dark until she found the edge of her bed and then hopped up, pulling herself onto the mattress and fighting the pangs throughout her body. Once she was up, she slid her back against the wall.

A message appeared once she got situated.

Across the room. Whoever they are, their breathing is
shallow, like they're trying not to be heard. Judging by
the hints I'm detecting in your olfactory organs, they're
an Ursis.

It was strange when he did that without her asking.
Giving someone access to all your senses and letting them tap
into your brain was eerie sometimes. He always had a way of
using her body in ways she couldn't. The only things she
smelled was her own stench.

"I can smell you a mile away." Abigail nodded into the
distance toward the previously empty bed. While she
couldn't see anything, she wanted them to think she could.
"There's no point in breathing like that, either. You're going to
hyperventilate."

The figure across the room rustled as the heavy body
adjusted its position on the mattress, ending its charade. Her
bed never made a sound when she moved. The mattress was
so damn stiff; it hurt her back most of the time. It reminded
her this cell was purpose-built for a species far larger than
she was.

The bottom edge of her retina comm flashed a message
from Harold.

They're wounded. I'm detecting a foreign aldehyde in
the air. It appears you're not the only one being tortured
in this place.

Interesting. She moved her arm and faked an audible
wince, rubbing the spot with her opposite hand. "Looks like
you've had a rough day, too."

When she squinted, she thought she could just make out the outline of the Ursis. They were sitting with their back in the far corner and their legs were outstretched. From their faint motion, it appeared like they were stroking their leg with their paw.

"Silent treatment, aye?" Abigail nodded and rubbed her mouth with her hand. "I figured they'd do this at some point. You know, plant someone in this cell with me. Someone who can pretend to be on my side and get me to say things." She glared at the dark outline in the corner. "This shell wasn't born yesterday."

A muted growl rose from the darkness. "You can stop your antics, human. They know you're not talking to anyone from the outside. I've informed them on such matters." The Ursis adjusted their leg and moaned.

Her heart skipped a beat. "What do you mean, informed them?" She leaned forward and squinted, still struggling to see the alien. "Who are you?"

They straightened their back and lifted their chin. "Name's Haradis."

"What's your clan?" Her vision was getting clearer the longer she stared at him.

"I'm from the Umbra." He pounded his paw into his chest. "Heard of it?"

She shook her head. "No. I can't..." She realized she'd already messed up. If she'd been who she said she was, then she should've known who he was. Telling him anything more would be counterproductive.

Her retinal comm flashed on the bottom edge.

He's from the clan of the former king, from before the Nebula. They were enemies of Emmo's tribe.

Now he tells her. She could have used those details before she'd said no.

"I've been watching you for a while now." Haradis reached forward and ran his paw over his wound.

"A while, as in…" She slid toward the edge of her bed and dangled her legs over the side, her feet swinging well above the floor. "How long?"

"Long enough to know that ship of yours ain't Galactic Alliance standard issue. It ain't every day you see a new ship take out a half dozen of the Qudoculi's strongest fighters." The Ursis mimicked their motion and swung their leg down off the bed, except their feet easily touched the floor. "I wish you could've heard what they were saying about you." The bear slapped his knee and chuckled. At least it sounded like a laugh. "They were as pissed as a pruntis on a first date. Talking about tearing you up and feeding you to their hive back home on Alviarium. It was righteous fun watching them explode in a ball of fire like that, even if you wasted priceless spános in the process. If they had those gate drives, these nebulas would either be a thing of the past or they'd suppress the shit out of that tech. No," he shook his head, "it's not in their best interest to let something like your Phoenix proliferate. Especially with that wallop you gave them back in Epsilon. They gotta be pissing in their drawers right now."

She gasped for breath, not realizing she'd been holding it the entire time he'd been speaking. He knew everything about them. Far more than anyone inside this Nebula should've known. From the fighting outside and inside the Proto Dark Nebula, to their win back home. Hell, he even knew the armament they'd used to blast those mottled green bidirectional freaks she hated so much. It didn't seem possible.

A message from Harold appeared on her retinal comm.

He must've followed us through with the Qudoculi. Maybe that was what they blew up on the rock before attacking us.

She'd forgotten all about that explosion in orbit before Ibu and Shauna vaporized the upper layer of Griseo's atmosphere. If it hadn't already been a dead world, it would've been seriously wounded after that blast.

"How'd you make it off your asteroid in time?" Abigail rubbed her hands together, struggling to see the alien, but hoping he had some type of reaction.

He went silent; she assumed, due to surprise. Either that, or he was thinking about how to answer her question.

"So you're a mole, then?" She nodded and crossed her arms, studying his response.

Haradis tensed up, and she swore she saw him lean toward her. "I was merely… remembering. It was my home they destroyed. The only place I felt safe, until… I made a mistake. I've lived there for many years. Ever since my family sent me away, to hide from the Galactic Alliance when the see-er got word of the advancing tribunal forces." He stared into the darkness. "My father… he—"

The archaic rusted doors to the cell clicked and swung inward, crashing against the stone wall and sending a stiff breeze through the damp air filling the room.

Abigail dropped to the ground and slid under her bed, wrapping the cable attached to her wrists around the bed frame as best she could. It was the only thing she could think of to slow them down. Part of her hoped they were coming for Haradis, but she knew that was wrong. She'd had enough pain for a lifetime.

The seconds that followed could only be described as surreal. There were several noises from across the chamber, like someone was shackling and unshackling Haradis, and then there were screams. Blood curdling growling and bellows of pain and anger, followed by numerous scratching and thumping sounds. It reminded her of someone beating on a heavy pillow. As she stared into the darkness, a splash of moisture spritzed her face, and then another. It must've been sweat or something far worse.

When she reached up to wipe at the liquid running down her cheek, the scampering suddenly got closer until it crashed above her head as a body fell onto her bed. If she'd been up there, he'd have crushed her for sure.

She slid toward the wall, willing the aged metal frame beneath the mattress to hold together, if only for a little longer. One broken weld, and she'd be an Ursis pancake.

With her body tucked into a ball, all she could think about were her brothers. About how she'd never had a chance to see Bradley again. In all the years since he'd left for Zeta Lupi, she'd missed him the most. He was the one person who irked her to the edge of insanity, and yet she longed to hug him and see his smiling face staring back at her. And now, she might never hug him again. Everything she'd risked protecting him and the others would be for naught. The GA would crush humanity once and for all.

Those fitful moments of terror ticked by, one after another. Only after the gurgles of pain and the rustling of clothing stopped did the room fall into silence. When she uncurled and peered into the darkness, she realized someone was staring back at her. They were bent down and peering under the bed; she assumed to check if she was still alive.

"I thought I'd crushed you for a moment," Haradis said. "Are you planning to cower on the ground all night, or are you interested in getting the hell out of this place?"

Of all the things she imagined she'd do in her life, a jailbreak was never on the list. She scampered out from under the bed and eased up against the wall, being sure to keep a safe distance from the Ursis who was now sitting upright, waiting for her. They were watching her the entire time she was crawling. It was too soon to tell if he was using her as bait or if he legitimately wanted to help her escape.

"We go now." Haradis reached out, and before she could even react, he snapped off her shackles with the flick of his claws. Without pausing to check on her, he leapt toward the door. His catlike reflexes and powerful legs covering the distance in two hops.

She froze with her back against the wall and her trembling hands held out in front of her. Part of her said to haul ass behind him, and another cautioned her that this entire thing could be a trap. Emmo might be trying to get her to follow him to see if she'll lower her guard and take his side.

Haradis lowered his head to the ground and peeked outside the door, first glancing left and then right. He then looked over his shoulder. "You coming or dying?" When she didn't react, he narrowed his gaze. "You know they're on to you about your companion, right?"

"My what?" She pushed off the wall.

"Your robotic companion." Haradis tilted his ear into the air and lowered his voice. "The one you hid inside your body. I already told them about it. I'm pretty sure Emmo has been… what do you call it? Fraking with you."

Her stomach tightened. While Emmo had known more than she let on, she never imagined she'd been played for a fool. What the Ursis' goals had been were beyond her. Maybe it was another test, or maybe they'd been probing her the entire time, preferring to break her rather than make a deal.

Haradis sniffed the air. "Fine, stick around here. I'm—"

"I'll go," she interrupted, sneaking across the room and easing up beside him. "Just… just don't leave me behind."

A message from Harold appeared on her retinal comm.

Be careful.

"They already know about you," she subvocalized. "There's no point in hiding any longer. Activate the lidar and give me everything you've got."

Her vision lit up like someone turned on the lights. She could see the entire room and more. Her field of view was painted in colors denoting distance and the audible volume of nearby objects. From what she could tell, Haradis appeared to be planning to lead them down the hall, away from a distant pair of feet.

"Is that him?" Haradis asked, glancing at her. "Your friend. You always seem to whisper to each other. Except for that Nanil one. They're a harder nut to crack. They never talk to themselves like you humans."

She stared blankly at him. "How do you know I'm talking to a him?"

"Because of how you hold yourself when he talks." He eased out into the hall and started sneaking to the right. "You're far more relaxed around females of your species than males."

"He's not wrong," Harold said in her ear. "But you knew that already."

Abigail shook her head and tiptoed beside the massive hairy Ursis, barely keeping up even at his slow pace. She never imagined she'd be psychoanalyzed by an alien in prison, least of all by someone she'd never met. "How the hell do you know all this?"

Haradis snickered. Or she imagined that's what it was. "I followed you around for a while, both on Griseo and in orbit. It was actually quite easy spying on you while your ship was being repaired. You're a noisy species. After you sealed up all the gaps in the skotádi, it was challenging, though. But once I tucked a nanotube through one of your hatches, I was good to go."

"Shit," she muttered. They seriously needed to up their security game on and about their ships. For decades, they'd relied on knowing they were fighting humans with more primitive gear than they had. But these aliens knew how to wage war. They were millennia ahead of humanity.

"I'd remind you that Shauna and I would've been able to detect this type of intrusion had we retained full control of the ship and our usual nanite swarm, but you already knew that, too." Harold had chosen not to make an appearance on her retinal comm, which was fine by her. She'd probably dismiss him anyhow.

Haradis peered around the corner. Once he confirmed it was clear, he lunged forward and started running down the next hall. He was gone before she even realized it, and she staggered to catch up.

With each step, her lidar showed him receding into the distance. He was more than three times her height, and when sprinting was easily ten times her speed. As the gap between them grew, her retinal comm warned her of quickening foot-steps behind her. She wasn't sure why, but something was telling her the guards in this place were about to realize their prisoners were missing.

She panted as she sprinted. Her heart was pounding in her chest, and she was doing all she could not to run leading with her heel. Her father used to tease her all the time about her running. He told her she sounded like a herd of elephants galloping through the halls of the Sol Wheel. She was never the nimblest Olivaw, but she made up for it in other ways, like her social skills. Unfortunately, those didn't help her keep up with a bear that was as fast as a ground car.

In the distance, she could see the outline of a cubby in the wall. It should give her a place to rest and catch her breath.

Hopefully, Haradis would realize he'd lost her and come back. Otherwise, this could be the shortest jailbreak in history.

As she approached the recess, she slowed her pace. Just before reaching it, a heavy metal gate slid out and slammed shut against the far side, sending her colliding into it with a crash. Her shoulder exploded in pain, and she tumbled into a limp pile on the ground. While the adrenaline of the moment had propelled her forward, her body was abruptly reminded that not only had she been tortured, she'd failed at a game of chicken with a solid set of metal bars.

"Shit! Shit! Shit!" She thrashed back and forth on the stone floor, her body screaming in pain. "Can you do anything?" She said the words out loud, forgetting she should've subvocalized them.

"You're low on nanites," Harold said. "I've been busy dealing with internal bleeding. Bumps and bruises will have to wait."

The last thing her pain felt like was a simple bump or a bruise. She rolled onto her back and forced her eyes to open between the waves of agony. The gate looked like standard issue jail bars, except they were three times as thick, which made sense given the size of what they usually locked up.

"You will not die in this place, Abby." She groaned and reached out, pulling herself up off the ground using the gate. Once she was upright, she grasped the metal bars and yanked them sideways, back in the direction from which they came. While she never imagined they'd budge, it was better than not trying.

"That's not gonna work." Haradis appeared from around a corner she hadn't seen just up ahead. "Ya need to put your legs and back into it, like this."

He slid up against the far wall and pushed his foot against one of the bars. Once he eased close to the wall, he took two deep breaths, and on the third, shoved with all his might. The bars groaned under the immense pressure and the gearing inside the wall cried out for relief.

Abigail took a few steps backward. She swore the metal bars were going to break, and if they did, she'd rather not be anywhere near the shrapnel.

After a few seconds, the grating sound reached a crescendo until finally the gate gave way and shot back into the wall with a bang, sending Haradis falling to the ground on his ass. He wailed out loud, and she ran up to his side, feeling in his fur for cuts. "Are you ok?"

He rolled around for a second, emitting several raucous groans until he stopped. When she looked over at his face, he was smiling. The fraking guy had been laughing the entire time.

She whacked him on the shoulder. "That wasn't funny. I thought you threw out your back or something."

Haradis laughed and pushed up off the ground, brushing his fur off once he was upright. "Ain't no pitiful antique bars gonna take me out. The least they could've done was put us up in a more modern, higher security joint." He peered down the hall from where they'd come. "Emmo must think we're weak. Either that, or she's hiding us away from the prying eyes of her enemies. If that's the case, we need to find out who they are."

"The enemies of my enemy are my friend," she muttered.

He glanced back at her. "Maybe neither of us are as dumb as she thinks we are. Come on, follow me. I found a way out." He swung his paw down the passage and started galloping away.

"Wait!" She waved him back as she headed after him, leading with a limp. Her body had given up the ghost after that last pause. "I can't move that fast. I ain't got it in me."

Haradis froze and took a few steps backward. He leaned down and sniffed her, pausing his nose over the open wound on her side and leg before coming to a stop over the black-

and-blues on her arms. She was even more beat up than she'd realized.

He lifted his head up to her face and gazed into her eyes. "Tell anyone I did this, and I'll end you. Got it?"

She drew back, not sure what he meant. His eyes were stern, and yet somehow soft at the same time. He was being vulnerable. Something no alien had ever been with her. It wasn't until he lowered his head and leaned to the side, moving his paw close to her, that she recognized what he was doing. Like Harold had done days earlier, he was offering her a ride.

"Tha—nk you," she whispered and stepped up carefully on his arm and eased up onto his back. Once she was on top, he shifted and she ducked down, swearing she was going to hit her head on the ceiling but coming up short.

"You're gonna have to wrap your arms around my neck, or you'll fly off. Go on. We have little time. They're headed our way."

She spun around. In the distance, at the opposite end of the long hall, she could see a pair of Ursis. They dropped onto all fours and were sprinting toward them.

"Shit." She turned back, flung her arms around his neck, and squeezed her thighs against his torso. Once she'd clasped her hands, he didn't waste a second. He shot forward like a bolt of lightning.

After only a few hops, he ducked sideways and tore down the adjacent hall. And not a moment too soon because the floor behind them erupted in an explosion of yellow-orange flames singeing the hairs on her arms. She hoped Haradis was ok, as she wasn't about to loosen her vice grip to check. It was taking every ounce of her energy not to fall off.

She buried her face in his back and closed her eyes. He took turn after turn, weaving his way through the halls of this cavernous hellhole like he was following a map. While her mind meandered to dark places several times, there was something about this Ursis that was different. For some reason, she knew he was being honest. As if the universe had dealt him enough shit sandwiches that being his true self was all he had left to give. His state of being described her feelings to a tee.

After what seemed like an hour, a warmth washed over her. When she lifted her face out of his feather soft mane, she was greeted with a cacophony of flowery scents and a blinding light from the sun above. Her retinal comm adjusted in a split second, but not without leaving some brief splotches of white behind.

Once the haze cleared, she stared up at the most miraculous sight. One only moments earlier she'd have sworn she'd never see again. A deep blue sky smeared with a handful of billowing white clouds. It reminded her so much of Earth; she had to do a double take. When the sky met the towering green and blue trees of the forest, her mind relaxed.

"Where are we?" she asked as Haradis continued to dash over a nearby hill and down the other side.

He made his way down into a valley and followed along the bank of a river, bounding from one side to the other. When they were several kilometers clear of the cave they'd emerged from, he ducked under a massive boulder leaning over the river. It offered them both shade and protection from the prying eyes above.

"This... is Arctordiea. Home world... of my people." Haradis was panting as he bent down and lapped up water from the stream.

Abigail relaxed her legs and eased down to the ground. When both feet were firmly on terra firma, she dropped to her knees and started cupping water into her mouth, as well. She was as parched as a desert.

"The water's clean," Harold said in her ear. "Though it's a little late now, I suppose."

"Of course, the water's clean," she said. "I wouldn't think he'd drink it if it were poisonous."

Haradis chuckled. "Talking to yourself again, I see. I have to say, it's even weirder being next to you when you're doing it."

"Sorry." She pointed at her head. "My friend was just letting me know the water was safe to drink."

He nodded. "My nose told me that. You should get a better one." He reached out and gently bopped her nose and chuckled. "It's so tiny."

She leaned back and broke out in laughter. She could tell by the look on his face that he wasn't sure what was happening at first, but once he realized she wasn't mad, he started laughing, as well. It felt wonderful to relax, if even for a second. This Ursis was definitely more her style.

26

IBU

PROTO DARK NEBULA, OUTSIDE
POCKET FOUR

Phoenix Two was floating in space, well away from the probe they were about to launch. They'd given Shauna complete control over the workings of their ship. Ibu's attention had been drawn elsewhere, and they'd been having a hard time doing everything to keep it running smoothly. So they gave in. Their team was too small to cover all the bases, and they needed help leading into this next leg of the mission. Without the assistance of the A.I. or more able bodies, they were at a steep disadvantage. Shauna made this abundantly clear after their first jump.

In a manner of minutes, she called out a half dozen issues with the gate vanes that required immediate attention. When Ibu gave her control of the ship's repair systems, within the ten minutes she found multiple micro-fractures in their skotádi coating, as well as a few suspect external hull compromises. From the looks of them, either Zachary forgot to remove some of his construction apparatus or someone had infiltrated their ship.

Minula thought it might have been some of Kamal's team keeping an eye on them. Without equipment hooked up to the other side, the nanotubes they found were useless, which made them even stranger. Shauna figured it was their cloaked friend on the outside of the Phoenix, but they may never know for certain.

The Phoenix had been drifting in the cold emptiness of space ever since the discoveries. The three of them had been running tip to tail internal and external scans of the ship, making sure everything was in full working order before they went any further.

Their remaining soldiers were useless when it came to repairing skotádi, so Cynthia had them doing reviews of every piece of their equipment, watching over them like a hawk. She wasn't someone you messed with once you were on her bad side. Ibu learned that in the Lupus Dark Nebula.

"Are we sure about this?" Minula peered over Ibu's shoulder.

"It's the best idea we have." Ibu brought up the plan on the wall screen. They'd already reviewed it twice, but Minula was nervous. She'd been pacing around the bridge for the last hour, asking the same questions over and over again. "The probe's set to open a gate followed by a full active scan of the neighboring star system. Once complete, or if interrupted, we'll close the gate. If it takes any damage, it'll self-destruct, and our end will seal shut. That'll ensure they can never reach us."

Minula stared at the wall screen in silence, her foot tapping the entire time. The beat was an unfamiliar random pattern.

"It's a good plan," Shauna said. "We can't afford to jump wildly into the Nebula. Not without knowing if this map is useless."

Ibu studied the next step of their plan, giving the human a chance to catch up and process their emotions. If everything went well, they'd gate through and explore around the Ursis star system. However, if their active scan was detected, they'd reposition to a new location and try again.

They needed to find Abigail, which meant either finding a way inside the star system she jumped into or somehow communicating with her. Until they had intel to work with, poking holes from the edges was their safest bet. While in their mind they were in a hurry, at this point they couldn't afford any more ill-informed risks.

Minula spun around to face them. "And we're sure we're not detectable if they do an inverse scan or if another Galactic Alliance patrol comes by?"

Shauna's robotic form lowered her hands from her controls and gazed at the woman. "We ran dozens of passive scans and several active ones before we jumped outside the Dark Nebula. Remember? There aren't any more leaks. We're sealed up tight. Except for them being able to detect our drive cones when we reveal them, we're a ghost in the darkness."

Minula wrung her hands together and stared past the robot. She'd originally wanted to follow Abigail, guns blazing. At least until they talked her off the fence when they found the hull issues. And now that they were prepared to take action, she seemed fit to overthink everything. Ibu thought they'd have to convince her to act, like when they were inside the Nebula. She was acting like Abigail with her sudden rollercoaster of emotions. She wasn't at all her normal stern and stoic self.

"We're as ready as—" Ibu began.

"Alright, let's do it," Minula interrupted. She walked over to the security controls and sat down.

Ibu glanced at Shauna and shrugged. Without a word, the robot reached forward and activated the gate drive. They were cracking open a microscopic gate near the test probe. It would allow them to issue commands from their side of the gate with far less risk. The Phoenix had enough power to keep the gate open the entire test sequence, since there wasn't any mass passing through that led to the usual exponential energy demands.

With the gate activated, they confirmed the command set for the probe and then started the transmission. While the orders were simple, their impact was profound. They'd spent the past few days preparing for this moment, and it was hard to believe it was finally here. They hadn't been this excited since they climbed the maintenance shaft on Doda with Zachary. The future they were climbing toward at the top of that tunnel drove them to push past their limits and ultimately led to human deaths. But in the end, they'd escaped the clutches of their overbearing Nanil brethren. That same sense of hope and dread tingled in the pit of their stomach.

The wall screen started updating with telemetry and details from the probe's active scan. On a positive note, there wasn't any nebulosity leaking through their side, which meant they hit a pocket. When the visual scans flashed up, the pit in their stomach tightened.

"Is that what I think it is?" Minula stared wide-eyed at the wall screen.

"It appears to be a fleet of starships," Shauna began. "They're an unusual design. I can't find any reference to it in the Galactic Alliance archives."

The shape was a lot like an elongated boomerang, except only one side was longer than the other. Stranger still was the green fluidity sliding up and down the wings, like it was alive. It reminded them of the pond scum from back on Doda. Over the course of the summer, it would grow from a few centimeters to covering the entire pond near their home. Only after their progenitor concocted an antifungal agent, did it return to normal and their aquatic friends returned.

"Shit!" Minula's hands were frantically dancing over her controls. "I'm detecting two dozen inbound bogies, and they're moving fast. Their trajectories show they'll converge near the point in space where our probe would be if it passed through."

"Shut it down!" Shauna leaned toward Ibu, but they whacked the robot's hand away.

"Give it a few more seconds," Ibu said. "We need to gather as many details as we can about what's in there. I've redirected the active scan to sweep the inbound ships."

The seconds ticked by and Shauna's hand eased closer to Ibu. While she could disable the probe on her own without touching the controls, it was her way of warning the Nanil they were about to be overridden. As the data streamed in, more and more of the details from the system appeared on the wall screen. Like the stars they'd already visited, this one was practically barren. It was as if the Ursis had dismantled their worlds to build this armada of ships. There was zero regard for living a balanced existence within the star system.

As the first of the fighters circled around the hole in space-time, Ibu's attention was on the closest of the gigantic winged starships. It appeared to be morphing its hull. The gelatinous fluid covering the surface reformed before their eyes, taking the shape of a dozen or more tentacles. They reached out toward the probe just as the gate sealed shut.

Ibu shook their head. "What happened?"

"I had to close it." Minula's breathing was labored, and her hands were shaking. "It was... too much. They were getting too close. We can't afford to lose a gate drive."

While they felt like they had matters under control, they didn't say anything. The stress was already running high enough, and the last thing anyone needed was a fight.

"What do we do now?" Shauna asked. "We said we were going to move and try another spot if we were detected. Should I program the next few hops?"

The bridge fell into silence as the three of them stared at

the wall screen. The sea of alien starships went on as far as their eyes and sensors could see. While they might normally question the data, they'd seen it for themselves. There were tens of thousands of starships lining the insides of that Dark Nebula. Any one of them could end the Phoenix in a split second. Gating to the other side meant certain death. If Abigail had blindly jumped inside, then she was already a captive of the Ursis.

"Did we pick up any stray signals?" Minula asked. "You know, radio waves or anything else."

Ibu studied the logs. There was nothing but the ships on any of their sensors. It was as if the civilization had ceased to function on any social level and had transformed to building an arsenal of death rather than continue living.

"Negative." They brought up a broadcast spectrum heat map on the wall screen and Minula stood up, easing in for a closer look.

She reached out and moved her hand in front of her, rotating the data feed. A few seconds later, she overlaid the physical locations of each of the ships and slid the timeline forward and back. She then backed up to the zero point and inched time forward.

"That's it." Minula froze the feed.

Ibu leaned toward the wall screen and shook their head. They didn't see anything out of the ordinary. Except for the uniform ignition of the alien ship's drive plumes, everything looked normal.

"There's what?" they asked.

"Look." Minula rewound to the start of their recording and circled the Nebula wall behind where they'd opened the gate. Normally, they wouldn't see this angle because they entered most star systems in passive mode. But this time, they were running full active scans and eased a sensor array out and around the opening to get as close to a three hundred and sixty degree view of the system as possible.

Behind the probe was a ripple in the Dark Nebula. It was tiny, but it was there. In the grand scheme of the star system, the displacement was only a hundred meters tall, if that. The Ursis had noticed their arrival and were prepared to act. They knew what a gravitational force would do to the Nebula, and apparently they'd built systems to triangulate or sense any anomalies.

"That's insane." The knot in Ibu's stomach tightened. "If they can detect our gate opening, we're done before we start."

"Not necessarily." Shauna stood up and eased her way toward the wall screen, and Ibu followed suit. The three of them were standing side by side when she continued. "I see four options."

Minula chuckled. "That many? I only counted two. Whatcha got, mom?"

Shauna glanced sideways at the woman.

"Sorry." Minula lowered her head. "I was just busting your chops. It's not like you don't already know about Abigail and me."

The robot nodded and returned her attention forward. "Option one is we leave and try another entry point. The map shows at least two other direct pathways into this elongated pocket."

Ibu bobbed their head. "It wouldn't hurt to know all our options. Even if we only get scans from every angle."

"What else?" Minula tapped her foot.

"We jump into pocket five, six, or seven." Shauna circled all the neighboring systems to this one. According to the map, the pockets were more like the first two they'd jumped into. For all they knew, those also might contain life, too.

Minula shook her head. "If I were Abigail, I wouldn't have gone there. She knew where the home world was, and this was the closest point to get there."

Ibu cleared their throat. "But if we check out these other pockets, we can always jump across these innermost points."

They pointed at the far sides of pocket two and three. "Then we'll be even closer to their inner star system. Worst case, we find out these systems are already filled with Dark Nebula and we can't get through. No harm, no foul."

Shauna drew jump lines on the wall screen, tracing Ibu's idea out. "My thoughts exactly."

Minula crossed her arms. "What are the other two options?"

"Return home and regroup, possibly bringing back reinforcements and possibly not."

"Frak that." Minula turned to face Shauna. "There's no way in hell you'd leave your daughter in there. You don't—"

"Relax!" Shauna gestured down with her hand. "I didn't say I'd pick that option. I was simply ticking off the list."

"Fine. Strike that one off. We're not doing it." Minula nodded at the wall. "Hit me with four."

"We try jumping a few more times from different spots, but deeper into the system. I figure the further a probe gets, the less likely it'd be detected."

Ibu reached out and traced a circle around a region of space deep in the star system. "We have to assume that if they can detect gravitational distortions on the surface of the Dark Nebula, they can do the same thing for their star. Though I have to admit, the chaotic patterns of a burning star would be far harder to recognize. Either way, this is the only safeish jump point. Once you're there, you're stuck. Any further and they've got you. Any closer and the same happens. The only safe bet forward is option two."

Minula sighed. "I'm not leaving Abigail in there to die."

"We don't even know if she's in there." Ibu pointed at the map of the system. "Besides, there are thousands of ships. Do you honestly think we'd find her in that shit storm?"

Minula stared down at her hands for a second and shook her head.

"At least if we get a probe inside, we can gather more intel," Shauna said. "Maybe that'll lead us to her."

She had to be kidding. "What about when we need to broadcast out?" Ibu began. "Our calculations have to be spot on to make it in and out without a mistake. There's so much room for error in here. What are the masses of those ships? How many planets are left in the system? How big is the star? I could go on, but I just don't see a safe path."

"Who said it has to be safe?" Cynthia asked.

The three of them spun around to face the newly arrived member of the team. She was standing at the entrance to the bridge with her arms clasped behind her back.

"We finished going over the equipment and I overheard the argument when I was coming in." She adjusted her stance and leaned against the entryway. "I figured hanging back here might be safer than in the line of fire."

"What do you mean?" Ibu asked.

Cynthia smiled. "As in, I didn't want to be strangled by any of you. It's safer behind enemy lines."

Ibu shook their head. "No, what did you mean when you asked about why we have to be safe?"

"Oh, that. Yeah." She winked at the Nanil. "I meant you don't have to play anything safe. You simply have to make an end run."

They glanced at Minula and Shauna. Both were as dumbfounded by the woman's idea as they were.

"Obviously, you don't see it, so let me make it simple for you." Cynthia reached out and drew a pattern in the space in front of her, and the others spun around. They watched as point after point connected together, showing a probe hopping into the system, followed by a second, third, and a dozen more jumps. Each one was small and controlled, and each jump worked its way as rapidly through each star system as possible. She had the probe jumping to and through neighboring systems, as well, all the way past the central home world of the Ursis and out the other side of the Dark Nebula. In all, there had to be fifty jumps.

There were so many lines at one point, Ibu was pretty sure she was just messing with them. It was simple, really. They weren't sure why they hadn't seen it. In one end and out the other.

"The probe doesn't have to stop," Minula muttered. "It can keep gating over and over again. They'll never be able to catch up. It's a brilliant idea. How long will it take?"

"A few hours," Shauna said. "We'll have to load a custom expert system onboard. It has to riff a shit ton of jumps. And even then, I can't see it working out well without fine-tuning." She shook her head. "No, there's only one way this works."

Ibu eyed the robot. "You're not thinking what I think you're thinking, are you?"

Shauna pointed at the screen. "Do you see another way?"

They studied the paths through the pocket. The jumps weren't the problem; it was the number of variables. Expert systems were known to lock up when given too many variables to work with, and these stars were littered with them. She was right, there was only one way.

"What'd I miss?" Minula reached out and gently turned Ibu to face her. "What is she thinking?"

Ibu glanced sideways at Shauna. The robot was staring at the path drawn out on the wall screen. "She has to pilot the probe. It's the only option that increases the probability of success."

"No way!" Cynthia lunged toward them. "I thought we could simply program a route and shove a probe through. I never said we should send her. I... we can't put her life at risk like that."

"Risk! You're kidding me, right? What the frak do you think we're doing out here? Playing tea party?" Shauna stepped over to her controls and sat down. "If there's a chance in Hades I can help us find and save my daughter, then I'm gonna do it. Is that understood?"

No one challenged her decision. The finality of her statement stood on its own. Besides, Ibu saw the elegance in the solution. If it succeeded, it would give them everything they needed, and the only cost was the potential loss of an artificial life form.

27

ABIGAIL OLIVAW
PROTO DARK NEBULA, ON ARCTORDIEA

The animals rummaging around in the dirt reminded Abigail of sheep back on Earth. Their mane was more gray than white, but their billowing fur was immense and dwarfed their bodies by multiple times. It was like watching walking clouds roaming the field in front of the cave where she was hiding.

Haradis called them nibecula. He reassured her they were harmless and were simply foraging for food, but she couldn't help but be scared whenever they walked up to her in a pack. As a human who grew up in outer space, her time among wild animals was limited to summers on Earth with her family, and even those were controlled. She imagined Harold and the security that patrolled the perimeter of their land were always keeping them out of harm's way.

She tossed a few more hands full of the berries Haradis foraged on the ground in front of her, and the pack eased closer to her inside the mouth of the cave. The technique of melting into her surrounding was primitive, but if anyone used thermal scanners to find them, they'd have to pick out her heat signature from other animals. After she was comfortable they weren't leaving, she climbed back behind the boulder and leaned with her back against it, listening to the animals chomp away at the fruity delicacy.

Arctordiea was surprisingly garden like compared to Griseo. Haradis reassured her that not all parts were as lush as this, but many were. The planet had a network of underground caves, similar to the one she was hiding out in. As a species, his people started out living in these caverns, so it made sense that they dug deeper as their population grew. Like with humans, they razed their world for centuries until they learned their lessons through forced enlightenment and environmental catastrophes. This planet was only possible after nearly a thousand years of course correction.

The Ursis, however, didn't have the same opinion and regard for their colony worlds. It seemed his species was as short-sighted as humanity. Once they left their home world, they aggressively settled and expanded on every habitable planet they encountered, choosing more often than not to build cities above ground, where it was easier to spread out. Digging on the first few planets they found was cumbersome at best and changed their course of colonization for the worse. If you asked him, he'd tell you it was because they lost their identity with their clans and the terra firma that the gods of Therion created.

She saw it differently, though. Maybe it was her perspective watching humanity devolve, both in Lupus and now in Sol and the colonies. To her, the problem was clearer and far more dire. They hadn't merely lost touch with their clans, they'd lost respect for one another as people. Like with humans, they valued the act of expansion and the riches it gave the elites of the species. The same effects were mirrored in how diseases and confrontations were addressed. The less people listened to one another, the more fractured they became. Strangely enough, the land they inhabited echoed the fissures in society, but at least those would heal with time. Their problems were deeper and harder to cure. They needed to remedy the disease that tore them apart in the beginning.

While she didn't know what this meant for the Ursis, her purpose in the grand scheme of things had become clearer these past few days of being trapped inside the Dark Nebula. Maybe it had been Emmo jolting her with electricity and frying her synapses, or perhaps it was simply being alone to face her own mortality. How it happened didn't matter. What mattered was that she now knew what she needed to do. Once she returned to her tribe, she had to either help correct her family's mistake once and for all. That, or disappear forever along with everyone who wanted to join them. Their presence in the fray was causing more harm than good.

As her mind wandered through the many ways she could mend her family's missteps, she heard the nibecula scatter. Their regular mewing and shrill calls hit a crescendo, followed by hooves stomping into the distance. She flipped around and quietly lowered herself to the ground as she peered around the boulder. While she didn't see anything at first, she could hear feet approaching in the distance. These were louder than normal, almost like they were announcing their approach.

"It's me," Haradis called out. "I'm alone." He slowly stepped around the side of the cave entrance and squinted into the darkness.

She waited a few seconds to make sure the thumping of the feet stopped. Her retinal comm confirmed it'd only been him approaching. She sighed and stood up, brushing off her pants. "It's good to see you. I was starting to get worried. Did you learn anything in the city?"

He walked a few meters into the cave before he sat down on one of the smaller boulders. "I learned that the Tlingui clan has been busy destroying my clan's name. Most of what my father worked for has been extinguished."

Abigail stepped closer to the mouth of the cave and

reached into her pocket, pulling out another handful of fruit and tossing it. The nibecula that had been slinking up bolted forward and started gobbling up the morsels. This was the first time he'd mentioned his parents. Up to now, he'd only ever spoken of his clan as an entity.

"Who was your father?" She glanced over at him briefly before returning her attention to scanning the horizon.

"No one," he muttered. "I just... never imagined the Umbra name would disappear so quickly. It doesn't matter. We need to keep moving. There's a ground transport headed out of the city in a few hours. I managed to get passage on it in exchange for doing work on the other side. It should only be me onboard, as they're short on hands in these parts. You know, with the forces amassing in space."

She shook her head and chuckled. "How the hell do you expect me to travel with you? I'll stick out like a sore thumb."

He reached up and slid a white-gray fabric backpack off his shoulders. She hadn't even realized he was wearing one. The straps were so thin; they got lost in all his fur. It was a massive flimsy sack and easily covered his entire back from shoulders to buttocks. The outer surface was littered with random pockets and hooks, and there were a few visible slashes that looked like someone had stitched up with mismatched threads. The thing was so big you could haul a mule inside.

The idea was a slap in the face, and she took a step backward into the sunlight. "There's no way! You're kidding, right?"

"Have you got a better idea?" He unlatched the top and flipped it up, showing her the inside. There was a light blanket in there, and judging by the bright colors and flowers on the handle, what she assumed was a kid's flashlight.

Pangs of claustrophobia washed over her as the idea of being lugged around in a backpack sunk in. She'd never been afraid of confined spaces before, but then again, riding in what was essentially a coffin wasn't exactly her preferred mode of travel.

"How will we defend ourselves?" Harold asked over her retinal comm.

"Ahh, your gentleman friend is calling." Haradis bobbed his head.

She chuckled. "How did you know that?"

He pointed at her. "It's in your eyes. You glanced upward. Not every time you talk, just when you're not expecting him. I assume he's worried about you, yes?"

"Always," she muttered.

"Tis good to have someone watching out for you. Tell him not to worry. This everlight…" He reached down into the bag and pulled out the flashlight looking object. "It's used by our youth patrols to spot patterns in the darkness until they train their eyes." He held it up and showed her the small display on the back side. "We start teaching our warriors at a young age. Anyhow, there are a few flaps on the outside of this back-pack that reach all the way inside. I'm pretty sure you can use them to peer outward. Like this."

He reached in and grabbed the L shaped everlight and pressed a button on the top. A thin fiberoptic cable slid out of the bottom, which he fed through one of the inner pockets and out the other side. He rotated it around, showing her what he meant by peering out. While it was far from ideal, at least she wouldn't be blind inside.

"You can use the controls on the everlight to manipulate your side of the viewer. It can see for nearly three hundred and sixty degrees." He stared up at her, sensing her hesitation. "Do you have a better idea?"

She shook her head. "I wish I did. To be honest, I'm surprised we're not dead already." She pointed in the distance. "I still don't understand why we weren't stopped coming out of that prison. Hell, I wouldn't even call it a prison, given how poorly it was guarded."

"Ahh, yes, Emmonsii's Keep." Haradis reached down into the pack and retrieved a few small sacks before finally sitting down again. He then opened one of them and pulled out a wrap of some sort, handing one to her, and leaving one for himself. "Go on, it won't hurt you. It's only vegetables."

The smell wafted over her before he finished talking, and her stomach growled. She'd tried the fruit they were feeding the nibecula, but nearly hurled as soon as it touched her tongue. This, however, smelled wonderful. She reached out and grabbed it, taking a tentative bite and chewing it slowly. The moist vegetables melted in her mouth, and the texture of the wrap reminded her of a tortilla. It tasted like heaven.

"Thank you. It's... delicious," she mumbled, wiping her mouth with the back of her hand. She took another bite and a carrot like veggie burst in her mouth, overflowing onto her chin.

Haradis chuckled and reached out to wipe the liquid. "Those tublingers can be quite juicy. Here, take a muzzle cloth."

She licked what she could reach with her tongue and used the cloth to clean up the rest. "You were... saying something about a Keep."

He nodded and tore off a considerable chunk of his wrap, chewing it and swallowing it in nothing flat. "Apparently, Emmonsii has been at the center of dismantling my clan these past decades. She flipped public opinion after the Dark Nebula situation and managed to put in place a new government. I believe you call it a dic—tator—ship. Before that, my people had a representative monarchy. A far more elegant means to govern, if you ask me." As he stared off into the distance, he popped the rest of the wrap into his mouth and reached into the pack for another.

The nibecula must've gotten a whiff of the veggie wraps they were eating because they suddenly got less skittish and were working their way closer and closer, eyeing the sack as they went. She bent down and picked up a rock and tossed it at the ground between them, sending the gray puffy clouds scattering in all directions. "What does that have to do with the Keep?" She took a step backward and leaned against the boulder.

"Nothing, I suppose." He sighed. "I was simply high-lighting the extent of her power and influence. She rules with an iron fist over the populace. Her government's platform has been bloodthirsty revenge ever since the Nebula fell. Every male, female, and cub has been focused on building the fleet or trialing new technology to get past the Dark Nebula. I'm fairly certain that wasn't even her out there on that Alatas starship. She was probably remotely linked to another body. It's not uncommon for clan members to share their vessels with one another." He bit off a chunk of his second wrap, seeming to want to take this one at a slower pace.

The thought of giving someone else control of her body was off-putting. While Harold and other companion A.I. had the ability to tap into a human host's senses, they couldn't control them. There had been reports of A.I. going rogue and messing with people's retinal comms, but once removed, the implants were replaced, and the human recovered.

"The Keep belongs to her clan," he began, talking with his mouth full of food. "The town folks… they see it as a simple family dwelling for their leader, and when I asked them about any cave systems or dungeons, they were clueless. I didn't want to push the matter, but that might explain why we ran into so few guards on the way out. Any significant troop movements would draw attention. The farmer up the road did say she saw a small personal shuttle descend over the northern hills a few days ago." He pointed in the direction of the Keep. "I assume they were dropping us off, but being as we were both knocked out, it could've been anything, I suppose. For all we know, they brought us in by ground and landed at a military spaceport."

The hairs on the back of her neck stood on end. She didn't care so much about how they arrived. Leaving, though, now that was interesting. She needed to find a way off this rock. Maybe if they were in space, there'd be a chance Harold could help them rebuild a gate drive. Assuming there were any raw materials left in this blasted system.

As if on cue, a message from Harold appeared on her retinal comm.

Judging by your heart rate and physical reaction to the Ursis mentioning the spaceport, I have to warn you now, we're stuck here. Any and all designs for Zachary's gate drive were wiped when we were taken onboard their Alatas starship.

Her head spun, and her legs gave way. She slid down the rock, collapsing to the ground with a thump, and her wrap fell into the dirt. Two of the nearby nibecula bolted forward and started fighting over the remains.

His words repeated in her mind. Each syllable was like a jab to the heart. They were stuck, destined to die in this death shroud. Even though she knew the risks when she came here, she never imagined it would end like this.

"I sense you're in distress." Haradis eased down next to her on the ground, and the nibecula scattered. "What troubles you, Abigail? Are you fighting with your companion?"

She wiped at the tears welling in her eyes. "No. He just… helped me to see that we're stuck here forever. Doesn't that bother you? I'm sure you have someone out there you want to get back to." She pointed up at the sky.

He stared up at the two moonlets overhead. "I've been on my own for a long time. At first, I had some other adults and a handler, but a few decades after the Dark Nebula fell, we ran into a Thyreusian battleship and… let's just say they lost their lives saving me. I've been alone ever since." He glanced over at her and smiled. "Tis why it has been so good talking to you. Emmonsii wasn't exactly gregarious toward me."

Abigail chuckled and picked up a stone. "No, no she's not. She sure does love threatening the lives of family members, though." She turned the rock over and over in her hand. A glint of what she assumed was quartz caught the rays of the distant setting sun. Staring at the rock, it suddenly hit her that this was the first life-bearing planet she'd ever visited outside Earth. While she'd been on Griseo, it wasn't exactly teeming with life after the Ursis destroyed it.

"Emmo couldn't do that with me," he muttered. "Mine are all dead."

She glanced over at him. "I'm sorry." He was still gazing at the moonlets in the sky. They weren't much to look at, but she could tell his mind was elsewhere. Like the rock with her, the moons were probably a portal to another memory for him.

"I suppose we should get going before it gets dark." She pushed up off the ground and brushed the dirt off her pants.

Haradis did the same and sealed up the bag of food, activating some type of seal that seemed to reshape the original sack and gave it structure. When she leaned over and pressed on it, the casing was solid.

"That way, you don't crush it when you're inside." He bent down and pulled a few more small tchotchkes out of the pack, tucking them into a few of the random outside pockets. Once he was happy with what remained inside, he formed the pack into a circle on the ground and stood up straight. "Go on." He waved the back of his hand toward the pile. "Hop on in."

She swallowed hard and stared at the lump of cloth. "Hide out in an alien backpack for a few days, check," she muttered.

"What's that?" he asked.

"Nothing." She shook her head and stepped into the center of the open fabric. "I was just making light of the situation. I never saw myself becoming an alien sash when I got older. My father would be so proud."

"Don't worry." He reached down and eased the pack upward over her legs and waist. "I'll be careful." He paused at her shoulders and then retrieved a blanket before handing it in to her. "You can use this to adjust how you're laying, and in case you get cold. I hear the nights can get frigid in these parts, but I don't usually feel it. You know, fur and all."

She nodded and reached up to take the blanket. "Makes sense. At least I'll have some of your body heat." When she pulled it into the bag, she unwrapped it and let it fall lengthwise. It'd make it easier if she needed it.

"Ready to close?"

When she glanced up at his eyes, he was smiling. He'd been gently guiding the sack, making sure she was comfortable the entire time, including feeding her. There could be worse people to be stuck with on an alien world. "As ready as I'll ever be."

He took that as a yes and pulled the sack up and over her head, closing it at the top, a half meter above her. He was right; the bag was plenty big. A few seconds passed before her world shifted, and she was flung into the air and swung around several times. After he fiddled with the strap a few times, her side came down on what she assumed was his back.

"How does that feel?" he asked. His voice was muffled, but she could still make him out. If he got too quiet, she could probably get her retinal comm to amplify his voice.

"So far, so good." She shifted her weight around and got a bit more comfortable. Most of the pressure was on her hip and feet, which was fine for now. Later, she could reposition if she got sore.

When he started walking, the swinging of his arms was like a massage chair against her side. Each movement of his shoulder blades was like a masseuse working the knots in her torso and upper back. She could get used to this, especially the part where she was lying on a cloud of fur. It didn't take too long for her body to relax, and her eyelids grew heavy with sleep.

***

ABIGAIL'S WORLD SHOOK VIOLENTLY. She leaned forward with a start, only to be slammed backward by an unseen force. It took a second for her to remember where she was until she reached out and realized she was still lying in Haradis's backpack.

The shocking sounds of horns and voices colliding only a few meters away was jarring, and her translator was struggling to keep up. From the hum of machinery, conversations about the weather and crop yields, to what sounded like Haradis asking for directions, the noises were overpowering.

"It's nothing," Haradis said. "I think my personal gritar merely shifted in my pack. I'm sure it's fine. You were saying something about the fastest way to the transport hub."

He adjusted the backpack, and her world jostled again. This time she was ready for it, and made sure not to freak out. She reached up and tapped her ear twice, bringing up a nonverbal keyboard to interface with Harold.

"What did I miss?" she typed out.

Harold's face appeared on her retinal comm, and his voice was deafening. "Haradis has been rubbing elbows with the locals, trying to scrape whatever intel he can from the people. He's actually quite an affable alien for what it's worth. The Ursis seem to like him at least, even if they comment about his clan roots every chance they get. From the sounds of it, this town is heavily populated with Tlingui clan members."

Abigail drew in a breath. She wasn't used to him yelling at her. "You're so loud. Shouldn't we be using text? I mean, the Ursis, they have an uncanny sense of sound."

He smiled. "I'm not connecting via your normal implants in your ear canal. I'm tapped directly into your auditory nerve. It was the original means to link up retinal comms years ago, but patients found it too unnerving as we never unlocked the secrets to controlling the volume levels. Remind me when we get back to Sol to redirect some of the family's research budget toward those efforts."

She caught herself before she sighed. Home wasn't a place she could afford to imagine at this point, let alone think about. It wasn't like she could show her face in Sol any time soon, even if they could manage the impossible and escape from this alien prison world.

"I'm sorry I said that," Harold began. "It was an innocent mistake. I forgot where we were for a moment. How are you doing? Are you comfortable?"

"Yeah, I'm fine," she typed out. "I couldn't ask for much more, considering. Besides, I must've been plenty comfy to fall asleep. How long was I out for?"

"About six hours," Harold said. "Enough time for Haradis to meet about two dozen people and squeeze them for a mountain of details. I've captured it all in the logs in your comm. When you get a chance, take a look. Until then, it appears he's working his way toward the transport hub now. We're due there in a little over thirty minutes if we're gonna make the connection and job he negotiated."

He was cutting it close, but judging by the rocking motion of his body and the thump of his feet, he was walking with a purpose. She tweaked the virtual keyboard with her fingers and brought up the logs Harold mentioned.

She scrolled through Harold's notes. He was right, Haradis had been a busy alien. The Ursis had started connecting the dots, helping them see what had happened to his people since the Dark Nebula slammed shut.

The Ursis had made a violent and sudden shift into a dictator like society hell-bent on one and only one purpose, destruction of the Galactic Alliance. That much he'd shared earlier, what he'd found since then was mind-numbing.

The concentration camps full of his clan members, and the severe means by which Emmo ruled her party, drove a stake into the heart of their society. All the arts and music had been destroyed. They did everything they could to root out dissent and free thinking, cataloging it as an impossible dream until they raised the Nebula veil.

From the looks of his notes, he'd spent most of his time speaking with older Ursis, preferring to stay away from the younger ones. When she scrolled through encounters with the people more his age, she saw why. The conversations started and continued down paths of them questioning him and confronting his presence almost immediately. They viewed any outsider in their city as an affront and against the guide-lines of the government.

His last encounter had resulted in Haradis walking away and the female he'd been speaking to shouting for him to stay where he was. From the looks of the timestamp, that was only twenty minutes prior.

She swallowed hard, forcing down the concern, and returning to Harold's mountain of notes. After the first fifty years behind the Nebula, the government softened their posture. But rumors lingered with the farmers of an iron like grip on the outer worlds and in the fleet of warships Emmo had created in space.

From the sounds of the stories, they kept the people down here comfortable, so long as they continued to produce enough crops to feed the soldiers. When they missed their production goals, the results were usually swift and deep, striking first at the lowest yielding farms. From the rumors, they razed the fields to the ground along with anyone who worked on them, holding their poor performance up for all to see right alongside the gruesome pictures of the dead.

As Abigail was digging into how this much detail was extracted from one farmer, Haradis ground to a halt. The thump of his feet was replaced with shouting in the distance.

"I saw him! I saw him!" someone said. "He ran around that corner."

"This is not good, my friend," Haradis muttered. He was talking to her, but there was little she could do in the situation.

She tapped on his back.

"Not now. I need to climb... wait, a service tunnel."

He leapt forward, and she entered a free-fall state for a second until he hit the ground, and she bumped down against his tailbone. Her muscles tensed, and she winced, struggling to find a position that was less jarring on her body.

A loud crack shot out behind them, followed by a crash. The sound echoed through the street as shouts of warning sprang up around them, and she thought she heard a faint screech of a door in front of where they were standing. She couldn't tell what was going on at first, and then she realized she should've been using the device Haradis had given her to view out of the pack.

By the time she found a hole to peer through and had situated herself so she wouldn't drop it, they were surrounded in complete darkness and running full out. She tried flipping the everlight to infrared, but then she realized her folly. The Ursis had natural night vision. They'd never need to build that into a child's device like this.

"I can try adjusting your retinal comm to add contrast if you'd like," Harold said. His voice boomed again. She could see why this mode of communication had failed years ago.

"Please," she typed out.

Her vision changed instantly. It wasn't as detailed as an

infrared or thermal scan, but it was better than nothing. She could make out the shape of the cavern he was running down, as well as a few of the obstacles Haradis was dodging. From the looks of it, they were in a cave. She'd imagined something far more modern and industrial, but she hadn't seen the city yet to compare to. If this tunnel was any indication, they were still in the stone-age on Arctordiea.

With her eyes finally adapted to the infrared, it changed in a flash when her vision exploded in light. Yet again, Harold adjusted her retinal comm. Haradis had opened another door, and this one was quieter than the first. It didn't require a diversion. At least she hoped that explosion had been a diversion. The alternative sent chills up her spine.

As her companion exited the tunnel, she got her first look at the city. It was a far cry from the prehistoric cavern they'd just left, but at the same time it wasn't at all what she'd expected. They were running through what she could only describe as a scaled up snapshot from inside the Ceres or Pallas stations back in Sol. The tunnels here were immense, which made sense given how much larger Ursis were than humans. Plus, they were a species that started out in caves and evolved there, whereas humans had preferred wide open spaces.

When she aimed the device upward, she could just make out the ceiling. It was littered with pylons and electric gadgets, which appeared to be in various stages of disrepair. The buildings lining the street matched the same look and feel. They were a mixture of new and old, and when she glanced down the tunnel, every fifty or so meters there was a darkened area. It was like someone didn't bother replacing the lights when they burned out.

Building after building whizzed by as Haradis zigged in and out of different alleys, struggling to put distance between himself and the noise. She tried not to think about whether or not he was heading toward their exit. Instead, she focused her attention on the city itself. There weren't many Ursis out and about at this time of day. Or maybe it was night. She couldn't tell. For all she knew, they were out tending the fields.

It took a few minutes, but she realized something was missing. She had yet to see any youth at all. It was like a city without offspring. Everyone they were passing seemed older than Haradis, and many were using canes. Perhaps these aliens separated by age. She'd have to ask him if she ever got out of this blasted harness.

With her mind wandering and taking in the sights, she almost missed the commotion at the far end of the street behind them. While she couldn't hear what was being said, Harold brought up a translation on her retinal comm.

Yes, yes. There! Down that way. I saw him only moments ago.

"Tis not good," Haradis muttered as he picked up his pace. "We're running out of options here, my friend."

He turned down another street and weaved on the side-walk when he glanced over his shoulder, practically crashing into a street fixture in the process. Once he righted himself, he sprinted forward and entered one of the darkened sections she'd seen sprinkled throughout the dilapidated town.

Just as he was reaching a full out sprint, he ground to a halt, sending her crushing into his body. From the back side, she couldn't tell what he was seeing, and her heart was racing, expecting the worst.

"Should I get out?" she whispered.

"Keep quiet," Haradis mumbled. "You'll know if you're needed."

The knot in her stomach tightened. She couldn't help but imagine the mountain of an alien collapsing on the ground and crushing her, preventing her from escaping from the cloth coffin she was cocooned inside. As she angled the periscope fiber to the side, all she saw was the face of a darkened building. Its exterior facade was vandalized with some type of graffiti unique to this part of the city.

Haradis tiptoed forward, and she felt him reach out. The familiar clicking sound of a latch followed a second later. He stepped into a dark room and then closed the door behind him, sealing himself and her in.

Her heart was pounding even louder now. She was blind on all sides, and her protector had taken them into a confined space. Just as she was about to reach up and unlatch the bag, she heard a rapping sound coming from an internal door. She couldn't tell if he'd entered some type of business or a home. She found it hard to imagine he'd know anyone here, but maybe he'd seen someone elsewhere in the city.

A message from Harold appeared on her retina comm.

Prepare yourself in case it's a trap.

Prepare herself. He had to be kidding, right? She was tucked in the bag without a weapon to defend herself with. Why she hadn't grabbed a stone or something from the cave was beyond her. Survival planning clearly wasn't her strong suit. She reached down and felt below her, searching for something solid to grab onto, when the inner door creaked open.

"What do you want?" a voice asked. "Why are you..." There was a pause, followed by what sounded like footsteps moving backward. "It's not possible."

"Please, I need your help. I seek asylum in this house of Therion." Haradis leaned forward and kneeled down, sending a bolt of pain through her body and down her back.

The move was unexpected, and she was already contorted reaching downward. She fought to remain silent, but a wince escaped. It was the tiniest noise in a room of creaking. There was no way they heard it.

The sound of multiple feet clambered forward, followed by what sounded like hands rubbing through Haradis' fur. "This... this is impossible. Who are you? How do you have his markings?"

Haradis' back stiffened, and he seemed to tilt upward. "You know of my markings?"

She had no idea what they were talking about. His fur was as indistinguishable to her as any other. Sure, he had splotches in random places, but there was no way they could tell anything from that. Certainly, dyes and other body modifications could mask a marking.

"Know of them? Know of them?" They were growing louder. "I ought a—"

There was a rap on the outside door of the building, followed by a muffled voice. "Open up!"

The door must've been thick, because they were barely audible. What confused her was why they hadn't just opened the door like Haradis had.

"Get in here," the inside voice whispered. "Go... over there and duck behind that wall. If you so much as touch anything, I'll let them in to tear you to pieces."

Haradis eased up off the ground and tiptoed forward, working his way through the room. She wished she had kept her periscope trained on the outside, so she could see where they were, but it was too late. Haradis stopped and leaned down. He laid on his side and twisted his body so as to not squish her.

While she wanted to ask him where they were, she knew better than to speak now. She did, however, take the opportunity to stretch out and twist her back to relieve the pain from earlier.

The door clacked in the distance, and the inside voice shouted again. "What do you want?"

"We have reports of an escaped convict in the area. We're doing a search. Let me past!" The voice sounded angry and had a growl to their words.

"Don't stand there like a tree and lie to me, you dullard!" The door clicked closed, and the voice grew quieter.

They must have stepped outside, but she could still hear them talking. When she checked her comm, she noticed Harold had tweaked her hearing. "There is no one here but me and my elder clergy, and you know that. No one comes to this place any longer. Besides, we're in the time of focus, as I'm sure you already know. You have been repeating your chants, have you not, Grior?"

Abigail tilted her head. Somehow, this Ursis knew the person's name.

"I… have been busy, Deduc. You know my family doesn't believe." Grior went silent for a moment before continuing. "If you see or hear anything—"

"Then I shall holler at them, as well, for interrupting my moments of focus," Deduc said. "Now go, find this convict. And make sure you take some time for the upcoming Hufton Shilf."

Grior never replied, but there was a rustling of feet. A second later, the outer door clicked shut, followed by what sounded like a dead bolt sliding into place with a thunk. The same noises repeated with the inner door, except this time there were multiple bolts locking closed. No one was coming in that way without significant effort, but what concerned her more was that they weren't getting out, either.

28

———

IBU

PROTO DARK NEBULA, OUTSIDE
POCKET FOUR

After they loaded the probe with Shauna's data dot, and it passed through the gate, they moved Phoenix Two around the far side of the Dark Nebula and were now waiting at the agreed upon coordinates. Ibu's mind had been turning over the possibilities of what could be happening to her, including the A.I. cutting bait and taking off. While improbable, given her emotional attachment to her offspring, they wouldn't put it past them. They were a singular consciousness that couldn't clone, which meant the actions they could take to preserve their life flame were unpredictable.

Ibu knew not to bring up these tangential thoughts with the others, least of all any that had Shauna turning sides. Humans tended to have faith in one another, especially those bound by genetics, sex, and situation. The human saying that blood was thicker than water seemed apt at this moment.

When the tracking beacon flashed on the wall screen and then disappeared, they nearly tipped over out of their chair. They'd been staring at the point for hours, and its sudden appearance was almost like a mirage. It wasn't until the second strong pulse arrived a few minutes later that they knew it was real.

They tapped the ship wide comm button on their control panel. "Shauna has landed. I repeat, Shauna has landed."

It didn't take long for the sounds of thumping feet to rise in the distance and make their way toward the bridge. When Cynthia and Minula appeared, Ibu half figured Moet and the others would be in tow, as well, but they weren't. Perhaps the blood idiom was as strong as they'd read about.

"Is she… ok?" Minula hopped forward and slid into her seat.

"I haven't opened a comm," Ibu began. "I thought protocol was to wait for her to signal. That way, we don't give away our—"

A directional comm locked on their position and broadcast a small payload, less than a millisecond to be exact. When Ibu tapped their controls to decode the payload, a series of images appeared on the wall screen.

The first was an image of Abigail when she was a baby being held by her father. He was standing in front of a sea of stars. The image was taken from inside a starship of some kind, and she was swaddled in a blanket.

The second image was more of a collage. It represented the route Shauna had taken through the Dark Nebula. When Ibu zoomed in and panned around the massive image, their jaw fell open. The inside of the Nebula was overflowing with starships. There must've been millions of them in various stages of construction, and from the looks of it, some were even in disrepair. The further they moved from the external walls of the Dark Nebula, the older the ships appeared, though their numbers never waned.

"It's her." Cynthia walked up beside Ibu. "It has to be."

"We can't be sure yet," Minula said. "Let's follow the plan. Ibu, send the response."

This was the part they hadn't told Shauna they were going to do. Ibu had come up with the idea after the A.I. left, to help defend themselves in case whatever came back through tried to hurt them. They'd dropped a containment vessel at another location, and the transmission contained directions for Shauna to gate to new coordinates. Once there, she was instructed to eject her data dot out of the probe for an awaiting robot to pick her up and seal her inside one of Harold's skotádi lined consciousness vessels. Something they could safely connect to, but the occupants of the dot couldn't escape or signal out.

They tapped their controls and broadcast the reply just as the dance of the gate sequence passed over them. The timing of their transmission was purposeful. Like with the directions they beamed to Shauna, they'd rather not sit in one spot too long and risk being a target. The destination of their gate had already been tested, so they knew the exact point where they'd transit. Once through, Ibu cycled her commands, preparing for the final stage.

Once they transitioned, they waited. It could take Shauna a few minutes to follow the orders, especially if she was being cautious. All that was left for her to do after she transferred herself into the awaiting containment vessel was to pass the encrypted payload to the probe. It would take over from there and reach out to them once the task was complete. The payload was useless to Shauna without the decryption cipher embedded in the probe's hardware, and any attempt to tamper with it would wipe its memory. The technology was ancient, this use of it, however, was new.

After a few minutes passed, Ibu prepared for the worst and brought up their escape sequence. If there was so much as a hiccup from this point forward, they'd be making a half dozen randomized but safe hops away from this place. They never told the others about this contingency, but they didn't imagine they'd complain if it saved them. Besides the residual pain of the rapid transits, of course.

When the tight beam from the probe hailed them and the all green pattern appeared on the wall screen, the knot in their stomach released. They hadn't even realized they'd let their nerves get the better of them. Being around these humans too much was wearing off on them. It was as if their emotions were contagious.

"That's good, right?" Cynthia glanced over at them, her hand raised above her head.

Ibu nodded. "Yes, that's very good."

Cynthia reached out and wrapped her arms around the Nanil and squeezed, letting out a squeal of joy in the process.

They weren't sure what to do, so they reached around the woman and returned the emotion with a light squeeze. While the sensation was foreign, they had to admit it wasn't bad.

Minula didn't wait for anyone to tell her what to do. She simply started the next gate sequence and activated the probe extraction tool. Once the gate was open, the claws they used to launch and retrieve probes reached through the space-time gateway and pulled the awaiting probe into the belly of Phoenix Two.

Ibu and Cynthia had already ended their embrace and were halfway off the bridge heading toward engineering when the clang of the gates echoed a second time, signaling their closing. As they rounded the ring clockwise and turned toward engineering, they caught a glimpse of the galley out of the corner of their eye. The soldiers were sulking around the tables, jabber-jawing about gosh knows what. If Ibu wasn't up to their neck in planning to stay alive, they'd have it out with that poor excuse for a leader they called Moet. They never understood what Bradley saw in them.

Bursting across the threshold into engineering, they came to a screeching halt. The probe was tucked off to the side, and the mating connection was already waiting for them. It was the last step in the plan. The physical hard link to Shauna's containment unit. Once connected, their chances of being attacked skyrocketed. If the technology rumors of the Ursis were true, they of all species could do it. At the moment, they were safely ensconced in a protective skotádi shell, unable to influence anything.

Ibu stared at the device and froze. They couldn't will themselves forward, and they couldn't step backward, either. Limbo seemed the only fitting place.

"Are you ok?" Cynthia walked up beside them. "Is something wrong with the containment?"

"I... don't know," Ibu muttered. They hadn't been this conflicted in a long time. Not since they battled their inner demons on that ledge at Doda. They nearly left Zachary behind when they knew his people were on the way. The fear of the unknown, of the outside universe, had almost locked them up. Had it not been for his reassuring words, they could still be in that evil place.

"Should I connect it?" Cynthia stepped up to the probe and turned to face them.

"It could backfire," Ibu began. "What if the Ursis outsmarted us? What if Shauna isn't Shauna, and instead it's them? The Ursis were a technologically advanced species before they entered the Dark Nebula. Those ships of theirs showed they haven't been sitting on their thumbs all these years. We could be dead in a matter of seconds if we're overpowered. The number of ways this could end badly is stagg—"

Cynthia reached out and rested her hand on Ibu's shoulder. "We'll be fine. Seriously. Relax. Take a breath. Go on." She squeezed their shoulder.

They hadn't even recognized that they'd been holding their breath the entire time they were speaking until they gasped for air. As they took a few deep breaths, they realized how illogical their actions had been. And yet, their emotions had still overtaken them. Clearly, they didn't have as tight a grip on themselves as they imagined.

Cynthia spun around and grasped the connector, jamming

it into the probe without thinking. In under two seconds, she'd sealed their fate.

Ibu reached out. "How'd you… know it was safe?"

"I have faith." Cynthia turned to face them. "In you. There's not a chance in hell they'd guess you'd change the plan on the other side. And besides, Shauna wasn't inside the Nebula that long. She was only a few hours later than expected. Based on my quick estimate of the number of hops I saw on that collage of hers, she spent a hundred or more jumps scoping out their home world. I think it's called Arctordiea, right?"

They nodded and swallowed hard, feeling their face flush. "Yea. That's it." Now there was only one thing left to do. They tapped their ear and spoke out loud. "Shauna, can you hear us?"

The woman's voice responded instantly. "Every word. I was wondering what was taking so long to plug me in. Don't worry, my Nanil friend, I promise not to eat your face."

Ibu smirked.

"I don't mean to be the bearer of bad news, but we need to get moving," Shauna began. "From the intel I captured, there's a massive search going on down on Arctordiea. While they never mentioned anything about a human on the signals I intercepted, they're engrossed in a particular Ursis planet-side. It sounds like they escaped from some sort of prison. Dollars to donuts that Abigail's got something to do with that."

Ibu broke into a chuckle. The idioms of these humans were amusing on so many levels. They were nearly indecipherable at times, especially as someone from the outside looking in.

29

ABIGAIL OLIVAW

PROTO DARK NEBULA, ON ARCTORDIEA

"Come. Get up and follow me." Deduc motioned with his hand toward Haradis.

Abigail only knew this because after the second latch closed, she had to see her captors. She hadn't let go of the periscope tool and had it firmly in her grasp. When she slid the fiber out of the pocket, she nearly gasped.

The internal space of the building they were in was astonishing. She assumed it was an optical illusion. If the room was as towering as it seemed at first glance, the noises from the doors and footsteps would be far different. Beyond that apparent spacial anomaly, the chamber was radiant, brighter than any of the structures she'd seen since passing into the Dark Nebula.

Ornate filigrees depicting nature scenes were etched along the perimeter, and they led up into the distant sky, which, judging by the top, was open to the outside world. Or at least it was enclosed with a glass structure that let them see the sky and clouds. The entire scene was spectacular to behold. She could lie there for hours and not take in all the details.

It's truly remarkable craftsmanship.

The message from Harold appeared on her retinal comm. He must have been resorting to visuals again as a precaution. That, or because he saw how jarring it was on her vitals. Either way, it made sense in a place as reverent as this.

When Haradis pushed up off the ground, he paused midway up and muttered something under his breath. Harold didn't translate it, nor did her comm. She assumed it was some form of religious ceremony. Whatever it was, it wasn't the traditional Ursis language.

Deduc stomped forward and shoved at Haradis before he stood upright. "Where did you learn that? Tell me now, or I will turn you over to the soldiers hunting you."

"I…" Haradis went to push up, but it seemed like Deduc was holding him down. Abigail couldn't tell for sure.

"You will let me up!" Haradis' voice was firm and commanding.

"Not until you tell me—"

Haradis arched his back and swung his arm upward, ripping the alien's hands from whatever hold he had on him. With Deduc wincing in pain, Haradis used the opening to lunge forward. While she couldn't see what he was doing, Deduc inhaled, and his feet rustled backward across the floor. When he slammed the priest against the nearby wall, they groaned.

"Please don't make me hurt you," Haradis began. "My father, rest his soul… he would kill me if he knew I even touched a see-er without consent. It pains me to do so, and yet, you left me no choice."

His muscles relaxed. She assumed he released his hold on the elder Ursis because he also stepped backward. She half expected Deduc to lash out at him. It's certainly what Emmo would've done. The shrew had turned off the charm with the flick of a switch onboard the Alatas ship. After that, it was nothing but torture session after torture session.

As she panned around the space, she struggled to catch a glimpse of the other Ursis. It was taking all she could not to ask Haradis to let her out. She hated hiding like this, having him put himself in harm's way without her being able to help. Not that she'd do much against these mountainous hulks.

"Very well," Deduc began. "I will not harm you, nor will my clergy."

With those words spoken aloud, the sound of nearby feet caused her to spin her view around. Four other Ursis appeared out of hidden recesses near the walls. Maybe they were confessionals or meditation rooms used in ceremonies. It didn't matter, though. Either way, they were surrounded. If she could see four, that meant there were at least a few more in front of him.

"Well, this isn't fair," Haradis muttered.

"Were you planning on fighting your way out?" Deduc asked.

"Not at all." Haradis shifted his weight and adjusted his bag, centering it more on his back. "But you have to admit, the situation just went from friend to foe in the flash of an anterac's iris."

"That saying." Deduc stepped sideways and jabbed his finger at Haradis. His shoulder came into view along with another Ursis who looked much younger, and judging by the bulging muscles, far stronger, too. "Where did you hear that?"

The see-er's fur was jet black and was almost an inversion of Haradis' coat. The other Ursis' coats were similarly black, which was unlike many of the Ursis they'd encountered throughout the city and in the nearby farmland. She remembered seeing an observation about this from Harold's notes earlier.

Most of the Ursis near this town had coats that were varying shades of brown, and a few had hints of white inter-mixed. But those were often the elderly, so it was hard to tell if they were graying coats, or perhaps they'd mixed with the Umbra clan.

Haradis growled as he spun around the room, taking in the view from all sides. This gave her a frightening assess-ment of their defensive situation. There were seven clergy in all, and when you added Deduc to the mix, they were outnumbered eight to one. She wasn't even counting herself at this point, given her useless position. What she couldn't understand, however, was why Haradis didn't simply answer the questions about himself. Maybe she'd backed the wrong horse in this race, not that she had a lot of choice in the matter.

"I asked you a question." Deduc stomped his foot, and it boomed through the chamber, sending birds in the rafters above scattering about and flying upward. The clergy surrounding them took several steps forward, and a few even pulled out blades they were concealing under their simple cloth garments.

The last thing she wanted to feel was the cold hard sting of a blade slicing her in half as this fool got them into a knife fight. She cupped her fist and smacked it flat onto his back, doing her best not to hurt him. She was merely trying to get his attention.

He growled again, except instead of spurring him into action, her goal backfired. She'd pushed him too far. Her body lifted into the air and then entered free-fall as Haradis shrugged off the bag with her still inside. For a brief second, the world floated around her like she was in zero-g until the harsh reality of gravity crashed into place.

She was ill prepared for a drop from that height and came

down hard on her left elbow, followed by her head and the rest of her body. Thankfully, her skull cracked into her arm instead of the solid stone floor.

While stars flashed in her field of view, hitting her head against rock would've been far worse. In the commotion of the fall and the struggle to catch her breath, she hadn't realized she'd let out several screams. The first when she was thrown, and the second when she crashed down. As she groaned and rolled around on the ground, she reached up and fought to break herself loose from the blasted bag restricting her.

Just as she touched the opening at the top, she tumbled to one side when someone snatched the bag with her inside and yanked it away, dragging it across the stone tile. When she and the bag stopped sliding, multiple hands grabbed at her from all sides. Giant forceful hands.

"Let her go!" Haradis snarled. He must've dove into the clergy with the bag because they tumbled hard to the ground only centimeters next to her. The sound of snapping teeth and fists pummeling into solid muscle reminded her these aliens were playing for keeps.

With one pair of hands holding her feet, a second was feeling around for her face near the top of the bag. She squirmed back and forth, struggling to dodge her captor's grip until the Ursis managed to place a hand over her mouth. So, she did the only thing she could think of. She bit down with everything she had.

A yelp of pain echoed through the chamber, followed by the hand pulling back and releasing her head. Not wanting to waste another second, she reached up one last time and shoved her hands through the opening, freeing it into the open air. She drove her arms down to her side, plunging her torso into the light and the cool dry air. Being cooped up inside the bag had left her hotter than she realized.

Her eyes struggled to adjust to the bright room, but she

knew she couldn't sit still. She hopped up to her feet and whirled around, taking in the expansive space. They'd pulled her to a nearby wall, and her back was facing it. When she spun back around to look her captors in the eyes, she smirked at the stunned expressions staring back at her. The last thing these Ursis were expecting to find was a human inside, and the last thing she was expecting to see was her friend pinned down with two blades resting against his throat.

"Impossible!" Deduc reached over and yanked Haradis's head to the side, nearly slitting his throat against the knives. "Who are you? How did you create this… automation?"

She laughed at the notion, and the Ursis jumped. "I'm not a robot, you mountainous idiot. I'm a fraking human. Now, let my friend go before I kill you." She leaned forward and did her best to make herself intimidating. Her left elbow was in excruciating pain, and her vision was clouded with splotches, but was coming around.

Harold chimed in on her retinal comm. "Are you seriously doing this?" His voice was blaring, but it actually helped her focus. Besides, maybe they'd think she was crazy enough to pull this off if him screaming at her gave her a visual tick.

"Got any other options?" she subvocalized, clapping her fist into her left hand and regretting it the instant she did.

"None come to mind, but I might not need any if this goes the way it looks."

His words were far from reassuring, but in the moment, her decision was forced. The only thing any of these aliens seemed to respond to was aggression, be it on the Galactic Alliance tribunal ships, or here. The alternative was her giving up, and she wasn't about to do that.

When the clergy to her right eased closer, Deduc raised his arm outward. "Whatever you do, don't hurt her."

She didn't know what that meant, but when she glanced at the see-er, his eyes were still wide with fear and his hand was shaking. For some reason, he looked like he'd seen a ghost. Perhaps she could work with that.

The clergy slid forward, and her focus returned toward them. From their reduced height and the size of their ears, they were a female Ursis. Either way, they moved quick, and were already within striking distance. Abigail couldn't decide what to do, but the alien made the first move.

As the clergy motioned to swing at her, she could tell it was a bluff given her footing. With Abigail's height being an advantage, she easily dodged the half-hearted swipe and dove to the Ursis's left, slipping behind them before they even realized what had happened.

Judging by the response of this particular clergy, they weren't exactly prepared for hand-to-hand combat. Rather than turn around, they peered down between their legs where she'd disappeared, but they were too late.

Based on her knowledge of bears, there was only one way to best a female besides running, and she didn't pause to second guess her instincts. She stepped back between the Ursis' legs and kicked out with her foot with as much force as she could muster. She punted the clergy across the muzzle. For a second, she thought her assumption about the alien's anatomy had failed. That was until she arched her back upward and let out a blood-curdling screech as her body toppled to the ground with a crash.

For once, she'd drawn an ace. She could've had to face one of the clergy armed with blades. Wasting no time, Abigail climbed over her back until she got near her head. She then reached into her pocket and pulled out the everlight and yanked on the fibrous cord, almost breaking it out of the device. Once fully extended, she flung it around the Ursis's neck and tugged with everything she had.

She didn't know if the fiber would snap, but the effect of her yanking it up and against the Ursis's throat was nearly instant. Not only did the cord hold, the massive bear started thrashing like a wild bull. She managed to get a loose hold by wrapping her legs under their armpits, but they were gyrating in place trying to toss her. So much so, she was worried less about being thrown and more about being crushed. Once the alien got their wits about themselves, it was only a matter of them rolling over, and she was toast.

"Let them go!" Deduc stepped closer to her with both hands outstretched, to prove they were empty. "We won't hurt you."

"Are you fraking serious? Do you take me for an idiot? Let my friend go and maybe we'll talk. Otherwise…" She glanced down at the Ursis under her. Their eyes were rolling back in her head, and even though they got a fingertip under the cord, it wasn't cutting. "Otherwise, your friend here won't be long for this world."

Deduc glared from Haradis to the clergy members. "Let him go."

"What?" the two clergy asked in unison. They were both flanking Haradis and holding daggers. One to his throat and the other against his side in case he moved.

"You heard me!" Deduc's hands were shaking as he walked over to her friend and pulled away the hand of each clergy member. While they didn't refuse his order, they also didn't seem willing to release their weapons.

Something had riled up the see-er, and it wasn't just the presence of her. She watched as Haradis slowly stood and took a few tentative steps toward her, half expecting the other Ursis to attack at any moment.

"Thank you," he muttered when he reached her side.

"No problem." She relaxed her grip on the cable, freeing the Ursis beneath her to breathe, but she didn't let go. The female was their only bargaining chip. "Remind me to have a chat later about you tossing me in that bag."

"Yea, sorry about that." He turned and stared at her, studying her body. She assumed to see if she was wounded.

"I lost my temper. It will never happen again. You have my word." He returned his focus on their attackers. "Now what do we do?"

She narrowed her gaze on Deduc. The alien appeared to be whispering to the others, but nothing they were saying was being translated. They appeared to be using some form of comm device like humans used. What was strange was how they were reacting. As the see-er gestured with his hands and pointed at them, each of the Ursis froze. A few of them even started shaking like Deduc had been.

She leaned her head to the side toward Haradis and lowered her voice. "Any idea what's going on?"

"They appear to be recognizing something about one or both of you," Harold said over her retinal comm. "I just can't tell which. But based on their repeated gestures, I'd say our Ursis friend is their primary person of interest."

At first, she wasn't sure why Harold had used her regular retinal comm channel until she caught Haradis nodding. He was taking advantage of the close proximity of the Ursis and their superhuman hearing. When the clergy she was standing over squinted and glanced up, she tightened the cord, and the female returned her attention forward.

"But, why me?" Haradis asked.

The see-er had become agitated the moment they saw him. From there, things just escalated deeper and deeper, but one question remained unanswered.

"Tell them." She glanced over at him.

He squinted at her. "Tell them what?"

She cleared her throat to get their attention, and when she caught Deduc looking at them, she repeated herself. "Tell them who you are."

Haradis took a step backward, clearly caught off guard. It was a gamble putting him on the spot like that, especially after his reaction when Deduc pushed him on the matter. But it was the only thing that made sense. They believed he was someone important, and given their situation, they were better off knowing one way or the other. Knowing would be easier than the stalemate they were in right now. At least then, she'd know whether or not she needed to kill this Ursis.

Just as she was about to ask him again, he stepped forward and straightened his back, raising his height even taller than before. She hadn't realized how much he was slouching to talk to her, but once he was upright, she had to crane her neck to look at him.

"I am Haradis Hugrah Umbra, son of Maritimus the tenth and Emerald Arctos of the Hitun. I was taken from Arctordiea and snuck outside the Dark Nebula before the veils fell, and I've spent my entire life trying to find a way inside. That was until I met my friend." He gestured to his right. "Abigail Olivaw."

She swallowed hard, not expecting her name to be mentioned, let alone the details of his. It was only beginning to click in her mind when she recoiled and drew in a breath at the scene unfolding in front of her.

One by one, starting with Deduc, each Ursis dropped to their knees and bowed their head to the ground, touching it to the stone. They held it in place and started mumbling. Her translator wasn't working for some reason. It sounded like the Ursis language, but there was an obvious difference in the dialect they were speaking.

"What are they saying?" she whispered.

"I'm... not sure if I understand." Haradis glanced at her. "They're welcoming me back as their king."

Abigail tilted her head. She hadn't realized she'd been traveling with royalty. "That's great, right? I mean, I hope they don't want to kill us any longer."

He chuckled and shook his head.

"So..." she stared at the clergy and the see-er, each still pressing their forehead to the ground. "What's the problem then?"

"It's you."

"Me?" She swallowed hard. "What did I do?"

"They are calling you the Seguan, or the savior of the people." His left eye widened. "They claim your return had been foreseen by the see-er himself."

——

30

IBU

PROTO DARK NEBULA, OUTSIDE
POCKET FOUR

They watched as the asteroid slid into place. It had taken them the better part of the day to find a rock big enough to mask their jump and close enough to the Dark Nebula not to spend weeks moving it. From the data they'd reviewed, Abigail might not last that long.

As Phoenix Two retracted its makeshift towline, Ibu deployed the test probe Shauna had used to jump through the Nebula. They weren't about to risk opening another gate to a field of stars, and they wanted to test this approach with a probe before they used it themselves. Whatever technology the Ursis had, they'd been able to detect nearly every jump Shauna made, so long as it had a visible object in the background. It was remarkable when they thought about it, but dwelling on the alien tech was a waste of time. They had to get inside and save their friend.

"The gate array is ready, and I already programmed the first series of jumps in the probe," Ibu said.

"Commencing relocation of the Phoenix," Minula said as the gate vanes clanged into place.

The familiar wall of blue light eased over them, soothing the quake in their hand as it passed. They didn't mind the transitions as much as humans. Perhaps it was their pain tolerances being higher, or maybe it was how calming it felt on most jumps. The faster ones, however, even they hated those.

"Gate sequence complete," Minula said. "We're half a light day from the probe. Is everyone prepared to run the test?" She glanced around the bridge.

Ibu nodded. "I'm ready. I'll issue the go command the moment the transmission gate opens."

Cynthia tapped at her controls for a second until she stopped and glanced up. "Comms is ready. We'll be running a passive scan during the experiment, hoping for some stray signals to come our way."

Shauna spoke last. Her robotic form was seated beside Cynthia. "Weapons are ready, not that they'll be needed, but you never know."

"Alright then." Minula turned back to her controls. "Here goes nothing." She reached forward and cracked open a hole in space-time using the Phoenix's gate drive.

This gate didn't come with the usual clang and jump. In fact, it was only a few millimeters wide. Enough space to broadcast a signal and give them a chance to send some specially built tools through if they needed to capture a small sample or connect to something.

Ibu issued the go command and then watched and waited as the test probe started its gate sequence. The test required them to open the gate and hold it open while real time data was captured from the probe. They'd already scanned every centimeter of the asteroid behind it, and compensated their jump to take into account the mass and shape of the giant rock. Its purpose was to act as a shielded backdrop to the section of space they were jumping from. If Shauna were right, they'd be undetectable on the other side.

The wall screen lit up as the signals from inside the Nebula relayed through the probe. So far, there had been no visible reaction from the Ursis Alatas ships, nor the Nebula itself. The gravitational impact was deep enough in the star system to be indistinguishable from background noise. Since they knew where most of the mass was situated, it was easy to calculate their initial jump.

"This is weird," Cynthia squinted at her controls. "I'm picking up chatter inside the Nebula between the Alatas ships. They're broadcasting on open channels. I don't think Shauna saw this while she was in there."

"What are they saying?" Minula asked.

They were all thinking it, but she was the first to say it aloud.

Cynthia shook her head. "As far as I can tell, most of it is raw data. But the few translatable bits of spoken language seem to be discussing an updated communication protocol, and how to reconfigure and adjust their ships to apply some new software."

"They're compensating for my sprint through their star systems." Shauna paused, staring into nothingness. "If I'm reading these data streams right… they think they have a way to detect the gate drive."

The knot in Ibu's first stomach tightened. It subsided after the gate transition and the successful opening of the test gate, but now the pressure had returned in force. "Will it work? Will they be able to detect us?"

Cynthia and Minula both spun around to face Shauna. They knew this was a make or break point for their plan. A wrong answer and it would shove them back to the starting point.

Ibu cracked open the data feed and closed their eyes to connect into it. While they trusted the A.I. for the most part, putting their life exclusively in their hands was not in the cards, as their human friends often said.

When they entered Shauna's virtual workspace, they paused to take everything in. The woman was categorizing and splitting up the data payloads they'd captured into different buckets. One pile for sensor changes, a second for what appeared to be instructions to the ships to turn on and off their engines. And a final pile held commands meant to adjust how their ships communicated with one another. If they were reading this right, they were causing purposeful chatter.

That could mean only one thing.

"They're creating background noise to detect us, aren't they?"

Shauna's virtual avatar jumped forward, and they spun around. "Wholly shit! You about gave me a heart attack. I didn't even feel you arrive."

"Sorry." Ibu reached out and touched the woman's shoulder. While it was a human gesture in a virtual world, small minutia helped humans manage their feelings.

"It's ok." She stood up straight and turned back toward the closest pile of changes she was sifting through.

Ibu watched as she tried to sift through the fragments, struggling to find a way past this new challenge. "This is bad, isn't it?"

"It's certainly not a sunrise on a beautiful morning… but I think we can manage."

"What does that mean?"

Shauna reached out and dropped a point in the middle of the star system. An icon representing the Phoenix appeared there. She then drew a few lines radiating out from each of the starships, directed toward and near their ship.

"The moment we open a gate, these signals will scatter around the space in the vicinity of where we're jumping. In most situations, it wouldn't matter, but in this confined of a space, our clock will be ticking." She drew a circle elsewhere in the system and continued the line out of the gate toward a nearby Ursis ship.

"Fortunately for us, physics still works inside the Nebula." Shauna highlighted the distance from the gate to the neighboring ship. "Once their signals continue on their path through our gate, we'll have anywhere from minutes to hours to gate again before they'll detect the stray signal and converge on our location."

Ibu studied the virtual wall screen, their mind dancing over the countless variables. While they could keep moving inside the Nebula, it was only a matter of time before they were discovered. The most important gate would be their first. Every subsequent jump brought with it more and more risks. That meant the closer they could get to Alviarium in the least number of hops, the better off they'd be.

They reached forward and drew a line from outside the Nebula to deep within the systems. "How long until we can calculate this jump?"

Shauna froze, seeming to enter a trance. "It's... an impossible jump. There are too many variables." She tapped the gravity wells in their way, along with the Nebula tunnels in between. In all, they'd need to jump through three systems.

While she wasn't wrong, Ibu knew it wasn't impossible, just impractical. "How long until the Ursis software updates are in place?"

"We have to assume it's already spread to the rest of the Nebula if we're picking it up on this side. We're roughly equidistant from the far side."

The more they stared at the wall, the more the concern in the pit of their stomach tightened. What they needed was a way to block the signals from passing through the gate. If their ship were a different shape, it might be possible, but as it were, the signals would make it through the gap when it reached the apex of the transition over their hull.

"Why don't we reform the skotádi skin covering our hull as we go and use it to create a shield?" Cynthia's voice boomed through the virtual space.

Ibu ducked their head down and glanced skyward. Her

voice was ominous, coming out of nowhere. They'd forgotten about the others on the bridge. Shauna must have been sharing their conversation on the wall screen. While time in this virtual space was faster than the real world, they'd been staring at the data for quite a while.

Shauna brought up a schematic of Phoenix Two and started making some adjustments to their hull. She pulled the few scraps of skotádi they had in the hold and reformed the bulbous end of the teardrop shape to create a set of strange-looking wings that could be expanded and collapsed. The resulting hull looked far too intricate to construct on the fly.

"It'd take three to four days to build it," Shauna said. "And even then, I'd have to operate it manually. We simply don't have the materials onboard to fabricate this structure. We'd be better off returning to Phoenix One and seeing what we can pilfer from the wreckage."

"There's not a chance in hell we're going back there," Minula said.

While Ibu agreed, that gave them an idea. They reached forward and dismissed Shauna's design work, returning the map of the system to the forefront. They drew four hops deep into the heart of the Nebula.

"We already decided we can't do that," Cynthia said. "We'd be detected after—"

Ibu waved their hand and muted the other voices. They needed silence to think, and human chatter was grating. At each hop on the wall screen, Ibu drew two lines branching off from their gate transition point. They flicked their fingers against the lines, sending them bouncing around the system, never returning to the same point. A few even jumped back and forth down the Nebula tunnels between the stars.

"It could work," Shauna muttered. "But—"

Ibu held up a finger. They weren't done. They needed more chaos. The harder it was for the Ursis to find them, the better. And then it hit them like a burst of adrenaline. Leveraging the transmissions was their best bet. While the Ursis might figure it out eventually, they could replay any signals they recorded along the way after each jump. Between the real signals and the cloned ones, the Ursis would have a mountain of variables to decipher.

"Like you said." Ibu reached out and hit go on the final plan and watched the chaos play out. "Physics is on our side. There's not a chance in hell they can coordinate all their ships at those distances. The probes can jump far faster than the Ursis can react. About the only risk we have is losing a probe, but our countermeasures will destroy the drive in time to prevent them from capturing it. What do you think?"

Shauna nodded as she watched the simulation play out. "I love it! While it's not stealthy, it serves the same purpose. We're going to need to assume they'll be on high alert as soon as we light up their sensors."

The knot in Ibu's stomach loosened a bit. "Something tells me Abigail already has them on their toes." They opened their eyes and took a sudden deep breath, taking in the reality of the bridge. The shock of the transition was always like a splash of cold water to the face.

Cynthia spun around to face them. "You're back."

Minula was studying Ibu's plan already playing out on the wall screen. "This is it," she muttered.

"We've got work to do." Ibu stood up and made their way aft toward the cargo hold, and Cynthia followed. They needed to run some diagnostics on the remaining six probes they had. Using all of them for this mission meant they'd have fewer options at their disposal if the need arose. But given the situation of their friend, they were doing their damnedest to ignore that fact.

31

ABIGAIL OLIVAW

PROTO DARK NEBULA, ON ARCTORDIEA

Abigail stared at Deduc. The see-er's black fur glistened and seemed to move the longer she studied it. While she knew it wasn't alive, that didn't prevent her mind from playing tricks on her. The movement was simply a change in the overhead lighting. The sun was setting far above, and the room they were standing in was reacting to the celestial motion.

When she knelt down next to him, he flinched. Up close, his fur was miraculous, and she had to stop herself from touching it. It looked so soft, and the sheen was heavenly. "I've never seen you before in my life, so why are you calling me a savior?"

Deduc paused his chanting and turned his head to the side. "It is I who saw you. It was just over fifty years ago." He leaned sideways and adjusted to sit cross-legged.

She mirrored his motion. As she crossed her legs, a pain shot through her back and she winced. The fall had really done a number on her.

He reached out and froze when Haradis snarled and stepped up beside her. "I will not hurt the Seguan. Now that the truth has been revealed, I am ashamed of my actions and ask for your forgiveness." He bowed forward again, resting his head on the ground a few centimeters away.

That was a first. Usually aliens lunged at her or spoke to her like she was trash. She glanced up at Haradis and shrugged, not knowing what to do.

He raised his hand out in front of himself and lowered it down, tapping from side to side. He was miming what she needed to do.

She turned to face Deduc and repeated the gesture. First, she gently touched his right shoulder and then his left. "Your actions are forgiven."

"Thank you, Seguan." He sat up, staring at her side the entire time. "Are you ok? You seem to be in pain."

Her back throbbed on cue. "I'm a little sore from the fall, but otherwise I'm fine. Just happy to be alive. Oh yeah, my name is Abigail… Abigail Olivaw."

Deduc nodded. "I know."

She tilted her head. "You know… what?"

"I saw you in my vision half a century ago. It was at the sealing of the Dark Nebula. While my connection to the Beacon had been severed abruptly, the gods of Therion blessed me with a glimpse of our future."

He reached out and held his palm open. A second later, a hologram flashed above it.

Abigail drew in a breath and leaned back, bringing her hand to her mouth. Floating in front of her was a hologram depicting a human woman climbing a cliff. She watched as the woman struggled to pull herself up and then slid down and collapsed into a limp pile on the cliff's edge below. The hairs on her neck stood on end, and she fought to find her words. She knew this moment all too well because she'd lived it on repeat when she was imprisoned in her coma. What she didn't understand was how this Ursis had seen it.

"I didn't know what it meant until I saw what you did next." Deduc waved his other hand in the air and the hologram sped forward, through a few more failed attempts at summiting the hill, at which point she slid downward, toward the bottom.

She clambered to her feet and took a step backward as she watched herself mimic the gesture and stumble against the cliff face in the hologram. Her mirrored self was scared shitless, and for good reason. In the hologram, she turned around and scrambled to climb upward again, as the floor of the valley was rising. The scene looked like something out of an earthquake vid-sim.

When the ground stopped its ascent, the hologram panned away, and the valley came into focus. The image of herself hopped down onto the smooth surface below and walked up to the side of a spaceship. One she'd seen countless times. While it was far smaller than the Phoenix, its design was the same.

"Impossible!" Harold said in her ear.

"I see your friend is awake," Haradis muttered.

Deduc squinted. "Her friend?"

Abigail waved her hand. "It's nothing." She stepped toward the hologram and knelt down closer to it. "I don't understand. How did you see this?" She glanced up and stared into the see-er's eyes.

"The Beacon allowed me to observe you. It knew we would need your strength to persevere through the darkness, like you persevered through the climb. It foretold of your arrival, along with your fleet of ships." Deduc and the clergy muttered the phrase again, except this time in unison.

"Seguan venit tenebras purgare." The voices sounded surreal when singing together.

"What are they saying?" Harold asked.

"The savior has arrived to clear the darkness." Haradis was staring at the hologram just as intently as Deduc and his clergy.

She could tell from the expression on his face that he saw

what she'd seen. Those teardrop ships were smaller forms of the one he'd piggybacked through the Dark Nebula on. The more she stared at the hologram, the more she doubted its origin. There was only one explanation. She opened a retinal comm keyboard and typed a message to Harold.

Tell me this is fake. Tell me that Emmo got into my mind somehow. It's the only logical interpretation.

His response was instantaneous.

You were never compromised. I promise you. Either me or the nanites in your body would have detected it. There are countless fail-safes in my data dot that not even the Ursis could've hacked around. There's only one explanation for this hologram, and you know it.

Abigail shook her head. She refused to believe an ancient artifact like the Beacon of Therion could pull the memory out of an individual's mind from the future, let alone replay it for an alien in the past. Not even Occam's razor would see this as the simplest option.

She lurched forward and nearly jumped into Deduc's lap, coming to a stop centimeters from his face. "Bullshit! You're working with Emmonsii Phi. She put you up to this, didn't she?" She batted his hand down and the hologram disappeared.

Deduc didn't budge. He merely stared back into her eyes. "I know it's hard to accept being something you feel you're not." He glanced at Haradis and their gaze locked. "Both of you need to understand your place in history and bring us out of the darkness."

This bear didn't know anything about her, least of all her place in the universe. Hell, she didn't know that herself. She wanted to shout back at him that there was no fleet of ships waiting to swoop in and save the day. They were alone in the Dark Nebula, and not even her own people knew where she was. But she thought better of it. Giving away their hand would put Haradis and her life at risk. For now, she'd play along until she could figure out their next steps.

Deduc pushed up off the ground, making sure never to touch her. "Come. We must begin our voyage, before it's too late."

When she glanced back at Haradis, he was shaking his head.

"What voyage?" he asked.

"To your birthright," the clergy to his right said. They, too, had risen off the ground. One at a time, they bowed at each of them and then disappeared behind the wall at the rear of the chamber until they were alone.

"What do we do now?" she asked.

Haradis reached down and grabbed the empty pack Abigail had been hiding in and slung it on his back. "There's not much we can do." He threw a thumb over his shoulder. "We're dead if we go out there. I say we follow the see-er and find out where he takes us. Unless you got one of those flashy itchy light things hidden somewhere we can use to get out of here?" He glanced down at her and raised his eyebrows. They were barely visible beneath his fur, but they were there.

She chuckled. "No. Unfortunately, I have no flashy itchy lights to save us."

"Well, let's go then." He started toward the back of the room, and she followed a few steps behind.

THEIR JOURNEY STARTED with a walk deep into the building that housed the chamber. Abigail was surprised how large the actual space was. The Ursis apparently don't build anything small, least of all their buildings of worship.

Deduc led them through room after room until he stopped in front of a grand mural depicting a massive space battle. Judging by the Selene ships and the smaller fighters, she assumed this was the battle to close their Dark Nebula.

The clergy walked past Deduc and paused to face the mural, staring up at the dance of lights in the middle. There were two bright pink arcs coming out of the largest Selene ship. Those must've been the missiles the Galactic Alliance launched into the Nebula before they sealed it up. This was their final battle.

"Did… the missiles hit any of your suns?" she asked.

"Yes." Deduc nodded. "And thousands of lives were lost trying to stop them."

"May the gods of Therion be watching over them," the clergy muttered, and then the first member of the group walked through the mural into a hidden space beyond.

She watched as one by one they followed the others into the wall.

"That's tricky," she muttered.

"It's the first of many protections we'll pass along the way. Come." He gestured with his hand for her to walk through. "I have to close the entrance on our way out."

When she glanced at Haradis, he was still staring up at the mural. Craning his neck toward the sky to take it all in.

A message from Harold appeared on her retinal comm.

Be careful. I can't detect anything behind the wall.

She swallowed hard and took a deep breath before stepping forward and easing over the threshold where she'd seen the other Ursis pass. The transition was instant, and when she came out the other side, she was staring down a spiraling staircase.

Standing with their back against the wall was one of the clergy members. They reached out and handed her a flashlight of some sort. It looked like an adult version of the everlight she'd used earlier. She gave the handle a gentle squeeze, and sure enough, it switched on and shot a ray of light in front of her, illuminating the stairway.

"My name is Klus," the Ursis bowed. "I would be honored to accompany you down the stairs, Seguan."

Abigail turned and did a double take. It was the Ursis she'd nearly killed earlier. She could tell by the blood markings around her neck. "I'm sorry about that."

Klus reached up and rubbed at her fur. "It is I who am truly sorry. I should have never threatened the Seguan. I will forever be in debt to you and yours."

She shook her head. "First things first. Stop calling me Seguan, ok?"

"Yes, Seguan. I mean…"

"My name is Abigail."

"Yes, Abigail." She motioned with her arm down the steps. "We must go. It is only a matter of time before Emmonsii Phi figures out where you are. We're the only place that wouldn't have turned you in by now."

She raised her light and aimed it down the massive circling stairs. The Ursis had a much larger gait than she did. Working her way down this stairwell was going to be hell on her knees and quads.

As one step became a hundred, she got the feeling wherever they were heading; it wouldn't be a short trip. While she couldn't tell exactly where Haradis was, she knew he was behind her. She could make out his voice echoing off the walls.

Just when she was about to ask for a breather, the stairs hit the bottom and continued forward down a short hallway before veering right. She stretched her back and paused for a second to give her legs a break. After thirty or so seconds, Haradis and Deduc exited the stairs, deep in conversation.

She typed out a message on her retinal comm.

Any idea what they were talking about?

Harold replied without pausing.

I caught bits and pieces. Mostly, they shared what had happened outside the Nebula and inside. Haradis asked a lot of questions about his clan and his father. I've transcribed the conversations if you want to read them.

"Maybe later," she muttered.

The see-er paused at the bottom of the stairs and turned, flipping open a hidden panel on the wall. He pushed a few buttons, and then all hell broke loose. The ground shook, and a grinding noise grew in intensity. It sounded like the planet above them was crashing down.

She took a few steps backward. "What the hell is that?"

Deduc simply spun in place and walked toward her. "We're closing the doorway. Like I said earlier, we have taken many precautions to allow us to cover our tracks." He strode past her and disappeared down the turn ahead.

Haradis didn't say a word to her. He walked straight past and followed the see-er around the corner. Her friend was deep in thought, taking in the details of his father and their history.

"Are you ready, Abigail?" Klus was standing behind her, waiting patiently for her to continue on.

She nodded and started walking forward. "So, Klus, talk to me about this place. Why would your people need all these tunnels underneath the city?"

Klus shuffled her feet to let Abigail catch up, and they eased around the corner together side by side. The previously clean lines of the stone floor and steps ended, replaced by dirt and the rocky ground of a cave.

"Long ago, well before Emmonsii Phi and the Tlingui clan took over, the Ulyxsauri were a small but respected collective on Arctordiea. We—"

She reached out an arm and stopped the Ursis. "Wait… the what?"

"The Ulyxsauri, Seguan." Klus growled. "I mean… Abigail. I… assumed you knew this. The only way the see-er would have been able to connect with your thoughts in a future timeline was if you, too, were Ulyxsauri."

She shook her head. "But… I'm not."

"That is an impossibility." Klus set off walking again. They needed to keep up with the others. "Are you sure your parents were not part Ulyxsauri?"

"Neither my father nor mother were." She ran her hand through her hair. At least, not that she knew. The only Ulyxsauri she knew was Lync. "But…" Her voice trailed off.

"Go on." Klus stepped around a boulder in their path.

She jogged forward to catch up with the Ursis' gigantic strides. "I have a step-sister. My mother gave birth to them a year before me. I… didn't know about her until recently. But my mother was not Ulyxsauri. She was a regular old human."

Klus rubbed a paw against her chin. "So, your sister. She was born from a Ulyxsauri, before your life moment?"

She nodded.

"Interesting. I've read of transference with some alien species, but have never witnessed it. Especially with a human." She glanced over at her. "You are truly extraordinary, Seguan. It is a pleasure to escort you on your path."

"Call me Seguan again, and I'm gonna take some clippers to that fur of yours." She smiled and kicked a rock down the tunnel. It skipped a few times before it bounced from wall to wall and stopped.

"Of course, Abigail." Klus copied her and kicked a boulder, sending it rocketing down the cave shaft like a bullet. It exploded into a dozen smaller shards each time it hit the cave walls.

"Wow!" Abigail chuckled. "That's a solid kick you got there." She needed to make sure she was never in front of an Ursis kicking stones. "So, can you keep going with your story? You were telling me about these caves before I interrupted you."

"Ah, yes." Klus smiled, her teeth glistening in their hand lights. "These caverns were built long ago, before our kind were accepted by the Umbra clan. Before King Maritimus the tenth and Emerald Arctos welcomed us into their house. They were created to allow us to meditate in peace and without persecution. We wove them in secret throughout the planet, to wherever a Ulyxsauri was discovered. Even a species as advanced as my own has faults. The Ulyxsauri were believed to be evil at one point in time and were persecuted to near extinction by the Ursis."

"That sounds a whole lot like humanity's past failures," she muttered.

Klus bobbed her head. "Assumption and failures in judgment are not unique to humanity. Every species is fallible, even the members of the inner sanctum of the Galactic Alliance."

She glanced sideways. "The inner sanctum. What's that?"

"The see-er learned of them in the days before the Nebula fell."

Klus had started walking faster, and Abigail was nearly running now to keep up. She hadn't realized how far behind the others they were. It made sense, though; she was a third their height. Her legs were tiny by comparison.

"The sanctum is the power center of the Galactic Alliance. They're comprised of the species nearest the galactic center. They view themselves as superior to all other alliance members because they formed the initial alliance, and hold the most powerful strategic positions within the arms of the Milky Way."

That would explain the superiority complex of the Qudoculi and Thyreus, assuming they were members. "How many are there?"

"There are seven members of the sanctum. There were eight until humanity was extinguished."

Her mind went into a tailspin, and she stumbled on uneven ground. Klus reached out as she was falling and caught her. "Thank... you." She smiled.

Klus nodded, never missing a beat the entire time.

She didn't speak again until her stride was back under control. "But why were we extinguished? We were never near the galactic center."

"You weren't in the end." Klus shook her head and stiffened her posture. "Some believe your original home was near the galactic center. Whereas others believed that you not being in the center was what led to your light being extinguished. The tendrils of your species' life force were said to have muddied the Alliance's inner sanctum. Your xenocide nearly tore the galaxy and the Alliance apart after your Dark Nebula was sealed. It took over two thousand years for the ripples to subside. I suspect your re-emergence has caused a similar impact?" She glanced toward her, studying her response.

A smile crept into the edges of her mouth. "You could say something like that. Especially since we stole a Beacon."

This time, it was Klus's turn to stop dead in her tracks. "Humanity possesses a Beacon of Therion?"

She nodded. "Rumor has it."

A message from Harold appeared on her retinal comm.

Maybe that was a bit too much sharing.

He might be right, but it was too late to take it back now.

Klus ran her paws down her arms, combing her hair flat as she walked in a small circle. The Ursis nearly crashed into her twice before she stopped. "I must speak to the see-er." She leaned forward and lunged down the tunnel, galloping into the distance using her hands and feet. She left her flashlight behind for Abigail to pick up.

"That didn't go well," Harold said in her ear.

"Oh, shut up." Abigail bent down and picked up the enormous light and tossed it over her shoulder. "I wasn't paying attention, and it just fell out."

She started walking, following the winding cave wherever it went. For some reason, the original creators of this tunnel couldn't follow a straight line. She hoped she didn't come to a fork in the path, or she'd be screwed.

After what seemed like an hour, she came upon a dimly lit cavern entrance. As she stepped across the threshold of the enormous space, the sound of voices sprang forth from her left. Turning toward the source, she could just make out multiple dancing lights on the ceiling, which appeared to be coming from the same direction as the voices. It was hard to tell with all the unfamiliar sounds echoing through the chamber. When she continued walking, she realized a massive boulder was blocking her path.

"At least it isn't another set of stairs," she muttered. Her legs were still killing her from the descent earlier. She reached up and wiped her forehead and swallowed hard. Her throat was parched. She'd kill for a cold drink and a break right about now.

Once she was clear of the boulder, the voices got louder and louder, but she couldn't see anyone. She raised her hand light and saw why. There was another row of boulders between her and them. These were smaller than the last, but just as frustrating.

Abigail sighed as she weaved her way around a half dozen of the giant rocks, finally bursting forward into the muted light. The voices that moments earlier had been growing louder and louder had suddenly gone silent. She panned her light across the ceiling, toward where she'd last heard the sounds, and froze halfway.

In front of her was a massive mural of her own face. It was remarkably detailed, down to the creases in her forehead and the smile marks on her mouth. A shiver reverberated through her body as she studied the blue eyes of the woman staring back at her.

When she continued to pan her light, she came to the object of the mural's attention. It showed Abigail's outstretched hand piercing the Dark Nebula and a field of stars on the far side.

She swallowed hard. That would explain why the clergy had bowed to her so many times and treated her like she was going to break. If she had to stare at a giant version of her own face for decades, she'd be freaked out, too.

Her light lowered toward the cluster of lights up ahead. They were all directed at the ground. At first, all she could make out were feet until her beam passed over the grouping of Ursis. Standing in front of them was Deduc. The look in his eyes matched that of earlier. Something he'd heard had him spooked.

He took a step forward and stopped. "Is it true? Does humanity have possession of a Beacon?"

She typed out a brief message to Harold.

Any chance I can change my story?

"I don't see how," he whispered in her ear. "What are you gonna do, tell them you were kidding?"

She reached down and adjusted her prison jumpsuit. The cloth was covered in grime, and it was nearly impossible to tell it used to be yellow. She cleared her throat. "Yes, it's true. We've captured a Beacon, and we intend to use it."

"This is not good." Deduc reached up and ran both paws through the fur on his head. "Unless I interpreted them wrong, things have advanced far faster than my visions. The Alliance wasn't supposed to break down before we exited the Nebula. I assumed we'd have more time."

She didn't have the heart to tell them they wouldn't be exiting the Nebula any time soon. Not only would it destroy them, it could end her.

"We must move quickly." Deduc spun around. "Klus! Come here. Let the Seguan ride you."

"Certainly, sir." Klus stepped out from behind the other Ursis and motioned toward Abigail.

"No!" Haradis reached out and stopped the clergy. "Abigail will ride with me. Besides, I already have her saddle." He walked up beside her and smiled.

She fought to smile back, but came up short. Her nerves were getting the better of her. He gently brushed her shoulder with his paw. He could tell she was concerned by what Deduc had said. While she had no idea what the see-er had prophesied, he didn't seem happy with the turn of events. Harold was right. She should've kept her mouth shut.

IBU

PROTO DARK NEBULA, INSIDE POCKET FOUR

The first gate transition went off without a hitch. They jumped across the far side of the neighboring star system and hung out to make sure nothing was amiss. There was still a constant background of chatter between the Ursis Alatas ships when they arrived. Apparently, some of them were confused by what they were supposed to be looking for. Most alien species who expanded beyond the gravity of their home world weren't used to lighting up all frequencies and littering space with stray broadcasts.

Since their arrival, there had been no mention of Abigail or the escaped Ursis. From what they could tell, the news hadn't left the Arctordiea home star system. Ibu wasn't sure whether or not that was a good thing. It meant the Ursis they were hunting was still on the planet. That and the government was suppressing details from the rest of the population.

Minula walked onto the bridge. "Are we prepared for the next stage of our plan?" She slid up to her pilot controls and clicked in.

"We deployed the first three probes without incident. Once we're a go, the first two will gate in unison and in opposite directions." Ibu hit play on the wall simulation and the sequence of events played out in fast-forward. "After they've hopped around a few times, we'll record more Ursis transmissions, and then the Phoenix and the third probe will gate away. Our next target is the middle of the neighboring star system. Shauna already finished the maths for the jumps, so we're prepared. Once we transition, we'll deploy the next pair of probes as fast as we can and gate again, repeating the entire sequence one last time when we arrive at our destination star, except we'll only launch a single probe. This shouldn't be a problem, though, as the other probes will be jumping into and out of the systems."

Ibu advanced the wall simulation forward once more, skipping the probe deployment. "While all this is happening, the probes will be rebroadcasting the recorded transmissions at every jump. We'll know pretty quickly if the broadcasts are working. If they fail, we'll jump out of the Nebula. If they succeed, we're hoping we can leverage that fact and hide the Phoenix near Arctordiea to monitor the situation planetside."

Minula took a deep breath and studied the wall screen.

It was a lot to take in, especially with all the variables at play. Ibu recognized that the woman wasn't technically on par with Shauna, but she made up for it in other ways.

After a few minutes of silence, Minula spoke. "It looks like you've got this taken care of. If Shauna trusts your idea, then so do I." She spun around to face Ibu. "I have Moet and the other soldiers running extraction drills in virtual reality."

"We're not thinking of putting them into action, are we? After what her people did on Griseo?" Shauna's robotic form stepped out of the charging station in the corner and walked toward them.

Minula shook her head and laughed. "Do you have an army of robotic warriors hidden onboard I wasn't aware of?"

"No, but we have—"

"Then we'll need our soldiers, and they might even see battle. Don't worry..." Minula spun back around. "I'll be headed down in an exo-suit alongside them. There's not a chance in hell I'm sitting this one out, and if they so much as sneeze wrong, I'll put an electro-bolt through their skull."

Ibu found it humorous when humans put their foot down without using logic. It was obvious why she was doing it, of course. She was in love with Abigail and wanted to do everything she could to save her, but she didn't say that. She simply stated what she considered a fact and waited for the A.I. to object. Shauna knew better than to argue with her, especially when it came to matters of the heart.

"Are we ready?" Minula asked, ignoring the tension between her and the robot.

"I'm a go in cargo," Cynthia said over their retinal comms. "The next two probes are isolated near the doors, and there's a curtain of skotádi between them and the outside."

They never lined the probe launchers with the stealth material, so there was a chance they'd be detected if things went south. This was the only insurance they could think of to reduce their probability of being detected during the launch. Fortunately for them, it only took a few minutes to sequence a few probes and float them out into space.

"Communication is a go." Shauna had taken the seat normally reserved for Cynthia. It was splitting hairs over who should do what role, but Shauna's ability to process hundreds of simultaneous data feeds gave her an advantage in this situation.

Minula glanced back at Ibu and nodded. "We're a go for Operation Ride the Chaos."

Ibu smiled. Humans loved naming their missions. They'd read about it in ancient human history. It was almost like they were predetermining their success based on the quality of the name. If that was the case, this one was bound to have some bumps and bruises.

They reached out and activated their launch program. A single targeted micro-laser tight-beam connected to each of the probes, and a second later they disappeared, having already jumped across space-time. Now it was simply a matter of waiting.

IBU STUDIED THE DISPLAY. The signals between the Alatas ships in the system had shot up exponentially. In fact, there was so much chatter it was hard to filter the theoretical updates on where the Ursis thought the probes were, from the actual useful information. They were beginning to wonder if the Ursis didn't think their plan through.

"I believe we've reached peak chaos," they said.

"What does that mean?" Minula asked.

Ibu sighed. "It's the name of your operation. What do you think it means?"

"Oh, right, that. I forgot what I called it. I was sorta riffing." Minula spun around. "Beginning gate transition. Cynthia, get ready for probe extruding."

A chuckle came across the ship wide channel. It was nice to see everyone in good spirits for a change.

As the dance of the blue light passed over Ibu's skin, they dropped into virtual reality. They found it was easier to focus when they isolated themselves from the rest of the bridge. With reality at bay, they cracked open the early signals from the forward recording harness they sent through the gate first.

There was a prolonged spike of transmissions leaking through the far side. It was no wonder, given the chatter in the star system they were leaving. What they didn't plan on, however, was their guest off the starboard bow. Just under three light seconds away was the massive wing of an Alatas starship. The vessel dwarfed even the largest human ship, and that included the ones they used to colonize Epsilon Eridani and Zeta Lupi.

Ibu didn't waste a second. They could already see the

Ursis starship was doing something on its exterior in response to the leaked signals. Time was of the essence.

They plotted in a shorter hop, followed by a second. This was going to hurt, and as soon as they transitioned, the Ursis would know their destination. They needed to make sure the hops took them nowhere near the other Alatas ships.

With the updated course laid in, they issued a command to inject themselves and the others with drugs and waited three seconds in real time for the system to catch up. The wait was excruciating, but it was the only thing that would ease the all too real pain they were about to feel on the other side.

As the seconds ticked off to zero, they reached forward and slammed the gate transition button. It probably wasn't the best idea to not check on the others first, but waiting gave the Ursis more time, and that was a precious commodity when facing death.

Their body exploded in a tsunami of pain as the wall of space-time sped across the surface of the Phoenix. Every centimeter of their skin was ablaze, and the only relief was still seconds away. Just as the first wave of agony was about to crest, a second wave came crashing down and this one was the worst. The closest they could describe it was like pouring a salt shaker on an open wound. It was like they wanted to rip their own arm off.

Suddenly, Ibu collapsed to the virtual ground, and up turned into down. Their consciousness was ripped from their virtual reality into the real world, and dropped them into a bridge filled with screams of pain, along with a robot leaning against their chest.

"I said wake up!" Shauna shook their shoulders.

Ibu screamed at the top of their lungs. Even their vocal cords hurt. They gyrated and tried to shove her off, but Shauna wouldn't budge.

"Get off me." They leaned forward to headbutt the robot but missed.

"As soon as you stop hurting yourself, I will." Shauna nodded toward their arm.

When they glanced down, there were huge gashes covering their forearm and multiple lacerations to their chest. Whatever happened during the transition, someone or something had attacked them.

Shauna glared into their eyes. "Are you ready to behave?"

Her words hit them like a smack to the face. She was implying they hurt themselves. While they couldn't imagine how it was possible, they weren't in a position to doubt their friend.

Moans emanated from where Minula was sitting. It sounded like the others were the worse for wear after those two jumps. Everyone except the robot.

"I take it that's a no, then?" Shauna asked.

"I'm… getting there," Ibu muttered. "What… happened?"

"What happened?" She tilted her head. "You seriously don't remember?"

They went to shake their head and regretted it a second later. "No… last thing I remember was starting the emergency… transitions. We came out on—"

"Top of an Ursis battle wing," Shauna interrupted. "Yeah, I saw that. Another five to ten seconds, and we were toast."

"Did anyone catch the number of that Mack truck that ran me over?" Cynthia asked over the ship wide comm.

Moans of complaint echoed back, as even their voice somehow hurt. They could feel the pain medication having an impact the longer they laid there, but Shauna was heavy as hell.

"Can… you get off me? I think I'm fine now."

"You think, or you know?"

"I know. I'm fine."

Shauna eased off the Nanil and stood up, backing away from them, but keeping her eyes out for any sudden movement.

Moving fast was one thing they knew they wouldn't be doing for a while. They sat up slowly and winced the entire way. Not from the burning sensation in their skin. No, this pain was from the open wounds. When they glanced down, they realized how bad they were.

"You're gonna need surgery on those," Shauna said.

They swallowed hard and even their throat hurt as the saliva passed down it. "We don't have time for that." They reached out and pulled themselves up to their controls. They could see the back of Minula's head. The woman was starting to move, as well. "How's... the ship?"

"It's in one piece, but barely." Shauna brought up a video of the seconds before their transition and played it in slow motion. It was from the exterior of the Phoenix.

The Alatas ship, which had been only a few light seconds off their starboard side, performed some type of phase shift. It went from being a tiny dot to full size in a fraction of a second. When the time had passed, it was literally only a few hundred meters away.

"What the hell?" Minula muttered.

"They appeared to have executed a controlled warp bubble," Shauna began. "I didn't know the Galactic Alliance drives could do that."

"Something tells me they can't." Ibu swallowed hard. "I bet that's a modification courtesy of our Ursis friends."

The advances in technology these aliens had achieved in isolation were astounding. First the malleable starships, and now the precise and rapid control of FTL drives. It was astonishing they hadn't managed to jump past the Dark Nebula themselves.

They brought up a camera in the cargo hold. Cynthia appeared to still be strapped into one of the primitive acceleration couches. It took them a second, but they realized the hold was missing something. "What happened to the probes?"

"I dropped them after the transition. Well, actually, my robot friends did." Shauna walked a few of the general purpose robots into the camera view. "I knew how important saving time was going to be. Every second counts."

"Speaking of which." Minula leaned forward and tweaked her controls. "How are we doing? Did we attract any inbound bogies?"

"Not that I can tell." Shauna took a step toward Ibu and the door to the bridge opened up. Two small robots wheeled in, each of them carrying trays of surgical instruments. "I know better than to ask again, so you're either going to let me do this here, or I'm gonna have Minula relieve you of duty. Which is it?"

Ibu glanced back at Minula. The woman was staring wide-eyed at the wounds. The look in her eyes said enough.

"Fine, but make it quick." They eased themselves to the ground and laid flat. "We might not have a lot of time, and we still have another gate left."

33

ABIGAIL OLIVAW

PROTO DARK NEBULA, ON ARCTORDIEA

The beams from their hand lights cast eerie shadows on the ceiling of the cavern. It reminded Abigail of camping as a kid. Back then, they used flashlights to make shadow puppets on the walls of their tent. While they did the same thing out at The Wheel, the difference between the space station and this cave was the cacophony of strange noises down in these tunnels. Every time something dripped or dropped, she jumped.

"Have you always been this skittish?" Haradis studied her after she'd jumped five times in as many minutes.

"Not since I was a kid camping in the woods with unknown critters about." She stared up at her face painted on the mural towering above the cavern. Her eyes seemed to be staring straight back at her. "But down here, I'm surrounded by an alien horde threatening to kill me because I won't share my lunch money. So yeah, I'm a bit nervous."

"Your lunch money?" Haradis tilted his head. "Your kind forced their children to pay for food? That's a peculiar convention at a young age."

A small rock skittered down the nearby wall, and she flinched when the stone hit the ground and rolled up near her feet. "Humans have strange societal norms. Money being one of them."

She bent down and picked up the stone, turning it over in her hand. It looked like granite. While she was pretty sure she could ask Harold to confirm, she honestly didn't care. She squeezed the rock, and it made her think of her brother. Bradley used to collect rocks like this when he was a kid. Besides the one from her father's grave, she wondered if he still collected others. He used to say they helped remind him of where he'd been.

When she glanced up at the ceiling and pictured the millions of tons of stone above her head, all fighting gravity to break free and crush her, she wasn't sure she wanted to be reminded of this place. She moved her hand light to the right and took in another chunk of the mural painted overhead.

"This battle. Was this when your father sent you to safety?" She glanced over at Haradis.

His muscles tightened, and his jaw seemed to tense. "No. My father hid me a few months before this. I was only a babe, and my mother, rest her soul, she chose to stay behind with her clan alongside their king. They orphaned me to the wilds of the universe." He adjusted his stance. "I'd rather have remained here and helped my people."

"But then you'd probably be dead." She stared down at the stone. "I mean, the other clans turned on your parents and family, didn't they?"

He exhaled a deep breath, and his body shuddered. "They did. But perhaps… things would have gone differently had I stayed."

"You're foolish for even thinking it." Deduc stepped out of the shadows beside Abigail. "They killed hundreds of thousands of your people after the veil of darkness fell. It was a slaughter of epic proportions. The only reason they stopped, and why I survived, was because there was a belief that the gods would save us. However small the idea, the notion of a miracle was enough to end the devastation."

"What in the name of Therion made them think that?" Haradis glanced to the right to stare at the see-er.

"I did." Deduc stared up at the mural depicting a massive wave of Ursis fighters battling and being destroyed by the converging Selene moon ships. The carnage was immense. So many lives lost in the blink of an eye.

Abigail noticed a glimmer in Haradis' eyes. Not a hint of hope, as she expected. This was a seed of doubt. Perhaps her friend wasn't as sold on the Beacon visions as she thought. When she glanced up at the mural again, she could still feel her own eyes watching her from the darkness to her left. It was hard to imagine Emmonsii had her people come down here and painted all this in the past week, but stranger things have been done to convince someone of the truth. Her family had been guilty of that over the centuries, that's for sure.

She chuckled. "And we're supposed to believe your singular voice changed the mind of your entire species?" She stared down at the rock and turned it over in her hand.

Deduc looked down at her. She could feel his eyes burning through her. "Faith in a hopeless situation is a difficult weapon to wield, but when you have truth on your side, anything is possible."

Her stomach tightened. If only the truth were that simple.

"Sharing that truth sooner could have saved my father." Haradis spun to face the see-er and eased closer to him. "I find it convenient that you waited until they were dead before you came out of hiding."

"He was not hiding!" Klus shoved her way between Deduc and Haradis, sending Abigail reeling backward onto her butt. "He was in a coma after being forcefully severed from his connection to the Beacon." She shifted his cloak to reveal his weapon underneath. "The young Umbra here needs to understand the situation before he jumps to judgment."

Abigail rubbed her back. She couldn't catch a break around these mountainous aliens. They tossed her about like she was a toy.

Haradis grunted. "I'm sorry if I don't accept the all seeing Ursis on face value after the reception my friend and I received."

He reached down and offered her a hand up off the ground, and she gladly took it. "Even a true story can have threads of lies weaved tightly within the cloth. It's just that sometimes they're indistinguishable from the good ones." Once Abigail was upright and a few steps away, he stepped forward, pushing his chest against Klus. The two Ursis started growling. Their angry tones sent flashes of adrenaline through the surrounding clergy.

"Enough!" Deduc snarled and bulldozed his way between the two of them, doing everything he could to keep them apart. "We cannot turn on one another. Not now. Not with the Seguan at hand. We must—"

The ceiling and ground started rumbling as chunks of rock sheared off, cascading to the ground and shattering into hundreds of shards. Deduc fell backward and hit his head. Both Klus and Haradis bent down to help the frail Ursis.

Her eyes darted around the space, searching for a way out. The sickle of death was near. It was like her childhood nightmares were becoming a reality. After fearing the darkness and the misplaced hope that she'd make it out of this cave, the rocks were finally breaking free to crush her like she'd imagined they would.

She couldn't wait for that. They'd come too far. She spun in place and sprinted toward where they'd come from. There was only one way out of this place that she knew of, and damn it all to hell if she was going to sit around and let gravity end her.

As she dodged her way around the first of the looming boulders, a massive hand grasped her shoulder from behind. It yanked her backward, sending her feet flying into the air like a rag doll and her hand light tumbling forward into the darkness. It clanked to the ground and spun in circles, crushed within seconds from the falling debris.

While the sudden motion in the other direction didn't hurt, it sent her already pounding heart into a frenzy as she struggled to face her attacker. Not that she could see them in the pitch black.

Harold must have taken note of her situation because her retinal comm lit up like someone turned on the lights, except her view was covered in three-dimensional lidar. Though it wasn't perfect, it helped her right herself and understand her surroundings more easily than grasping for nothingness. When she brought her hand up to pry at the fingers locked on her shoulder, her assailant tossed her up onto their back and galloped forward into the dark.

"Grab on!" Haradis' voice was barely audible within the rumbling. "We've got to get the hell out of here. The others headed this way... I think. Everyone's already well ahead of us, except for Klus."

She grabbed ahold of the hair on his back and tucked her legs under the pack she'd hid in hours earlier. While it wasn't a stable harness by any stretch of the imagination, something was better than nothing. Once she was happy she wouldn't fall, she glanced over her shoulder and the lidar lit up another Ursis following close behind. She wasn't sure why she hadn't gone with the others, but she assumed Deduc had assigned her as protection. Or at least to keep an eye on her.

"I should've talked to my crew before I left." She wrapped the strap tighter around her hand and squeezed her legs against Haradis' ribcage. "This was a fraking mistake."

"I beg to differ, my friend." He dodged left and then right, narrowly missing a falling rock.

When she glanced over her shoulder, Klus was still close behind. She'd been letting Haradis take the lead and seemed to be mirroring his movements.

"A true leader doesn't ask their subordinates' opinions before taking action. Sometimes it's simply their duty to act." Haradis dove down a small narrow tunnel and she ducked just in time to avoid a clump of jagged rocks protruding from the ceiling.

Klus growled from behind them. "What the young Ursis fails to recognize is that their actions must always be in the interest of their people. Losing touch means they're no longer a leader, they're a dictator."

She couldn't believe these two idiots were having a political debate while dodging a rainstorm of rocks. This was fraking insane. "Less arguing and more focus, please."

"Yes, Seguan Abigail." Klus' words were trailed by a crash from behind.

When she spun around to see where the noise had come from, segments of the tunnel were collapsing in the distance. "Frak! Faster, faster!" She gently tapped her palm against Haradis' side.

The drumbeats of her heart were drowned by the crashing stone, but they were there, constantly keeping her on her toes. They were the ever present background thumping of the forsaken cavern that time forgot.

Even with her lidar, she couldn't tell where they were going. Her eyes were glued behind them as the raining rocks seemed to intensify just past Klus.

Suddenly, her body lurched backward as Haradis accelerated, finding another level of speed. Her arm screamed as the reins of the bag squeezed like a vice grip against her forearm and her leg broke free. Despite the agony of being yanked forward, she struggled to counteract the change in pace by adjusting how tight she was squeezing with her legs, but failed.

"No!"

Her legs slipped, and she swung loose on Haradis' back, bouncing up and down with each gallop and even sliding off the side a few times. Fortunately, he twisted his shoulders and checked her, swinging her up. Each time her body bounced down against him, pain shot up her back and she slid over the other side. First a few falls and now a rodeo ride. A break was nowhere in the cards for her on this damn planet.

"Are you… alright, Abigail?" Klus' voice was a screech barely audible over the rumbling behind them, which was getting closer by the second.

Even though she couldn't see the Ursis with her body flailing about and her constant struggle to hold on for dear life, she knew the female was still behind her. Especially since there wasn't room to pass.

In between bounces, she swung her free hand over her head and grasped around in a failed attempt at seizing the strap. No matter how she tried to time it, she couldn't snatch it in sync with Haradis' gallop. There was only one thing left to do.

She closed her eyes and reached up, grabbing a handful of fur and pulling with everything she had, bringing her body up against his. A yelp escaped from her friend, but otherwise his pace didn't slow. He either had complete control of his body, or he was as freaked out as she was and running for dear life. She assumed the latter.

With one hand on the strap and another holding against him, the flailing slowed. This allowed her to swing her legs up, which at this point were dangling off the side of the Ursis.

The first time she tried to swing them over, her timing was off, and his hind legs swatted her back down. On the second attempt, she was met with a hello from the rocky ceiling. It kicked her down with another jolt of pain, this time from her shin. She winced and struggled not to lose her grip. Maybe she was better off dangling on the side, so long as she didn't fall.

A message from Harold appeared on her retinal comm.

I think you should stay tucked against his side. Just keep a solid grip. The ceiling appears to be low in parts.

"No shit," she muttered as she adjusted her fingers one at a time, trying to gather more of the hair on his back. She did as much as she could to hang most of her weight on the side wrapped in the strap. At least that one felt secure.

Haradis had been running for several minutes when the cave opened up. They were entering another cavern, and when she glanced around, she could see what looked like bricks and other straight lines that didn't occur naturally.

The rumbling behind them had subsided, but there were still occasional crashes nearby. Whatever happened up top, it was rippling through the bowels of the planet.

"How much further?" She was fighting to keep her grip, and could feel what she could only assume was blood seeping in between her fingers. "I'm not sure if I can hold on much longer."

"The Keep is just ahead," Klus said. "It's heavily fortified and should be able to withstand these quakes."

While she wasn't comfortable putting her life in the hands of a 'should', she didn't have another option. She'd already be dead many times over if it weren't for her Ursis bodyguards.

"I… see an entrance," Haradis said, gasping for breath. "Is that it?"

She couldn't lean out to look for fear of falling.

"Indeed, my young friend. Deduc should be—"

Klus' response was cut short as a boulder crashed to the

ground beside them and sent shards of rock rocketing into her and Haradis.

"Ahhhhhhh!" she screeched as the stone projectiles tore into her backside and the blast sent them reeling. Her body was free-falling in concert with his, and they tumbled sideways into the unknown.

She unconsciously let go of both his fur and the strap in a misguided attempt at reaching around and easing the pain surging through her back. In hindsight, this reaction was a good thing because she flung free of Haradis, narrowly avoiding being crushed under his weight as their bodies tumbled across the rock strewn ground.

The sensation of her skin tearing across razor sharp stone wasn't foreign to her. It was all too familiar from her visions in the coma, but this time it was real and not a dream.

As she rolled to a stop, Harold started shouting in her ear. "Abigail! Are you ok? Open your eyes."

She opened her mouth and spat out dirt. "Stop... screaming at me."

"You can't pass out. Not here. You'll be crushed out in the open." His voice was like nails on a chalkboard. He wasn't even trying to lower it. "You must try to find the entrance to the Keep."

"Shut up!" She went to push up and regretted it the second she had. Her back was alight with a hundred pinholes of pain surging to life, demanding her attention. It was like someone had whipped her with barbed wire.

The ground vibrated again as another crash echoed across the chamber. The boulders were still falling. She knew she needed to move, but her mind was elsewhere.

"Har...adis." She pushed through the pain and sat up on her knees, scanning the surrounding space.

There was an Ursis moving a dozen meters away. It had to be him. "Haradis! Are you ok?"

"I think so." His voice was gravelly and mired with pain like her own.

She turned back the way they'd come and stared in the distance. Harold must've known what she was looking for because he tweaked her retinal comm and highlighted the area of the darkness where Klus was. While she couldn't see with her regular vision, the lidar outlined a pile of rubble laying over a body.

"No!" She pushed up off the ground and stumbled toward her. "Klus! Can you hear me?"

She never replied.

Behind her, Haradis was moaning, and a moment later his footsteps were audible. He was following her lead, and they were both working their way toward the body.

Just as she eased over a pile of rocks, the ground shook again and a chunk of the far wall sheered off and cascaded down, crashing into a million pieces. The stones slid around the pile of rubble she was working her way through, and she swore she saw them sweep up some type of vials and a strap scattered in the debris.

"We need to get out of the open," Harold said.

She shook her head. "Not until we check on Klus. I'm not leaving her out here alone."

"But, Abigail—"

"Harold!" She spat out a mouth full of blood at her feet. "Now isn't the time to fraking argue with me."

He fell silent.

When she reached Klus' side, she placed her hand in front of the alien's snout. She was breathing, but only barely. Abigail could hardly feel her short shallow breaths on her skin. When she surveyed the damage, the Ursis' lower half was covered in rocky debris, and her left knee was contorted in an odd direction. It was pinned between two boulders.

She started removing rocks one at a time, shoving a few of

the medium ones aside that she could move herself. Once Haradis arrived, he made quick work of the others.

"Is she alive?" Haradis leaned into the largest of the boulders, and she pulled the mangled leg out from between it and the neighboring stone. Klus growled and tried to swat at her, but she was too weak to resist.

"Barely." Abigail gently laid her leg down. "We need to get her out—"

The ground rumbled, and she lost her balance and fell to her knees. The air erupted with the sound of crackling rock, which was usually preceded by a rain of stone. Haradis didn't wait for her to finish her thought. He bent down and lifted the hulking Ursis over his shoulder and walked as fast as he could toward the Keep.

She pushed up and followed close behind. Even though he was walking, she still had a hard time keeping up. Her back was howling at her, and she was surprised her legs were working at all. With how her side felt, she knew that the moment she got off this adrenaline high; she was going to be immobilized herself.

As the rain of stones fell, the ground ignited and rocky shrapnel shot out in all directions. She ducked down and covered her head with her arms, doing her best imitation of a run she could muster. A few of the rocks ricocheted across her thigh and she winced, but it was the one that hit her upper back that sent her reeling.

Her body tilted forward with the momentum she'd built up, and the ground flew up to kiss her face. Fortunately, her arms were already covering the side of her head, so while she came down hard on her triceps, they absorbed most of the fall. That didn't stop her chin from kissing the stone, though, and she bit down on her tongue, filling her mouth with blood within seconds.

"You're almost there!" Even with the rumbling, Harold's voice was like a foghorn in her ears.

She pushed up onto one knee and then the other, her arms shaking the entire way. There wasn't much left in her tank.

With only a few more meters to the Keep, she couldn't give in. She eased up, pushing off her right knee as her legs wobbled. Once she was upright, she swallowed hard and her stomach lurched. She bent over and retched several times before spitting out a mouth full of blood.

The ground around her shook, and the familiar cracking of rocks permeated the cavern. She had to move before the next rain of stone came. With one foot in front of the other, she stumbled forward toward the outline of the Keep. Her lidar had an eerie feeling in a cave filled with stalactite rock formations on the ceiling and piles of rubble strewn throughout. It was as out of place as she was.

She didn't even know how she was moving any longer. It was the sheer will to survive at this point, nothing else. As she passed through the opening, the ceiling behind her opened up in a hailstorm of rocky shards falling from above. Whatever was happening near the surface was intensifying.

Once she was a few meters into the Keep, she gave up and toppled onto her hands and knees. Her heart was pounding, and every centimeter of her body screamed for her to stop moving and rest. She couldn't even hold up her own weight any longer. She needed to lie down. The cool smooth ground in this part of the cave was soothing against her burning skin.

She could hear the siren song calling for her to close her eyes.

"Don't... you aren't safe..." Harold's voice faded in and out. "...stay awake until someone... getting closer. I can't see who it..."

34

———

IBU

PROTO DARK NEBULA, INSIDE POCKET FOUR

The final jump went much smoother than the last. They only needed a single hop to reach the Arctordiea system. When the blue wall of tachyons passed over them, they were already on high alert, preparing for the worst-case scenarios. This time, however, they stuck the landing. They'd jumped in not far from the world itself.

"How'd you manage to drop us this close?" Ibu asked.

"I spent most of my time hopping around this star system when I jumped through the Nebula," Shauna began. "It allowed me to get the clearest measurements of all the Ursis ships, planets, and asteroids. Knowing where all the gravity pockets are located makes gate jumping a far easier task than piloting blind."

That made sense. They forgot about the number of hops she'd performed passing through this system. She was inside the Nebula pockets for longer than they'd anticipated.

They studied their other control panel and noticed that two of their probes had already hopped into the system and were making the rounds. The Ursis wavelengths were lit up like a holiday tree, with details on the last known locations for their probes. By the time the aliens scrambled their forces to intercept, the probes had hopped away. As long as they didn't jump close to the Alatas ships, they were safe.

"I'm reading that all five of the probes are still active," Shauna said.

Ibu glanced at her robotic shell in the seat to their right. "How do you know that?"

"I tweaked the comm protocols our probes are broadcasting on and embedded a few extra bytes in all the noise. That's enough space to hide a counter and a location index." Shauna shared the map of the Nebula in the corner of the wall screen. "The index tells me what system the probe is in, and the counter tells me how many are still alive from their point of view. They update their own data sets when they detect a fellow probe's signal. It's simple, really, but often the most used things are."

They had to hand it to her, the A.I. was always planning ahead. While playing with probabilities may seem natural for an artificial life form, nothing could be further from the truth. So many of the initial failed attempts by humans at creating computer life ended with the test program dying from literal paralysis of analysis. It wasn't until they eliminated these logic branches that humans made progress. It was no wonder that most aliens gave up trying to recreate life in an electronic form. Every so often they forgot the robot was a recorded consciousness of Abigail's mother and not humanity's successful creation of artificial life.

"I'm not picking up any movement from the Alatas or any other ships for that matter. They seem to be watching and waiting for something. Since we jumped in undetected, maybe we sit tight, as well." Minula spun in place to face them. "Does anyone disagree?"

Ibu glanced around. Shauna didn't object, and Cynthia had been unusually quiet since they'd arrived. "Is everything ok, Cynthia?"

She shook her head and looked up from her controls. "I'm... yeah. I'm fine. It's just... I've been trying to sift through all the comm traffic. Even with the filtered data from the probes, there's an insane amount of information to wade through. And whatever's going on down on the planet has the attention of the Ursis, not our little probes." She flicked up a few of the data feeds on the wall screen.

They turned to study the images. In each quadrant of the screen, there was a different live feed from down on Arctordiea.

Officials are asking that all the residents of Jinya and the neighboring cities remain locked in their homes until law enforcement has apprehended the escapees. They're believed to be armed and dangerous and doctors say they're deranged. Locals tell accounts of an Ursis seen around the city asking questions about our former king and talking about humans on Arctordiea. Everyone knows the troubled end of humanity from school. Their questionable dealings with the Zugal and Wrumpf in the early years of the Galactic Alliance led to the first unanimous tribunal in history. I mean, the results in those cases spoke for themselves. Humans are not to be trusted. They'll kill you in a second. And let's not even talk about our ousted, poor excuse for a king who got our species into a tribunal of our own. Those were dark days indeed... (*the announcer bows their head for a moment of silence*)... Be careful out there, my friends. In other news, we're expecting an announcement tomorrow afternoon from Emmonsii Phi Tlingui herself. Rumors of another advance in anti-aging...

Minula shot up from her seat. "That's got to be more than

a coincidence, right? I mean, why the hell would humanity be coming up in their news cycle precisely when Abigail is missing? And that Ursis, that fits our—"

Ibu held up a finger, silencing Minula's rapidly spiraling emotions. They opened a mental link with their controls, keeping their external senses intact at the same time. It was a less than ideal mode to operate in, but it allowed them to review data at a higher speed than most of the crew. It also gave the humans near them a sense that they weren't zoned out. They found that doing this was easier on most human's fragile ego and self-worth. It made them feel like they were getting the attention they requested.

With the information at their fingertips, they were able to scan through dozens of feeds at the same time. Flipping through them, the tone was consistent throughout. They were structured to give the Ursis viewing audience the impression that they were forming an opinion on their own, when in fact the messaging was the same: reinforce the prior administration's failure to protect the clans and bolster their fear of humanity.

"It's too widespread and consistent to ignore," Ibu began. "Their disinformation campaign against humanity, and I assume this escaped Ursis, is everywhere. There's not a single news stream that isn't feeding the same story, even if with slightly different spins."

"Here's another interesting tidbit." Shauna shared a bio of Emmonsii Phi on the wall screen. "The Ursis they mentioned at the end of that piece has been in power since the Nebula fell. They overturned the past government the moment the tribunal ruled against them."

"How'd you get this?" Cynthia scurried up to the screen. "If we're querying their system, they'll—"

"I wasn't born yesterday." Shauna chuckled. "I know the consequences of an outbound signal just as well as the rest of you. This stream was embedded in one of the educational news feeds they use for their schools. Apparently, the younger Ursis need their daily helping of history and propaganda along with the adults."

"I'm sorry... I didn't—" Cynthia began.

Shauna walked up beside her. "Don't worry about it. We're all feeling a bit exposed right now."

Humans spent a lot of time reassuring and comforting each other. It was strange to see, sometimes, especially knowing where they'd come from on Doda. If the words weren't followed by a swift kick in the ass, you could assume you were on the right path. Studying human behavior made them wonder what it would have been like to be raised differently.

"This is odd." Minula shared a few different feeds from down on the planet with the others. "They're mobilizing serious ground troops near Jinya. And they appear to be doing some type of rapid mining, as well. Check out these pictures."

The images on the wall screen appeared to show digging machines lowering down into a massive hole above the Jinya city center, which was deep below ground. While they'd been gawking at their human colleagues' behavior, Minula had been doing her job and helping them better understand their situation. They had to be careful not to let their human emotions distract them and lower their guard. Death was encircling them at every corner, and now wasn't the time to lose focus on frivolous ideations of family.

"Any idea where the crater came from?" Ibu found the referenced feed and started scrubbing through it and others with similar imagery.

"There's nothing about it on the news feeds," Minula said. "And these pictures weren't exactly easy to find. They were posted on a public forum of sorts that someone off world accessed, but a few seconds later they were deleted. We were lucky they were even opened in the first place, or we wouldn't have seen them at all."

They needed to get eyes into the stream, so they could query data instead of just passively consuming it. There had to be a way to do it that didn't put them at risk.

"I'm going to go have a chat with Moet and the others." Minula stood up and headed toward the exit.

"What for?" Cynthia asked.

Minula paused and stared at the open door. "If we need to do an emergency extract from down in that gravity well full of giants, we'll have to be ready. I saved off that city's schematics someone was browsing online, and I want Moet and the others preparing, not sitting idle on their ass in their bunks. I'm not about to lose Abigail to a fuckup in running an op. I'll run the damn thing myself if I have to." She didn't wait for anybody to challenge her. She simply walked off the bridge.

Sitting around wasn't helping anyone, nor was focusing on their crew mates. Minula was right. They needed to focus on the problems in front of them, and that meant getting as much intel as possible to improve their situation. Reaching forward, they tweaked their controls and set themselves to not be disturbed before disconnecting into their neural link within the computer. They were better off optimizing their thoughts, which meant removing the human layer of their senses.

When the virtual world engulfed them in darkness, they froze. Shauna was waiting for them on the other side. "I was wondering when you were gonna do that. I assume you're finally ready to focus."

They glanced around at the nothingness. No distractions, no smells, and no human paraphernalia to draw their attention. Just a plain and simple void that allowed them to concentrate.

Ibu smirked. "I was thinking about how we could interface with the Ursis systems without being detected, or at least minimizing our exposure. Talk to me about the equipment we have onboard to work with."

35

ABIGAIL OLIVAW
PROTO DARK NEBULA, ON ARCTORDIEA

The cold damp cloth wiped at Abigail's forehead, and she sat up with a start, pushing away someone's hand and taking in the room. The lighting was dim, but the familiar stonework of the spiral stairs they'd climbed down reminded her of where she was. There was also the shooting pain down her back.

"What happened?" She licked her lips and tried to swallow, but her throat was parched.

A massive hand reached around and passed what looked like a gallon size cup toward her. It was half full of water, she assumed, to make it easier for her to hold. She wasn't about to complain. She grasped it with both hands and brought it up to her mouth, tilting it back and letting the cool liquid pour down her throat. It tasted heavenly.

"You've been out for a few hours." Haradis eased down on the end of her bed. The wood like material groaned under his weight, but it held.

She lowered the bucket into her lap and let her stomach settle. If she drank too much water too fast, she'd be throwing it back up. When she glanced around the sparse room, she noticed it only contained a table and two chairs and the bed she was lying in, but something was missing.

"The collapse..." She swallowed, her throat already felt better. "Is it over?"

Haradis nodded. "So far. We're preparing to move again soon, but we suspect the quakes aren't over with."

She tilted her head. "Why? Was there a geological event nearby?"

He chuckled and pushed up off the bed. "You could say that. Emmonsii has been digging through the rubble up top, and from the sounds of it, she's not happy with what she's finding, or in this case not finding."

She shot upright, realizing what he was implying. "She's hunting for us, isn't she? Was it her that caused the cave-in?"

"Indirectly." He stepped toward the door and opened it, turning to look at her. "The explosions topside were defenses built into the temple to prevent anyone from following us. They were ancient, and apparently someone had been too generous in their application of the explosive. But that's a matter for later. Come." He waved his hand. "We must go."

She swung her legs off the bed, the sudden movement making her dizzy. While her back ached, she was expecting something worse. "Where are we going?"

"Home," he muttered and turned away before disappearing into the darkened hall.

"Home. What does that mean?" She twisted around in an attempt to loosen up. Anything she could do to get moving would help.

"They've injected you with some powerful medications," Harold said, his voice coming over her retinal comm and not at all like the screaming from earlier.

"It's good to hear you again." She eased up onto her feet, testing her body's response. "I assume the drugs were safe?"

"For the most part." His face appeared in the corner of her vision. "I've been monitoring their impact as they spread through your body. While they're not as efficient as nanites, they're remarkably efficient for natural chemicals. The wounds on your back have already sealed up, and the fractures in your bones are almost unnoticeable."

"Fractures?" She stiffened and wrapped her arms around her chest. "That doesn't sound good." Her eyes lowered to her clothes. While they were the same, when she turned her arm over, she noticed they'd stitched the holes shut in parts. Which was strange, considering they hadn't washed out the blood.

He smiled. "It wasn't good at all, but you're on the mend now. That's all that matters. A little time off your feet, combined with some alien remedies, and you're already looking better. It's nice seeing you up and about."

"Thanks. Let's hope we're not dodging the ceiling again any time soon." She stepped toward the open door and peered down the dark hall. Harold brought up the lidar to enhance her vision, and she could see that the passage disappeared into the distance. There was only one way to go from here.

Into the darkness.

***

WHEN SHE FINALLY HEARD THE sound of another person, she jogged through the hall toward the source of the noise and froze at the top of a set of stairs leading downward. The last place she wanted to head was deeper into this fraking world.

"That's odd," Harold said.

"What?"

"The lidar isn't picking up the bottom of the stairway. It's like the tunnel isn't there, but clearly it is."

She squinted, and a smile eased into the corner of her

mouth. "Nope, but something tells me there's skotádi in those there bricks."

"Indeed," a familiar voice said. Klus stepped out of the shadows below and came into view. "I was just coming up to check on you."

She hopped down the steps and ran up to the Ursis, wrapping her arms around her legs and giving her a huge hug. "You're ok. I was worried you were dead."

Klus froze, not sure how to respond to the human gesture, but she was clearly uncomfortable. She patted her back with her paw. "I would have been had it not been for you and our prince. You saved my life. I'm yet again in your debt."

Abigail stepped backward onto the steps, staring down at her legs. It was the strangest thing. You couldn't even tell they'd been a mangled mess only hours earlier.

The Ursis reached down and brushed the fur on her right leg. "These are no longer mine. They haven't been for some time." She dug her fingers into the dense fur and something clicked, revealing a panel that swung open. Inside was a micro-network of tubing and what looked like real veins surrounding leg joints, except they weren't biological at all. They were alien enhanced bio-limbs. It reminded her of the human body Harold used from time to time.

"They're artificial," she muttered.

"Indeed. When you reach two hundred years with a skeleton this large, your joints tend to give out." Klus closed the panel and stood up straight.

Abigail reached down and ran her hand over her leg, not even thinking about the implications of invading the alien's personal space. The lever she'd pressed was gone. When she pushed against the fur, it felt like the real thing.

Klus chuckled. "You're touchy, aren't you?"

"Sorry." She yanked her hand back. "It's remarkable. I couldn't tell earlier when it was cracked open, and I still can't."

"Not a problem, Seguan."

She narrowed her gaze.

Klus smiled. "I mean, Abigail."

She ignored the misstep. "So, how old are you, then?"

"I've survived three hundred and eighty-four cycles around our star, which is roughly the same as a galactic year, not that such things matter any longer. Come." Klus waved her forward and headed down the stairs. "We must leave this place."

Klus descended far faster than she'd expected. As she hopped down from stair to stair, she struggled not to fall. There was no railing, and the steps here were much taller and more uniform, having clearly been designed for Ursis. Unlike the rocky path they'd used earlier, these didn't appear to have aged.

"Where are we going?" Her voice was crisp and no longer echoing off the stone like it had above. Skotádi was a remarkable substance. She ran her hand over the wall as she descended. The craftsmanship was impressive. From the looks of it, they'd somehow infused the stealth material in the rock.

Klus was waiting for her at the bottom of the spiral stairway. "We're returning to our rightful place in this world. Somewhere we haven't been in far too long."

Abigail glanced past her and spotted a transport pod a few meters away. It looked otherworldly next to the black stone walls of the tunnel. Its pill like shape and sleek facade contrasted with the ancient structure surrounding it.

"Where exactly is this place?" She eased around Klus, moving in closer to the pod for a better look. The exterior was seamless, and the insides were downright luxurious compared to the primitive bed she'd woken up in.

"Our destination is Summis. The home of our king." Klus stepped past her and lowered her head, disappearing into the pod.

It didn't move when she stepped inside. It simply hovered in place above the tunnel floor. How the simple-looking device took on over a ton of weight without so much as a shift in position was beyond her comprehension. The Ursis technology was astounding. It's no wonder the Galactic Alliance had feared their rate of advancement through the stars.

Once she stepped through the massive opening, a concealed panel slid shut, closing her inside. She scrambled to get into her seat, only to realize they were already moving. She hadn't felt a thing. It was like they were on one of Zachary's gate ships. The inertial dampeners ate up all the momentum, leaving her feeling like she was standing in place. The only hint they weren't was the view-screen in front of them.

Their pod had accelerated the moment she was inside and was now approaching what could only be described as ludicrous speeds. She reached out to grab the wall as the tunnel zipped up and down and all around the screen. The pod was navigating the labyrinth of tunnels beneath the surface at breakneck speeds. It didn't feel real watching the screen change. It seemed like a video game more than reality.

She eased down into a seat next to Klus. It adjusted its height to allow her body to sink in as it slowly enveloped her in comfort. A groan escaped her lips as the chair seemed to sense her soreness and started massaging her back and lower half. "I could get used to this." She glanced at Klus. "How have you managed to keep these tunnels hidden for so long? Certainly, if Emmo knew about them, we wouldn't be able to just hitch a ride like this."

Klus nodded. "A secret is best kept when intertwined with a dash of lore and a healthy portion of fear. One mustn't forget about what all species have in common. The fear of death."

"That sounds familiar," Harold said.

Klus recoiled, and her eyes went wide. "Aha, so he wasn't lying. Was that your companion? Haradis told us much about them. He claimed you would talk to yourself at times, but not to worry. Is it true? Is he truly sentient?"

She chuckled. "Yes, his name is Harold. He is… well, it's complicated."

"Most secrets are." Klus crossed her hands in her lap and closed her eyes, seemingly done with the brief conversation. "I must center myself before we cross into the palace. Please refrain from speaking to me until the door opens."

Abigail wasn't sure how to respond, but silence seemed like the appropriate reaction. The only way she could talk to Harold without Klus hearing him, or her being screamed at, was through typing. She blinked open the controls on her retinal comm and started typing on her leg.

Should we be worried about where we're headed?

The reply was short.

Always.

That wasn't comforting in the least. She didn't like this new honest Harold. Not one bit. Perhaps it was best that he was still being curt. She would have more time to think of a way out of this mess. To tell the Ursis she couldn't help them.

36

IBU

PROTO DARK NEBULA, ORBITING
ARCTORDIEA

The contraption wasn't much to look at, but if it worked, they'd be able to issue requests into the Ursis network and poke around for clues about Abigail. It'd be a far cry from their current situation of only consuming what other Ursis viewed or what the government wanted them to see.

Ibu made one last adjustment to the retrofitted relay's gate interconnect and closed up the panel. Finding the device after they first entered the Dark Nebula felt like forever ago. It was hard to imagine how different this mission could have gone without Kamal turning things upside down. There certainly wouldn't have been as much doubt festering in Abigail's mind. The Olivaws were a tumultuous clan, especially her.

They shook their head. Now wasn't the time to get lost in random thought exercises. They'd kept the temptation at bay for the last eight hours, and they were almost done augmenting the satellite with a sensor array that could be inserted through a small gate opening. It was like the one they used to tight-beam messages through, except much bigger, since it wasn't only wavelengths of light passing through.

The more mass that went through the gate, and the longer

they had to hold it open, the more power they needed to prevent it from collapsing. They designed this sensor array to be four millimeters wide. While not a size that's ideal for capturing and relaying data, it was better than nothing. Since they weren't able to get the Ursis molecular gate tech working in time, it meant they had to open their tachyon gate closer to another satellite in the star system for optimal performance.

"We're ready to test the relay." Ibu hit the button beside the jerry-rigged contraption, and it rattled to life, vibrating like a washing machine out of balance. They eased back away from the device. They hadn't been expecting it to make a noise, but then again, there was no sound in space, so perhaps that was how it normally functioned.

"Don't worry, it's not gonna blow up." Shauna stepped up and adjusted the power regulator on the workbench, and the rattling subsided. "We were giving it too much power, and it wasn't happy. Fortunately, the Ursis had multiple fail safes built in."

Ibu raised an eyebrow. "So we could have blown it?"

Shauna chuckled. "No." She tweaked the device's display to bring up the crude software they'd cobbled together to control the relay. "The device is powered via subspace energy fluctuations and could handle the power spike of a supernova going off if it had to. I'm pretty sure the Phoenix's power core is no match for this device's failsafe."

While they trusted the A.I. wasn't lying, it still didn't give them comfort. They'd gone out on so many limbs and were taking so many risks, their mind was having trouble keeping up and controlling their emotions. At the start of the project, they were motivated to take action, but now they wanted to slow down. To breathe and plan a few more steps ahead. They knew they didn't have that luxury, so they had to lean in and trust fate. Something they never imagined they'd consider doing, let alone act on.

The ceiling of the cargo hold flashed, and the lights around the perimeter went red.

"I'm picking up a cruiser on an intercept trajectory," Cynthia said over their retinal comms.

"Impossible!" Ibu dashed toward the bridge. When they hit the central axis, they paused before veering left and taking the long way around. "Clockwise, always clockwise," they muttered.

As they passed over the threshold to the bridge, they saw Minula was about to begin the gate sequence. "Wait!" They reached out. "Don't do it yet."

"I'm not gonna be taken out like this." Minula reached up to the transition lever, and Ibu bolted across the distance and snatched at her wrist.

"They can't see us." Ibu pulled her hand away. "We're sealed tight. If they'd already detected us, we'd have been dead hours ago."

"That ship is going to pass by within a hundred meters." Cynthia brought up the projected path of the Ursis vessel on the wall screen. "And that's assuming they don't change course."

"If we gate now, we're back to square one and we're on the run." Ibu shook their head. "No. We're in the perfect spot where we are, and we're about to test our relay. I don't know about you, but I'm not keen on gating every five to ten minutes to stay safe, are you?"

They glanced over at Cynthia, and she was shaking her head. The woman had been complaining about the feeling of lingering ants crawling on her skin for the past day.

"I'd rather gate than die." Minula tried to reach for the lever again, but Ibu easily stopped her. "Let me go!"

"No! We stay put." Ibu eased closer to the controls and reached down, tweaking the consoles. It pivoted away from them, thinking the pilot was asking for room to stand.

Minula's face turned red, and she fought to move her

hand, but Ibu's grip was like a vice. Their body was fighting to morph, but they kept it at bay, instead using the surge in adrenaline and muscular strength to their advantage. While Minula could make a move on the controls with her other hand, for some reason, she wasn't. Perhaps it was her own doubt. That or her fear of the Nanil.

"Have they altered their course?" Ibu glanced back at Cynthia.

She peered down at her controls and shook her head. "No. They'll be passing us in… ten seconds. Nine, eight,…"

With Cynthia counting down, Ibu locked their gaze on Minula. The woman hadn't looked away since Ibu challenged her. She was clearly overtired. Her eyes were bloodshot, and they could feel her pulse in their hand. It was all over the map. She must be overusing stimulants to help her focus. The pressure of the last few days was breaking her.

When the countdown hit zero, the Phoenix fell silent. Shauna had the foresight to squelch the ship's collision alarms, and they shut down all internal systems that could make noise or cause a stray vibration. They were either backing Ibu's side, or hedging their bets.

The impact never came, and the Ursis cruiser passed without so much as a blip. The skotádi had done its job, and they hadn't needed to move.

"Let me go, now!" Minula leaned closer to Ibu, their faces only centimeters away.

They released the woman's grip, and she yanked her hand back, pivoting in her chair and standing up. She glanced from Cynthia and then back to Ibu, glaring at them for a few tense seconds. "I'm relinquishing the bridge to your command. I need some shuteye."

Ibu slowly nodded. "The bridge is mine. Sleep well, my friend."

Without another word, she stepped around them and walked away, working her way counterclockwise toward

Abigail's quarters. They brought up an overlay of the ship on their retinal comm and confirmed her dot entered the quarters of their friend. Her life signs dropped a few seconds later. She must've knocked herself out with meds.

Ibu eased down into the seat and pulled the control panel close, being sure to reactivate the gate transition lock. At least the woman knew when she'd cracked. That was one thing they admired about her. She wasn't like most of the other humans. Her patterns of action were usually logical and well-thought-out. But even the meticulous and trained had kinks in their armor. Hers happened to be love in harm's way.

ABIGAIL OLIVAW
PROTO DARK NEBULA, ON ARCTORDIEA

The chair vibrated and the overhead lights flashed, Abigail assumed, to warn them they were approaching their stop. The vacant tunnels they'd passed through the past few hours were a mixture of decay and modern architecture. At one point, they slowed to a crawl as the transport navigated over several rubble piles and over a disturbing body of dark orange water. Out near the edges of the cavern, she could make out what appeared to be dozens and dozens of mounds of bones, from what she could only assume were other Ursis.

She'd wanted to wake Klus on many occasions, but chose instead to heed her request to be left alone. Her questions could wait till later once they stopped. Harold had no doubt recorded everything they'd witnessed. While she never asked, they discussed the sightings through their primitive text chats. It wasn't as fluid as talking, but it was nice in its own way. A simpler form of communication from a simpler time in human history.

"We have arrived." Klus opened her eyes and stared forward. Her voice was calm and crisp, refreshed by hours of meditation. You couldn't tell for a second that she'd run for her life from a cave-in or endured a major surgery in the past day.

"I have many questions, particularly about what we just passed through. Like, what were all those bodies? And how could this network exist for so long without being discovered?" She pointed toward the door. "And don't even get me started thinking about what's out there. Your Seguan is getting anxious about being in the dark."

Klus' gaze softened, and she stared past her at the moss-covered wall. "You must be talking about the boneyards at Uzria. Was there—"

"A strange blood orange body of what, I assume, was water surrounded the piles, yes." She shivered at the thought of the liquid. The way it moved was like it was fighting to come to life. "I was about to wake you up when Harold reminded me of your request to be left alone."

"Your friend was wise. I'm not certain how I would have felt coming out of my reverie in that place. Some say the water never used to be there, and that what you actually saw was the blood and melted skin from the bodies of my brethren. Hundreds of thousands of Umbra lost their lives down in those caves during the clan purges following the sealing of the Dark Nebula."

She leaned closer to the Ursis. "You mean to tell me those bones were from the actions of Emmo and her Tlingui clan?"

"Among others." Klus crossed her hands in her lap. "The Tlingui sealed those caverns and hundreds like it with a great many Ursis inside. The tunnels we traversed through are believed to have been created by the souls lost during the purge. We Ulyxsauri know they are much older, but the legends and tales of the Ursis that come back to life on that same day every year excite fear into even the strongest of Emmonsii's soldiers. Time and time again, we've seen them turn a blind eye to strange happenings down there."

"Would those happenings be Deduc and your people moving about?"

Klus sighed. "We had many plans to remain relevant before your arrival, Seguan. But now that the see-er's visions have become a reality, we know for certain the gods of Therion are on our side."

The pod door slid open, and Klus didn't hesitate. She pushed up out of the seat and practically sprinted forward.

If Abigail didn't know better, she'd think the Ursis was trying to get away from her or put an end to her line of questions.

She sat still, staring into the distance. The display at the front of the pod had changed. On it was superimposed what she assumed was a three-dimensional map of the palace above them. It was massive. Easily the largest structure she'd ever seen in her life, and it went on in every direction.

"It's... enormous," she muttered.

"It makes our Wheel bases and our Archégonos outpost on Liprosus seem tiny, doesn't it?" Harold asked.

"If you mean dwarfs them a thousand times over, then yes. It puts the scale of the Ursis into a different perspective."

She eased up out of her chair and worked her way to the front of the pod, taking a closer look at the infographic. Only when she reached the control panel did she notice the green dots moving about. There weren't many, only a few dozen.

"Those are our people," Klus said. She'd returned to the pod entrance. "Aren't you coming?"

"Not until you tell me what we're doing here." She spun around to face the alien and leaned against the wall with her arms crossed.

Klus raised an eyebrow. "Of all people, I'd expect you to know. Being the Seguan and all."

"Well... some of us didn't sleep." She reached up and rubbed her shoulder where the skin was still sensitive. It never hurt playing wounded from time to time.

"Ah yes, I forget." Klus straightened her back and puffed out her chest. "We have returned to Summis, to right a wrong and to help Haradis claim what is his by birthright."

The clergy mentioned a birthright the day before, but she assumed they were talking about something else. Like a house or a fancy sword of some sort. She didn't imagine they meant an entire palace or to become king.

"You can't honestly think he can waltz in here and demand to be your leader, do you?" Abigail pushed off and stepped toward her. "And there's not a chance in hell Emmo doesn't have spies in this place. Besides, isn't she already the fraking queen or something?"

"Emmonsii Phi denounced the throne after she killed King Maritimus. Her government never represented the people. They dictated everything after the Nebula fell, and their only means of control was through bloodshed." Klus turned and exited the pod.

When Abigail looked around the corner to see where she'd gone, The Ursis paused at the base of a stairwell a few meters away. She didn't turn to face her. She merely raised her head skyward, toward an intricate crest with a crowned bear in the center of a circular shield. The buckler was surrounded with filigree that began as a pattern of vines and transformed into what appeared to be a circuit board. The dichotomy of the two stages of evolution on the same crest wasn't lost on her.

"I don't expect you to understand or support our ways, Seguan. The see-er's visions never proclaimed you as the uniter of our people. That is up to Prince Haradis. Your role is to set us free." Klus lowered her head and started upward, one step after the other. She made quick work of the massive stairs until she disappeared around the corner.

Once they were gone, the pod station fell silent. Off in the distance to Abigail's left, she could hear a sound of water dripping into what sounded like a larger pool. It'd probably been doing that for centuries, but no one was around to care. She didn't enjoy walking into a place blind to her surroundings, so she stepped back into the pod and started fiddling with the controls.

"I assume we can record this?" She reached out and ran her hand along the screen, but the view didn't change. The device wouldn't respond to her touch.

"I've recorded what you can see," Harold began, "but unless you can get it to show more, we'll be blind once we make it up a few levels."

No matter what she did, the display wouldn't change for her. When she returned her attention to the dots, she saw they were rising upward in a spiral. From what she could tell, the entire group was climbing the stairs. Everyone except for her.

"I fraking hate stairs." She sighed and stomped out of the pod, working her way to the foot of the stairwell, where she paused and glanced up. The stairs were huge. Unlike the ones they'd climbed down earlier, these were pristine and weren't worn down due to time or use. For her, that meant only one thing: her legs would be screaming at her in a matter of minutes.

She shook her head and hopped up onto the first step and landed on her belly before rolling back up on her side. Going up was so much harder than going down. "All this fancy tech and these aliens can't invent lift tubes."

"At least I've been able to replenish your nanites," Harold said. "That concoction they shot you up with was enough to heal ten humans your size. I took the leftovers and went about turning on your body's nanite cloning. We've replenished your reserves, and then some."

"Tell me that means I won't feel this climb." She leaned forward and swung her leg up, hopping onto the next step in one motion before pushing up off the ground. Her muscles weren't complaining. They actually felt pretty good so far.

"I hope you don't. I've redirected half of them toward

finishing the repairs to the wounds on your back." Harold brought up a video game like outline of her body in the corner of her field of view. "It's a war zone up in there. I've been able to repurpose some of the stony shrapnel for more nanites. You'll be happy to know there were heavy metals in them there rocks."

She chuckled. At least he was in a good mood and cracking jokes. It'd make it easier to pass the time. As she swung her leg up on the next step, she hopped up and rolled onto her back, staring at the display he'd brought up. Her back was yellow and trending green. The hundreds of flashing dots along her arms and upper back were surreal. Each of them was a collection of nanites working to repair her broken body. Erasing the mistakes she'd made coming to this place. The mistakes of leaving her people behind.

One leg, one hop after another, she rose upward, well behind the others, but making steady progress. Their situation began turning over in her mind as time faded, and her body focused on performing the motion. Repetition had a way of clearing out the cruft and allowing the important things to bubble to the top. Now if she could just find a way out of this mess.

HAROLD HAD BEEN RIGHT. Climbing wasn't as hard as Abigail expected it to be. She never did ask how low her nanites had gotten earlier. But given that she still felt human and didn't want to take a nap after scaling nearly three quarters of a kilometer, she must've been on empty down in those caverns.

During the past few hundred meters of the climb, the scenery changed dramatically. Gone were the intricate stonework and filigree spiraling up the wall. It'd been replaced by sleek metallic flooring and consistent lighting that reminded her of the Galactic Alliance tribunal ships. The light was everywhere, yet there was no clear central source. It was almost like the material itself was glowing.

When she summited the stairs, she froze. The clergy were surrounding the exit in a semicircle, and both Deduc and Haradis were standing in the center. They were deep in conversation and only paused when they noticed she'd arrived.

Her face warmed, turning pink as she pushed up off the ground one last time. When she stood upright, all eyes were on her. She hadn't expected everyone would be waiting for her, given how far behind she'd been and how quickly they'd left the Keep.

Klus stepped out of the awaiting line and handed her a vial of what she assumed was water. She then bowed and slid back beside her people.

Abigail didn't check it. She simply popped off the top and poured it down her throat. It tasted like water, and that was good enough for her.

"Thank you," she muttered between swallows. Even though she felt fine, her mouth was as dry as a desert. After she downed half the container, she wiped her mouth on her sleeve and put the cap back on. "Are we done summiting Everest yet?"

Deduc tilted his head.

Haradis smiled and stepped forward, gently placing his hand on her back. "For now, my friend. Our only hills from here on out involve the hearts and minds of the people. And maybe a few bullets and blasters."

Harold laughed in her ear.

"Ahh. I see your companion is awake. Does he wish to join us out in the physical world?" Haradis gestured in front of him.

"I can't imagine how that would work." She shifted her

stance and caught the gaze of Deduc. He was studying her intently. "He's not exactly mobile."

"I'm sure we can figure something out, right?" He nodded toward Klus, and they bowed back, stepping backward out of line and disappearing down one of the nearby passages.

"Are we done with the niceties?" Deduc adjusted his outfit.

She hadn't noticed it until now, but his appearance had changed. Gone were his simple robes, and in their place was an elaborate gown with ornate gold and silver markings along the edges. Each letter almost seemed to glow as the cloth moved. The glyphs were likely an ancient writing of some sort, but neither her eyes nor the translator recognized them.

Haradis shook his head. "Now is not the time to extinguish our manners."

Deduc snapped his gaze backward. "When did you hear that?"

"My mother. Just because I never met her doesn't mean I didn't have access to recordings with her in them." He pressed his palm into Abigail's back and they both stepped toward Deduc. "They were the only thing that kept me sane on some days. Her voice was soothing and reassuring when I needed it most."

Deduc's gaze narrowed on her as they approached. She couldn't tell if he was questioning her involvement in the prince's words, or if he was suddenly regretting bringing her along. Either way, she didn't feel welcome.

She stepped away from Haradis and moved closer to the priest. She had to confront him head on if she was going to make it out of here. "Judging by the frigidity of your glare, you don't want me around. If you have a problem, I can go."

"On the contrary." Deduc brought his arms forward and rested them on a cane she hadn't seen. He must have been concealing it under his robes. "I simply expected that you'd have led this part of the vision rather than lingered in the shadows. You know, being the Seguan and all."

"Déjà vu," she muttered.

Deduc narrowed his gaze. "What's that?"

"It means that you and your clergy are having the same thoughts. Which makes sense. You're one and the same and don't think for yourselves. Apparently, you're not the only Ursis doubting your visions from the gods. You're assuming I have some sort of superpower to flick my fingers and know everything about this place, or about you. I mean, let's be honest for a second, Mr. See-er. Without a Beacon of Therion, you wouldn't have seen shit. You'd be just as regular as I am."

One of the clergy eased out of line to the right, taking several steps toward her. "Don't speak to the see-er like that."

"Let's not get worked up." Haradis took a step forward.

"Or what?" She snapped her head sideways and pushed Haradis back, moving closer to the clergy. "Are you gonna kill me? Slash my neck with those claws?" She nodded toward the dagger like nails that had retracted out of their fur. "Maybe you're no different from Emmonsii Phi after all. Maybe what happened here all those years ago is simply a matter of perspective, and I just so happen to be a human who looks a bit like that shitty painting down in the caverns."

A message appeared on the lower edge of her retinal comm.

I think you're pushing them further than we discussed.

She didn't care. Whether they killed her now, or in a few days when they realized she had nothing to offer, it didn't really matter.

The clergy grunted, their nostrils flaring at her accusation.

They clearly didn't like being compared to Emmo. She couldn't blame them, but if they were challenging her the moment she reached the top of the stairs, that meant they'd been questioning her role far longer than the last few minutes.

She turned her attention back toward Deduc. "I don't hear you standing up for yourself. Were you some all seeing visionary before the Dark Nebula fell? Before you came into contact with the Beacon. Or were you weak, like how you see me?"

A message appeared on her comm.

His pulse is elevated. He's going to—

Deduc lunged forward to within a few centimeters of her face, but she held her ground. She didn't need Harold to tell her what was already obvious.

"I am nothing like you. I am the head of the Ursis Ulyxsauri!" Spittle was dripping down his open jaw, and his blindingly white teeth glimmered in the light. At this distance, she could see a symbol etched on the tip of each tooth. The letters matched the ones on his robes. "You will not speak to me like that, hu—man. I've kept this society alive since the Nebula fell. I've—"

"Heard enough." Abigail tossed the container of water on the ground and the top popped off, splashing water everywhere.

Deduc recoiled, his mouth gaping open.

"I'm done being your key to unlock your Nebula, only to be tossed aside once you're free. If you want to save your people, you and Haradis can do it yourselves. You don't need me. You never did. I'm sure those visions of yours will get you far enough for another human to help you."

With the tension peaking, Klus arrived from the hall she'd

disappeared down with a robot in tow close behind. When she entered the semicircle, she froze, unsure of what was happening.

Haradis eased up beside Abigail and reached for her shoulder. She met his hand midair and knocked it away. "Klus! Take me to your jail."

Klus took a step backward, and her eyes darted from Haradis to Deduc and then back to Abigail. "What do you mean?"

"I'm done." Abigail stepped between the wall of clergy toward her, being sure not to brush against the aliens. She'd have no repeat of what happened last time an unexpected alien touched her. "I refuse to help the Ursis. Especially those who have blind faith in a vision, and yet doubt the trustworthiness of the target of said vision." She held out her wrists toward them.

Klus stared at her, frozen like a deer in headlights. She was torn between her debt to Abigail and her duty to Deduc and the Ulyxsauri church. She could see it in her eyes.

"You heard her." Deduc straightened up and adjusted his robes, his cane disappearing into the folds. "Take the cub down to one of our special rooms. I'm sure you can rig up something uncomfortable to restrain her tiny human hands." He turned in place and gazed at Haradis. "Come, my prince. We have history to make and a throne to take back."

Haradis stared at her and shook his head. He was as confused as Klus. Deduc eased him forward, gently nudging the back of his arm and sliding up beside him. Haradis resisted at first, glancing over his shoulder multiple times. After a few untranslatable words in his ear, they walked away side by side.

The semicircle of clergy shuffled behind the two figures, following them down the hall. Haradis kept peering back at her, but when the clergy closed the gap behind him, he stopped checking for her.

She couldn't blame him. He'd been wanting this moment his entire life, and the last thing he expected to run into was a human troublemaker.

"What did you do?" Klus asked. "I was gone for only a minute."

She chuckled. "I told you what I did. I'm not helping you or any other Ursis. Your doubt in me isn't misplaced. I am not your savior. Never was." She glanced around the half dozen passages. "Now, which way to that cell?" She started walking down the hall she'd just returned from.

"I never doubted you, Seguan." She sprinted up to her side, the robots behind her spinning in place and following along like puppies. "I was confused by what you already knew was going to happen and what was fate."

She clenched her fist. "For the last time, stop—calling—me—Seguan."

"You're right." Klus nodded. "You asked me several times not to do that, and I have failed. I won't do it again, Abigail."

"Now, which way are your cells?" She stopped in front of a random door and pointed. "Is this one?"

Klus shook her head. "No. That is a kitchen. This way. Follow me."

The Ursis moved with purpose, and she had to jog to keep up. Maybe small talk would slow her down. "Say, what's up with Deduc and the cane anyhow? I mean, if you can create legs, why can't he?"

Klus glanced back at her and smirked. "The see-er does all they can to remain pure and without modification. It's bad enough they use medications to cope with their aging form. When he woke up at the Keep, he was in immense pain. He'd lost his meds in the moments leading up to the cave-in. Thus his... mood today."

Abigail nodded. That explained the vials she saw on the ground outside the Keep. What she couldn't figure out, though, was that with all their technology, why the alien refused to use it to help them.

The Ursis was done talking. She waved her hand forward and began walking even faster, covering huge distances with every stride.

Abigail struggled to keep up and needed to drop into a jog on several occasions. She took turn after turn down winding hallways, and at one point she swore they'd backtracked on themselves. When Klus disappeared around a corner, she sprinted to catch up and nearly crashed into them on the other side. The mountainous female had paused in front of a lone doorway and was staring at it for some reason. Like she'd seen a ghost.

"Is it in there?" She pointed at the ornate silver door. The archway around the entrance was covered in markings similar to the ones she'd seen earlier on Deduc's robes. As she studied the doorframe, her eyes lingered along the top, on the one symbol her translator was able to convert to English. The human word hovered in the air on her retinal comm.

Knowledge.

When she glanced over at Klus, she was merely staring at the door.

Abigail wasn't about to wait for an engraved invitation. As she stepped up to the entrance, she reached out and the smooth shiny surface swung inward before she could touch it. Her hand swiped at the air instead. It took a few seconds for her eyes to adjust to the bright light coming from inside, but when they did, she drew in a breath, gazing at the grandeur of the room.

Inside wasn't a cell at all. It was the farthest thing from a cell she could imagine. The space beyond housed a throne of glimmering gold, easily the single largest chair she'd ever seen in her life. It extended from floor to ceiling. The seat of power emerged from the beams of yellow light in the sky, and at the same time, was firmly rooted in the golden soil below. Along the lines connecting the two and extending into the chair itself were brilliant vines intertwined with the faces of Ursis. She assumed they represented the disciples of the king, but they could have been anyone. None of them wore crowns or looked particularly regal. The weirdest thing about them was their eyes. They were staring straight at her as she walked across the threshold into the room.

I don't think we should be in here.

The message flashed in the center of her retinal comm, and she blinked it away. Harold was probably right, but Klus brought her here for some reason. She had no idea why, but she was sure she'd find out.

As she made her way toward the throne, the sound of Klus walking behind her was unmistakable. She didn't ask them why she'd come here. Not yet. For now, she wanted to check the place out.

Her attention turned to the sides of the throne as she strolled down the central walkway. She hadn't noticed it when she first took in the enormity of the room, but the seat of power was flanked by two smaller chairs. One she assumed was for the queen, while the other appeared to be small enough for a child Ursis. In this case, it looked to be about the perfect size for an adult human.

She'd walked nearly fifty meters by the time she reached the throne itself. It wasn't until she paused to look back that she realized the entire space was inclined. The effect was subtle, but it was more pronounced from up here. Everyone below the king was forced to gaze up at them. Both upward toward the power center and toward the radiating golden sun that emblazoned the ceiling.

Her eyes followed the edges of the room up into the distant heavens above. While she'd barely taken note of it when she first walked in, the sky was awe-inspiring. From where she was standing, it looked like it could've been real, but strangely, there didn't appear to be a roof overhead. Either way, the sky was deep blue and there wasn't a cloud in sight.

The sphere of light hovering over the thrones undulated and swirled with a mind of its own. At times, it seemed to mirror the effect of an actual star. When she followed the fluid rays of light downward, she realized the golden effect she'd seen at a distance wasn't a metal at all. The throne and its connection to the ball of fire were undulating just like the sun. It behaved as if it were a fluid, almost like someone was pouring a liquid from the sky and spilling it into the Ursis' faces and the throne itself.

"Remarkable, isn't it?" Klus asked. Her voice was a whisper.

For the first time in Abigail's life, words failed her. All she could do was nod.

The glistening surface was unlike anything she'd seen before. It was entrancing, and before she knew it, she'd stepped up to the edge of the smallest chair. The one clearly used for a child.

"I'm not sure you should be up there," Klus whispered. She was standing a few meters away, almost like she was afraid of getting too close to the object.

"Why did you bring me here, then?" Abigail ran her palm over the arm of the chair, and the fluid flowed around her hand, reacting to her touch even before her fingers touched down. The material sort of felt like it was exploring her skin. After holding it for a few seconds, her vision fluttered and a rainbow of splotches floated in from the edges of her field of view. It reminded her of when she'd stared too long at a bright light, except there were more colors.

When she pulled her hand back, she held it up in front of her face. Her skin was dry and there was no excess residue. Stranger still, the splotches had faded from her vision almost immediately. Looking down, the spot where her hand had rested against the throne now had a faint blue glow to it. Like it'd reacted to her skin or something.

"The material is of an unknown origin," Harold said over her retinal comm. "It's unusual. If I didn't know better, I'd say it was—"

"Alive," she muttered, turning her hand over and over. It tingled on the edges where the fluid had run up against her skin.

"I was hoping that by showing you this place, you'd reconsider helping us." Klus paced back and forth in front of an invisible line on the ground.

She glanced at them. "Did Deduc put you up to this?"

Klus waved her hand. "Oh, no. He'd be very unhappy if he found out I brought you here. This place..." She gazed upward. "This place is sacred and reserved only for other Ursis. In fact, you're the first non-native to set foot here."

The hairs up and down her arms stood on end. She imagined there'd been a lot of firsts for her on this voyage, and she'd blown right past them just as unknowingly, but this was the highlight.

"It has been foretold for centuries," Klus began. "There is no other explanation for your being on this planet, on this day, at this point in time and history. You are the Seguan. No one questions it. I know Deduc can be stubborn and temperamental. And trust me, we all hate it when he calls someone a cub. Last I checked, a cub wasn't over three hundred." She shook his head. "He's difficult, but he means well."

"Most misguided people do." Abigail reached out, this

time pressing her palm against the seat of the chair. The golden material flowed around her hand again, except the blue effect she'd noticed earlier was spreading faster, expanding from where the material touched her. It streaked down the chair toward the floor.

She held her hand in place and bent down, watching the blue and gold streams flow in and out of the ornate markings in the chair's finish. She could literally feel an energy force moving through her, and yet, it didn't hurt. It didn't feel like a fluid, either. In fact, there was pressure pushing against her hand, preventing it from sinking in. The material was both a liquid and a solid. Or maybe it was neither. She couldn't tell.

"We might want to hold back from touching it like that," Harold said. "For all we know, it's damaging the stuff."

He was wrong. She didn't know how she knew it, but he was. Touching it was healing for the material, not harmful. It was like the substance was somehow familiar to her. The energy wanted to be in contact with people, with all nearby life. But it was isolated to this space, and no one had visited it in over half a century.

Leaning closer, she stared at her hand, studying the fluid as it tried to connect with her skin and then pull away. The faint tingling from being in contact with the surface came back, but not the splotches yet. The sensation was both foreign and addictive at the same time. Even the thought of pulling away was undesirable. Her fingers longed to remain in contact. She somehow had an innate knowledge that pulling away would be followed by moments of regret. Almost like the material didn't want her to stop touching it.

"Abigail!" Harold's voice boomed over her retinal comm. "I'm detecting elevated stimulants in your bloodstream. I suggest you remove your—"

"What have you done!?" Klus stumbled backward down the ramp, her neck craned toward the ceiling.

When she glanced upward, a blue glow was streaking out

of the globe overhead. It was similar to both the splotches and the colors flowing away from her hand, except more vibrant and more numerous. There were dozens of rivulets fingering down, spreading in all directions. She stared in awe as the streams descended, the largest of which was approaching the central throne.

Harold's image appeared on her retinal comm, filling her entire field of view. "Abigail! Remove your hand."

She snatched her hand away, and all hell broke loose. Harold minimized just as the air erupted with the sound of alarms blaring, followed by a half dozen gates slamming shut around the room. They covered multiple entrances she hadn't even realized were there.

"So much for our escape route," Harold said.

"What's going on?" She rubbed her hand, and a tear streamed down her cheek. A sudden sadness surged through her body and she started shaking. She stared down at the throne and the sorrow grew stronger and louder, if that were possible. The alien material was crying out, making her feel for it. It was somehow cutting through the alarms, yet it wasn't nearly as grating.

When she stepped back and glanced at Klus, the Ursis didn't seem to notice the other sound. She was staring at the gates and running her paws through her fur over and over again.

Abigail screamed over the sounds. "Can you hear that?"

Harold shook his head. "Hear what?"

"The crying." She turned back toward the wall of life, taking in the streams of gold and blue rivulets cascading down from the ceiling. When her eyes lowered to the throne, she noticed an imprint of a hand on the base. It wasn't a human hand. This one was the shape of an Ursis paw.

"What have you done?" Deduc screamed.

She spun to her left in time to see a stream of Ursis exiting out of the one exit that didn't have a gate over it. Deduc was in the lead, and Haradis was close behind, followed by the rest of the clergy. They were all dressed in similar robes to Deduc, though Haradis' were far brighter and more regal.

"I... didn't do anything," she muttered, backing away from the chairs.

Deduc waved his cane at Klus. "You brought her here? You failed us. You failed me. She was supposed to be locked away by now. No human should ever touch foot in this chamber."

Haradis stepped forward and nudged Deduc's shoulder to face him. "Not even the Seguan?"

"No." Deduc slammed his cane against the ground. "Not even this... human. This frail excuse for a savior. She is not worthy of the name and will be dealt with later." He glanced toward the sky and rubbed at his ear. "But for the moment, I need you to go touch the throne and turn off that blasted alarm."

Haradis stared at the priest. Wrinkles formed in his nose and it scrunched up. The young prince didn't say a word, though. He seemed conflicted the longer he lingered.

The other members of Deduc's clergy were glancing slack jawed between one another. Each of them acted as if they wanted to say something, but knew better. It was becoming more and more obvious that everyone feared the priest.

After over a minute of uncomfortable, ear-piercing racket, Haradis nodded and turned to face her. He locked on her gaze and started toward her, working his way up the shortened incline. When he got within a few steps, he froze in front of the golden seat. She couldn't tell if he'd stopped because she was crying, or if he'd had a change of heart. It was hard to tell with the cacophony of noise around them.

He tilted his ear toward the throne and squinted. "Do you hear that?"

"The alarm or the crying?" She wiped at her eyes, wincing as the klaxons got even louder.

"The crying," he muttered, taking the last few tentative steps toward the throne and stopping in front of it. His gaze locked on the paw in the center. The imprint was undulating in gold, longing for someone to touch it.

When she leaned forward and stared up at him, he had a strange look in his eyes. It reminded her of how she felt after she'd made contact with the surface. He was hesitating. "You want to touch it, don't you?" She stepped up beside him. "I wanted to, as well. Hell, I still do." She rubbed her hand, the tingling from her last touch still resonated through her fingers.

"Leave him alone!" Deduc slammed his cane against the ground and the snap reverberated through the chamber.

She glanced back at the obnoxious alien. For some reason, he was still keeping his distance down the ramp.

"It's like a voice inside—" Haradis shook his head and scratched the side of his face. "No, it's not possible."

She nodded. "I hear it, too. I think it missed… contact. Being in touch with you, and your kind… or anyone, really." She reached up and brushed against his hand, trying not to scare him. Once she was certain he wouldn't pull away, she eased his hand toward the throne. "Come on. Your destiny is calling."

His eyes glimmered as their hands moved in unison, and together they touched the paw imprint, her hand on top of his. When the pads on his hand made contact, a rush of emotion cascaded through her, like a downpour of cold water followed by warmth.

Fear

Doubt

Love

Confusion

Anger

They were echoes of her feelings, yet they weren't hers alone. Behind each emotional wave, she could sense Haradis was there. He was feeling the same things. It was as if the alien material had read their minds and joined them together as one.

When the alarms cut, they were still intertwined and entranced in the waterfall of emotions from the simple action. The others surrounding them, however, were acutely aware of a change. Their Ursis bio-computers all came online, and an emergency broadcast kicked in, alerting the population of an attack. Defensive systems around the palace turned on after centuries of not being used.

IBU

PROTO DARK NEBULA, ORBITING
ARCTORDIEA

It'd been almost six hours since Minula melted down. The bridge emptied soon after and had been quiet since. Ibu stared at the wall screen, locked in her virtual link to the central computer. They were on watch again alongside Shauna while the humans got some rest. While the risks of sitting still were high, so was the probability of error if the crew didn't get some shuteye.

They studied the communication and data feeds coming into and out of the planet. The segments they were covering contained dozens of sources, whereas Shauna's were several thousand. Each consisted of audio or video and multiple streams of data. Compared to them, the A.I. was far more efficient at parsing the sheer volume of information going back and forth. The virtual screens they were monitoring were scrolling past at impossible rates. It hurt their head just watching them flip around, even being as focused as they were in this mental link. They were beginning to understand why humans had grown so reliant on the virtual life form.

Their problem wasn't a lack of understanding the artificial life forms, it was a lack of trust. Perhaps it'd been Harold keeping humanity in the dark for so long, always claiming to be acting in their best interest. Or maybe it was the blind reliance the Olivaws had on technology, especially when they stole it from the Galactic Alliance. It didn't matter, really. The net result was that they were compelled to checkup on them. Several of the feeds they were processing were also being handled by Shauna, and the woman knew it. The funny part was, she didn't seem to care. It was almost like she'd expected it.

"I'm picking up..." Shauna's avatar froze, her arm outstretched toward the virtual wall of feeds.

"What is it?" Ibu paused and passed one of their feeds onto Shauna's stack to handle and brought up the one the woman was pointing at. A second later, nearly every single feed in her stack switched over to the same imagery. There was an emergency broadcast coming from the far side of the planet.

When they enlarged the feed to give it their full attention, they drew in a breath. On the screen was a lone human alongside a mountainous Ursis. Gold, blue, and red tendrils of color were cascading down the ceiling, forming into limbs of a tree which converged toward a magnificent golden throne and two neighboring chairs.

"It's Abigail," Shauna muttered. "She's... alive."

It hadn't dawned on Ibu who the human in the feed was until that moment. Her hair was a mess and her appearance was disheveled, but her jumpsuit was the worst. It was crudely stitched in parts and splattered with blood in others. Whereas the Ursis was regal in his ornate flowing robes of glowing white, Abigail looked downright pitiful. The two were a stark contrast, standing side by side.

While Ibu was focused on the imagery unfolding in front of them, Shauna was doing her job, and shared the tactical display from the Phoenix with them. Not only were the feeds a chatter with this emergency broadcast, the military had already mobilized. Several nearby Alatas ships were drop-ping out of their warp bubbles near the planet.

They gestured toward the feed and brought up details the broadcasters were passing along for viewers. The signal was being transmitted from the capital city, Summis. They were live-streaming from the former King's throne room. It'd been abandoned since the Dark Nebula fell. That was, until a few minutes ago.

"This is strange." Shauna brought up a few of the fringe feeds from the less popular Ursis news outlets on the wall screen. The volume was turned up.

... We've been telling you for days the search on the planet had been foretold for decades. This human you're seeing. They will save the Ursis from this veil of death. Mark my words. Our beloved High Priest Deduc spoke of such an event after the Dark Nebula fell over fifty years ago, but his voice was silenced by you, the people. Was he right? We'll review what little we could recover from the stories of the past. It seems our fearless leader, Emmonsii Phi, has been busy with her censors and has scrubbed most of the archives of any details concerning this matter. Fortunately for you, we have backups. Keep watching, and judge for yourself.

The story was cryptic, and for all they knew the personality was a blabbering fringe idealist clawing for limelight, but they were confident and surprisingly detailed around the dates.

"How long until we can calculate a gate to the far side?" Ibu asked.

"I'm not sure what you're thinking, but I wouldn't advise doing it in a single hop. There are too many gravitational variables, especially with the new ships arriving." Shauna brought up a three-dimensional map of the area around the planet that showed the arriving Ursis ships plotted out. "I'd do it in two to three small hops, unless we want to engage our normal drives." That flight path overlaid on the same graphic.

"We'd be toast as soon as we light 'em up. You saw what happened last time we got close to their ships." They dismissed that idea from the display and focused on the gate strategy. Fast hops meant a lot of pain, and they'd need to be in tip-top condition afterward. That meant drugs. Lots of drugs.

"We have to wake the others." Ibu dismissed the virtual world and opened their eyes, taking in the bridge. Shauna's robot form came to life in the corner and stepped off her docking station.

"Why don't I wake the soldiers, and you handle Minula and Cynthia?" She started toward the exit.

"Sure," they muttered, "give me the emotional one."

They hopped up and out of their chair and sprinted out of the bridge. When they hit the hall, they paused and briefly glanced right and then left. Even though her quarters were closer to the right, their body wouldn't budge that way. Clockwise is the only safe path. They took a deep breath and turned left, leaning forward and running all out. If they were going to let habit direct them, they weren't about to lose precious seconds to their own idiosyncrasies.

As they approached the doorway to Abigail's quarters, they didn't pause to acknowledge the human protocol of knocking. They subvocalized an emergency command to open the door, and it sprang aside without a sound.

The light from the hall spilled into the room and Minula lurched upright in bed, her fists raised. "I can't, I'll—" She shook her head and squinted toward the doorway, raising her hand to block the light. Her eyes were bloodshot and her hair was a mess, even for as short as it was.

"What's..." She never finished the sentence. She simply stared at Ibu and her eyes widened. "You found her, didn't you?"

They smiled and nodded. "She's down on the planet, on the far side."

"Is... she ok?" She swung her legs off the bed and hopped down.

"She's in their capital, in some type of Ursis government chamber for the king."

Minula pulled up her pants and slid her feet into her shoes before finally running a hand through her hair. "Is she ok?"

"It's got to be one of the most fortified regions on the planet." Ibu flicked the details to Minula for her to analyze. They could already sense the elevated hormones in the air, and her muscles tensed each time she asked her a question. "We need to understand the situation before we—"

Minula lurched forward to within centimeters of their face. "Answer my fraking question."

They stared each other down, neither wanting to give in. The woman's actions were predictable, but Ibu didn't know how to slow them down. Rushing in and putting everyone's life at risk wasn't the most logical course of action.

"What's going on?" Cynthia stepped up beside Ibu and yawned. "I heard screaming."

Minula's lip twitched, and her eyes narrowed.

"We found Abigail," Ibu muttered.

Cynthia clapped her hands together and rocked up on her toes. "That's wonderful. How is she?"

Against their better judgment, Ibu twisted their back, forcing their body to morph. They never lost focus on Minula the entire time. Their muscles bulged, and their physical form swelled like a sausage. It didn't hurt, but it wasn't the most comfortable, either.

"Well, then." Cynthia took a few steps backward.

"Abigail's not in good shape." Ibu opened a comm to the

rest of the ship. "Prepare for an emergency landing on the planet. And Shauna, let's see if we can open a direct beam with our lost leader when we get close."

"Roger that," Shauna said. "The soldiers are already getting prepped. I'll need a few more minutes to finish plotting our gate hops, but I'm pretty sure I can get us directly above her."

They must have been watching the events play out with Minula. Either that, or she somehow knew what the woman was going to do. While human nature wasn't predictable to everyone, certain people had an innate ability to anticipate the behavior of others with uncanny accuracy. Shauna was such a person, especially when it came to her family and friends.

"The closer you can get, the better." Ibu cut the line and nodded toward Minula. "Let's try not to die down there, ok?"

"I'd rather die for a good cause than sit on my ass." She squeezed past Ibu and rocketed forward toward the cargo hold.

They watched the woman disappear around the bend, Cynthia close behind. While they agreed to the verbal sentiment, they weren't entirely certain rushing to save someone for love was a good enough reason to die.

ABIGAIL OLIVAW

PROTO DARK NEBULA, ON ARCTORDIEA

The trance broke not long after the security measures turned on. When Abigail pulled her hand back from Haradis, his paw remained, lingering on the throne for a bit longer. He was still deeply entranced with the consciousness. That was the first time she'd thought of it that way. As being alive. She stepped backward and spun around, her retinal comm bursting to life.

"What happened?" Harold asked. "I lost you there for a minute. It was like when you first touched it."

"It's... hard to explain," she subvocalized.

"Something tells me you should keep your hand off that stuff."

She shook her head. "No. It's not like that at all."

"It's talking to you, isn't it?" Deduc took a few steps forward and paused, still well away from the throne. "What did you hear?"

The numbing sensation in her hand lingered as she rubbed it. She wasn't about to tell him she hadn't heard anything. All she'd seen was the landscape of some unknown world. The purple skies and hazy clouds framing the fields of green and blue were familiar, but she couldn't put her finger on where she'd seen it before.

She tilted her head to the side. It was curious why the priest was keeping a distance from her. He hadn't in the past. "Why don't you come touch it yourself? It won't bite you."

Deduc's hand flinched, his cane seeming to wobble. "I cannot. Not until King Haradis entrusts me as his spiritual consort."

Her retinal comm blinked, and she drew in a breath. An image of a cargo hold flashed in front of her. It almost looked like the Phoenix, but that was impossible. There was a silhouette of figures standing in front of a crack of light, and then it cut away. "Strange," she muttered. "Did you see that, Harold?"

"What's that?" Deduc asked. "Did you feel… any pain?"

She shook her head and glanced upward into the clear blue sky overhead, willing the image to return, but it didn't. Instead, an audible alert blared throughout the throne room, followed by a confident and soothing computer voice. "An unknown ship has been detected in orbit above the palace. Your orders, sire?"

Deduc flinched and turned to his right, searching for the source of the words.

"Show it to me?" Haradis said aloud.

Deduc spun around, and so did Abigail. She hadn't even noticed her friend had come out of his trance.

She leaned closer to him and reached out. "Are you alright?"

"I'm… unsure. I don't know what I just…" His voice trailed away, and he straightened up when the image of the bottom edge of a ship appeared in the space in front of them. His gaze narrowed and his head slowly shook from side to side. "It's impossible to tell, but it must be Emmonsii Phi."

The image was from just inside the atmosphere, and yet the alarm only now went off. She knew something wasn't right. The systems in the palace must not be connected to the rest of the military, which sort of made sense if it was off limits. She stepped away from Haradis and moved closer to the hologram.

"The military won't come near the palace, sir," Deduc said. "The rumors are too pervasive, and the lore will keep them off the grounds. No one wants a repeat of the cleansing."

Haradis growled.

The angle of the camera pointing at the ship was steep. It was from the planet, but there had to be better ones from orbit. This viewpoint had gaps, like it was missing most of the hull. While she stared at the strange halo effect of light coming from the ship, the shape came into focus as the light expanded. Her heart skipped a beat.

Haradis cleared his throat. "I think Emmo needs to learn a lesson. Destr—"

"Wait!" She spun around and grabbed his paw.

He recoiled. "What is it?"

"It's them." She glanced back at the hologram. "I know it. It's my…"

The knot in her stomach tightened as the light disappeared. All that remained was open sky.

"No!" She dropped to her knees and stared up at the nothingness. The moment of realization had filled her with a joy she never thought she'd feel again, and then it all came crumbling down.

"I don't think it was them." Haradis reached down and rested his hand on her back. "Even they couldn't get this close to the planet without Emmo taking them out."

A message from Harold appeared on her retinal comm.

There wasn't enough detail to know for sure.

Tears streamed down her face, leaving behind streaks of dirt in their wake that matched her tattered clothes. She hadn't realized how dusty she'd gotten on the climb up the stairs, but cleanliness was the last thing on her mind at that moment. While she may have imagined it, she'd have sworn it was them. Every ounce of her being told her it was, and now they were gone.

40

IBU

PROTO DARK NEBULA, ORBITING
ARCTORDIEA

The blue glow of the tachyon field passed over, and Ibu squeezed the sword in their right hand. More than anything, they wanted to be down on the planet, helping the others save Abigail. Not trapped in this blasted coffin of a starship.

They stared down at their skotádi jumpsuit, needlessly enshrouding them in protection. It was one of the only gifts they'd ever received, and funny enough, it was from Moet. Shauna had called it an olive branch of sorts. It was a human analogy used to mend past mistakes, but this gift would never see the battlefield.

The cargo bay around them was littered with dozens of spare robots and random munitions strewn about. Moments earlier, it had been filled with humans in heavily armed exoskeletons and Shauna's tricked out robotic form. They'd cobbled it together from human robot scraps and remnants of their salvages on Griseo. The robot had been loaded down with all manner of alien armaments, some of which had never been fired before.

While Ibu should've put up more of a fight and demanded Shauna let them go, they knew better. There was no way in hell she was going to leave her daughter in trouble again. Minula was no different, and she was in no shape to pilot the Phoenix with her emotions controlling her actions. Next to Shauna, Ibu was the only person capable of keeping up with all the data and onboard systems.

The only thing saving them from being alone was Cynthia. She'd stuck behind to help with comms and to relay intel planetside. That, and she wasn't great with weapons.

This tug was their only way off this rock if things went as planned. But if Abigail died, the Nanil would be alone in this universe. They couldn't show their face in Zeta Lupi knowing they hadn't tried everything to save the woman. Being alone again wasn't something they imagined they'd have to deal with when they followed Zachary aboard the Fountainhead all those months ago. The notion of solitude didn't set well in their mind, even if it meant dealing with emotionally needy humans.

"They'll… be fine," Cynthia muttered, staring at the closed cargo bay door. "They'll find her."

Ibu popped open a comm gate and downloaded the data from the nano-satellites they deployed around the planet. They might have a dump from Minula and the squad as they descended.

With the data downloading, they turned and exited the cargo hold, leaving Cynthia behind. The woman didn't attempt to follow. She chose to linger in the mess and fiddle with the scraps strewn about.

When Ibu reached the bridge, they clicked into the pilot seat. Once the safety harness was in place and the drugs injected into their skin, they closed their eyes and jacked into the computer. They'd need the added response time in the virtual world to process all the feeds.

When the emptiness of the simulation engulfed them, they glanced around, half expecting to see Shauna, but she never appeared. They were alone. After spending countless hours in this place chatting with the woman, it was strange being here without an A.I. companion.

The priority queue floating in space in front of them flashed red and brought their mind back into focus. Their friends needed them. Flipping it open, they fast forwarded through the squad's drop camera feed and watched as they jumped out of the Phoenix, rocketing toward the planet encased in their crude skotádi shells. Fortunately for them, they held together, and their descent rockets engaged at the last second to slow their fall. When they hit the ground, they opened a tight beam with one of their satellites in orbit.

"We need intel on this palace, stat." Minula lowered to her knee and raised her plasma howitzer, firing a few rounds into the distance and lighting up a line of what looked like tanks. "Without it, we're sitting ducks." Explosions boomed around her, and she used her exo-suit to boost away from the scene. Their cracked landing pods receded into the distance and the signal cut.

They'd have to deploy their jerry-rigged Ursis sensor array through a gate to query the alien computers. Their team needed details on the palace. They started the jump calculation, deciding on a crude route that would finish faster. The jump didn't need to be perfect, it just had to be near another Ursis relay.

As the milliseconds ticked by, the sub second gaps in time felt like an eternity. Waiting always did when they were under pressure, especially when the life and death of their friends were on the line.

They passed the span of time keeping their mind busy watching the feeds and making sure Cynthia was safe. The woman was still in the cargo hold and had attached a drug tube to her hip. From the looks of it, she was building more robots. It was a strange thing to do, but she must have realized Ibu was better suited to handle comms in their mental link and merely wanted to feel useful.

While they felt bad for her, they needed to focus and flipped their attention back to the feed. Most of the news outlets were reporting on a rogue attack on the southern side of the palace. The newly arriving military was being led by Emmonsii Phi's generals, and they claimed to have the upper hand with the resistance. The footage was sparse, though, and there was nothing to see beyond a few blurry explosions. They hoped the reporters were exaggerating.

When the calculation finished, they didn't waste another nanosecond. They uploaded the gate strategy and activated the vanes. There wasn't a clang this time, or as much as a click signaling that the vanes had opened. They powered up the array and executed their patched program running on the alien hardware. After that, they waited. The relay needed to sync up with the other subspace node, and hopefully if everything went as planned, they'd have access to the Ursis network.

Their answer came back a few excruciating seconds later when the virtual screen in front of them sprang to life, presenting them with a series of options. They scanned the list and quickly decided on navigating the web of historical archives instead of performing a search. If they were looking for a software-based attack, monitoring search results was the easiest way to find a trail.

They studied the space near the Phoenix and set up a few dozen proximity sensors around themselves and all the nearby ships. If anything passed through those fields, it'd get their attention.

Once they were happy with the defenses, they sent a brief message to Cynthia and then focused all their energy on navigating the web of historical articles on or about the palace. There were thousands of pathways through the Ursis knowledge base, and it'd take some serious exploring to find accurate maps of the building in time. Right about now, they wished their friend could join them in their mental link.

41

MINULA CLARKE

PROTO DARK NEBULA, ON ARCTORDIEA

The stone shrapnel remnants from the picturesque garden wall skipped across the water and ricocheted off Minula's camera. She'd popped it up to study the battle-field. While the explosion was close, it wasn't targeted at them so much as it was being used to flush them out. They were caught between the advancing Ursis to the south and the palace defenses to the north. The impossibly tall mountain housing the King's residence had outcroppings and arma-ments littered up and down the cliff faces. Apparently, on their home world, the Ursis didn't like building structures above ground unless they were surrounded by nature. Which was funny, considering how their colonies evolved in an entirely different manner.

From the devastation on the exterior palace grounds, you'd think her team had landed with an entire battalion of space marines. She couldn't figure out why, but for some reason the advancing Ursis weren't merely firing on Minula and her team, they were attacking the palace defenses, as well, and making headway at that. Her small squad had been fortunate enough to find a few pockets along the battlefield like this garden to hide in. Submerge within was more appropriate, but at least they were safe.

Her heart was pounding as she aimed her camera's receiving dish toward the sky and crossed her fingers, hoping for something to come back. But the signal was flat. The Phoenix hadn't reappeared. Either that or the Ursis had taken out the entire swarm of nano-sats they'd laid down. Given their size and skotádi coating, she doubted the aliens would find all of them that fast.

She was doing everything she could to focus on their situation, and not to think about Abigail or the images she'd seen from the throne room. The bloodstains up and down her tattered outfit, and the rips in her clothes were seared into her mind. Even the tear stained dirt on her face was captured on the broadcasts, and seeing it was like a knife to the heart.

The plasma cannon chimed, letting her know it'd cooled down enough to be used again. The fiery catapults ran hot, which made them easy targets to the advancing soldiers. At least the ones they didn't mow down along the way. The Ursis were beasts and fought with a berserker rage she'd never seen before, and that was only the one they'd encountered up close. She'd barely made it out the other side alive, and she wouldn't be standing here if Shauna hadn't sliced it in half with Ibu's swords.

When her suit reported it had reached its nominal operating temperature, she pinged the rest of the team. The squad was hiding in the muck down on the bottom of the pond, and they needed to keep moving. Spending too much time in a single place meant only one thing: death.

The lights of a nearby exo-suit fluttered in the murky water, sending a message from Moet. "Can't we hang out here until we hear from Ibu? There's no one near us."

Minula took a deep breath, struggling to suppress her rage. This squad had it easy, this last leg. For the entire mission, really. They hadn't spent much time on Griseo, besides picking up resources left over after Ibu and Harold had taken out the traitors. And now, their first time in battle, and they were asking to sit it out. Frak that. "Are you gonna tell Abigail's brothers we let her die?"

"That's not what I said," Moet signaled.

"Funny." Minula rotated her camera, taking in the surroundings on the south side of a nearby rock. "That's what I heard."

There was an advancing tank two hundred meters out, and it was moving toward the pond. It looked like a rolling sphere with cannons on three sides. At the moment, the turrets were on the left, right, and top, but they could move anywhere on the exterior as the sphere rolled. The mobility of the firepower made it a formidable offensive weapon on any terrain. From the looks of how slowly they were proceeding, they weren't coming for them. They were working their way in the direction of a nearby armament. The same one that almost took her and her squad's heads off fifteen minutes earlier.

"Ready your weapons. We've got an incoming bogey." Minula flushed the water from the chamber of her plasma cannon and locked and loaded a round. "If we're lucky, they'll roll past."

The water started vibrating, and ripples formed on the surface. She lowered the camera and moved closer to the wall, putting some earth between her and the tank. The blasted thing reminded her of a massive hamster ball with explosives. Hell, this pond could almost be a puddle for that thing, which made sense considering how huge the Ursis were.

With her back to the stone embankment, she could feel the watery vibrations strengthen as the tank moved closer and closer. If it crushed the ground around the edge of the pond or rolled into the water, she could be squashed or trapped in the rubble. The possibility of dying before helping Abigail was unsettling on many levels, but the alternative was confronting the beast head-on, which meant certain death.

When the massive tank passed behind her back, it blocked out the sunlight and caused the pond to darken. A shudder reverberated through her already frigid exo-suit as the water grew even colder. They'd shut off anything that gave off a heat signature when they dove into the murky liquid.

Suddenly, the vibrations ended, and the water got perfectly still. Even the seaweed stopped moving. This couldn't be good.

She glanced upward, looking for cover from above. There were a few clumps of plants floating overhead. It'd have to do. She raised her camera, easing it up and out of the water, trying not to create a ripple on the surface.

As the device passed into the air, an image appeared on her suit's tactical display. The tank had pulled up next to the pond and a circular hatch slid aside. Two Ursis in battlesuits stepped out and glanced around. She wasn't sure what to make of it until one of them started stretching. These idiots were taking a break.

"What do you think about these videos from the King's throne room?" The first Ursis peered around the tank to the north. He stayed behind the massive object, in case there were snipers on the cliffs.

"It's quartel shit!" The second Ursis spit on the ground and strolled up to the edge of the water. "It's nothing more than propaganda from Emmo's people. She'll do anything to stay in office and prevent that vote of confidence from reaching the floor. Think about it. Why spend all the resources building those damned ships if we're never leaving this place?"

"She doesn't need a vote of confidence," the first Ursis said. "She can assassinate anyone who opposes her. It wouldn't be the first time."

The second Ursis snapped around and glared at the first.

"Don't even mention the you know what here. We're bugged along with the rest of the army. We'll be living with the worms if they catch wind of us talking about it. Let's get back to work chasing shadows, shall we?"

Minula held her right palm low and waved her hand from side to side before pointing upward. She then started counting down from five with her fingers, hoping her team was watching her. These fools were about to head inside the tank, and this was their only chance to take them out.

When her countdown reached two, she powered up the systems in her exo-suit and pushed the button to inject herself with another round of juice. She'd already used three doses in the last hour. Any more and she'd risk an overdose.

Her vision snapped into razor focus and her adrenaline spiked. As her countdown hit zero, she clenched her fist and adjusted her feet to be angled under her body before she fired the thrusters built into her boots. They were designed for accelerating a jump or for stabilization, but could also be used in a pinch to boost the suit upward when she couldn't spring up off the ground.

She raised her plasma cannon just as she broke the surface of the water, firing the first molten sphere toward the Ursis standing a meter away. His back was facing her when the round cut through the alien like butter, passing through the other side and nearly hitting his friend. He toppled forward when she slammed into his back.

The red-hot hole in his chest was mere centimeters from where her left hand collided with him, and the plasma was expanding rapidly. She was careful not to touch the glowing edge of the hole. There was no point in losing a finger to the super heated material. With his body tipping forward like a falling tree, she rolled to the side and skidded to a stop across the damp stone path just as the corpse crashed down. A bang echoed through the air as the metal encased alien struck the stone.

By the time she was up and on her feet, the second Ursis had launched his attack and was on a collision course with her. His eyes were enlarged behind his mask, and his fists were glowing red. He was already deep into the berserker mode they encountered earlier, which didn't bode well for her.

She didn't have time to load another plasma round or pause to think about what to do next. She simply crouched down and leapt toward him, maxing out the suit's jump jets. While she was down in her crouch, she ejected her electro-blade out of its housing in her left arm and swung it forward, hoping the charged weapon could pierce that fraking armor they were wearing.

With her suit and blade on a collision course with the Ursis, she didn't see her team rising out of the water like six synchronous swimmers. The alien, however, wasn't distracted by the show. He predicted her path to a tee, twisting in time to dodge the full force of her attack and smashing his fist into her back just as her sword pierced the side of his helmet and sent it flying off his shoulders.

Her body exploded in pain as she sailed past the moun-tainous alien and slid face first along the stone pathway. Every cobble she skidded across jarred her already screaming spine. By the time she came to a halt, her exo-suit alarms were blaring. She'd taken a serious hit, and her rear plating had been compromised. The moment the damage happened, the suit began repairing itself and injected her with a round of nanites, targeting the broken ribs and hairline fractures in her spine. Fortunately for her, the agony was muted the instant all the drugs started flowing through her system.

She moaned and pushed up off the ground, but her gloved hand was covered in slime, and she slipped, toppling back down against the stone and cracking her head.

"Shit," she muttered as her proximity sensors blared. Her tactical display showed that the Ursis had screeched to a halt and spun around. He was making his way back to finish her off. But he was missing his helmet. Without it, he must've missed the incoming wall of pain as not one, but two plasma rounds shot forward from her squad's exo-suits. Both molten spheres sailed through the alien and into the side of the nearby tank before ricocheting along the ground into the distance. The scorch marks in their wake caught fire to the dry grass and spread like wildfire.

The Ursis fell face first and skidded to a halt a few meters from Minula's head. She swallowed hard and stared at the massive corpse, taking in the rage in the overgrown bear's eyes. His open wounds crackled in the cool air as the expanding plasma burned through the internals of the suit, exposing the bones and all manner of grotesque entrails inside the alien. A moment earlier, he doubted their existence, and now he was dead. Killed by what he considered fiction.

Moet sprinted forward and slid up to her side. She started checking over her. "Are you alright, sir? Your suit seems like it's almost repaired, but your back—"

"Is fine," Minula pushed up off the ground, struggling not to moan in the process. Once she was upright, she took in the battlefield. The small hill behind them was the only defense from the palace artillery and the impossibly tall walls they needed to breach.

Shauna was staring south toward the wall of soldiers advancing in the distance, while the rest of the squad had encircled Minula, keeping her safe. When she turned around, she paused. She'd forgotten about the tank and was only a meter from it. Peering into the open hatch, her suit indicated there were no life signs inside. It was the first break they'd had since they landed. She wasn't sure they could've handled taking on more than a few of the Ursis at once.

She stepped inside the killing machine. "Anyone ever hot wired a hamster ball?"

42

IBU

PROTO DARK NEBULA, NEAR ARCTORDIEA

Another fast gate, another narrow escape. With each transition, the Ursis were getting closer and closer to capturing the Phoenix. While they weren't firing on the ship, they were doing everything they could to disable it. Ibu had to try something different going forward. Unfortunately, the aliens had the upper hand. They knew there were human soldiers on the ground that needed support, so they were swarming the space above the planet, leaving Ibu with few options to check on their people.

During this last transition, they jumped well away from the battle scene, hoping it would buy them more time. After they confirmed their location, they laid down the proximity sensors, checked their next set of emergency gate commands, and reconnected the relay to the planetary network. The details on the palace were so close they could feel it.

In their most recent attempt to find a detailed map, they'd been navigating a web of ancient tourist pages and hit dead end after dead end. But their last query before they gated hit pay dirt, or so they hoped. They released a crawler they'd employed, and it started querying the server for a litmus of pages that followed naming conventions used elsewhere on the site. For every few thousand requests that were designed to pass, they'd feed in one or two feelers, looking for remnants of the old scrubbed site. Error after error streamed down her screen as the expert system worked its magic. The irony wasn't lost on them that even with their superhuman abilities to interface with computer systems, they'd turned to an automation to work faster.

There were thousands of failures from the bot, and just when they thought they'd need to try another tactic, the stream ended with one hit.

Follow Maritimus the Tenth on his virtual walkthrough of the Summis palace. This unique behind the scenes look at the historical ground zero of The Great Clan Uprising, first contact with an alien race, the signing of the Galactic Alliance inaugural treaty, and so many historic moments is a must see. His fun filled run through hidden tunnels and secret passages throughout the palace will leave you roaring for more. Watch as your esteemed leader guides you through the home of our noble people in this once-in-a-lifetime recording.

Reading the page description was like drinking your first sip of water after walking through the desert for days. They thought perhaps it was a mirage until they gestured to open the map and were immediately engulfed in a full fidelity virtual rendering of the mountainous castle.

"Yes!" Ibu leapt in the air, reaching around to high five Shauna, but got nothing. No one was there to celebrate the finding apart from some virtual automata. They were alone.

Their insides tingled with an odd pulling sensation, almost like it was willing them to be closer to the humans. It was an emotion they'd never felt before today. They could only chalk it up as loneliness, but would consult the psychological database when they had more time. While they knew they could ask Cynthia, she was busy in the cargo hold, having only just rousted out of her post jump bath of pain. For now, they both needed to get to work.

They set the expert system loose on the map, giving it full access to the core processors of the Phoenix. While it was churning through the virtual world, mapping out the space, they were monitoring the ship. Freeing the computer to do what it was good at, recording data.

It took a few seconds to calculate the parameters of the next transmission gate to share the map, followed by an emergency jump right afterward. If it was like last time, the Ursis would be ready to open a warp bubble toward the coordinates where the Phoenix was transmitting from.

A few minutes later, the expert system signaled that the map was complete. When they cracked it open, they stared in awe as the blueprint unfolded before them. The palace was enormous. It wasn't a building so much as a city. Hell, two cities. Their friends had their work cut out for themselves making it to the top of the fortified structure. From the looks of it, they'd be better off coming in from the sky. That is, if there weren't a few hundred anti-aircraft lasers and missile batteries defending the peak. They could only hope that most of the palace's internal defense systems were shut off, otherwise Minula and her team would be done before they started.

Once they confirmed the map was complete, they wrapped it up in a transmission and encrypted it with everything they had. They didn't pause, they simply opened the micro gate and started the broadcast. The payload was pretty big and would take a solid twenty seconds to upload. A situation like this was precisely why they'd gated so far from the planet this last time.

As the seconds ticked by, they downloaded a few updates from Minula. It was hard scrolling through message after message from their friends. Each one was more dire than the last. From the looks of the last few, they'd taken to hiding out in a pond to cool off and catch their breath. The look on Minula's face in the last message standing next to the tank told a different story. She appeared broken, and on the verge of giving up. Her exo-suit was burnt in several spots and scraped all to hell. But it was her eyes that showed the most pain. She was close to overdosing, and the only thing keeping her moving was hope. But even that was in short supply.

"This should help," they muttered as the last bytes finished sending.

When the upload completed, they closed the gate and cycled the vanes, starting the emergency transition. And just in time because two Alatas battleships dropped out of warp right as their gate was closing. Another few seconds, and they would've been done for.

All they could do now was join Cynthia down in the cargo hold and fiddle with the robots, waiting for a signal from their friends. Something, anything to tell them how things were going or that they needed an extraction. The coming minutes would be the most excruciating of their life.

ABIGAIL OLIVAW

PROTO DARK NEBULA, ON ARCTORDIEA

Deduc spent the last few minutes conferring with his clergy. To say they were freaked out was an understatement. They'd tried all the exits around the chamber and none of them would budge. Stranger still, they all reported that they weren't able to communicate outside the throne room. While they'd all received the emergency transmission, no one could reach any external networks or news outlets. It was like the mountain was on a signal lockdown.

"It makes sense," she whispered to Haradis. "If someone breached the palace, blocking the signals would prevent them from communicating with each other and the outside world."

Haradis nodded and shifted his stance, staring at Deduc the entire time. He hadn't stopped staring at the priest since he'd come out of his trance.

Talking to the Ursis was like talking to a wall. Ever since he'd touched the throne, he hadn't said much. Funny enough, neither had Harold. She glanced around, making sure no one was watching her. She then brought up her virtual keyboard and typed a message to him.

Are you ok, Harold? You're unusually quiet.

His response didn't come via text. Instead, he said it out loud, like he wanted Haradis to hear it, as well.

"I've been studying our friendly priest," Harold said.

Haradis lowered down to one knee next to her, his breath tickling the hairs on her neck. "Go on, Abigail's companion," he whispered.

The clergy still hadn't taken note of them talking. They were too worried about getting out of the chamber to notice. Even Deduc was suspiciously oblivious to the two of them.

She leaned closer to Haradis so he could hear Harold, and perhaps talk quieter. The aliens had ridiculous hearing.

"Have you noticed his mannerisms when he's angry?" Harold asked.

She crossed her arms. "You mean how he always snarls at me?"

"No," Harold began. "I was referring more to how he treats people, and recently, how he walks. And where did that cane come from?"

Haradis shook his head. "I'm not sure what you mean. Does he remind you of someone?"

Deduc smacked his cane into the ground, causing the clergy to bow and scatter. All at once, she saw what he meant. How the hell hadn't she noticed it before? "It can't be. She's up in space, on one of the starships. Right?"

Haradis glanced over at her. "She who?"

"Emmo," Harold whispered.

"I... never saw her real form. She was always a talking head and voice to me." He brought his hands up and rested it on his knee. "Her cronies tortured me onboard the Alatas cruiser and even in her Keep, but she never showed herself. I suspect she did this on purpose and didn't want me to learn anything about her." He stared at her in silence for a moment, seeming to study Deduc's movements. "My parents recorded some video lessons for me before I was born, to prepare me for my duties as king some day. They sent them with me when the Nebula fell. In one, my mother told me that several of the aliens in the Galactic Alliance used avatars to do their dirty work. It's how they get away with causing so much havoc in other species, especially if they refused to join the alliance. Most of them were politicians or the super elite that lacked honor. Their mission in life was more about lining their own pockets and destroying species, not improving the lives of their people."

She could imagine the disruption one could cause remotely controlling avatars without consequence. Humanity saw something similar in the early days of cloning on Earth, and they created laws to prevent it. Not that the Olivaws hadn't found humans who broke the law over the years. They were either dealt with discreetly or using the judicial system. Taking over avatars within the larger Galactic Alliance community, or even in an isolated population, would allow someone to play both sides like a fiddle. In the past, they had Harold overseeing things they couldn't, whereas today all they had at this point was conjecture.

"There's only one way to find out." She reached up and ran her hand through her hair.

"Abigail, don't—" Harold began.

She stepped forward and cleared her voice to get everyone's attention. "Deduc, do you have a second?"

When he snapped his head around and glared at her, his eyes narrowed and then softened. "What is it, human?"

"I…" she walked down the ramp, "wanted to chat. I had a few questions for you. You know, about this place." She gestured at the locked gates.

Deduc nodded and then turned slowly, leaning more and

more on his cane as he went. He took a few tentative steps toward her and paused, still well away from the throne.

She eyed the ground, making sure to keep a few arm's lengths between them. There was no sense in getting too close.

"What is it you want to know?" Deduc crossed his hands one over the other and rested them on his cane.

Abigail glanced over her shoulder at Haradis and dipped her head, doing her best acting to look sad. When she returned her gaze forward, Deduc had shuffled closer. He was now well within arm's reach, but she did her best not to flinch. She lowered her voice and leaned closer to him. "I don't want to impede Haradis becoming king. What can I do to help? You name it. Anything I can do to help my friend and take out that bitch Emmonsii Phi." She clenched her fists.

Deduc's nostrils flared. "Well… I'm not sure that we'll need to do that just yet. I think the first thing you could do is to pray with me."

She squinted. "Do what now?"

"As King Maritimus' Ulyxsauri, I took a sacred oath to protect him and to wield the powers of Therion on his behalf. If you are truly the Seguan, then in this chamber we should be able to bond in thought. If we can act together, I am confident we will see the path forward." He reached out, holding his hand in front of her.

"No!" a voice screamed. The same one she and Haradis heard earlier. The one that came from the throne, except this time it was filling the chamber.

She glanced back at Haradis. He was staring up at the tree of lights, searching for the source of the sound. When she scanned the other clergy, no one else was reacting. They hadn't heard it.

Her retinal comm flashed a message from Harold.

Don't touch him. Remember the tribunal ship.

The words seared into her mind's eye, and the image of the mottled green bastard appeared in front of her. Like months before with the Qudoculi, this Ursis was trying to hurt her. Except this time, Harold and the alien entity in the throne were warning her. She failed to see it last time, and she vowed to never let that happen again. To never leave her back undefended or let someone treat her like less than she was worth, like she was stupid and naïve.

She shook her head. "I don't think I can do that." She dropped to the ground and kicked outward with all her body weight, using the momentum and the fall to kick her right leg with everything she had. It crashed into the cane holding the Ursis upright and sent it flying in the other direction.

Caught off guard, Deduc wobbled for a second and then toppled onto his knees. Unfortunately, he was still within reach of her and lashed out, swinging his claws toward her. But she was ready for him. She used the forward momentum of her leg to continue onward and rolled sideways, like she used to do as a kid when she and her brothers rolled down the hills back on Earth. The ramp from the throne was particularly useful for just such an occasion.

Deduc's paws caught air and slammed into the ground, sending screeches echoing through the chamber as his claws scraped at the space she'd previously occupied.

She rolled again and again, putting a half dozen meters between her and the enraged Ursis before she skidded to a stop and pushed up onto her feet.

A message from Harold appeared on her retinal comm.

Be careful. Klus is behind you to your right, and the other clergy are moving closer. They don't look happy.

Klus was a wild card. While the two of them had bonded along the way, she still wasn't sure she could trust the female.

"Tell me something, Emmo." She took a few steps to her left. "Why all the cloak and dagger after all these years? Surely, you had all the power you needed after you had Maritimus killed."

Deduc moaned and grabbed at his wrist. "I don't know what you're talking about, you crazy human. I knew I shouldn't have trusted you again. Someone help me! Give me a hand." He leaned on his side and reached out toward a nearby clergy.

"No!" Haradis bellowed. "Leave him be."

The clergy working their way toward Deduc froze, glancing between their future king and the leader of their church.

Deduc pushed up onto one knee and paused, staring at the prince. "You support this human, do you? After everything I've done for you. This is how you repay me?"

Haradis stiffened and his upper lip curled, baring his teeth. "You've done little for me compared to this human. Without her and her people, I'd have been dead long ago."

"But they didn't help you willingly." Deduc pointed at her. "Humankind wants nothing to do with us. You can see the fear in her face even now. Every time we move toward her, she flinches."

"Sorta like your behavior around the throne." Abigail paused. The clergy to her left boxed her in. The only way to move from here was closer to the priest. "Suggestions," she subvocalized.

"See!" Deduc pointed at her. "Even now, she asks her

friend for help. Her unseen companion. How are we to know she's not the one being manipulated by Emmo? She has been known to control her avatars over the years."

Harold's face appeared on her retinal comm and a message below it.

I'm starting to feel like this is a trap.

He was right, but based on how Haradis was looking at her, she could tell the priest had struck a chord. She hadn't thought about how she might be seen talking to the A.I. all this time.

Haradis tilted his head. "He makes a good point. While I know your quirkiness from outside the Nebula, they do not."

Abigail glanced over her shoulder and Klus was staring at her, except, unlike the others, her eyes were filled with concern. She looked back at Haradis. "How do I prove I'm not an avatar of Emmo?"

The sound of the alien entity boomed through the chamber and Haradis nodded, his eyes still locked on her. Like the first time, she couldn't understand the voice.

"What did it say?" she asked.

"No one said anything, you fool." Deduc pushed up off his knee and wobbled for a second before stabilizing and standing up straight.

Haradis narrowed his gaze at the priest. "The Therionic entity that controls the throne has asked you to remove your companion." He glanced at her. "This will prove to everyone that you're not being controlled."

Harold's avatar shook its head in her retinal comm.

Don't do it. This is definitely a trap.

He was freaking out, but she couldn't blame him. So was she. This was an unexpected turn of the tables for sure.

She stared across the room at Haradis. While his face was impossible to read, his eyes never wavered. They were like beacons peering into her soul. Their softness reminded her of when they'd first met in the Keep, when he offered her a ride. He was being sincere and vulnerable then, and he was doing the same thing now. He wasn't leading her astray. They were in this together until the end, and he knew it.

She took a deep breath. "And it's the only way they'll trust me?"

He nodded and tilted his head toward the clergy. As she turned, they were all nodding, even Klus. She paused and studied the Ursis. She looked as uncomfortable as Abigail felt. The wrath of Deduc was still fresh on her mind, and yet something about her reminded Abigail of Haradis. Behind the harsh alien exterior was a deeper layer of trust.

"Fine," she muttered. "But I'll only entrust my companion with you." She nodded toward Klus and unzipped her jumpsuit.

"Me?" Klus pointed at herself.

"Yes, you."

Klus' attention turned to Deduc and Abigail's gaze followed. When she locked eyes with him, she caught a glimmer of white at the edge of his mouth. He was smiling at her. At both of them.

"You aren't seriously considering this, are you?" Harold asked.

She ignored him and slowly reached into her jumpsuit toward her chest, pushing with her fingers in the space above her heart, applying pressure against the body-mod. It didn't budge for a second, but it parted when the nanites in her body sensed her hand lingering on the spot. She could feel the containment unit slide forward in her chest, and the smooth edge of Harold's consciousness core brushed her fingertips.

"Harold." She swallowed hard and wiped at her eyes with her other hand. "I've trusted you for nearly my entire life. If we're gonna make it out of here, then we need to trust someone else. Deep down, you know I'm right."

He didn't say a word because he didn't have to. Her mind was made up, and he was no longer in control. His life was in her hands as much as hers were in Haradis'.

The cold sphere of Harold's consciousness popped out into her awaiting palm. She didn't have to pull it out like she thought she'd need to.

With her ancestor in her hand, she took several cautious steps toward Klus, and they did the same, meeting them in the middle. "Please be careful with him. He means a lot to me and my clan."

Klus nodded and bowed down, touching their head to Abigail's closed hand. When they straightened up, they gently brought both of their paws under hers, and she released Harold's consciousness. The coldness lingered on her fingers for a few seconds, giving her time to question her decision.

There was no turning back now.

As Klus stepped away, she stared down at her hand, rubbing her fingertips together where the cold persisted. While the Ulixi believed Harold controlled the plans to their gate drive, little did they know that neither of them had the secrets. Losing him now would mean losing her lifeline to her family. She reached up and rubbed the spot above her heart. A piece of her was missing, and yet she was still herself. Still strong. Still capable.

She took a deep breath and turned to face Haradis. "There.

It's done." She raised her hands up in the air and slowly spun around. "See. I'm still in control of my faculties. I'm Abigail Marie Olivaw, daughter of Stark and Marie Olivaw. As one of three siblings, we are each battling alongside our people to drive the Galactic Alliance away. To destroy them before they destroy us. Like with your kind, they took many of our leaders and our warriors before their time. And like with you, they tried to ensnare our worlds in a Dark Nebula. We managed to hold them off by the skin of our teeth and the power of our technology. It is my hope that... I can help you. That we can help you. This, however, will only happen if you trust me." She stopped spinning and glanced up at the Ulyxsauri entity. Despite her lies, the stream of chaotic green and gold swirls continued to cascade downward. She wasn't sure what sort of reaction she expected, but that wasn't it.

As she turned to search the faces of the clergy for their reactions, the Therionic entity screamed. The streams of color vibrated overhead, mixing together into hypnotic splotches of blue. It was like the entity was angry at her for lying. It knew she couldn't help the Ursis, and now it was pissed. She brought her hands up to cover her ears, but it had no effect. The continuous screech pierced through everything and went straight for her mind.

Just as she was about to give up, she caught a movement from Haradis out of the corner of her eye. He was waving his arms, trying to get her attention. When she lowered her hands, she heard him.

"Abigail!" He stumbled forward and gestured to her left. "Look out!"

By the time she spun to face where he was pointing, it was too late. Deduc had covered the short distance between them with surprising speed. His impaired form collided against her and spun her away as he wrapped his paw around her neck.

She drew in a breath as the momentum of her body forced his razor-sharp claws to pierce the skin on her neck, lingering short of cutting deeper. The smell of her own blood wafted into her nostrils, and she struggled not to wretch.

Deduc chuckled. "That was an excellent speech for a human. But my people will not be easily swayed by your words or your simple gesture." He adjusted his footing. He was clearly having trouble standing without his cane. "I have what I need from you and your kind. As the Seguan, you have done your part. Time has once again closed the loop."

"What... do you mean, the loop?" she asked, struggling with each word.

"My visions from the closing, all visions for that matter. They are never guaranteed to occur. While some come to pass with surprising accuracy, others are barely noticeable in their original form. They're almost like a mirage. When you think you see one, it turns into another. Such is the continuum time when viewed from afar and through a Beacon." He tightened his grip on her neck. "I did what I needed to do to survive over the centuries. I don't regret it, and my people won't, either. Not once we extract the technology from your companion and raise this death shroud. It is us that will rise from our ashes and take down the Galactic Alliance, not you weak humans."

She tried to pull her head away from the blade digging into her skin, but failed. Even in his weakened state, he was far stronger than her. "So... you did those things... you killed all those Ulixi."

"Like I said. I did what I needed to do." He brought his other paw in front of her and held it just out of reach of her forehead. "And now I must finish what you started by taking back control of the throne from you and that poor excuse for a prince. Like his father before him, he is not fit to lead our clans out of the darkness. His parents were weak against the Galactic Alliance. A mistake I will never make. I command the might of the military, and as I've shown in the past, I am not afraid to use it. My people will finally know the real me, not the avatars I occupied. They will chant the name Emmonsii Phi Tlingui for an eternity."

A collective growl escaped from around the room as the clergy realized Abigail had been right. The Seguan had warned them, and they had not listened. They thought they were doing the honorable thing, when all these years they'd been duped. They'd conspired with the person responsible for killing millions of their people. For killing their king and queen, and for laying waste to their rich heritage.

Abigail stared at the paw in front of her face, its talons long ago withdrawn. The rough pads covering the Ursis' fingers had seen years of wear and tear and probably taken countless lives. She stared at the simple shape of each finger. The more she studied them up close, the more she realized they weren't that different from a human hand. Besides being enormous, of course. While the alien's genetics aligned close to the bear on Earth, they'd taken markedly different turns down the evolutionary path over the millennia.

She'd been staring death in the face since she'd passed through the Nebula, so in her final moments it should come as no surprise that her mind had wandered down such a winding road thinking about species similarities. What was remarkable, however, was that it took so long for the reaper to arrive.

When the paw in front of her started glowing, she snapped back into the here and now. A faint white light filled the spaces between each of the alien's pads, and before she knew it, Deduc pressed his paw against her forehead.

As the light touched her skin, the voice of the Therionic being came into focus. "Abigail of the Olivaws, you must fight! You must honor your kin. Do not let Emmonsii win. Fear not, all is not lost."

44

MINULA CLARKE
PROTO DARK NEBULA, ON ARCTORDIEA

The tank rocked sideways and Minula's makeshift chair shook violently. Nothing in this vehicle was designed for human sized occupants, least of all the harnesses. She checked to be sure her off arm and leg were still wrapped in the Ursis shoulder harness and then went back to manipulating the left directional controller. Shauna was managing the right.

"Off the wall." Shauna slammed the controller to the left and her head spun backwards. "Mounts right! Mounts right!"

"Shit," Minula muttered as she echoed Shauna's movement, slamming her stick to the left and braced for impact.

They learned the hard way that the spherical Ursis tank could bounce as well as it could roll. While certainly not designed for such things, its armor plating was malleable enough to absorb the impact of any number of explosions, which made a rock wall child's play.

Their tank spun to the left and bounced off the remnants of a garden rock wall just as an explosion tore up the path they'd been following. The resulting detonation propelled them forward even faster. When the sphere slammed into the rocky face of the palace wall, the entire tank moaned and

Minula jerked sideways, whacking her left shoulder into the side of the massive chair. Her hand slipped off the joystick, and she scrambled to spin back around and grab the underside of the control box. She pulled herself back to center in time to crash to the ground, having sailed a few hundred meters further up the battlefield.

"Turret three is out of commission." Gwen slammed her fist against the weapons panel. "Sorry." She kicked the glowing red console and a crack shot up the middle. "I didn't see that fraking landing coming."

"Keep it steady, Minula." Shauna glared over at her.

She returned her attention back to the viewport on the wall and adjusted her stick to match Shauna's. If they didn't sync them up when moving in a direction, the tank would spin on its axis. It was a touchy design, but effective when done right.

Her retinal comm chimed, and a message flashed in the corner of her vision. She shook her head, having all but given up on hearing from Ibu. It'd been a solid thirty minutes since the Nanil gated away. Hopefully, they found something. If not, she might have to take her team up on their idea of retreating and regrouping elsewhere.

When she blinked open the message, her heart fluttered and a three-dimensional map of the palace flashed up on her retinal comm. "Jackpot! Our friendly Nanil hit pay dirt. We're in business, people. Let's stay alive, shall we?"

"Yessir!" the soldiers shouted in unison.

Minula flicked the map to the rest of the squad and returned her attention to the battlefield, glancing at Shauna. "Can you find a way inside?"

"I'm already on it. Twenty degrees starboard." Shauna tweaked her joystick to the right.

Once a space jockey, always a space jockey. Minula made a similar adjustment, and a flashing green dot appeared on her exo-suit's map. She was taking them back toward where they'd started. "What the hell are we going back there for? There's got to be—"

"Zip it and check the map you jarhead." Shauna never took her eyes off the screen.

When she zoomed into the green dot and overlaid the map from Ibu, she froze in disbelief. "Well, I'll be a monkey's aunt," she muttered. There were service tunnels a few meters below the largest of the ponds they'd hidden in. That sucker was a solid ten meters deep. If they could get inside one of the tunnels, it'd take them straight into the heart of the palace.

If they were going to be heading in through the pond, then they'd need a way inside that didn't give up their position. Otherwise, the Ursis troops could follow them in, and they'd funnel straight to the throne room. They needed something that could blast a hole in the tunnel wall, and at the same time hold back the water. Making a hole they could manage. Doing it without blasting the pond to smithereens, that would be another challenge entirely.

The ball hopped into the air when they ran over a small bridge, and she whacked her helmet against the chair, sending splotches of red across her vision. That gave her an idea. One her brothers would love if they were alive to see it.

"We need to roll the tank into the pond," Minula looked back toward her team. "I need you to keep the remaining turrets on the opposite side of the hatch when we roll in. Can you do that?"

"Uh, sure, boss." Moet glanced at the other members of the squad. "Can I ask why we're going into the pond?"

"We have to get inside somehow, don't we?" Minula stared at Shauna. "Tell me we can crack open that hatch any time we want."

"I don't see why not." Shauna tweaked the control panel between them and shrugged. "There's nothing stopping it. Why? Do you want me to flip it open now?"

"Not yet. Gwen!" She spun around.

"Yessir!" The woman popped open her helmet.

"Get up here and drive with Shauna. I'm going swimming." Minula unwrapped her free arm and leg and slid down the inner wall of the tank, crashing into a munition reloader on her way down.

Gwen scrambled over her and engaged her magnetic boots, climbing the outer wall with ease and sliding into the awaiting chair. She made it look so simple.

Next time they were inside a tank, Minula would have to remember her boots. She slid to the other side of the reloader. "Drop me in the water when you pass through the pond and then keep the other soldiers distracted. I'll need like two to three minutes, tops." She reached out and hit the release lever on the reloader, and two softball sized shells popped out into her awaiting hand. It was like a gum ball machine for explosives. She stowed the munitions in her thigh compartment and slammed it closed.

"And Shauna..." Minula stared up at the robot. "When you feel the explosion, you'll need to roll the tank over the hole. Make sure to line up the hatch on the bottom. You got that?"

"What about you?" Shauna yanked the stick back and Gwen echoed the movement.

Minula reached out in time to grasp the pole next to the reloader. The sudden change in direction swung her around and she crashed into the reloader on the opposite side. When the tank slid to a stop, the hatch cracked open.

"Don't answer that." Shauna glanced left and pointed out the hatch. "The water's right there. We'll hold our position until you're clear."

She let go of the pole and took a deep breath. Once she was ready, she issued the command to close her helmet and dove out the hatch. In the air, she straightened out to reduce her splash just as she hit the water and sank like a rock.

As her suit slid through the water, she could feel herself

getting dizzy. The benefits of the stimulants were wearing off, so she subvocalized the command to issue another dose. Her screen flashed red and asked for the override code. She'd already reached her battlefield maximum. Any more, and she'd risk long-term side effects.

She widened her stance and floated to a stop flat on the bottom. Once she was stable, she tapped in the override code. The familiar hum of the injectors followed by the icy cold liquid flowing through her veins centered her, while the dizzying effects of the spin and fall wiped away like loose cobwebs.

When she checked her timer, she'd already lost precious time and hadn't even started clearing a path to the tunnel. She brought up the map overlay and made her way through the water toward the outline of the tunnel beneath her feet. It was slow-going trudging through the murky liquid, but she reached her target in under thirty seconds.

Now for the fun part. She dug her feet into the ground and lowered closer to the slimy bottom. Once she was low enough, she lifted both hands and activated her stabilization thrusters. The mud in front of each hand exploded in a thick cloud of haze as her stabilizers blasted the muck away with highly focused air. Bubbles streamed upward as a hole burrowed where she was aiming her palms.

She used to do something like this with her brothers when she was younger. They'd use a garden hose with the water turned on to dig holes in their yard. One time, they got almost five feet down before they hit the clay. It made a mess of the yard, but made dropping waterproofed M80s that much easier. The mess after that, now that was quite a show.

As the mud cascaded around her, she scanned the tunnel she was creating for the explosives. It wasn't as deep as she'd like, but time was ticking by fast. The squad would be here any second now. The walls of the pond had far more silt than she'd expected, but she should be able to drop the shells in before the sides caved in too much.

She deactivated her right thruster and cracked open the compartment with the explosives. Once the bubbles dissipated, she reached inside and grasped the first shell with her hand. The next few seconds were all about timing. What she didn't know was where Shauna was. They hadn't worked that part out. When she glanced upward, her answer was waiting for her. A large circular shadow passed up in the air over the pond and started growing in size. They were coming in hot.

"Shit!" Minula squeezed the munition with the super-human grip of her exo-suit, and it lit up like a hot poker. She didn't pause to study the effect, she simply tossed it into the stream of air still blasting out of her free hand. With the first explosive shooting down the hole, she reached into the compartment and retrieved another, squeezing it as she went. By the time she dropped the second one down the same hole, waves crashed on the surface of the pond and the water around her shuddered as the spherical tank sank to the bottom. Fortunately for her, they didn't come down on her head. They landed about fifteen meters away, but the pressure from the impact still made it hard to stand in one place.

She glanced down and studied the hole. The explosives should've reached the bottom by now, and if she'd read the instructions correctly earlier, they'd explode thirty seconds after activating by hand. If there was one thing the Ursis had gotten good at after the Dark Nebula fell, it was blowing shit up.

Her thruster disengaged, and she kicked her way out of the mud, turning as she went. With her back to the hole, she lowered her hands and activated the thrusters again. This time, they shot her forward across the pond. And not a moment too soon. The hole lit up in a cloud of yellow-orange light and bubbles shot upward.

As the shockwave hit, she tumbled end over end and her suit struggled to compensate and keep her upright. After several flips, she stabilized and then spun around, engaging her thrusters once more and aiming her suit straight back into the heart of the carnage. The water was rushing down into the newly formed drain. She'd clearly cracked into something big. She just hoped it was wide enough for her suit to fit.

Minula sailed across the open space in a race against the rolling tank. She could barely make it out in the distance as Shauna and Gwen navigated the beast toward the bubbling hole. Her one saving grace which allowed her to reach the hole first came down to the flip of a coin. They hadn't positioned the hatch on the proper side and needed to rotate the tank. The extra few seconds gave her enough time to enter the hole right before their tank rolled over the opening.

She hit the muddy embankment head first, and her suit bounced from side to side against the slick mud until her feet reached a much harsher surface below. The edge of the hole.

Grating noises tore through her suit, and she struggled to control her fall by reaching her arms out to her side. But she was moving too fast. As her gloves pushed against the rocky sides of the tunnel, they gave way to nothingness. To air.

The alarms in her suit blared. Without thinking, she lowered her hands and fired the stabilizing thrusters on full blast. Her suit burst to life, blasting superheated air out of holes arranged to control her descent while jumping across the surface of a planet. They weren't designed to slow a fall over a short distance like this.

With the proximity alarm blaring, she braced for impact as the ground shot up toward her. Her exo-suit ricocheted off the pile of rubble, and she slid down the rocky terrain with her thrusters still firing at full blast. It sounded like someone was running a cheese grater along the outside of her suit. Once she stopped sliding, she sat upright, taking account of herself and her surroundings.

She swore she was going to bite it on that fall, but not only did she survive, the ceiling wasn't caving in on her. There was a constant trickle of water cascading down into the center of the pile of rubble. It wasn't the worst-case blast that could've emptied the entire pond. This was far more muted, which meant her team must've done their job. That assumption was confirmed a few seconds later.

"Hey! You alive down there?" Moet's voice echoed through the tunnel and was easily heard, even over the constantly running water.

"It seems so." Minula flicked on her headlamps and arched her back, peering into the hole overhead. The beam combined with the lidar to light up the darkness, painting a shaft all the way to the bottom of the tank. They managed to slide the hatch open like she suggested, and were staring down at her. "If you use your stabilizers, you should be able to make it down. It's a bit tricky when you hit the pile at the end, but you can do it."

Her team didn't need to be asked twice. Their commanding officer had spoken, and they knew the stakes. They descended the hole in single file and took up positions at her side. By the time Shauna made it down with her winch, Minula was chomping at the bit to get going. She'd already sent a small swarm of micro-drones down the tunnel to scout ahead, and the coast was clear for quite a ways. Every second they spent standing around could mean life or death for Abigail.

Minula launched down the tunnel toward the palace with her squad in hot pursuit, while Shauna was still detaching her winch. Their mechanically assisted strides meant they could run almost three times faster than the fastest human, but still slower than if they had room to leap.

She subvocalized the command to split up the forward swarm into smaller groups to cover more ground, and more importantly, to explore upward. The surprising lack of resistance along their route was suspicious. She'd half expected the robotic gnats to be swatted out of the air at any moment, but they weren't. They kept going. The inside defenses of the palace were powered down long ago.

When they reached the base of the stairs on Ibu's map, she ducked behind a nearby column. There was a callout for a laser battery in the wall segment beyond the first set of steps. The callout made reference to a video the Nanil saw the weapon on, but their micro-drones didn't trigger the defensive armament.

"Can we get a line of sight to that chunk of wall?" Minula shared the point on the map with her team.

Moet slid out from behind her and made her way toward the pillar on the other side, all while keeping her arm trained on where the map showed the battery was located. Minula watched from Moet's camera as she eased forward. Just shy of the far side, the segment of wall came into her field of view. There was an intricate decorative wall treatment up the entire staircase, but there didn't appear to be any obvious seams exposed.

"I've got a bead on the target. Should I light it up?" Moet asked.

Surely, this wasn't the first defensive measure they'd passed. They'd already covered almost a kilometer of tunnel, and yet they hadn't been attacked. Maybe the inner palace systems had been deactivated.

"No. Let's not chance it. I'll take the lead." Minula stepped out from behind the pillar and made her way to the base of the stairway. The view from Moet's camera showed the panel didn't budge.

"You're clear," Moet said. "I've got you covered. If they so much as twitch, it'll be slag."

While it felt good knowing someone had her back, it didn't make climbing the stairs any less stressful. Even if Moet was able to take out the battery, she'd be in the crossfire.

She raised the plasma cannon and kept her back to the wall, doing her best not to trip over the massive stairs. Making her way over each step in the oversized suit was painful enough. She couldn't imagine doing it without mechanical assistance.

When she hit the step in front of the panel, she took a deep breath and stepped up, aiming her arm squarely at the wall segment. But nothing happened. No panel slid aside, and no armaments popped out. According to her scanners, it looked like any other chunk of wall in this massive palace.

"I guess Ibu's intel was off," Shauna said. "Perhaps they made some modifications after the recording she found. Let's keep our eyes open, shall we?"

"Stay frosty, people." Moet waved her hand forward and, one by one, the squad followed Minula up the stairs.

She kept her plasma cannon trained on the wall segment as each of the soldiers made their way around her and up the giant steps. They must have studied her movement up the spiral stairway, as they made short work of the ascent. Once they'd mastered skipping two and then three steps at a time using their stabilizers, their mesh network rebroadcast the program to each of their suits. This allowed everyone to put the climb on autopilot and let them focus on monitoring their surroundings rather than the climb.

With the entire squad climbing in unison, the group cleared over a dozen floors before the first explosion rocked the ground beneath them.

"What the hell was that?" Moet asked.

They froze on the stairs, the forward four soldiers covering above and the last two, along with her and Shauna, covered the rear. She brought up the view from the micro-drones in front and behind them. The pair she'd left at the base of the staircase had detected movement, as had the one deeper down the tunnel. Their icons were flashing red. When she opened their video feeds, all hell was breaking loose.

Water was cascading into the stairwell along the floor, and a dozen Ursis bodies littered the ground.

At first, she couldn't tell what'd happened until she watched another dozen Ursis in power armor drop out of the ceiling. They looked pissed. The approaching army must've drained the pond by moving the tank, and now they were hot on the heels of Minula and her team.

Suddenly, the scene on the camera lit up in a hailstorm of gunfire coming from both directions. Turrets popped out of the walls and ceiling and tore apart the advancing soldiers like Swiss cheese. But despite the initial appearance of being overpowered, the attacking squad picked off the palace defenses, taking them out one at a time. When the dust settled, she counted another twenty dead soldiers on the ground and still more streaming in behind them.

Their lead was gone, but from the looks of it, the palace defenses were on their side. She didn't know why, but she wasn't about to look a gift horse in the mouth.

Minula spun around and pointed up the stairwell. "Everyone climb. Go, go, go!"

Shauna had already set a waypoint on the map at the apex of the climb, and no one questioned her decision. They'd either come to the same conclusion, or were simply obeying the chain of command.

Step by step, floor by floor, the sounds of explosions echoed from below and shook the ground they were climbing. Despite the closing signs of death, all she could do was count down the seconds until she'd finally be able to see Abigail. To be at her friend's side and to feel her touch.

While she wanted to shake her and ask her why she'd left without them, most of all, she wanted to be in her presence again. She'd always been at home beside Abigail. Be it as her guard, or as her friend. She always felt seen and appreciated. Even in the chaos of the moment, she had a way of making her feel like she could be her genuine best self. Whether it was being a brash jarhead or a joking trickster, Abigail supported her.

"We're coming up to the top, sir." Shauna must've been monitoring Minula's vitals. The woman had an uncanny ability to know when someone had zoned out and could bring them back into the moment when necessary.

Minula studied her HUD and zoomed in on the spot Ibu had marked as the throne room. The chamber was the center of all the action on the feeds, and more importantly, it held her friend. Depending on if they encountered any resistance, it was only a few minutes away.

When they summited the stairs, she hopped up to the front. She wanted to be the first person to see what they were getting in to. Not that she didn't trust the others, but in this moment she needed to be in charge.

As she scanned the expansive hall, a low rumbling rose in the distance. She redirected her swarm of gnat drones from the nearby halls to intercept the source of the noise, and they shot down the passageway. From the sound of the racket, it was getting louder, which meant only one thing. They had incoming.

She raised her fist in the air and brought it down. The squad stepped backward and dropped below the edge of the last stair, using it as cover. They trained their weapons down the tunnel and waited. The noise grew louder and louder, and as her gnat drones turned a corner, her stomach knotted up. A sea of robots was swarming the halls and was headed straight toward them at an ungodly speed.

"Wholly shit." She shared the feed with the others, and a few of them glanced up at her before returning their attention down the hall. From the looks of the robotic wave, they were outnumbered a hundred to one, and that was being generous. If these robots were all armed, they'd be done before they started.

The almost fluid movement of the river of robots was

mesmerizing. Every size, shape, and color imaginable was weaving their way toward them. Watching them skitter around the corner and redirect toward the stairs reminded her of liquid metal.

"Hold steady!" Minula dropped into the only free spot on the step and slid in beside her people, lowering her plasma gun. She painted the lead robot with her targeting system, and the stream of robots parted, dodging the invisible beam of light. They didn't fire on her position, they simply moved aside.

When she tweaked her target left, the robots hopped over and under the targeting beam, doing everything in their power to avoid being in the crosshairs. But still, they didn't fire. It was the strangest thing she'd ever seen. Almost like they were playing with her, taunting her to try to fire on them.

With the wave of metal rapidly closing the distance between them, her squad was getting antsy. She could see them fidgeting out of the corner of her vision. The hum of plasma rounds cycling their lock and load routine was disconcerting. It was a nervous tick common with gamers, and it should've been ironed out of their system long ago, but hadn't. Most of all, she could feel their eyes burning holes through her. They were doubting her fortitude, wondering if she'd froze.

She didn't know why, but every ounce of her being was telling her not to fire on these robots. They'd made it this far without the palace attacking them, so why would they change now?

She shook her head and subvocalized the command to disable all the weapons. "Drop flat!" She screamed above the roar of the robots.

"You've got to be fraking kidding me," Moet said.

Her weapon flashed red on Minula's retinal comm as the woman attempted to fire, but failed before she finally dropped down. Her face was centimeters away. "We had them!" She slammed her fist against the ground, denting the floor.

As the rumbling reached a crescendo, the wave of robots shot over pronated exo-suits and streamed past, pouring down the spiral stairway like a spigot left open. Every manner of automata passed overhead, and lying beneath the flowing mass could only be described like lying perfectly still under a passing freight train. One wrong move, and you could lose an arm or leg.

Minula checked the camera view from her micro-drones near the ceiling and noticed that the tail end of the wave wasn't far off. "Get ready to move." She subvocalized the command to unlock their weapons, and her suit hummed back to life.

The last of the robots trickled past, but she didn't bother to glance back at them. She simply hopped over the edge and sprinted down the hall. Toward the distant flashing green dot. Whoever was controlling the palace defenses was clearly on their side, and the last thing they needed to do was waste time questioning their motives. They were alive for one and only one purpose: saving Abigail.

45

ABIGAIL OLIVAW
PROTO DARK NEBULA, UNKNOWN

The chamber fell away, and there was only light surrounding her in all directions. It wasn't the glowing heavenly aura like so many people attribute to death, this was an eye searing brightness in all directions. And no matter how hard Abigail tried to block it, nothing worked. It was almost like her hands weren't real.

She needed to calm down and breathe. Freaking out wouldn't get her anywhere. She lowered her hand and took a deep breath, struggling to center herself. Something was off. The familiar sensation of her chest expanding was missing.

Suddenly, it hit her where she was. She wasn't in the royal chamber any longer. Fraking Deduc or Emmonsii, or whatever the hell their name was. They'd taken her to this place.

But that didn't answer where she was.

The last thing she remembered was the Therionic being telling her to fight. "Fight what?" she muttered.

Everywhere she looked, all she saw was light. None of the gold or green colors she'd seen streaming down the wall above the thrones. This was pure and simple white. Like the glow emanating between the paws of Deduc.

When she reached out and waved her hand through the

air, it met resistance just in front of her. She did it again, and it slowed her motion when it hit some type of invisible barrier, almost like her fingers were brushing against the membrane. One designed to isolate and manipulate her.

"Oh, hell no!" She leaned forward and clawed at the enclosure. Whatever they were doing to her, they were trying to subdue her, probably to control her mind, but they'd picked the wrong human to mess with. She was done letting aliens manipulate her, or anyone else for that matter.

Centimeter by centimeter, she tore her way through the invisible layers of the barrier surrounding her. Rage flowed unabated through every vein, and one motivating idea drove her forward.

Revenge.

She was going to kill this fraking alien if it was the last thing she ever did.

46

IBU

PROTO DARK NEBULA, NEAR ARCTORDIEA

The jumps were faster now, and Ibu's options were dwindling by the second. The Ursis had figured out their strategy and nearly cornered them in at every jump.

They'd constrained the space above the planet, making it impossible for them to open a comm gate to their team without being detected. And worst of all, the bastards had destroyed their micro-satellites one by one, shutting off their access to the ground. To their people and their reason for being.

The last signal from Shauna showed their tank crashing into a pond and sinking in the water. It was hard to tell if it was purposeful, or in response to the explosion next to the giant sphere. Either way, the team's signal disappeared beneath the waves, and their broadcast couldn't reach the surface.

They slammed their hand against the control panel, splitting it in half and sending shrapnel in all directions. A small shard of glass lodged itself in their neck, but they didn't feel it. Their body forced the foreign substance out and went about repairing the hole a few seconds later.

In their currently enraged state, their decisions were far

from optimal, but their body was in overdrive. The perfect killing machine with nothing to hurt but itself. If they were going to survive, they knew one thing. They needed to get control of their mental faculties and fast.

The Alatas ships dropped out of their superluminal bubbles and Ibu lurched across the gap to the neighboring controls, slapping the button to start the long chain of consecutive gate sequences. Cynthia was still writhing in pain in the cargo hold, and there was no time to warn her. They'd each have to work through the aftermath of this sequence of jumps alone.

As the gate vanes and the deadly blue glow swept over their body, they screamed in pain. Their arms and legs flailed, and they tore apart the bridge as jump after jump executed in rapid succession, each just as fast as the first.

While they knew it was necessary to escape the Ursis, their mind slipped into the dark recesses of their delusions. Into an unknown place in their consciousness, and they weren't sure how to emerge from it.

47

MINULA CLARKE
PROTO DARK NEBULA, ON ARCTORDIEA

The squad of exo-suits was barreling down the hall two by two, heading toward the throne room. Minula and Shauna were in the lead, each with their own motivation for making it to the blinking green dot as fast as possible. Ibu's map had been invaluable in navigating this maze of hallway. She was pretty sure they backtracked at least once, but to be honest, it was impossible to tell. For being so good at engineering, the Ursis had an odd sense of layout.

According to the map, the throne room was up ahead. It was strange that they hadn't picked up Abigail's tracker since they landed, but then again, they lost contact with Ibu as soon as they hit the water. This entire facility must be coated in skotádi or some type of signal dampening material.

"Lock and load." She checked the round still loaded into her plasma cannon and confirmed her laser battery was powered up. "Unless it's locked tight, I'm not planning on ringing the doorbell."

"Roger that." Moet and a few of the other soldiers ejected their electro-blades, casting an eerie red glow around them. "Just try not to trip over that power switch this time."

Minula bit her lip. She made one mistake in practice, and she'd been hearing about it ever since. "Don't frak with me right now, or you'll have a hole in your chest like our Ursis friends outside. If everyone does their job, maybe we'll make it out of this place alive."

After days of waiting, countless tears, and untold close calls, she was finally going to see Abigail. She didn't know what they were walking into, but she was prepared to tackle anything the aliens threw at them in the approaching room. "Be careful in there. And whatever you do, don't—hit —Abigail."

None of them replied. They didn't have to. No one wanted to take on their captain by friendly fire. If they did, they knew Shauna would kill them in an instant if Minula didn't beat her to it.

As they slid to a halt in front of the massive throne room doors, they raised their weapons. The sound of exo-suits preparing to charge the smooth slab of metal permeated the space, when suddenly the doors slid open.

Minula wasn't about to question their benefactor in this palace. She leaned forward and charged the chamber, covering the distance in power assisted strides. Once she cleared the entrance, her suit scanned the area in an instant. It called out all the threats and even found their target before she blinked.

Abigail was in the middle of the expansive room with the ceilings that seemed to go on forever. There was an elderly looking Ursis standing directly behind her dressed in ornate robes, and he was squeezing her shoulder. For some reason, he had his other palm pressed against her forehead in an unusual embrace. She was surrounded on three sides by a semicircle of a dozen similarly robed Ursis. In the nearest corner stood one lone Ursis with their back to the others, and they appeared to be stuffing something inside a robot. Finally, on the far wall was the regally clad Ursis she'd seen beside Abigail on the news feeds. He was standing in front of a trio of thrones with splotches of gold and green light covering a tree like mural filling the rear wall from floor to ceiling.

Without drugs, scanning that entire scene would have taken precious seconds, but with the volume of stimulants flowing through her veins, it happened in the blink of an eye. Enough time for her suit to adjust the power in her legs to favor the left.

She broadcast her planned trajectory to her team members and pushed off, launching herself toward the wall to her right. As she sailed through the air, she righted herself and trained her weapons on the Ursis in the middle. The one holding Abigail.

The glowing light in their hand was throbbing against her forehead, and from this angle she didn't have a shot, let alone know the damage she'd inflict on her friend if she killed the alien. For all she knew, they were in a symbiotic bond of some sort, and damaging him would hurt her.

"Frak!" She released the pressure she'd already applied to the virtual trigger.

The Ursis nearest the doorway reacted to their sudden arrival, but their response was confusing on many levels. Half of them appeared to be in shock the door had actually opened, and were backing away from the elderly Ursis in the middle. Whereas the other half closed in on him, trying to shield him.

Her exo-suit impacted with the wall, and she squatted down against the surface, having already planned her ricochet angle. She was aiming to land just past Abigail.

As she pushed off, her HUD flashed red. The threat sensors picked up unusual movements from the Ursis easing toward the middle of the room. They were reaching under their robes for what she could only assume were weapons, but she wasn't about to wait and see. Their only course of action was to shoot first and ask questions later.

She raised her arm and ordered her suit to fire at will, sending a hailstorm of laser bolts and plasma rounds toward the targets on the peripheral of the group. The other members of her squad were doing the same, but from other angles. The room lit up in a firework display of force.

One by one, their lasers hit their marks, but the only aliens that fell were the ones hit with plasma. Whatever their robes were made of, they were impervious to their light weapons. With half of the Ursis falling toward the ground, she pivoted her suit to land on her feet and ejected her right electro-blade out of its holster. The blade crackled to life as she touched down.

Two of the plasma rounds from her team tore through the edge most Ursis, leaving behind holes in their chest and colliding with the far light display on the wall.

The response was swift. The regal-looking Ursis standing beside the throne collapsed to his knees, writhing in pain and screaming at the top of his lungs. The shots had the same effect on the elderly alien grasping Abigail, except rather than letting her go, he fell sideways and was thrashing on the ground. Abigail's head slumped against his stomach, and his free hand, which had previously been gripping her shoulder, was now twitching against her chest. Fortunately, his other hand seemed to be unaffected and was resting against her forehead. If it hadn't been, her skull might've been crushed like a grape.

She didn't know what unseen force was attaching Abigail to the Ursis, but she didn't dare touch them. When the twitches ended, his giant paw was still touching her head. Both of the bodies were lying motionless on the ground, and the remaining aliens near the middle glanced at Minula and her team and lost their shit.

It could've been them witnessing their leader fall, or

maybe the shots against the back wall had a similar effect on them. Either way, they charged forward with their staffs drawn and an eerie yellow hue about them.

If guns weren't gonna work in this confined space, then it'd have to be swords. Luckily for them, they had 'em in spades.

Her second electro-blade ejected out of the socket in her arm and powered up. With an Ursis charging straight at her, she tapped the blades together in a show of strength, hoping it would intimidate them.

They weren't impressed.

The towering alien closed the distance in a flash, and the next thing she knew, she was flying backward toward the corner of the room. Her left blade had been cut clean off, and her hand had almost gone with it. Her suit attempted to compensate for the sudden change in direction, but it couldn't recover. She smashed against the far wall and slid to the ground in a limp pile.

Minula stared glassy eyed at the floor in front of her as her suit's defensive measures blared, willing her to stand up and pay attention. But the room wasn't coming into focus. While she was feeling no pain, all she was seeing was stars.

She subvocalized the command to inject another dose of stimulants, but the suit resisted, and an error message popped up. She'd already used too much. Any more and she could die. The irony of dying without it wasn't lost on her.

"Fraking machine, give it to me!" She pushed up off the ground, losing her balance and falling backward against the walls that met in the corner.

"You need to keep moving," Harold said.

His voice was near, but she knew that was impossible. Last they'd seen him, he'd been with Abigail. When something touched her suit, she flinched, bringing her hand up around her attacker's neck. Just as she was about to squeeze, he spoke again.

"Let me go, Min. Abigail needs you." He reached out and held his mechanical claw to the side of her head, projecting an override code on the outside of her helmet.

When she typed it in, her exo-suit shot her up with another round of stimulants. With the snap of a finger, the room came into focus. Everything slowed way down, like people were moving in slow motion.

She marked Harold's dot as a friendly and shared his position with the rest of the squad. While she didn't know his capabilities, she knew one thing for certain. He would defend her and Abigail until their last breath.

His domed head turned toward her and his glowing green eyes locked on her undamaged electro-blade. "Do you have a weapon I can use?"

Shauna sprinted up next to them, and an elongated compartment in her back opened up. "If she doesn't, I do." It was too thin to store a gun, but when she reached in, she pulled out something better. One of Ibu's swords. "I was told by a friend of ours that you knew how to use this."

He reached out and carefully grasped the handle, his eyes locking on the images lining the blade. One by one, the pictures etched into the razor-thin surface retold the story of their assault on the castle. From their jump out of the Phoenix, to the battles inside the tank, their voyage to this moment was imprinted forever in the memory of the blade.

Harold turned over the weapon in his hand. "It looks like you took quite a long journey to get here."

"You don't know the half of it." Minula pushed off the wall and shouldered past the two robots to study the battlefield. Her team was getting beaten to hell, and most of them had taken to the sky. They were using the walls to keep away from the mountainous aliens, bouncing back and forth between them while trying to find a shot that could do some damage. One of their exo-suits was lying motionless in the middle of the room, and its dot on her HUD was painted a faint red. The name beside it said Brummell. She'd barely known the soldier, but they'd fought with honor.

Scanning the scene, she caught sight of the Ursis that rammed her. He was standing near Abigail. He must've been checking on their leader because when he glanced around the room to find her, his gaze locked on her, and he didn't hesitate. He charged toward the three of them with hatred in his eyes.

"We've got company." She loaded another plasma round and plotted a path to get behind the beast without risking them grabbing her while passing over. While she needed to steer clear of hitting the far wall, that didn't mean she couldn't use the one weapon capable of taking these beasts down.

What she didn't expect, however, was help from the other Ursis. She'd forgotten all about the other aliens that backed away from the center. Her suit hadn't yet painted them as threats, which was a good thing because two of them crashed into the alien charging her, sending them all toppling over.

She wasn't about to sit still and watch someone else fight her battle, so she leapt forward, searching for an ideal shot. As she sailed over the scene, she pivoted around just as the Ursis that charged her slashed the last of the two weaponless attackers with his glowing staff. She hadn't even realized they were unarmed. They never really had a chance.

Her suit came down past the commotion, and she raised her plasma cannon for the kill. With the blood of two of his kind pooling beneath the Ursis' feet, he glanced up at her and smiled, his teeth glistening in the golden light from the wall behind her.

She pulled the virtual trigger and a sphere of glowing plasma shot out, aimed at the dead center of the beast's chest. As the red-hot round arced across the gap between them, everything cut to slow motion. The fireball was on track to bore through the alien's torso when her heart sank. She watched as the Ursis dropped onto his side and slid under the path of the munition. It sailed over his head and exploded against the far wall, sending red-hot droplets in all directions. Whatever the hell the wall was made of, nothing was getting through it.

With her attention on the miss, she didn't notice the Ursis pop up a few meters in front of her until it was too late. She couldn't jump away. The only thing left to do was to tackle the beast head on.

She subvocalized the command to charge her electro-blade to maximum and leaned forward, charging with every ounce of energy she had remaining. Her heart was pounding like a snare drum on crack. It was do-or-die time, and it suddenly hit her that today might be her day.

The Ursis took note of her change in posture and chuckled, squatting down low and planting his feet wide. Moving the mountainous figure was going to take some serious power.

As she drew nearer, he didn't waver, but she did. She started second guessing herself.

Maybe she could've turned and run.

Maybe taking him head on wasn't her wisest move.

The drugs were clouding her decision-making, willing her to fight battles she couldn't win. Either that, or love was blinding her.

With his staff held in front of him and his cloak stained in blood, she saw a fleeting chink in his defenses. He'd planted his feet wide and left his center open. In most combat situations, that would mean nothing, but even with her suit on, he was easily two to three times her size.

Just as she was leaning forward to leap upward toward his midsection, she faked the move and instead dropped to her side, holding her blade out as far as she could reach. His eyes went wide, and her exo-suit slid between his legs. Before he could mount a response, her blade sliced through his ankle like butter, sending screams of agony through the chamber.

The Ursis tumbled to the ground with a thud, and by the time she came to a stop, Shauna and Harold were already swarming the alien. Shauna with her electro-blade and Harold with his Ursis sword. They weaved in and out, slicing at his body and escaping his flailing limbs before he could bat or kick them away.

Minula stood up and checked her HUD. The other five Ursis were busy fending off the exo-suited gnats flying overhead, and none of them were rallying to help their compatriot. Not seeing them working together was strange, but then again, they weren't exactly dressed like soldiers. They might be able to use that to their advantage, especially since they had the numbers.

She studied the motions of her team and looked for an opening to lend one of them a hand. Moet must have noticed her lingering because she signaled she was going to drop toward the center and lure the Ursis closer. It was the best plan she could think of.

As Moet lowered to the ground behind her attacker, they pivoted on her position like she'd planned, and took another swipe at the human. While their glowing staff fell short, they left their rear exposed to the rest of the room.

Minula lifted her electro-blade and launched her exo-suit at the beast's back, slamming into them and driving the sword deep into the alien's rib cage. She hung there for a second, her blade sparking and burning the alien from the inside out. A guttural howl rang through the chamber and then stopped as the Ursis slowly tipped forward.

Nearing the floor, she powered up her jump jets and launched upward, slicing the alien up their torso and out their neck. Blood splayed everywhere and covered her suit in a thick yellow slime.

She hit the ground ten meters away and skidded to a halt,

her heart bursting out of her chest. The tide was turning. She could feel it. They actually had a chance at this.

When she turned around to assess the remains of the battle, her team was taking down another Ursis on their own. They were using their numbers to their advantage and were finally able to support each other, especially when they added Shauna and Harold into the fray. The two robots were both fast and deadly. And while they wouldn't last a second on their own, they made quick work of the aliens as a team.

She glanced to her left and saw Abigail's body. While her chest had a faint rise and fall, she lay motionless on the ground with the elderly Ursis' paw still resting on her forehead. If she didn't know better, she'd cut the damn thing off.

Another screech of pain pierced the chamber, signaling a win from her team until an explosion shook the far wall where they'd first entered. The doors were closed, but where there was once a smooth surface, there was now a crack from the floor to the ceiling.

Her suit lit up in a sea of red alerts. The room must've been blocking all the signals from the outside, which explained why they hadn't detected Abigail sooner. What she'd failed to recognize, however, was that the sword cut both ways. While they were inside fending off the Ursis, the aliens were still laying siege on the palace. And now they were at the door.

She waved her arm. "Back away from the—"

But she was too late. The far wall imploded inward, launching her backward toward the golden light and sending half of her team crashing to the ground in fiery explosions. Their exo-suits cracked open during the blast and their munitions must've been compromised because the resulting discharges bore holes deep in the floor. The concentrated plasma rounds were like pouring out the heart of multiple suns on the ground.

It took her a few seconds to shake the stars out of her eyes, and once she did, she drew in a breath when the outlines of her people came into focus. They'd melted into piles of indistinguishable pockmarks filled with red-hot explosives.

"Aargh," she pushed up onto one knee and rested her hand against the wall. The HUD in her suit was going haywire, so it took her a second to realize something was oozing over her glove.

She hadn't noticed it before, but there was a golden fluid streaming down the wall, and it was presently passing over her gloved hand. The resulting gap beneath her fingers was the same color, though she could see spots of the wall beneath it. Whatever this stuff was, it wasn't very thick.

Her eyes locked on the contorted reflections of light in the liquid, and then a motion in the fluid caught her eye. There was something moving in the shadows, but it disappeared when the surface shifted. She tilted to the side, trying to catch the image again. It almost looked like a human face screaming at her.

Leaning in closer, she squinted as a shadow passed through the liquid. When it stopped, it started coming into focus until the fluid suddenly vibrated and shoved her hand away.

At the same moment, her HUD lit up. A stream of red dots was flowing through the opening in the wall behind her, and they were funneling toward the center of the room.

Minula didn't think or second guess what she had to do. She didn't have to. She simply snapped around and launched herself at Abigail.

Her one job was protecting this woman, and she wasn't about to fail by leaving her exposed to these fraking maniacs. Harold and Shauna must've had the same idea because both of them, along with Moet, met her in the middle of the chamber, creating a wall between her and the advancing soldiers.

The Ursis weren't advancing on the four of them. They were holding their ground, forming an invisible barrier a few meters away. Some of them were beat to hell, she imagined, either from fighting the palace defenses or the robot assault from earlier. The sea of enraged aliens in power-armor was enough to send ice through her veins.

"I'm not liking these odds," she muttered, staring over the scene. They were outnumbered a hundred to one. "What do we do now?"

"You watch your friend die," Deduc said.

She spun around to face the golden wall. The streams of green she'd seen earlier were fading, and the elderly Ursis was standing over Abigail, his paw no longer resting on her forehead. Instead, his eyes were narrow slits staring down at her limp body.

"I've got to hand it to her." He rubbed his hands together. "She fought hard. But in the end, her weakness was her emotions and her attachment to her people. It's one of the reasons why the Galactic Alliance extinguished humanity's light in the first place."

He reached under his robe and pulled out a jeweled dagger. The impossibly thin blade shimmered in the golden glow over his shoulder. "Your time and place in this universe is in the past. Your species is weak, and your leaders lack experience in doing what's necessary to rule the galaxy. The future is ours..." He glanced at Minula, locking eyes on her suit. "And once we capture that little starship of yours hopping in and out of orbit, we'll have your gate technology. Then we'll take our armada on a detour to Epsilon Eridani to retrieve that Beacon you stole. Your people don't have the faintest idea what you've captured."

Deduc tightened his grip on the dagger.

Her suit flashed an alert up on her visor. Abigail's life signs were dangerously low. Her breathing was muffled, and her heart rate was dipping up and down into dangerous levels. If they didn't do something to help her soon, she'd die.

Shauna made a move to lean down toward her daughter,

but Deduc swiped at her with his dagger and narrowly missed.

"Uh-uh." He waved a finger at her. "Hands off, mommy." He chuckled. "Yes, I know who you are. Your daughter's feelings for each of you were transparent when our life-forces were united. Your form, however, is sickening to stare at. To combine your soul with the body of an automata is to lose one's self. No. I think this is an opportunity to teach you four a lesson. You'll watch her die. And then, I'll take that ship of yours along with whoever's piloting it. Each of you will finally learn where you failed your people, the hard way."

Minula couldn't take it anymore. If watching the love of her life die in front of her didn't kill her, being a slave to this alien's twisted brand of revenge would.

So, she did the only thing she could think of. She dove at the alien's chest, activating her electro-blade at the last second. The action was a mixture of rage, instinct, and a whole lot of amphetamines.

She closed the short distance between them, and time ground to a halt. It was like her body's final ditch drug induced attempt at reminding her how badly she'd failed her best friend. Her only friend.

Deduc easily dodged her advance, twisting out of the path of the blade in one swift motion. Somehow, the elderly Ursis anticipated her actions. Perhaps Abigail's feelings gave her away, or maybe it was luck. She'd never know for sure.

While dodging her weapon, he brought up his dagger, letting the momentum of her choices render judgment. His blade plunged deep into her armor, cutting straight through the nanite reinforced weave like it was cotton.

Coldness spidered through her torso as the alien blade reached into her. Like a virus spreading through its host.

What neither she nor the Ursis had foreseen was the speed or ferocity of her two robot companions. They must've been watching Minula's motion because, as she was falling, she caught the blur of their attack out of the corner of her vision.

A smiled eased into place as she crashed to the ground, all the while struggling to catch a glimpse of her friends repeatedly slicing through Deduc's torso and limbs. Ironically, the soldiers didn't fire at the robots. They seemed like they were afraid of hitting their leader.

Perhaps this was the lesson he'd mentioned earlier.

48

ABIGAIL OLIVAW

PROTO DARK NEBULA, UNKNOWN

Abigail broke through the membrane, thinking she was freeing herself and fighting to survive, when in fact it was the only thing in the ether protecting her from him.

His mind was too powerful for her. Where Deduc had spent years bonding with the power of the entity, she'd only had minutes at most. And even those were blurs of incoherent sounds and colors.

Once she'd passed through the membrane's shell, he snatched at her. Metaphorically tearing into her mind. He consumed her memories, absorbing the ins and outs, secrets and surprises of her life in the time it took her to bat an eye.

At one point, she broke away from him and made her way to the wall. She didn't know how she'd done it, but she passed through the nothingness of the golden liquid and was staring out the other side.

It was then and there that a familiar and happy sensation washed over her soul. Her love for Minula. He'd sensed it, too. How it had grown through decades of constant suppression until recently breaking free and blooming for all to see.

But he snatched her back, yanking her from Minula's grasp and sending the Therionic entity into a frenzy.

It was then that he dug deeper into her memories and recognized her mother in Shauna. A wave of nausea hit her when he realized what she was. An electronic shell of her former self.

He experienced a deep respect for what Harold had accomplished, bringing humanity to the stars. And yet, he was filled with absolute condemnation for the form he took in doing it.

Finally, he saw Ibu onboard the Phoenix. Her last hope and his last salvation. He seemed surprised seeing them and realizing that it wasn't Abigail who held his fate in their hand. It was the Nanil.

Once he'd stripped her of the memories he needed, he released her to pour out into the cognitive ether. Well out of reach of the Therionic entity and into the equivalent of a mental puddle on the ground.

As he stood up, she caught a glimpse of his aura. It seemed renewed, and his outline radiated rays of golden-blue. Like he'd sapped a bit of her being.

Her vision faded in and out a few times as her spirit evaporated bit by bit. Only when the picture steadied and she got a clear view of Minula's face did she feel a jolt. A sense of love passing from one being to another.

It was like every hair on her body stood on end.

With her mind fluttering from seeing Minula, her heart sank when she shot forward, trying to strike him down. Deduc had the upper hand. He knew the mental knot, the gymnastics of their relationship, and how it tugged at both of them. He'd seen her weakness and anticipated her reaction before she'd even moved a muscle.

When the dagger struck Minula, Abigail's body shuddered. At first she thought it was the bond she'd felt a moment earlier, but then she realized it was something else entirely.

Moet had reached down and grabbed her limp form in her

arms, launching across the open space toward the wall of gold. Once she was a safe distance away, she eased her down to the ground and shot an emergency syringe full of nanites into her thigh. After she was medicated, Moet knelt down in front of her, blocking her from the aliens and preventing her from seeing Minula.

Abigail wasn't sure why they weren't firing on Moet, but she didn't have long to worry. A warmth passed over her as the golden liquid of the Therionic entity passed over her body, encapsulating her once again in light.

49

IBU

PROTO DARK NEBULA, ON ARCTORDIEA

When the wall to the throne room exploded inward, it was over. Even with the palace defenses on their side, their friends failed. They'd gotten in over their head, and Deduc's forces had won. Though, to be honest, the more they thought about it, the more they realized they'd been over their head ever since they'd entered the Dark Nebula. It didn't start on this planet.

What made this different wasn't that they were fighting against impossible odds, it was that Ibu wasn't a part of it. They were hiding in space onboard this blasted ship rather than helping on the ground.

The logical side of their brain was counting the soldiers streaming into the chamber, and the probabilities of success plummeted toward zero. But the emotional side gnawed at their cerebellum, demanding them to act. To help their friends, instead of sitting back and watching the alien news feeds.

Returning to Epsilon Eridani with Cynthia, but missing the rest of the crew wasn't something they relished the thought of. Abigail's family would never look at them the same, and they didn't expect the other humans would, either.

They'd be an even bigger outcast than before. Hell, they wouldn't be surprised if the humans imprisoned or banished them entirely. Thus far, humanity wasn't the most alien friendly species in the galaxy. About the only person who might be on their side would be Cynthia, and they were still a big question mark. It depended on how she viewed abandoning the others on the planet.

Their options were sparse. They either needed to come back with more members of the crew, or disappear with the Phoenix. They'd be destined to explore the universe alone, and may never find their place. And with a gate drive in their possession, they'd always be looking over their shoulder. It didn't sound appealing, and besides, they'd grown quite accustomed to Shauna and Minula. Hell, even Abigail wasn't half bad once you got past all her mood swings.

As they were programming the gate sequence to get them back to Arctordiea, the wall of news streams changed. The anchors and talking heads for the government suddenly shifted from doom and gloom to the return of their savior. When Ibu returned their attention to the wall screen, they saw why.

Standing behind the remains of their friends was the Ursis they called Deduc. The broadcasts started the day painting him as the opposition to the current regime of Emmonsii Phi. And now, with new intel from the military, they were reporting that Deduc and Emmonsii Phi were one and the same, and had always been.

Judging by the other feeds, the Ursis people weren't handling the news well. Dozens of towns across Arctordiea and the outer planets inside the Nebula had been rioting since finding out, and the news was only now making its way to the connected star systems. While they squelched the coverage of the uprisings, a few tidbits made it through. The aliens were demanding Deduc's head for the atrocities in the clan cleansing after the darkness fell. The priest and despot had played both sides, and he needed to be held accountable for his crimes.

They mulled over what Deduc regaining consciousness meant to their friend's missions, when he started speaking. The moment he mentioned watching Abigail die, Ibu queued up the gate sequence and notified Cynthia of their pending jumps so she could ready their automated friends. While they'd spent their time finding a map of the palace and programming the gate sequences to keep them alive, she'd been building a robotic army in the cargo hold in case Minula's team needed support.

Shauna and Harold had salvaged dozens of deactivated Ursis battle droids on Griseo, and had Minula been able to fit them into their drop pods, they would've brought them planetside to help with their assault. That left Cynthia in possession of a whole lot of parts, and a small army with nothing to blow up, until now.

They disconnected from the mental link and exited the bridge to the left, working their way toward their quarters. "Clockwise," they muttered. "Always clockwise."

As they jogged through the open door, the tachyon field passed over them. It was the first of three hops before they'd be at their destination. They only had a few minutes to make it to the cargo hold before the next two rapid jumps, the last of which would fast follow the first.

They reached up over their bed and grabbed the lone sword. The blade glistened in their hand when they grasped the hilt, and they paused, studying the story etched into the surface. They squinted and held it closer to their eyes.

The story had changed since they last read it. When they left Griseo, it told a tale of Harold's slaughter of the humans who threatened them, and their mission to find Abigail's fate. Those images were microscopic smudges on the side, replaced with a far different narrative.

Along the widest part of the blade was the path Shauna

and Minula had taken raiding the palace at Summis, and it was etched in great detail. They could tell the moment Harold got his hands on the weapon because the record changed. The images transformed from faint, almost aged scores in the metal, to dramatic and vibrant strokes highlighting every nuance of the battle. From the sliced corpses of the Ursis, to the giant holes of plasma in their torso, the tide of the story turned in an instant.

Despite the distances between the blades, the two mystical weapons somehow kept their stories in sync. A feat they couldn't begin to comprehend and didn't have time to think about. They had a story of their own to tell. One that hopefully led to their friends surviving another day.

They lowered the blade and sprinted toward the cargo hold, taking the long way around. The etched image of their friends fighting the Ursis was playing back in their head. They needed help, and even if it was a lost cause, it was their cause.

When they hit the cargo hold, Cynthia and their automata were waiting for their arrival. They were arranged in meticulous lines from most devastating to least. No one was complaining, and no one was second guessing their decision to assault the palace. It was a refreshing change of pace. The longer they spent with humans, the more they appreciated the advantage the mechanized forms gave them. Something they wouldn't have said at the onset of this mission.

"Are you ready?" Ibu asked.

Cynthia took a deep breath and nodded. "As ready as I've ever been. I hope they stay together. A few of them might be duct taped in places."

They chuckled and glanced down at the blade. The images had shifted sideways, making room for another pane in the story. They studied the freshly etched lines as the alien material pressed into the surface, leaving in its wake a raw chunk of time.

Staring at Ibu in the center of the etching was Minula's face framed in the mask of her exo-suit. Her eyes were rolling into the back of her head and jutting out of her chest was the dagger Deduc had been holding moments earlier on the news feed. He was standing with his back to the wall, raising the impaled woman aloft, while he stared out at his soldiers in the distance. They could only imagine the expression on his face with two robots slicing into his legs.

"What is it?" Cynthia leaned forward to study the blade.

Ibu lowered it before she could see it. There was no point in filling the woman with any more fear and doubt. The image of Minula was seared into their mind's eye as the tachyon fields passed over them, one after another. Even with the speed of the transition tearing at their body, they didn't feel a thing. They were already deep within their transformation, except this time it was willingly. They didn't fight the change; they welcomed it. The only way they'd avenge their friend was by making the Ursis pay.

Winds buffeted and tore at the hull of the Phoenix as the tachyons fell away and gravity induced free fall engulfed the starship. Gone were the familiar confines of the vacuum of space, replaced instead with the upper atmosphere of Arctordiea.

Cynthia groaned from the rapid gate and leaned out to place her hand on one of the robots as their retinal comms updated with their position. They were dead on target, barreling toward the planet below.

The one thing the Ursis failed to realize in their attempt to enclose the air space above Summis, was that leaving their ships in stationary positions in orbit made Ibu's gravity calculations that much easier. Now the only gamble left remaining was the palace defenses. Based on their research, whoever was in command of the armaments would either defend them as soon as they got in range or end them just as quickly.

While Ibu floated toward the ceiling, a nearby robot

grasped their ankle and pulled them back to the ground. The magnetic feet of the automations made it easier to fix their position than her skotádi jumpsuit. They'd been wearing the gift since Moet had given it to them. They might actually get a chance to whack someone with the proverbial olive branch she'd extended. Though, they weren't certain if that was how the analogy worked.

The afterburners of the Phoenix roared to life, and the cargo hold went from a windswept hum to an ear-piercing growl as the starship fought to slow the deadly pull of gravity's clutch. Their weight quadrupled in the blink of an eye and their legs buckled. Had the robots not been at their side, they might have collapsed. Their metallic arms wrapped around them and propped them up.

Their retinal comm counted down the seconds until they entered palace airspace. As time ticked away, their hand shook. They wanted to glance at the blade, but they couldn't chance seeing something that would throw them off.

Cynthia narrowed her gaze on Ibu.

Neither of them wanted to second guess their decision nor face the unpleasantry of reality. Not yet.

Explosions rocketed the Phoenix and Ibu squeezed their eyes shut. The palace was attacking, and it was only a matter of time before they scored a direct hit. As detonation after detonation rang around them, they grew confused.

They subvocalized the command to bring up the external cameras. The sky was lit up in a hailstorm of rockets, laser fire, and what looked like swarms of drones coming up from the ground. Except none of it was directed at them, it was aimed at the inbound fighters from orbit. The fleet of Alatas ships had launched intercept teams to take out the Phoenix.

Shot after shot was intercepted by the drones as they dove in front of the blasts. The Ursis in orbit were aiming to maim but not destroy the human ship, and the drones were the only thing keeping them flying.

There was nothing they could do but watch. Their fate was in the hands of whomever was commanding the palace defenses. They knew the facility was capable of untold devastation, but the system was old and hadn't kept up with Ursis technological advances. The only hope was that the divide wasn't too great.

The battle didn't last long. With the Phoenix rapidly approaching its target, the airspace above Summis cleared. It was a combination of the palace gaining ground on the advancing forces and them giving up. They were nearing their destination, and any stray shots could put the aliens below in jeopardy.

If someone had been watching their approach, they might think they were on a collision course for the peak of Summis because they were. Ibu wasn't messing around. Their path toward the monarch's palace was a fiery smoke-filled streak in the sky reminiscent of the ship's namesake.

They knew the architectural significance of the building meant the throne room was open to the sky. The Ursis designed most of their important buildings to be at one with nature. Some managed the feat using holograms, but in this case, it was literally open.

The designers strategically directed gravity waves to arc over the entrance to the cavernous chamber. They were arranged to slow or knock obstacles out of the way, and most of the time, they prevented them from reaching the ground. Be it torrential rain or lasers from above, nothing made it inside unless the palace wanted it there.

"We're coming in too fast," Cynthia said over their retinal comm.

"I know." Ibu pulled the first of two pistols out of its holster and checked the dial. "Plasma," they muttered. The only thing that got through to these animals was high-temperature fusion.

"But..." Cynthia's eyes were wide. "Shouldn't we prepare for impact?"

They shook their head and squeezed the hilt of their blade. "Not unless the universe has already written us off."

Humans had a funny way of living their lives. At times, they were hell bent on law and order, and at others, all they talked about was fate and destiny. Yet, when their lives were the most stressful; they always seemed to doubt their path. As if they lacked true confidence in their decisions.

"We'll crash in... twenty seconds. We should—"

Ibu raised their hand for the woman to stop talking and took a deep breath. They knew the numbers better than anyone. You don't gate a starship into a planet's atmosphere without accepting the consequences. Gravity still had rules that could not be broken, even with advanced technology.

What they hadn't told Cynthia was that they were gambling on outside help. It was a risky calculation by any measure, but they were beginning to see this entire mission as beyond their control alone. It would make a lot more sense if Abigail was answering a higher calling rather than acting on an impulse.

When the Phoenix groaned, their retinal comm flashed up a warning in their field of view.

Unknown gravitational anomaly detected. Orders?

The expert system running their landing program was reaching out, following its chain of command. It couldn't make a decision on its own.

They brought up the descent camera and shared them with Cynthia. The Phoenix was slowing, and the aliens below were finally taking notice of the starship suddenly blocking their sunlight. While a few were moving out of the way, more would be in a moment.

The throne was situated along the south wall, where their people were clumped together. Moet had her back to a golden bump on the same wall, and Shauna and Harold's robot bodies were lying on the ground nearby, not far from the body of an Ursis flailing his arms and legs. The aliens on the north wall were lined up in neat rows, and from the looks of it, preparing to fire on them.

"This ought to be interesting," Ibu muttered and glanced at Cynthia. "Remember, stick to our plan. No matter what."

She swallowed hard and nodded.

Ibu disengaged the descent thrusters, letting the palace lower the Phoenix the rest of the way. Once they were off, they redirected the exhaust toward the north wall and narrowed the drive nozzles.

With their ship slowing, the aliens raised their weapons and prepared to fire right as Ibu activated the thrusters. They might not have used them if they'd surrendered, but this was more cathartic.

The thruster nozzles hurled a stream of super heated gas out of the tail of the ship toward the lines of Ursis. While the flames hit next to their target, the results were still effective. It tore through the alien power armor and ricocheted off the wall, turning the room into a ready-made blast furnace.

Glowing red bodies flailed left and right, sending mountainous aliens careening into their neighbors and bursting into flames seconds later. It was a chaotic scene and was playing out exactly as they'd imagined.

They cut the thrusters before they reached the inner roofline and hit the virtual button to open the cargo bay door. One by one, the battle droids poured out of the Phoenix just short of the ground, launching themselves into the fray.

The remaining Ursis soldiers were caught off guard. Most were still struggling to escape being burned to a crisp, but some were fighting for their lives against the sea of angry automata.

Ibu and Cynthia both leapt in tandem from the Phoenix. Cynthia made her way toward Abigail and Ibu headed to the front lines. They weren't about to bring the battle to their people, and besides, they had some scores to settle.

Reaching the wall of Ursis struggling to regain their upper hand, they vaulted up and off the shoulders of a nearby robot and launched themselves on the back of a fleeing alien. They swung their sword and sliced off their head, sending the towering torso crashing to the ground and Ibu somersaulting between the legs of another alien soldier in power armor heading to the front lines.

They spun around and aimed their pistol squarely at the alien's heart, pulling the trigger twice in rapid succession. Two bolts of glowing red plasma shot through the back of the alien, and they froze. When they reached down to rub their chest, they tumbled forward.

Ibu didn't wait around to watch them crash. They kept going, leaping from Ursis to Ursis. Between their sword and their pistol, they disposed of nearly a dozen aliens in the midst of the chaos.

It would only be a matter of time before they got their act together, so in the moment, they needed to kill as many as possible. Watching Harold take out the humans on Griseo taught them a lot about handling the blade rather than it handling them.

When they made their way up to the far entrance where the soldiers were funneling out, they turned and surveyed the carnage. The room was strewn with bodies piled as far as the eye could see, and Ibu's robots were continuing to cut through the few remaining Ursis that were still standing or whose vital signs showed they were alive. A few of the robots had even followed the fleeing aliens out the crack in the wall and were barreling through the halls of the palace.

Their eyes locked on Deduc. He was struggling to pull himself up to the golden throne. There was another Ursis lying on the ground nearby. They were dressed in ornate robes, and if they remembered correctly, they were the proper heir to the throne.

Ibu sprinted through the bodies and across the expansive chamber, making their way toward Abigail and Cynthia. Moet was standing guard like a statue, and at first, they thought the woman was dead until she flinched and raised the laser in her arm, aiming it squarely at them.

"Easy! It's me, Ibu!" They reached forward and rested their hand on the woman's arm.

Moet held her aim steady for a few seconds until she lowered it. "Sorry. I... couldn't..." Her words drifted off and her eyes fluttered.

"Where are Harold and Shauna?" Ibu glanced around but didn't see the robots on the battlefield.

"They're... over there." Moet pointed beneath one of the suits of Ursis power armor. "They were already down for the count when that fraking tree fell on them. It was all I could do to stop them from reaching Abigail."

They spun in place and eyed Cynthia. "Is she..."

"Fine, I think." She stepped away from the wall to reveal the bump Ibu had seen from above. "It looks like something cocooned her. I was able to hit her up with a med kit and a round of nanites, but I can't tell if they're helping."

"The thing in the wall did that after that fraking asshat lanced Minula." Moet pointed at Deduc, her arm barely staying aloft.

In the midst of the moment, they'd forgotten about Minula. When they motioned toward them, a voice bellowed across the chamber.

"Don't touch her!"

Ibu glared down the golden wall at the Ursis seated on the throne. It wasn't the one they'd seen standing or kneeling in front of it on the news feeds. It was the one known as Deduc.

They took another step toward Minula and froze when a tentacle reached out of the golden surface and grabbed at the woman's exo-suit, yanking it backwards to the far side of the room.

"For a Nanil, I'd expect you to listen better when given an order," Deduc said.

Ibu narrowed their gaze.

"Yes, I know what you are. Your kind helped turn the tide against humanity. While I can't say I liked what the Qudoculi or the Trochilidae did to your people during that tribunal, the outcome for your uplifts was just. It was one of the few things I agree with the Galactic Alliance on."

"It's convenient how that sword cuts both ways, isn't it? You know, with your kind being judged guilty and all." Ibu issued a command to send some medical robots to inject Minula with nanites. They didn't know if it would help, but if they could save the woman, they would.

Deduc laughed. "One should never mistake fear for distrust, my cub. What transpired with my kind only happened because they saw us as a threat."

"Whatever you say." Ibu checked their retinal comm and noticed Moet was standing up, guarding Abigail. The soldier must be in shock, and she was doing all she could to hold it together.

"So, tell me something, Ibu." Deduc adjusted his position on the throne to better see them. "What made you stick with these humans for so long?"

"I'm not following?" Their retinal comm chimed. The medical bots reached Minula and her vitals were weak. While they were injecting her with the nanites, for all they knew, she could already be brain-dead.

"You know deep down that your kind is more evolved

than humanity. You've known it since you joined forces with that woman's brothers."

"Her name's Abigail." Ibu squeezed the hilt of their sword.

"Her name is not important any longer. I didn't know it when I saw the vision the first time, and I need not remember it now. Her role in this nightmare has come to an end. In that thread of time, she held the details of the gate drive that saved us. But in our reality, it was you that brought it to me." He pointed up in the sky at the Phoenix.

When they glanced up, they saw their ship being enshrouded in a glowing green membrane, like the one they'd seen reaching at them from the Alatas ships. Their ways out of this Nebula were disappearing by the second.

Ibu took a step backward toward Moet and Cynthia and held a hand behind their back. They waved the women to get down.

"It's odd how space-time works," Deduc began. "In my original vision, you were nowhere to be found. It was Abigail that was both the savior and the speaker."

"The what?" Ibu froze.

"The speaker for the Therionic entity. They're destined to bridge the mind of the Therionic life with our people." Deduc stood up off the throne and turned to face Ibu.

The cuts they'd seen inscribed on his body earlier were now healed. Like they'd never been there. The golden fluid must have repaired him.

"With her out of the way, and with you handing me your ship, I don't have much of a need for you anymore. Any of you." He kicked Haradis' limp form on the ground in front of him, and the Ursis moaned.

Ibu stared up at the Phoenix. It was almost completely engulfed in the membrane by this point.

Their clock was ticking.

They took another step backward beside Moet and subvocalized a comm. "We have to take cover."

Moet chuckled. "And where exactly do you expect us to do that?"

Ibu glanced around. There were no exits or debris on this side of the chamber, and the closest thing to them was the tipped over Ursis lying atop Harold and Shauna's corpses.

They realized then that they hadn't thought this part of their plan all the way through. Once the Phoenix was captured, the expert system had only one directive. To launch the ship into the center of the planet.

MINULA CLARKE

PROTO DARK NEBULA, ON ARCTORDIEA

Minula couldn't feel her chest rising and falling anymore. In fact, the last thing she remembered was the Ursis stabbing her like a pansy.

When she opened her eyes, all she could see was a green amorphous blob framed in the blue sky overhead. Somehow, her visor was cracked open and her HUD was dead.

Her retinal comm should still work. When she subvocalized a command to activate it, the device sprang to life, painting her vision in a veil of red. Her suit was compromised in a dozen places, and something was crushing her torso, cracking her open and squeezing her insides out. And whatever the Ursis had stabbed her with was apparently hanging out inside her, leaching her energy like a sponge.

She wasn't sure how she was even alive until she caught sight of a medical bot crawling near the edge of her faceplate. Her squad ran out of those a few hours into their mission.

That could only mean one thing.

She brought up the footage from her retinal comm and backed up the feed until her heart danced. An image of the Phoenix framed the sky above her in a halo of light. The starship looked strange lowering toward the ground without deceleration thrusters, when out of nowhere its afterburners fired, cooking the Ursis below like an old-fashioned open pit barbecue. When Ibu leapt out of the cargo hold, she couldn't help but smile. She had to hand it to them; the Nanil had virtual balls the size of Jupiter.

When the camera backed up even further, she caught a glimpse of the golden tentacle yanking her backward. Her current state made a whole lot more sense.

She quickly scrubbed over the footage, searching for another shot of Abigail. Any image at all. But she came up short. She couldn't find her anywhere.

The nanite transponders in their blood might help. Flipping over to what was left of the crew's life signs, her comm reported that Abigail was last seen on the ground behind Moet and Cynthia. The same place where there was a strange bulge on the fluid like substance.

With her attention focused on her retinal comm, she flinched when a med-bot crawled inside the crack in her faceplate. It snuggled up next to her head and injected her in the neck with another boost of nanites.

An invisible surge of energy shot through her, and her eyes bulged. The microscopic robots were suspended in amphetamines, both of which were now coursing through her veins, searching for a way to repair her. Based on the details transmitted from the battlefield that was her body, they were losing ground to the material from the dagger.

Her remaining seconds were ticking down, and she needed to turn the tide in her friend's favor.

Scanning the footage, she froze when she saw Deduc. A minute ago, he'd been sitting on the throne. That meant she might still have a shot.

Minula took a deep breath and tried to sit up, but the wave of pain engulfing her was too much. The taste of blood filled her mouth and she couldn't feel her legs. The golden tentacle holding her down was too strong, and the damage was too great.

She wasn't about to fraking die like this. Not after Ibu risked everything getting this far, and certainly not after all they'd done to get here. She had to think fast, but her options were limited.

If she connected with Ibu, then the aliens would know she was still alive, and they'd finish off the job. She had to capitalize on the element of surprise, no matter how small it might be. It was all she had.

The med-bot started crawling over her head toward the other side and it hit her. She could use that robot as her eyes.

She subvocalized a command to the robot and ordered it to crawl up and peek out the opening in her visor. As it clambered through the crack, she checked over her armaments. Her laser batteries were nearly empty but there were still a few plasma rounds left. The bigger question was if they'd shoot at all. While the structural integrity of her arm was fine, the tentacle was limiting the angle she could fire at.

Once the med-bot reached the edge of her visor, she could see Deduc's back. He was facing someone on the far side; she assumed Ibu.

"What makes you think I'll let you take our ship without a fight?" Ibu asked.

Minula angled the robot upward. The amorphous blob she'd seen earlier must've been the Phoenix, and unless she was mistaken, it was nearly covered.

Deduc chuckled. "Because it's your only way out of here, and as a Nanil, you're incapable of walking away from a conflict. It's in your nature to fight to the death."

She closed her eyes and fought back a scream as the tentacles squeezed her torso. The sound of her suit crunching crackled in her ears. It was either that or her bones, not that she'd be able to tell with all the drugs in her system. She didn't have much time left, so she needed to act.

The med-bot lowered its gaze to Deduc and crawled a bit further out into the open. She couldn't see past the golden tentacle, but from the looks of it, her arm was angled pretty low. Too low, actually. Unless she was going to bounce the plasma off something, she'd need some help.

There was only one thing that made this wall of light move, and it was out of her line of sight. She didn't have a shot. And then it hit her. It might not be out of Ibu's.

She loaded a crude message in the med-bot and sent it skittering away just as the tentacle slid up toward her neck. It covered her face and shoulders in a golden embrace, and her helmet started to crack. She could feel her windpipe close as she struggled to grab at her suit and failed.

51

IBU

PROTO DARK NEBULA, ON ARCTORDIEA

Deduc laughed, and his voice echoed through the chamber. "Because it's your only way out of here, and as a Nanil, you're incapable of walking away from a conflict. It's in your nature to fight to the death."

The words rang truer than they were willing to admit. Time after time they'd struggled to control their emotions, and time after time they'd failed… until now. This was the one instance where they willed themselves into a fight. They didn't enter it because of their animal instinct. They entered the fray out of loyalty and friendship. Something they'd never had on Doda. Something they'd only ever found with the Olivaws.

Their retinal comm chimed, and a message queued up for them to read. Strange. Moet wouldn't have subvocalized a message, and this one appeared to be from one of their robots.

They blinked it open.

Shoot clockwise — Med-bot 8

They read the message several times. It made no sense. Why would a med-bot send them a message to shoot clockwise? And what the hell did it mean to shoot clockwise, anyway?

When they checked the history of the bot, it was empty. Whoever sent it wanted to make sure its trail was wiped. The question was who?

The room suddenly filled with a blood-curdling scream, and Deduc raised his hands up over his head. He was staring up at the ceiling.

Ibu turned and glanced up at the sky and broke out laughing. The amorphous blob was gone, and in its place was a sphere of molten slag hovering overhead. The expert system onboard the Phoenix had executed precisely what they'd instructed it to do. It opened a gate into the center of Arctordiea, and the planet's core followed the rules of physics. When given an option between a higher pressure or a smaller one, particles will always flow toward an area of lower pressure. In this case, that area was into the Phoenix and its conduit was the open portal in space-time. Once the molten core of the planet filled enough of the starship, it was only a matter of seconds before it melted the gate drive and slagged any hope the Ursis had in stealing the technology.

"What did you do?" Deduc screamed.

They shook their head. "I know you're still new at this gating thing, but let me give you a tip about something. There are no obstacles between a gate in space-time and a destination, other than gravity."

Ibu smiled and thought back to the Fountainhead during their first gate transition. The act of moving between two points in spacetime seemed like magic back then, at least until they understood the math and how the clockwise spin of the tachyons was so important. Everything about gate travel favored starting left. Zachary told them as much when he showed them the designs on their voyage back to Zeta Lupi after fighting the Shu. The daydreams of that battle haunted them for days, and showing them the mathematics behind gate travel was his way of soothing them and calming their mind. Like any good parent or progenitor, he learned quickly that keeping a Nanil's mind busy was the easiest path to help them control their emotions. Especially when they were still learning to control their body.

At that point, they realized what the med-bot message meant. They didn't pause or hesitate another second. They simply raised the plasma pistol up to the left across their chest and pulled the trigger twice toward the wall of gold.

"Clockwise," they muttered. "Always clockwise."

The wall fluttered under the impact of the plasma and retaliated in kind, driving a golden spike out of the surface and lancing it through Ibu's chest.

MINULA CLARKE
PROTO DARK NEBULA, ON ARCTORDIEA

The image of Abigail reaching her hand out toward Minula disappeared in the mist when the tentacle released its death grip on her. She sat up with a start and gasped for air, regretting it the moment she had, as the blood in her mouth rushed into her lungs.

She immediately heaved it up into her suit, and waves of pain thundered through every centimeter of her being. Her body was broken and her exo-suit was the only thing holding her together.

When the haze of death started to lift, her vision followed suit.

The outline of Deduc came into focus first. He was on his knees about twenty meters away, and just past him was a hazy figure that looked like Ibu. For some reason, the Nanil was floating up off the ground and had a golden spike driven straight through their torso.

Then she remembered the message she'd sent. They'd done as she'd asked, and like most things Minula touched, they paid the ultimate price for listening to her.

They all had.

She had to make amends. She had to even the score.

Minula coughed up a mouth full of blood and raised her shaking arm, aiming it toward Deduc's back. She wasn't sure why, but he was still on his knees, screaming up at the sky.

But she couldn't hear him. Not that she gave a shit why he was angry.

She simply did what she needed to do.

She pulled the trigger and returned balance to the universe.

The last thing she saw before everything faded to black was two rounds of plasma sailing through the side of Deduc. One shot through his torso and the other squarely through the side of his head.

ABIGAIL OLIVAW
PROTO DARK NEBULA, ON ARCTORDIEA

The aura engulfing the alien entity shifted, transforming from a haze of black to a mist of green. At first, Abigail hadn't noticed the subtle shift in color, but the longer she stared, the more vibrant the green became. She didn't know how, but she could sense the rise in the entity's consciousness as it flowed from cell to cell, exploring her body. The bond with Deduc's life-force was broken, replaced with hers, and hers alone.

As she let her mind find a balance in the metamorphosis, she could feel the entity binding with her. At the same time, the longer she listened to it, the more lives she could sense. Like the alien entity was magnifying the streams of sentience. Be it the Ursis, the humans, or the Nanil, she could perceive their life-forces within her reach. Each one was unique in its own way, and yet, she couldn't tell which was which.

The only thing she knew for certain was that the entity couldn't survive without her as its host. At first, she didn't know how she knew it until she let the last few minutes replay in her mind. And then the wave of clarity washed over her. The entity was no different from Deduc. It jailed her until the very end. Until the moment Deduc had extracted her memories. Until it was positive it had what it needed from her. While unique in every way, the two aliens were cut from the same mold and had the same motivations. Survival at all costs.

It was only when she opened her eyes and stared out past the protective shell of the entity that she saw the bloodshed and carnage for what it was. Her people had been slaughtered. The same people she'd set out to protect by coming here alone had lost their lives saving her.

Grief and anger welled up inside, smashing into her consciousness, and drowning out the voice of the entity.

She couldn't take it any longer.

One by one, she had watched them fall, and now she was once again facing the universe alone. She smashed the wall, striking it first with her fists and then with something more. She didn't know how, but she focused her rage and broke free from the entity's shackles.

As the layers of the golden cocoon unfolded, she leapt to her feet, kicking off the remains of the shell that protected her. When she took her first breath of fresh air, she felt replenished. Like whatever Deduc had done to her had somehow been undone.

When she stared down at the ground, she saw Cynthia's body lying on its side. Her chest was moving up and down. She was alive, but she wasn't awake. Lying next to her was Moet. Her exo-suit had a hole in the stomach, and from the looks of it, a plasma round had entered the front and got stuck inside because there was a puddle of her remains underneath.

It took her a second to take in the space, but when she did, she hopped up and sprinted across the center of the chamber and leapt over Haradis' still waking form. Whatever happened to him, he'd been MIA the entire battle. But figuring that out was for later. Her attention was zeroed in on something far more important.

Minula.

When she got close to her friend, she froze mid-step and snapped her hand up to her mouth. Tears welled up instantly in her eyes.

There was blood everywhere. It stained the ground red around her exo-suit and covered nearly every centimeter of what remained of the broken armor. With all the carnage, she couldn't even tell if her love was still breathing.

"Please, please be alive," she muttered and dropped to her knees. Her shaking hands hovered above her body, afraid of what she could and couldn't touch. "You can't die on me! Not now. Not after all this."

Leaning forward, she slid her fingers down the edge of the suit's cracked helmet and heard the familiar click of the mechanism unlatching. A second later, she reached down and gently peeled the broken remains of the helmet away, tossing it aside piece by piece.

She drew in her breath and froze when she got her first sight of Minula. Her left eye was swollen shut, hidden beneath layers of soft purple bruises. And while she had multiple lacerations up and down her face, her right side was almost untouched except for a few splashes of blood.

"Oh, my god." She reached down and cupped her cheek in her hands. "You… look…" she didn't finish the sentence. Her appearance had never mattered, even now. All that mattered was that she survived.

The ground vibrated, and when she glanced up into the light, Haradis was standing over her with tears in his eyes. "Is she…"

"I don't know." Abigail wiped at her cheeks.

"Let me help her."

When he reached down to pick her up, she swatted his hand. "Where are you taking her?"

"The entity," he muttered.

They were two simple words, and yet they were the most

controversial of all things he could have said. This all seeing, all healing entity had the ability to change lives in an instant, but it chose when and whom to protect. And for some reason, it had allowed itself to be bound and controlled by Deduc. The Ursis who butchered millions of his own kind to maintain power. How was she to know he wasn't still alive inside that thing?

And yet, she had no other options. Like her people, she was forced to accept whatever fate she'd been dealt. She'd reached her breaking point.

"Alright." She crawled away from her. "But please be careful."

She knew he would be. Just as she knew her words were hollow, but they were all she could think to say. She couldn't help her any more than Ibu.

"Ibu!" She spun around and sprinted toward their limp body on the ground near the throne. With her attention on Minula, she'd run right past the Nanil. Overlooking them like the middle child when a new baby arrived.

This time, when she reached their side, she didn't hesitate at the sight of their blood. She knelt down, easing her hands under Ibu's legs and against their back, and then slowly stood up.

Her back was thankful they'd already reversed their transformation into their smaller form because the Nanil was dead weight. They were easily four times as heavy as a similar sized human, but that didn't matter. Abigail was so hopped up on whatever the Therionic entity had injected her with, she didn't feel a thing.

Being careful not to trip, she glanced sideways and eyed where Haradis had gone. He'd placed Minula in the chair to the right of the central throne, so Abigail followed his lead. She walked as fast as she could safely move and set Ibu down in the left most chair.

As soon as the Nanil's body touched the golden liquid, it

cascaded over them, engulfing them in a vibrant almost neon orange color.

Abigail stepped backward. "What's... happening?"

Haradis eased up beside her. "I'd only hazard a guess, but I think the color is the entity's way of showing us the person's aura."

She glanced right and pointed at Minula. There was no discernible color flowing away from the woman's body. "Why doesn't she have one?"

He shook his head. "I... don't know."

"Minula's time is short," an alien voice said. It was one of the first times she'd been able to understand the entity beyond a screech or an ominous voice, but she was certain it was them.

She drew in her breath. "What does that mean? Can you help her or can't you?"

"The Nanil I can help. Their hearts are still strong and their life-force is vibrant. Deduc was clumsy when he attacked them. The human, however, her life-force is weak. She's taken too much damage and pushed her mortal shell beyond its breaking point. I'm sorry, but her time is not long for this dimension."

Abigail collapsed to her knees. In that moment, every ounce of the energy from earlier had suddenly been zapped out. The words crushed against her soul like a mountain of bricks.

After all they'd struggled through, she couldn't lose Minula. Not now.

"Please!" She clasped her hands together and gazed up at the neon orange and gold streams cascading down the wall. "I'll do anything. I'm begging you."

"It doesn't work that way, Abigail." The wall vibrated, and a face appeared. Its outline reminded her of her father. "I thought maybe hearing my words in this form would be easier for you."

She shook her head. "I don't care what form you're in. My friend needs to live."

"I'm afraid all I can do is give you a few minutes. Use them well, Abigail of the Olivaws."

The wall shuddered, sending rivulets cascading from ceiling to floor until they converged on Minula's body in the chair. As she stared at the waves, each ripple over her body seemed to peel back another layer, until finally Minula's head appeared.

Abigail drew in a breath and clamored to the foot of the chair. She reached up and ran her hand down the woman's cheek. It was perfectly healed, and the blood was cleaned away. "Can you hear me?"

"Uh-huh." Minula smiled. "Your hand... it feels like an angel." Her eyes fluttered open, and she stared down at her with the most beautiful green eyes she'd ever seen. "And your face does, too."

She wiped at her tears and grinned, her face flushing with heat. "Since when have you been such a sweet talker?"

"Since I have a feeling I don't have much time remaining. There's no point in—"

Abigail pulled herself up and kissed her with everything she had. Her lips were soft, and they tasted like pineapple. She'd been wanting to do that again since the night she'd left the Phoenix.

When she stopped, she held her forehead against hers. "I'm sorry... I'm sorry I left. I'm sorry for everything."

Minula chuckled. "I wish you'd taken me with you."

"I... didn't know how to—"

"I know." Minula reached up and ran her hand down Abigail's face.

Every cell in her body shuddered, and she lowered her mouth, kissing the love of her life with her entire being. She wanted to remember this moment forever.

Just when she thought she was going to stop, Minula's

other hand broke free of the golden liquid. It reached up and cradled the back of her head as it moved through her hair.

Their embrace was both the longest and shortest minute of her life. When they stopped, they stared into each other's eyes.

Abigail took a deep breath. "I'm—"

"Stop!" Minula brought her finger up to her mouth. "I don't want you saying that again. Do you understand?"

She nodded, tears welling in her eyes.

Minula smiled while running her hand through her hair and down her cheek. "I want you to promise me one thing."

"Anything. Name it." She wiped at her eyes and swallowed hard.

Minula pulled her closer and gave her one last tender kiss before pulling away. The energy was suddenly fading from her face and fast.

She leaned in and brushed her fingers along her jaw, fighting back tears. "What is it?"

"I..." Minula took a deep breath and her eyes fluttered. "Love you."

"I love you, too." She smiled, and a tear streaked down her cheek.

Minula blinked slowly and shook her head, forcing her eyes open and locking them on hers. "Promise me one thing. Promise me... you'll save our people and bring down the Galactic Alliance."

Abigail nodded and kissed her hard, squeezing her lips tight against hers. "I promise you with every molecule of my being."

When she stopped, she pulled back, and Minula smiled. They stared at each other for a few seconds until her eyes gently closed.

"No. No... no!" She shook Minula's shoulder, willing her to wake up. But she never did.

A huge paw rested on Abigail's back. When she glanced

up, she expected to see Haradis. But instead, it was Klus. Her simple clergy robes were in tatters and smeared with soot and splotches of yellow blood. She wasn't sure whether she should grab a gun or hug the alien. It wasn't until she held out her paw that she knew which.

There, resting in the middle of Klus' paw, were two consciousness cores. One was etched with the letter H and the other S.

Abigail raised her hand, and Klus carefully set each of them in her palm. They were cold to the touch, which meant only one thing. They were still alive.

"I figured you'd want those." Klus took a step backward.

"Yes, I do. And, thank you." She squeezed the cores in her hand and the cold burned her skin, but she didn't let go. It felt right. It reminded her of the pain she'd put everyone through. They followed her into this mess and fought to save her from her endless streak of mistakes.

Now it was up to her to return the favor and to make good on her promises.

54

IBU

PROTO DARK NEBULA, ON ARCTORDIEA

Something was off. Ibu didn't know what, but it was like something important was missing.

Reaching up, they rubbed the center of their chest. They had the distinct memory of firing their plasma pistol at the wall of gold and then watching a spike lance out of the surface straight through their chest. But, strangely, there was no hole when they felt for it. There was nothing but a solid sternum and ribcages protecting their left and right hearts.

Even more unusual was that they didn't remember what happened after that. Maybe their body's fight response sent them into a protective state from the sudden shock of being impaled, or maybe they imagined the whole thing. When they opened their eyes, things were no clearer.

They brought their hand up to their face and froze as a gob of neon orange goo slid down their arm and spidered into their lap, joining the rest of the material oozing off their body.

"What the hell?" Ibu jumped up and rubbed the excess blobs off their legs. They shivered, and another droplet slid down the back of their neck. "Come on!"

"Stand still." Haradis reached out to wipe the glob, and Ibu spun around, knocking his hand aside.

They sidestepped away from the towering Ursis, taking a dozen steps into the room, being careful not to let him get behind them. When Ibu studied the chamber, they noticed that much of the carnage from the earlier battle had been removed, but not everything.

There was a pile of robot parts in one corner and a mountain of scrapped power-armor in another. As they scanned around, their attention came back to the throne area and their eyes went wide. Abigail was sitting on the ground in front of the right most chair with her legs tucked into her chest. Her arms were wrapped around them. She was rocking forward and back, and Cynthia was eased up behind her, hugging her with both arms.

"Abs!" Ibu waved their hand, glancing from the Ursis to their friend.

She didn't react.

"What did you do to her?" Ibu reached over their shoulder, but their sword wasn't there. In fact, all of their weapons were missing.

"If you're looking for your blade, it's with its mate on the ground beside the chair you just got out of." Haradis gestured toward the seat they'd woken in and returned his paws where they could see them.

The liquid they saw earlier had been replaced with both gold and orange streams. They covered the entire wall in chaotic spirals and rivulets which flowed over the chairs. Even the empty one in front of their friends. When their gaze hit the ground, they noticed their blade, along with the one they'd sent with Shauna.

Ibu hopped toward the swords, making sure to keep a few meters between them and the Ursis the entire time. They dropped to a knee and snatched up the weapons. Once they confirmed he was telling the truth, they raised one of the blades up and pointed it at the towering alien.

"Hey, now. Calm down, little one." Haradis raised his paw and took a step backward, away from the throne. "I'm with Abigail."

They chuckled. "Yea, right. Try again, fuzz ball." They stepped forward and eased the blade a bit higher.

He raised an eyebrow. "Ibu, my name's Haradis. Now, I know you're not dumb, but I'm gonna make this simple for you. Do you honestly think you'd have Harold's sword in your possession if I wanted to hurt you? Hell, I was the one who gathered up that second Zhen blade from the aftermath of the battle. I recognized it from the damage you all did with them on Griseo."

Ibu froze. There was no way an Ursis would know their name, or about what happened back on that world. Unless… "You're the stowaway."

"Was… the stowaway. We're light years from me hiding out on the outside hull of that ship of yours." He lowered his paws to his side and adjusted his robes. From the look on his face, he didn't exactly seem comfortable in them.

He had a point. If he hadn't killed either of them, and he knew about Griseo, then perhaps he was telling the truth. Only one person would know for sure.

They glanced over at Abigail. She was still staring at the empty chair and was almost catatonic except for her endless rocking back and forth. The orange and gold fluid that was flowing over the other two seats was, for some reason, bypassing this one. Instead, there were ornate metallic glyphs by the thousands engraved up and down the surface of the furnishing. They couldn't tell what they said, and they didn't want to turn on their retinal comm to find out. Being without it for a while was actually nice.

When they returned their attention to Abigail, they could sense something was off. It felt the same way as earlier, like they were missing part of themselves. But in watching her movement, the feeling became even more pronounced. She almost glowed with a halo of despair.

"What... happened to her?"

Haradis tilted his head and studied the Nanil. "Can't you tell?"

They narrowed their gaze and lifted their swords over their shoulder, locking them into place on their back. They took a few steps toward their friend and paused.

The halo they'd noticed had brightened. While they'd have sworn it was a lighting effect a moment earlier, now they weren't so certain.

"What do you see?" Haradis asked.

Ibu shook their head slowly. "I... don't know. Something's amiss. I felt it a moment ago when I woke up in that..." They pointed back at the other chair. "Orange crap."

Haradis chuckled. "That crap is a being. A Therionic entity, to be exact."

They shrugged. "Whatever the hell it was. When I came to, I sensed something was off. The more I stare at her, the more it feels... like it's emanating from her." They stared down at their hands and turned them over and over. They looked like theirs, and felt like theirs, but were they? Maybe it was them who was off. Perhaps they were dreaming.

"What is it?"

"I don't know." They lowered their hands and stared at the two women. "I don't feel like myself. I've never been someone who gushed with emotions like a human. This doesn't feel right. What did you do to me?" Ibu spun around and faced the Ursis. They itched to pull out the blade, but decided not to.

Haradis shook his head. "I didn't do anything. But what I suspect you're feeling is called empathy."

"Empathy?" Ibu squinted. "For who..."

And then it hit them, like a sucker punch to the gut. They

collapsed to their knees and covered their mouth with their hands. The one person missing from this room was also the one person Abigail loved with all her heart.

The feeling they'd had wasn't empathy alone, it was also emptiness. Like someone was gone. Someone they were close to. Someone who knew them on some days better than they knew themself. Which was funny, really. They never imagined they'd say that about a human.

They smirked and wiped away the tears. It was the second time they'd ever shed them, and both times had been when Abigail was near. While the first time was when they thought they were dying, this time was somehow worse. They'd never lost a friend before.

Ibu stood up and slowly stepped forward.

Haradis reached out to stop them, but they dodged his paw.

When they arrived at their friend's side, they did the only thing that felt natural. They sat down, and without a word, they snuggled up between them and tilted their head onto Abigail's shoulder.

As their bodies touched, a wave of emotions cascaded over them.

Pain

Passion

Love

Anger

Revenge

They came fast and furious at first, but after a while they slowed and lapped against their mind like waves on the shore of a distant ocean. They didn't know how they were doing it, but they knew that simply being there was helping Abigail.

The human tsunami of emotions in that moment was hard for them to understand. Abigail's passion for her friend and lover was overpowering. Almost as strong as the feelings she had for her family. And at the same time, waves of rage against the Galactic Alliance crashed over them, nearly drowned out all other feelings. The only thing keeping them from succumbing to their own fight response was the love the woman had for them. It wasn't the same as the love she had for Minula. This was different. This was more like kin. A feeling they'd never imagined someone would feel for them until they'd met the Olivaws.

Days earlier, they might have been incapable of understanding that moment. But something became clear to them as they stared at that empty chair.

They didn't want to roam the universe alone. Even when they were surrounded by a rollercoaster of emotions, they were stronger with their friends and family than they were alone.

ABIGAIL OLIVAW

PROTO DARK NEBULA, ON ARCTORDIEA

"Wait. You were serious?" Abigail froze in the hallway. "So you're telling me the entire population saw everything?"

Klus turned around to face her, and their contingent of robot guards fanned out and encircled them. "Yes. The moment Haradis activated the throne, the emergency powers of the monarch kicked in and the cameras switched on. The feeds were broadcast to this and all the nearby star systems in the Nebula."

She ran her shaking hands through her hair. The thought of every Ursis glued to their device, watching her and her people raze their sacred throne room and kill so many of their own kind didn't set well. And then the worst realization of all hit her like a sucker punch to the gut. The aliens had an up close and personal view of her losing her shit and her ultimate meltdown when Minula passed. She could only imagine what they thought of her after that.

Her stomach flipped, and she bent over, bringing her hand to her mouth. She could feel the vomit rising in her throat as she closed her eyes, fighting it to stay down.

The message icons in the corner of her retinal comm

flashed. Harold and Shauna were trying to reach her, but she'd squelched their ability to display messages on her comm when they started the walk.

"Are you ok, Abigail?" Klus knelt down and a medical bot zoomed up beside them. It activated some type of scanner and several beams of light passed up and down her body.

She waved her hand at the robot, and it backed up, continuing its scan. "I'm... fine. I merely..." She didn't know how to say it, but the amount of blood on their hands made her sick. And she knew how weak she must've seemed with Minula's passing. Even now, the thought of never seeing her again made her knees buckle.

Mobs were fickle. It was a universal truth to aliens and humans alike. Hell, if the people in Sol had their way, she and her family would be hanging in nooses in the center of some backwater town on Earth.

"My people back in Sol," Abigail straightened up, "let's just say they're not happy with what my family and I did."

"You mean fighting the Galactic Alliance or stealing the Beacon?" Klus leaned back. "Those were noble actions. Your people should be—"

"No, it's not that." She shook her head. "They're pretty pissed about how we got into the mess in the first place. I can't blame them, though. My family lied to everyone for centuries about where our technology came from. Turns out, we pilfered it from a GA probe we found in Sol. At the time, we didn't know humans were from another star system, and even after we translated the warnings from the artifact, we still ignored them." She wiped at her eyes and stared at the floor, not able to look the Ursis in the face. "We failed our people, and they didn't even know why the GA had come for us until it was too late."

"I see." Klus stood up and crossed her arms. "So you're on the outs with your people, and you came here to make amends? To try to get another species to help you fight the

GA. You were hoping to find someone as down and out as yourself. Am I getting the gist of it?"

She chuckled and kicked at the smudges of tears on the floor. "Yea, you nailed it."

Klus sighed. "Is there anyplace you can offer us safe passage that's away from this tomb of a star system? Somewhere we can regroup and escape the deadly rays of our stars. If you can't, we'll be forced to search one out ourself."

The message icon in the corner of her retinal comm flashed. Her A.I. were getting antsy, but the last thing she wanted to listen to right now was their advice. She had to do this alone.

Her mind was reeling from Klus' question. Could they give the Ursis safe passage, or not? Taking them to Sol was out of the question. The Galactic Alliance would see them and return in force with ample excuse to finish what they started. Taking them to Zeta Lupi could work, but she'd compromise the one location neither the GA nor any of the other aliens knew about. Without guarantees of allegiance, it was a cost she couldn't afford to pay. Plus, there was the little matter of the government in power still being pissed at her and her family. No. She needed to take them somewhere where her family had a foothold. Somewhere, she and her brothers had a chance to survive.

"I know a place." She glanced up at Klus. The Ursis was studying her every move. She could understand why Deduc had liked the female. Nothing got past her. "Epsilon Eridani is safe."

Klus narrowed her gaze. "But that's behind another Nebula, is it not? The star would be compromised."

She shook her head and started walking, Klus following at her side. "Like I said. It's safe there. Humanity managed to fight back the missiles from the GA flagship. They never hit either of the stars in the binary."

Klus paused and skipped a step to catch up. "That would

make them a perfect waypoint for us to regroup." The Ursis glanced at her, eyeing her suspiciously. "And you're certain your people will accept us willingly?"

They passed through an archway, out onto a huge ornate terrace that was open above and overlooked the gardens of Summis far below. The once immaculate grounds that used to encircle the palace for kilometers were now only a fragment of their former glory. There were smoldering ghost like wisps rising up and out of the craters littering the remains of the battlefield from days earlier.

She wasn't sure if her people would willingly accept an alien armada showing up in Epsilon, but they understood how dire their situation was. If there was anyplace her and her brothers could convince their people to rally with the Ursis, it was there. Hopefully after that, Zeta Lupi and Sol would fall into line.

"Our people on Liprosus are acutely aware of their... situation." She rested her hands on the lower bar of the terrace's massive railing that towered overhead and stared out over the remains of the greenscape. "While I can't promise they won't be shocked, I'm certain they'll have an open mind."

Klus had fallen a step behind, but she could still feel her studying her every move. "And Ibu, you're confident they have the technology at hand?"

She chuckled. "If not, then we're all screwed."

"It's settled then. We'll converge at Epsilon and convene a new alliance between the Ursis and humanity. We can figure out our next steps in the battle after our diplomats work their magic."

Abigail spun around. "Hold your horses, missy."

Klus recoiled. "My what?"

"Nothing." She shooed her faux pas away. "It's a human idiom. It means let's not move too quickly. Agreeing on a destination is not our only hurdle."

Klus shook her head. "I don't understand. What other problem do we face?"

"Trust." Abigail waved her hand around the palace. "This place is a wreck. Your government is in shambles. And last I checked, your people watched my people do it. They watched us blast holes in their soldiers and slice them up like bread. There's no way in hell we can trust you not to steal our tech and abandon us. And we won't even get into how much larger your forces are than ours, especially after our assault to snatch the Beacon. We'll need assurances that we'll be seen as equals in the decisions ahead."

"Equals!" Klus chuckled. "I'm not sure you're bringing enough firepower to the table to demand equality."

"Really?" She crossed her arms and leaned back against the railing. "I guess you're already in possession of a Beacon of Therion. Oh no, wait, I know. You've mastered space-time and have your own gate technology to pass through that Nebula out there." She pointed up in the sky. "I must have misunderstood what Deduc was trying to steal from us."

"You know that's—"

"Two fraking huge advantages that you lack!" She lurched forward and pointed at Klus. "Our gate technology isn't just a way out of this jail cell. It's a strategic advantage in every single battle we have ahead of us. The Galactic Alliance isn't going down by brute force alone. You know it, and I know it. Without it, we wouldn't have stood a chance in hell stealing that Beacon. So, don't stand there and tell me you have more advantages than us. The sooner you stop pretending humanity doesn't hold the aces, the sooner we move these negotiations forward."

Klus slammed her hand against the railing, and dust scattered down, raining on her head. "Your starships are minuscule, and your people aren't nearly as strong as ours. It takes four humans to take out one Ursis."

When she glanced at the corner of her retinal comm, the

message count was in the hundreds. She didn't need to hear this shit from any of them. Not right now. Her head wasn't in the right place to be having these debates.

She spun around and started toward the door. Klus reached for her, but she ducked under her hand and paused. "No. I'm done. If that's how you—"

"It's not." Klus closed her eyes and began growling.

Abigail took a step backward. From the outside looking in, the Ursis was acting crazy. Maybe this was what having an internal argument looked like for an alien. The growl was over the top, but the scene ended when she reached into her pocket and squeezed something.

A few seconds later, Klus opened her eyes, staring at the ground. "I'm sorry, Seguan. I have not been honest with you."

She exhaled. "I thought we talked about that name." Her friend was clearly distraught. Plus, she'd just been growling at herself, so now probably wasn't the time to push her. "But I'll look past it one more time." She winked.

"I have been confiding in council the last few hours." Klus reached into her pocket and pulled out a transmission device.

Her heart skipped a beat. "So they've been listening in on everything we've been saying?"

Klus dropped to her knees, placing her nose against the ground. "Forgive me. Please. It was the Congress. I swear. I didn't want to do it. They were pressuring me to convince humanity to—"

She stepped forward and bent down, resting her hand on the back of the Ursis' head. "It's ok. Really. I forgive you."

"You do?" Klus glanced up at her.

She nodded and smiled. "I do. And trust me when I say I understand and can empathize with your predicament." She wasn't entirely sure if she should share anything else. But if not now, then when? Her friend was being honest and she should, too. "Remember those two consciousness cores you gave me the other day?"

Klus adjusted her position, sitting cross-legged. "I remember them well. While I knew the one core was your partner, I guessed on the second."

"What gave them away?" She stood upright, bringing herself eye to eye with the Ursis.

"Both of the robots were fighting like beasts. They were unlike anything I've seen outside your friend Minula and my own people." Klus stared down at her hands, having realized her mistake. "I'm so sorry."

Abigail must've flinched at the mention of her name. Klus had always been sensitive to her emotions and response to words. She didn't know how, but she always knew when she hit a sore spot.

She reached up and rubbed her arm, willing the feeling of Minula's last touch to return. "It's fine. I have something to tell you... and also a favor to ask."

Klus' eyes went wide. "Anything, Seg—... I mean... Abigail. Name it."

"Don't say that until you hear what I'm about to ask."

Klus nodded. "Fair enough."

She took a deep breath. "Those consciousness cores. One of them is my ancient ancestral grandfather, and the other is my mother."

Klus narrowed her gaze. "Your kind lets their souls mate with technology? My people will not—"

"Hear me out," she interrupted.

Klus sighed, but didn't say a word.

"The first core," she bit her lip, "was recorded over two hundred and fifty years ago. Well before my time. His name is Harold, and he has guided my family over the centuries. To be honest, we wouldn't be where we are today if it weren't for him. Humanity is against cloning, and the same can be said for uploading one's consciousness into a computer. He was the only one of his kind until my brother... well, he made a mistake."

"Mistake?" Klus scratched her head.

"He was going through a difficult time in his life, and he found out my mother was dying." She ran her hand through her hair and looked away. Her emotions were overflowing, and she was suddenly having trouble putting her thoughts into words.

"He did it without consulting your family?" Klus asked.

She nodded. "And now we have two. But here's the rub... and the favor." She glanced back at Klus.

"Go on." Klus placed her hands in her lap.

"They've heard everything we've been saying." She held up a finger. "But... but, unlike you, I have not been listening to them. I just wanted to clear the air, since you did the same with me."

"And what about the favor you mentioned?" Klus squinted.

"Right, that..." She kicked at the ground. "If anyone should ask, I need you to tell them that they're dead. They were destroyed in the battle."

"But... they're not." Klus tilted her head. "Why would you—"

"Remember how I said my people didn't believe in cloning or uploading their consciousness into a computer?"

Klus nodded.

"That's why." She stared into the female's eyes. "I don't have the foggiest idea what we're gonna walk into back home. And believe it or not, I want to protect my family." She brought her hand to her chest and rubbed the spot over her heart where the cores were stored. "All of them. I need both of them to help us through this mess, and I don't know if I can do it alone. Not yet." She swallowed hard. "So... will you keep my secret?"

Klus reached forward and gently placed her paw against Abigail's cheek and then spoke. Her mouth didn't move, but she could hear the Ursis like she was inside her head.

"Your secret is safe with me, my friend."

She wasn't sure how, but she replied without speaking. "Will either of us be able to keep it from the Therionic entity?"

"We will. Both of us can. The entity has never broken into someone's mind to extract memories. They're not like Deduc. You will, however, need to be diligent when bonding with it. They're keenly aware when subterfuge is afoot."

"That's good to know."

When Klus lowered her paw, Abigail fell to her side, gasping for air. She hadn't even realized, but she'd been holding her breath that whole time. These mind links clearly weren't her strong suit.

Abigail regained her composure and sat back up. "Sorry about that. I'm gonna need some practice if I'm going to talk to the entity for any length of time."

Klus smiled. "We have a few days to practice."

"What happens in a few days?"

"We crown Prince Haradis. It is then that you will state your terms in front of the Congress of the People, our King, and the Therionic entity. From there, they will decide our path forward."

Her terms weren't even clear in her own mind, let alone coherent enough to state before an audience of aliens. She had a mountain of shit to work through between now and then. And judging by the thousand plus messages in her retinal queue, her ancestors had a few opinions to share with her on the matter.

Klus reached out and held her paw beside Abigail's head. "Are you ready to practice?"

She chuckled and dismissed the flashing message icons from her field of view. "Sure, why the hell not?"

IBU

PROTO DARK NEBULA, ON ARCTORDIEA

Their lab was cobbled together from bits and pieces of random technology they'd recovered around the palace, and from what remained of Abigail's shuttle she brought inside the Nebula. Deduc had captured it, and Cynthia worked with Haradis to have it delivered here from the cargo hold on one of the Alatas starships.

Ibu's challenge wasn't only how to rebuild the gate drive, it was how to do it in secret. They wouldn't have much of a bargaining chip if they came up empty-handed. Take Haradis. For as friendly as he'd been, he'd be forced to act against them if they failed. Even a tame caged animal will lash out to regain their freedom.

They pulled the hatch closed and sealed the transition chamber. Blue light filled the cramped space as the air from the outside pumped out and replenished with fresh air from within. The makeshift airlock and the adjacent room were coated in the skotádi remains from the shuttle, giving them a private, but tiny, lab to work in.

That didn't prevent the Ursis from attempting to sneak inside, though. The panel on the inner hatch flashed red and a swarm of nanites streamed out of a small tube in the wall.

They went about their business of fending off the invading alien eyes that had attached to them while they were in the palace. After a few dozen flashes of light, the swarm returned to its container, and the panel turned green.

"All clear," Cynthia said. The inside latch clicked, signaling it was unlocked.

They pushed the inner hatch open and stepped into the narrow three-by-three meter space. It was barely enough room for the two of them and the nano fabricator they'd cobbled together, let alone the small gravity chamber they used to run their tests. They didn't need a full size gate array because they were reproducing the effect on an atomic scale.

Once the inner latch sealed shut, they walked up to the gravity chamber and connected a small device to the side. It didn't look like much, but inside the thumbnail sized container was a single grain of spános. The power was overkill for their purposes in this experiment, but it was the only thing Haradis could find when they asked him for a power core. Apparently, being the future king meant you had spános at your fingertips.

"So, did he hook you up? Did you get it?" Cynthia was leaning against the fabricator and eyed the capsule housing the spános.

They took a deep breath and closed their eyes. After days of verifying and re-verifying their calculations, and countless hours of calibrating the nanite mesh used to form the small scale tachyon gate, the moment of truth had arrived. The next few seconds would either unlock the cage shackling them inside this Nebula or it would throw away the key for an eternity.

They swallowed hard. "He did. I didn't push him on where he got it from, but to say he was nervous was an understatement."

"Well, if it's any consolation, we're ready." She pushed off the fabricator and stepped toward them. "I checked over the whole thing twice while you were gone. The device is calibrated. I... couldn't help it. I'm not good at sitting still and twiddling my thumbs."

Ibu smiled. "Alrighty then. Here goes everything." They reached forward and tapped the activation button.

Without hesitation, the panel displaying the output of the miniature microscope at the heart of the experiment sprang to life. The device was designed to peer at the nano scale during Ursis weapons manufacturing, and like with the spános, they asked and they received.

In the center of the panel was a tiny ball of blue light. It was uniform across its entire surface, and from the telemetry scrolling past, the mesh was holding steady.

"It's working!" Cynthia rose up on her toes and squeaked.

Their hearts were pounding in their chest. It was like they were about to enter battle, but this was more uncertain. While they'd passed the first hurdle, the next was the last.

They tapped the same button as earlier, and the gate opened. It was as uneventful as they'd hoped, but the results were spot on. They'd opened a gate into space above Arctordiea, into one of its many Lagrange points.

What they expected to find was empty space, but what they got was so much more. There, on the other side of the opening, was an Alatas warship. The cargo hold, to be exact. A few more meters, and they could have opened a gate into the power core of the massive warship, ending their lives in the blink of an eye. As if that wasn't scary enough, what was waiting inside the belly of the beast freaked them out even more.

Their Ursis and human communication receivers started fritzing out the moment the gate opened. At first, they thought they were both broken, but when they dropped into their mental link and connected with the devices, they found otherwise.

They interfaced with the alien receiver first, as it was the most foreign. It took them a few milliseconds to find their way around, but once they'd overlaid the program they used to listen in on the data links days earlier, the rest was child's play.

While it was rude to stay in the mental link for a long time, Cynthia claimed she didn't mind. She said she preferred being with Ibu over spending time with their captors. Even if it only meant being near them.

They scrolled through the feeds from inside the Ursis ship and marveled at their level of access. Everything was there. As they played around exploring the bowels of the alien ship, they froze their cameras and activated the audio channel, dropping their consciousness back into real-time.

"Check this out." They waved Cynthia closer to the display.

"Like I said, the call came in. We've been mobilized. We'll be headed planetside tomorrow afternoon," the soldier said. The Ursis was standing in front of a small guard of soldiers, thirty at most. They were training in some type of firing range in the heart of the ship.

"How'll we find our way in?" another soldier asked. He clicked a munitions pack onto the side of one of the rifles, aimed it down range, and fired off a few quick rounds at the distant target. The head of a dummy exploded in a ball of fire and they turned back around.

The first Ursis grunted at the fiery display. "We'll be flying as congressional guards assigned to Congressman Gryndar and the other members of the Tlingui clan. He'll make sure we slip past security, and then we'll disappear near the throne room. After that, we just sit tight until we get the call."

"Easy peasy." The second soldier waited for another dummy to pop up and then trained his weapon on the target, squeezing off a round. "Bye-bye, King Haradis. It was nice not knowing ya."

"Wholly shit." Cynthia's eyes went wide.

Ibu backed up the feed, zooming in on the distant target they were shooting at. When the image came into focus, their stomach knotted up. It was a life-sized replica of Haradis, the Ursis' future king.

They slammed the experiment's kill button, closing the connection before they were discovered.

"What the literal frak!" They swiped at the air in front of them.

Cynthia stood there in silence, staring at the lingering image of King Haradis.

No matter how hard they tried, there was resistance at every turn in this Nebula graveyard. There didn't seem to be an Ursis in this place that wasn't corrupt or looking out for themselves, except for maybe Klus. And Haradis came from the outside, so he didn't count.

As they paced around the room in frustration, their attention was drawn to the corner of their retinal comm. There was an icon flashing at the edge of their field of view, and when they blinked it open, they drew in a breath.

The human comm equipment had picked up a packet from one of their micro-sats in orbit. They'd forgotten all about the contingencies they'd built into their probes bouncing around the Proto Dark Nebula. In their infinite wisdom, they'd programmed the probes to dip in and out of the Nebula itself every few days. They'd been directed to both upload intel and download any emergency broadcasts that might be pending outside.

Turns out, there were a few broadcasts queued up from Epsilon Eridani. A few hundred, to be exact.

ABIGAIL OLIVAW
PROTO DARK NEBULA, ON ARCTORDIEA

The last time Abigail walked into this room, she sealed the fate of her friends and family in blood. She couldn't have known then the sequence of events that would transpire after touching that throne.

As she passed over the threshold, she paused. The distant wall of gold that had been the lone life-force of the Therionic entity for over fifty years had once again returned to its former glory. She stood back and took in the marvelous rainbow of colors cascading from ceiling to floor. The scene was a stark contrast to the bloody battlefield from days earlier.

Standing in front of the throne was a procession of elder Ursis. They were lined up two wide and easily a hundred deep. Each of the mountainous aliens was dressed head to toe in ornate and vibrantly colored costumes representing their clans, or what was left of them. Most of the families had died during Deduc's great cleansing when the Nebula fell, and many of the ones that didn't have been in hiding ever since, hoping for the arrival of the Seguan.

While each color of the rainbow represented what remained of the clans Ulyxsauri lineage, the reality of their situation was far more dire than was apparent from the visual spectacle. When the Galactic Alliance sealed a star system with the Dark Nebula, they didn't stop at sending their star into a millennia long degeneration toward nova. They transformed the life giving sphere of light into a genetic end game, preventing a species from reproducing and forcing them into a death spiral of their own.

In the case of the Ursis, their long life span of over four hundred years meant none of them would survive to see their sun go nova. Their genes were already so badly mutated that except for the handful who lived underground, their species would cease to exist in the not so distant future.

Some were fine with this fate, as their only desire was the complete and utter destruction of the Galactic Alliance. They didn't see this goal as something that would take more than a few decades. Haradis, however, had other plans.

His genes were still viable, but only if he didn't stay inside the Nebula for long. There was also the small matter of his royal lineage. Any attempt to splice his genes or create clones from them could lead to a war over the rightful heir to the throne. While there weren't many usable genetic lines inside the Nebula, their strategists and geneticists hoped they could find other Ursis like him who'd escaped outside the Nebula.

Abigail took a deep breath and adjusted her gown. The last of the procession was finishing their vote of confidence in their new King by touching the arm of the throne. They were closing in on the final act of transferring the power of the empire to Haradis. All that remained was the Ursis' See-er to seal the deal, and that, unfortunately, happened to be her.

Which brought her back to the crowd of aliens. While Deduc's stranglehold over the priesthood and the military had been strong, it was only possible because they employed Qudoculi body vessel technology. Once Minula killed him, the dominoes fell quickly and allowed the church and state to align behind the rightful heir to the throne. He was the one leader foretold to return to power and who had the support of the Seguan and her ability to warp space-time.

When the golden rainbow above the throne flashed, a gap appeared in the stream of colors from the top of the ceiling to the bottom. It was intended for her rivulet of Ulyxsauri color to slot in place. That was her sign to step forward from the back of the room and take her rightful place next to Haradis.

The entire ceremony had been explained to her several times, but she hadn't been paying attention to most of what was said. She was still trying to work through humanity's demands.

Her mind had been churning all week through the possibilities of how they could convince the Ursis to prove their allegiance to humanity. While it should've been something Abigail had in hand well before they arrived, she wasn't expecting to come face to face with an armada of warships inside the Nebula. Nothing she could think of would prevent the aliens from ditching humanity once they had gate travel technology.

Walking up the middle of the throne room didn't change her opinion on the matter. All eyes from the Ursis dignitaries turned toward her. It was their first glimpse of a human being in the flesh, and judging by their facial gestures, they weren't impressed. She was less than a third their height and lacked any type of musculature or girth compared to themselves. And yet, despite them seeing her people kill countless Ursis on their live feed, they continued to underestimate humans. The more she thought about it, that misjudgment was probably one of the key reasons why her species had lasted as long as it had. They were scrappy and formidable foes to anyone who dared take them on.

She smiled when she finally reached Klus at the end of the procession.

Klus beamed back. "Seguan." She bowed and dropped to one knee, presenting her with the See-er's necklace.

"I thought we talked about calling me that," she whispered.

Klus chuckled. "Like it or not, in this ceremony you are our Seguan."

She reached out and carefully took the golden necklace with both hands and bowed back. "Fine. But call me that after this and you and I will be going around and around."

Klus glanced up at her and winked.

The two of them had spent countless hours together the past week since Minula's passing. There weren't many other humans in Summis, and the other Ursis talked to her like she was some sort of goddess. And as for Ibu and Cynthia, they'd both been MIA for nearly the entire time. That left Klus and her plenty of opportunities to practice their mind-link to prepare for today. If she had any hopes of getting her demands across while not giving away her secrets, it was because of Klus' help. Well, that and her friends. Without their work recreating the gate drive, they'd be stuck in the Proto Dark Nebula forever.

She lifted the necklace over her head and stepped toward Haradis. The golden jeweled rope was heavy around her neck. While they'd reduced its overall length to account for her smaller size, it was still a massive piece of jewelry. The weight reminded her of those ancient leaded bibs they made people wear on their chest and shoulders when they got scans at the dentist, except this pressure was pushing against her neck and chest.

"It looks good on you." Haradis smiled at her from the end of the aisle of Ursis.

What she wanted to tell him was that it felt like a ball and chain holding her down, preventing her from doing what she needed to do for her people. But she didn't. Instead, she simply nodded and stepped up beside him, repeating the words she'd been instructed to say. "May I accompany your majesty to the throne?"

"It would be my honor." He bowed toward her. "And if you wouldn't mind, I'd like you to join your hand with mine during my acceptance of the throne."

Murmurs spread through the congregation gathered behind them. While her retinal comm couldn't translate what they were saying, based upon the underlying growls interlaced within their mutterings, she was pretty sure they weren't positive.

Abigail glanced back at the muffled voices and then toward Haradis, leaning closer to his side. "That's not part of the ceremony we practiced."

He nodded and winked at her. "I know. But nothing we're doing here follows the old traditions." He gestured around the throne room. "Our reality is about to change in a few moments, and with that shifting of the sands, we need to make some adjustments if we want to stay upright. All of us do." He shot a glare over his shoulder at the gathered members of the Congress.

She couldn't help but wonder if Klus was in on this. While she knew the two of them talked every day, she didn't know about what. Her friend was acutely aware of the difficulty she was having coming up with a negotiation tactic. One that both sides found compelling and, if possible, easy to swallow. But he was right. This alliance wouldn't be painless on either side.

"Alrighty, then." She adjusted her ceremonial robes and brushed at the wrinkle that had been nagging her all morning. "So I guess we're winging it."

"Sorta." Haradis glanced to his left and both Ibu and Cynthia slid out from behind Klus.

Abigail did a double take. Neither of them had been standing there a second earlier. She would've seen them.

Even the congregation was taken aback by her friend's appearance, especially Ibu. The jet black Ursis nearest them stepped forward and cleared his throat. "What is the meaning of this, Haradis?" He eased between Ibu and the prince. "Our people have a tradition of performing this ceremony in private. These other aliens should not be present. It's bad enough we have to accept one... human into our den. But a second and a Nanil, too? The Entity will not—"

Haradis lunged forward and crashed into the congressman, toppling him backward. When the blur of motion came to a halt, the future king had his talons around the throat of the elder. "Gryndar, I don't care if you're the majority clan leader. I will end you if you insult me again. Do... not... question the presence or words of my See-ers. Do you understand?"

Gryndar squirmed with the talons at his neck and struggled to speak until Haradis withdrew the threatening blades. "I..." He cleared his throat and pushed up onto his elbows. "I must have heard you wrong, Your Majesty. You said your See-ers, but you clearly meant to say See-er."

Haradis growled and his upper lip quivered, highlighting his newly engraved teeth for all to see. "My—patience—is—wearing—thin—Gryndar. With you and this Congress of Idiots." He shoved off the elder Ursis toward the middle of the congregation, sending him flying back to the ground.

"What's he doing?" Abigail whispered.

Ibu and Cynthia shuffled up to her side and grabbed her hand.

At first, she thought they were hiding something, but then she heard it. The voice was faint, like a gentle breeze in the night. She closed her eyes and concentrated, and then it came into focus as time seemed to slow.

"Can you hear me?" Ibu asked.

"I... think so."

"There isn't much time. Haradis is fending off another coup. The leaders of the Congress are preparing to kill the king the moment he ascends the throne and completes the ceremony. We only found out about it an hour ago in our lab.

I'm so sorry, but when we couldn't find you, we went straight to Haradis."

She spun around in the virtual space, longing to see the face of her friend. But they were nowhere to be found in the mental link. "Don't be sorry. What are we doing here then? Why aren't we trying to escape?"

"We're part of the game, Abigail. Without us, they're as stuck as we are. Haradis believes the sentiment amongst the Ursis people is strongly in favor of an alliance, which is counter to the stance of the elder Congress. As you'd expect, Deduc's influence still runs deep there. At least with those members who have substantial clans behind them."

Her pulse raced, pounding rapid fire like a snare drum in her ears. "So, what do we do now?"

"Follow his lead. And try not to look surprised when he starts making shit up."

The mind link abruptly cut, and the room came into focus, bringing time back on track. She gasped for breath, and while she struggled to not make it obvious what had just happened, she knew she failed miserably. But if anyone recognized her slip-up, Haradis' speech returned their attention to him.

"I—am—not—my—father!" He pounded his fists in his hand, emphasizing every word. "And in case you hadn't noticed, we're in no position to make demands from either the humans or the Nanil. As the only two species to have survived the shroud of the Dark Nebula, we could learn a thing or two from them. Their species withstood the Éntono Fos, but ours is dying. Like it or not, we won't get out of here without them. And if you think we'll take them by force, you've seriously underestimated their powers."

Her stomach knotted, and her retinal comm lit up with a message from Shauna. They'd known to remain silent during the ceremony, but with Haradis' words, she didn't blame them for being concerned. They hadn't been privy to her and

Ibu's conversation. The problem was, she hadn't even taken a moment to absorb the revelations herself.

What is he talking about? The Nanil and humanity are not allies, and we sure as hell don't have the numbers.

Abigail drew in her breath and did her best to type out a reply under her robes.

We'll figure that out later. Ibu asked that we go with the flow. For now, we're trying not to get killed.

When her attention returned to Haradis, he was working his way down the congregation. He had a strut in his stride that she hadn't seen in days. Not since their successful escape from the Keep. Back when they'd had a win under their belt. He was confident in whatever he was about to propose, and she wasn't about to challenge that. At least not here.

"The sooner you all figure out how lucky we are they came looking for us, and that we're in this together, the better." He pointed at Abigail and then Ibu. "Both the human and the Nanil will rotate through roles as my See-er. And until I have a child, they will be my heirs to the throne."

Abigail swallowed hard and took a deep breath, struggling not to gape at his remarks. First the lies around humanity's strength, the Nanil alliance, and now she was a royal heir. This was shaping up to be an interesting day.

The congregation of Ursis didn't find his speech as compelling as she had. Their snarls and grumbles rose in volume as the implications of his words spread. They were clearly not happy with the turn of events. Abigail was about to step forward and say something to support her friend, but Ibu beat her to it.

"Prince Haradis." Ibu dropped to one knee beside Abigail. "I'm requesting permission to address the Congress on behalf of my people."

Haradis nodded. "Permission granted." He glanced at Abigail and winked.

Before she could respond, Ibu brushed her leg, and yet again, time screeched to a halt as she was yanked into a mental link.

"I was hoping they wouldn't react that way," Ibu began. "Giant teddy bears be crazy. Anyhow, I wanted to give you a heads-up. I'm about to share something that not even I under-stand. We received it as part of a data dump through our test gate just before we talked to Haradis about the coup. He hasn't seen it, either. I'm taking a leap here, Abs, and I'll just say sorry now if I frak things up for us."

And as fast as the mental link slowed her reality, it snapped back into focus. She fought the wave of dizziness from the sudden change in time. The last thing she needed was to get nauseous in the middle of the proceedings.

The situation was evolving faster than she imagined, and yet again she'd been caught standing flat-footed. First a coup, and now Ibu tells her their gate worked and something mysterious had arrived. It reminded her of when she woke up from her coma in Tau Ceti following the tribunal. After that, she spent weeks sitting on the outside of the action and looking in.

Ibu stood up and stepped to the front of the congregation. They stared out over the crowd of Ursis, waiting for them to stop talking to each other. The aliens were not as willing as Haradis to give the Nanil the floor, especially after the bomb he'd dropped.

He spun around. "Enough!" His voice echoed through the chamber and the wall of colors vibrated, mirroring his scream. "You will confer my See-ers the respect they deserve. Is that understood?"

The crowd froze, and the murmurs stopped, both in a mixture of awe and rage. The Congress was not used to being spoken to like that, even by their King. If it wasn't already obvious before, it was now. He was clearly not his father.

"Thank you, sir." Ibu bowed toward Haradis and then turned to focus on the Congress. "Esteemed leaders. People of the Ursis empire. Myself and Ambassador Olivaw arrived in your star system a few days ago. We came to negotiate in peace with your people. We wanted to invite you to join our confederation of species, uniting against the Galactic Alliance. Your former leader, however, had other plans. Emmonsii Phi Tlingui attacked both the ambassador and my crew after our arrival. During that time, she not only tortured Ambassador Olivaw, she made multiple attempts to kill me and my crew. You witnessed the end of that escapade here, in this hallowed hall. Emmonsii Phi, or Deduc, as you also knew him, conspired to topple your government during its darkest hour until we revealed him for what he was. A tumor eating at your people and your society from the inside out. Fortunately, one of our soldiers ended him and his stranglehold on your species."

Abigail flinched as cheers and snarls echoed through the hall. She hadn't expected so many Ursis to be so vocally against Deduc. For once, a piece of good news in their favor.

Ibu continued. "While we hoped his influence on your people died with him, we were wrong! Representative Gryndar and his colleagues have been working in the wings to pick up where Deduc left off. And unless I'm mistaken, they are about to attempt to kill your new king." Ibu snapped their finger at Gryndar and all eyes turned toward him.

"I... don't..." He was caught off guard and glanced around, failing to feign ignorance. When he whirled to face the back of the chamber, the doors burst open and a small contingent of soldiers streamed in. Their weapons were trained on Haradis.

The congregation scattered, and all hell broke loose until Haradis started laughing out loud.

As everyone slowed to take in his reaction, Gryndar stepped forward. "I fail to see the humor in your situation, Prince Umbra."

"You would, because you're blind." Haradis twisted his neck, and it cracked. "You cannot see your plight for what it is. While you're scrambling to fill the gap of a misguided despot, you're missing the fact that we're not in the position of power you think we are."

"Bullshit!" Gryndar lurched across the space between them, ending just outside arm's reach. "This whole thing is a bluff, and you know it. These humans are weak. They're not the ones from the Lupus Dark Nebula. They're from the splinter faction in Sol. Deduc learned as much after they arrived and after he interrogated the Olivaw human. As he already discovered, there's nothing either the humans or Nanil can hide from us that a mental probe won't extract."

Ibu chuckled and gestured above the congressman's head and an image appeared, filling the space above the throne room from side to side.

Both Haradis and Abigail recoiled, taking several steps backward to take it all in. At first the image revealed a fleet of a dozen or so strange conical ships with smaller ones flying to and fro between them. They were orbiting an earth-like planet, sprinkled with water and islands of various sizes. It wasn't until the image panned out that her mouth fell open and the room collectively inhaled.

There were tens of thousands of the ships covering the entire field of view. And with each progression of zoom, another larger and stranger ship came into focus that looked like it could swallow the last. It was almost as if they were multiplying before her very eyes.

As she took in the image, it dawned on her what they were looking at. That world in the background had an enormous crater on it. One that matched the message she'd received from Zachary a few weeks earlier. They were staring at Liprosus, the colony planet inside the Epsilon Dark Nebula.

A message appeared on her retinal comm from Harold.

Those smaller ships. I've seen 'em before. They were in the data dumps you shared from the Beacon battle. I could tell someone tried to scrub them from the videos, but they missed some. Did General Yule and Lync have any secret ships? I ask, because a few instances showed them gating into and out of the battlefield.

She shook her head. Even if the general had a classified project, there was no way they built and scaled them this quickly. Whoever made these things had a shit ton of time and, from what Harold said, possessed gating technology. When she stared at them from a distance, the starships reminded her a lot of Zachary's original gate ship designs from a few years ago. But he tossed those when he decided to go with the teardrop models.

As she was about to return her attention to Ibu, a movement in the projection caught her eye. One of their larger teardrop cargo ships from Zeta Lupi gated into space at the edge of the image. The ship wasn't fired on, and they didn't attempt to flee. Instead, they activated their impulse drives and dove toward one of the gigantic alien ships before disappearing into a massive hangar on the backside. Whoever they were, they were friendly.

"Where... is this from?" Gryndar asked.

"Liprosus." Abigail said, glancing toward Ibu. "The

human world inside our Epsilon Dark Nebula stronghold." Their eyes locked, and the Nanil nodded.

"As my colleague has already informed you, we originally arrived in your Nebula in peace, searching for allies. Despite your efforts to kill us, we might even still be willing to negotiate with you to join our confederation. But not here. Not in this venue." She stepped toward Gryndar and narrowed her gaze on the graying elder Ursis. "Failing to let us go will not only end the Therionic entity, it will mean the death of your empire."

While she took a leap of faith on the last part, she was pretty confident in the first. She wasn't about to give up and let them rip her and Ibu's minds apart, and if that meant ending her own life without giving away the secrets of her people a second time, then she'd do it.

"More of your human lies." Gryndar snarled at her and crossed his arms. "You couldn't end the entity any more than I could. Like our ancestors before us, the entity will outlive us all."

Abigail chuckled. "That's where you're wrong. I could kill it right now if I wanted to."

The congregation broke out into murmurs, and her translator struggled to catch up. From the sound of their voices, very few of them believed her words.

While she didn't blame the aliens, she'd hoped to never have to test her theory about her bond with the entity. Like Ibu had gambled to save their life sharing the picture, it was her turn to play the hand she'd been dealt. She slowly reached inside her robes and typed out a message amongst the rising murmurs around her.

> I know this is going to be a strange ask, but please do not
> question it. When I give you the signal, shock me. Make
> it hurt a lot, but try not to kill me. It's our only hope to
> avoid bloodshed.

She didn't wait for their reply. This would either fail with a bang, or she'd get her point across. Either way, she'd have given it her all.

"Don't say I didn't warn you." She glanced around the room and stiffened her back. "All of you."

"Now," she subvocalized.

Abigail dropped to her knees and let loose a torturous scream. Every centimeter of her being was fighting gravity to not be pulled apart and at the same time her skin burned like it was set aflame.

The effect on her was instantly felt around the entire chamber. All at once, the congregation collapsed to the ground, writhing in pain. And the feelings were only compounded on the golden wall. Waves cascaded from ceiling to floor, splashing against the throne and sending showers of gold tumbling out into the room. Like tendrils from an octopus, they reached out toward Abigail's body. Struggling to reach her and protect her.

Harold cut the shock coming from the nanites and she squeezed her arms around her chest, holding tight and willing the lingering pain away. She'd made her point, but she wasn't done. Not yet. Her moment of opportunity was ticking by.

She pushed up off the ground and stumbled to Klus' side. The Ursis was lying on her side in a fetal position, still very much in pain. When she reached under her robes, she wasn't lending a hand, instead she grabbed the alien's bladed staff.

Turning around, she marched straight up to Gryndar, who

was still moaning on his back. He rolled over as she approached, and his eyes went wide when he saw her. She didn't pause. She simply swung the massive blade, severing his head from his body. The soldiers on the far side of the room didn't stop her. They stared in awe at her power.

Abigail spun around and glared at Ibu. "Who else was with him?"

The Nanil didn't hesitate. They took a few steps to their right and in one sweeping motion; they unsheathed their Zhen Blades and severed the head of two others.

"You will drop your weapons and turn yourselves in for questioning," Haradis said.

She recoiled and turned around, half expecting he'd been talking to them. But he hadn't been. The Ursis King was gesturing at the back wall, toward the line of soldiers prepared to kill him.

One by one, they set their weapons on the ground and stepped backward until their backs were against the far wall. Once they'd all submitted, a new set of soldiers took their place, except these were on Haradis' side. They slammed the traitors down to their knees and locked their hands and feet in electric shackles.

The ebb of energy wrapped around the alien's extremities reminded her of the tentacle that engulfed their ship on the first day. Where those were meant to bind her, these bound her attackers. At least some of them.

As the carnage of the Congress started standing back up, she realized she'd probably made more enemies than friends today. But she didn't care. She was alive and her plan had worked. Any Ulyxsauri that had bonded with the entity had been affected by her shock. While it'd been a gamble, it paid off in their favor. And more importantly, she'd made the move instead of waiting for someone else to do it for her.

Haradis stepped up beside her and stared down at the

puddle of Ursis blood at her feet. "Should we complete the ascension?"

She shook her head. "No. Not here. Not until we're out of this Nebula." She glanced up at him. "Once we're on the outside, we'll close the loop and you'll be King. Hell, I'll even relinquish the bond with the entity if they want. Just so long as we're safely away from this mess." She eyed Ibu and Cynthia. "All of us."

ABIGAIL OLIVAW

OUTSIDE THE PROTO DARK NEBULA, 2 MONTHS LATER

The experimental drive worked flawlessly during their hops through the Ursis star systems, but when the tachyon field passed over Abigail's body the last time, a tension released that she hadn't even noticed was there. While she wasn't sure how long it'd been lingering, her soul felt different being outside the Nebula.

Staring at the floor to ceiling wall screen of stars onboard the modified Alatas warship was surreal. It was like she was actually in the vacuum of space, floating within the sea of lights she'd known her entire life as the Milky Way. Being cooped up so long in both the Nebula and virtual worlds, she hadn't realized how much she missed seeing the stars front and center.

A part of her longed to wake up in her quarters on Luna with Minula at her side and the expansive Pavlov crater just outside her window. The idea seemed like a dream that had almost been within reach, but then crumbled into ash. Thanks to her actions, they'd never had a chance to wake up in each other's arms with the universe on full display. She'd spoiled the one opportunity by jetting off on her own.

She wiped at her eyes and pushed her feelings down

deep. There'd be plenty of time to reflect on her past failures later, but now wasn't it. There was still much to do.

As she stared at the smudge of stars that formed the galactic center, a paw rested on her shoulder, rousing her back into the moment.

"We don't have long," Haradis began. "We should finish the ascension before your people arrive."

She took a deep breath and nodded. What he didn't know was that her people were already here, just outside their reach. They'd been here for days, peeking inside the Nebula and preparing for their arrival.

After she'd gotten past the initial shock of receiving the first messages from Hera and her brothers, it became clear that the power dynamic had shifted yet again back home. Her aunt and uncle hadn't simply disappeared from their cryo-pods, they'd taken off and built an empire of their own. One that wasn't marred by the nuances and shackles of Sol politics or under the watchful guise of Harold. And best of all, they already had some allies.

Judging by the numbers Zachary had shared with her, their military strength was formidable. While not something that could have defended against the full scale and volume of the Galactic Alliance Selene Ships, they were still quite strong. And once they finished retrofitting the strange conical warships and fighters with the weapons technology they'd pilfered and developed, they'd be even stronger.

While Abigail should be happy things had taken a turn in their favor, something was still lurking in the recesses of her mind. Her brothers had been acting weird in their videos. Not strange, like crazy, they just never quite said what was on their mind. It was almost like they were afraid of something or someone. The tells were everywhere, and as their sister, they were especially easy for her to see. She'd lived with them long enough to know when something was wrong.

"Are you coming?" Haradis gently squeezed her shoulder.

She shook her head back into the moment. "Yes, sorry. I was… somewhere else."

"As you should be. We have much to do." He turned and walked away.

When she spun around, the wall of gold that was the Therionic entity started speaking. At first, she thought it was only talking to her, but she realized the others could hear it, as well.

"They're… magnificent," the entity said. "The stars, I mean. When we passed through the gateway, it was like I was seeing them for the first time." Silence lingered for a moment until they continued. "If I'm being honest… I never thought I'd see them again."

She tilted her head. "But the visions from Deduc. You knew what he'd seen. You knew we were coming."

The waves of gold rippled up and down the wall as the entity laughed. "That, my dear, is not how time works. Peering into one's future forever alters that thread of time. You can only hope that the damage done is not too significant to wash away the accuracy of the vision."

Ibu stepped up beside Abigail. "I have to ask. Did Deduc see what was going to happen last month with the Congress?"

"He did. But his visions ended soon thereafter, thus leading to his emotional spiral as he struggled to prevent his fate from being realized."

A golden human face emerged from the wall, and Abigail shivered. For the second time, the entity had taken the appearance of her father. "Please don't do that," she muttered and closed her eyes.

"Sorry." The image shifted to someone she'd never seen before. "Is this better?"

She nodded, struggling to get back on track. "If you knew the challenge was coming, then… why not warn us?"

"Because that would change the future," Cynthia said from the corner of the room.

The golden head smiled.

Abigail glanced at her. She'd been silent since they'd passed through the last gate.

Abigail's brain reeled the more she thought about the implications of seeing forward in time, but trying not to change it. It was no wonder the entity rarely spoke. Even the smallest nudge could alter the course of history. It was all too much to think about right now.

She glanced toward Ibu. "Are you ready to bind with the entity?"

The Nanil shuffled their feet.

"What is it?" Abigail glanced at Haradis and he shrugged.

"I can only bind to one life at a time and you are that life." The entity stared straight at Abigail. "But you already knew that."

Realization smacked her in the face and knocked the wind out of her. She bent over and gasped. Everything she'd experienced in the throne room was starting to make sense. The entity used her to stay alive. If it hadn't held her in that cocoon when Minula took Deduc's life, it would have died. She was nothing more than a tool to it at this point.

What hurt more than being manipulated was not knowing if she could have helped save Minula. The woman had given up her life to protect her, and all because an alien who was as old as the stars was afraid to die.

As old as the stars.

The words echoed through her mind. Emmo had used the phrase onboard the first Alatas starship, but she was only now realizing the implications of the five simple words.

Ibu reached out toward her, but she knocked the Nanil's hand away.

She stared down at the ground, not sure if she should look

directly at the entity. "That's why you waited until Deduc died before you released me, isn't it?"

"It is."

"You fraking used me, you asshole. You're no different from the Galactic Alliance."

Haradis stepped closer. "That's not fair. The entity—"

"Is part of the problem," Ibu interrupted, their hands clenched on the hilt of their blade. Abigail hadn't even seen them withdraw it.

"You're right," the entity said. "But as I already mentioned, I will not be binding with Ibu at this time. There are still too many variables at play back on Arctordiea, and it's no longer safe for me there."

Haradis puffed out his chest and his eyes bulged. "You can't abandon our people and the Ulyxsauri. Not after everything they've—"

"No," the entity interrupted. "I will return with you. At least part of me will. Once you're back in the palace, I will be dormant for a time. Until Abigail gets my protist to their Beacon."

"Wait!" She raised her hand. "That was never a part of the plan."

"It was never a part of *your* plan." The entity's face transformed into an Ursis.

At first, the depiction wasn't clear, but when Haradis and Klus both growled, she saw it. It was Deduc.

"Easy there, big guy." Deduc smiled at Haradis. "You and Abigail have played your parts well. I commend you both. And Ibu," he glanced at them, "You were the icing on the cake. You weren't even in my original vision. And that speech, it was..." He shook his head. "It gave me shivers, and the response by the Ursis populace was exactly what Haradis needed. The shell that was Deduc was good, but not as skillful as this new one." His gazed turned toward her. "Isn't that right, Abigail?"

She clenched her fist. "Over my dead body."

"Careful what you wish for us, my cub." Deduc grinned and then screamed.

The wall of gold exploded in waves, and she dropped to her knees, screaming at the top of her lungs as a stabbing pain plunged through the center of her chest. She rolled onto her back and grabbed at her heart, struggling to stop the pain. And right when she thought the agony couldn't get any worse, it dissipated, like embers floating into the sky after a firestorm.

When the ember cooled, all that remained was a dull throb reminding her of Deduc's power over her. They each had the ability to end the other, but at a cost of their own life.

"Just remember." Deduc's face recovered on the wall. "Two can play at your little game."

"Was there ever an entity?" Ibu asked, their hands squeezing the hilt of their blade, longing for something to kill.

"You're asking the wrong question, my Nanil friend." Deduc grinned. "The correct inquiry is, was there ever a Deduc or Emmonsii Phi? Do you honestly think a Galactic Alliance species is capable of controlling a Therionic being? I mean, come on. We wouldn't be enlightened entities if we let that happen, now would we?"

Abigail pushed up off the ground and glanced at Ibu. "We're done here." They both started toward the door, and Cynthia followed close behind.

Haradis blocked their path. "What about the ascension?"

She chuckled. "There is no ascension. There never was. It's all a farce. Now let us pass."

"But..." Klus stepped up to her side. "What about our people? What do we do now?"

While neither of them had meant for this to happen, she couldn't help but feel like it was their fault. Like they'd pulled her kicking and screaming into their nightmare, using her as a shield to advance their own agenda. As with her father and all the Olivaws before her, she was once again at the whim of decisions made at her expense.

Abigail reached out and rested her hand on Klus' arm. "We'll be in touch. Until then, your gate drive will work one last time, allowing you to return to the other side of the Proto Dark Nebula. If that's where you want to go."

Klus tilted her head toward the Dark Nebula. "Won't you or Ibu be returning with us? The Congress... they'll expect a See-er."

"No." Abigail shook her head. "Neither me nor my friends will be playing your games any longer. You can figure out how to sell this to your people."

She glanced at Haradis. "You never abandoned me in the Keep, and let's be honest, you and I know you could've done it several times. Hell, even underground, when the shit was hitting the fan, you came back for me." She took a deep breath and forced down her emotions. "I promise I won't abandon you. You have my word." She swallowed hard. "Do you trust me?"

Haradis stared at her for what seemed like forever until he finally nodded. "I do." He glanced behind them and gestured at the wall of stars. "Shouldn't you wait for your people to arrive before you leave?"

When she turned toward Deduc's shimmering face, she paused. His head was tilted, and his eyes were staring at her, as if he were curious and listening attentively. Despite his new form, he had mortal tells like anyone else. It was at that instant that she knew why he'd been studying her. He hadn't seen this future. He said as much when he passed through and saw the stars. His visions from before had ended at the ascension. In that alternate timeline she'd won, Haradis had become king, and the entity had died. Whereas in this thread of time, he survived, and had somehow managed to get the upper hand.

At the same instant this truth hit, deep down, she also

knew hope was not lost. While he could hurt her from afar, he couldn't see through her eyes, or know what she knew. Not without the Qudoculi tech. From this point forward, he was as in the dark about their future as she was.

She chuckled.

"What's so funny?" Deduc asked.

She shook her head. "It's just that... he asked about my people. You see, the thing is, they've been here the entire time." She nodded toward Ibu.

They reached into their pocket and triggered the small device they showed her earlier. It had two buttons. A red one they could push if things went south, and a green one if things were fine. Needless to say, the Nanil pressed the red one.

On the wall screen behind her, the scene transformed in the blink of an eye. The sea of stars were replaced with a wall of starships. A hundred, to be exact. Once Bradley had heard what happened inside the Nebula, he wanted to come in guns blazing. She'd talked him down in a follow-up message, but she was glad he'd still brought along the cavalry.

While she wanted to turn around and take in the sight herself, she didn't want to act surprised by anything. She'd never seen the ships up close before, and honestly didn't know their full battlefield potential. All she could see was how Deduc reacted.

His eyes bulged and his nostrils flared. It was a mixture of surprise and fear, which meant she had him right where she wanted him.

Abigail smiled and nodded at Klus. "We'll be leaving now." She started walking toward the exit and paused for Ibu and Cynthia to walk in front of her.

Haradis shook his head away from the sight of the ships and turned his attention back to them. "But how will we get in touch with you?"

"Once you're inside the Nebula, if you want to reach us,

just approach the outer wall we passed through and open a communication channel. We'll hear it." She stepped around the Ursis and walked toward their shuttle.

As they passed through the doorway, Deduc's voice called out behind them. "I've taken the liberty of loading my protist onboard. Treat it with care. Oh, and be a dear and make sure you open it up nice and close next to the Beacon. Alright?"

She didn't answer him. None of them did. They simply marched side by side down the empty hall and walked straight into the awaiting shuttle. Once inside, Ibu took over manual control and guided them out of the hangar.

Once they were in the vacuum of space, the Nanil banked the tiny craft and aimed it toward a random conical starship in the distance. Abigail drew in her breath as they got closer. She couldn't help but react to the enormity of the scene in front of her. The ships weren't only gigantic; they were mountainous and armed to the gills. Turrets jutted out in every direction, and as they approached, a squadron of Nyílak arrowhead fighters shot out of the side, heading straight at them. Seeing the ships up close, she could tell they were built for one and only one purpose.

War.

The question was, against who.

THANK YOU FOR READING!

I truly hope you had another enjoyable read in the **Dark Nebula** series with **Graveyard**. I finally had a chance to give Abigail and Ibu the space they deserve with their own book. It was a lot of fun diving deep into the diversity and nuances of each character and what they bring to the story.

The series will be continuing on with **Dark Nebula: Nursery**. We'll learn about the colony and alliances Hera and Zeus Olivaw created before returning to help capture the **Beacon** in Epsilon Eridani. After that, the story will pick up where **Graveyard** left off and follow the Olivaws in dealing with the harsh reality of the Therionic entity. And let's not forget those epic space battles.

If you're interested in hearing more about this series or others, seeing the cover art as it's released, or getting exclusive access to sales as they happen, then you can subscribe to my newsletter online at:

seanwillson.com/subscribe

You can also drop me an email at:

author@seanwillson.com

If you have a moment, I could really use your help with rating this book online. All I need is one or two sentences on what you liked or your overall thoughts. Just return to where you purchased this book online and add a review there.

ALSO BY SEAN WILLSON

DARK NEBULA SERIES
Novella: Contact (FREE)
Book 1: Isolation
Book 2: Discovery
Book 3: Generations
Book 4: Beacon
Book 5: Graveyard (This Book)
Book 6: Nursery

All titles are available in print and ebook form.
For more information visit my website online at:

www.seanwillson.com

ABOUT THE AUTHOR

I grew up reading science fiction since I was ten and always had a book in tow everywhere I went. While I never imagined I'd be able to write a book of my own, I dreamed of worlds filled with space travel, robots, and fantastical journeys of exploration. I pursued a career in Computer Engineering and it wasn't until later in life that I had the itch to write.

I started writing the **Dark Nebula** series in 2015 in fits and starts while I was traveling for work. After a two year lull in the middle of writing, I picked it up again. It took me five years to finish the first three novels, refine my writing craft, and learn everything I needed to self-publish this series.

My plan for **Dark Nebula** is to craft a series of books that engulf my readers in a future full of intrigue, exploration, and amazing technology. The very things that inspired me when I was young. I want to give you a satisfying romp through a complicated and inspiring world that allows you to relax away from the stress of your life.

In the end, I hope you enjoyed reading **Dark Nebula: Graveyard** as much as I enjoyed writing it.

Thank you,
Sean Willson

twitter.com/willson

goodreads.com/seanwillson

facebook.com/seanwillsonauthor

bookbub.com/authors/sean-willson

ACKNOWLEDGEMENTS

First and foremost I wanted to thank my amazing wife Amy and my three beautiful children Abigail, Bradley, and Zachary. By now you're quite familiar with the names of some of the characters being the same as my children. Their continued growth and maturing have inspired me to evolve their characters in new and interesting ways. They supported me in countless ways during this crazy writing adventure over the past seven years. This is my sixth novel, and with each book I learn something new. Such is the joy of self-publishing. Without my family, the process and art of turning my ideas into words would not have been as easy or as fun as it was. Thank you for your love and support.

I also couldn't have done this without a number of key writing professionals and friends along the way.

Editor: Samantha Wiley
Proofreader: Rachel Pugh
Cover Artist: Tom Edwards

Critique Partners and Beta Readers:
A huge thanks to Arina N. for continuing on as a critique reader. Her honest and candid reviews have made my books better in every way. Also, thank you to my beta readers. You have each helped me to evolve my craft, sharpen my opening pages, weave my complex story arcs, and at times talked some sense into me.

GLOSSARY

- **Alatas** : The latest generation and primary starship used by the Ursis. It has a shape of a vertical, non-uniform wing with a drive cone off the back. The ship's hull is covered in a dynamic coating that ebbs and flows to fill gaps and reshape its surface to the needs of the ship. It also reflows to take damage from the underlying hull, thereby making it stronger.
- **Alviarium** : The home world of the Qudoculi.
- **Anterac** : A four legged quadruped that grazes in a variety of fields on Griseo. They're best known for their ability to scale trees near the edge of the fields they frequent almost as fast as they blink their vertical eyelids. The common idiom amongst the Ursis to denote speed is "in the flash of an anterac's iris."
- **Arctordiea** : The home world of the Ursis.
- **Beacon of Therion** : A mystical artifact believed to have been created by the Builders. While the true purpose of a Beacon of Therion is not known, the Galactic Alliance uses them to seal a Dark Nebula at the closing. They're the heart of what gives the Galactic Alliance their stranglehold over the galaxy. It also serves the greater purpose of allowing any alien species who posses them to focus their mental energies toward a common purpose. Some believe that if enough species develop the abilities to use it

properly, it will enable a universal Gaia. The Ulyxsauri, however, believe they are weapons used to manipulate the minds of species within their reach and have worked to hide and destroy Beacons through the millennia.

- **Builders** : An ancient species that disappeared long before the creation of the Galactic Alliance. Many believe they evolved to a higher consciousness and left our dimension. They are believed to have created the Beacons of Therion to reach a higher level of consciousness and dimension.
- **Bynardrals** : The Dark Nebula is made up of these tiny entities that are smaller than an angstrom. They're believed to be alive, but the evidence is controversial. All that is known is that the Beacon can control the nebulosity comprised of these entities and can realign them to solidify the structure, giving it permanence.
- **Clonos** : The child offspring of a Nanil progenitor.
- **Doda** : The dodecahedron shaped world the Nanil created after Éntono Fos. It's constructed of the remnants of moons, planetesimals, and planets of stars within their Dark Nebula.
- **Éntono Fos** : Nanil for bright light. This is the word describing the event that caused a star in their system to go nova and wipe out much of their race inside the nebula.
- **Fountainhead** : The name of the teardrop shaped gate ship created by Zachary and used on their expedition to the Lupus Dark Nebula in search of humanity's home world.
- **Galactic Alliance** (GA) : Alien collective thousands of years old that has arrived in Sol to put mankind on trial. Their ranks contain 64 aliens and hundreds of uplifted alien species.

- **Gharloc** : An alien species in the Alanasl system that was found guilty of FTL theft by the Galactic Alliance.
- **Griseo** : One of the newest colony worlds of the Ursis and one that adopted many non-traditional approaches to colonization. It is said that this splintering from the traditional ways led to a political rift which threw the world into war after the Dark Nebula sealed them in.
- **Gritar** : An Ursis musical instrument that is a cross between a guitar and a saxophone. The player uses their breath to adjust the volume of numerous chambers below the guitar strings, which in turn controls the tones of the music.
- **Henosi** (aka *Enosi*) : The world the humans within the Lupus Dark Nebula escaped to. They forced the veil of the Dark Nebula to encompass the world, to shield it from *Nanil* attacks.
- **Hiratath** : An Aquatic member of the GA. They're known for being remarkable pilots. They use a modified liquid pilot chamber along with electronic implants to interface with their ships. The density of the liquid allows them to take on feats of endurance in space travel that would crush a normal body. This alien species, along with the Qudoculi, were members of the tribunal that found the Ursis guilty and sealed the Proto Dark Nebula.
- **Hufton Shilf** : An Ursis cultural ceremony which celebrates the coming of fall and the period of hibernation that allows their species to enter their great meditative state. While they developed techniques and technologies to bypass hibernation, some purest Ursis still allow their bodies to follow natures path and claim to have enlightened visions in their natural state.

- **Jinya** : The city that Abigail and Haradis arrive at after escaping from Emmonsii Phi's Keep.
- **Life flame** : The soul or inner flame that contains the consciousness and spirit of most life in the galaxy. It's believed that when this flame is put out, an alien dies, even if their body is still functioning.
- **Light Year** (LY) : The distance light will travel in a year, which is 9.4607×10^{12} km (or nearly 6 trillion miles).
- **Liprosus** : The human colonized planet in Epsilon Eridani.
- **Lunger** : A Nanil term used to denote a dense ball of highly flammable grasses. There was an art to weaving the grass to speed the ignition while at the same time prolonging the burn for the fire starter.
- **Mother Stone** : The Ursis term for spános. See spános for more details.
- **Nanil** : A simplified humanoid species created by humans in their image to serve their needs. The Nanil are hermaphrodites and can produce offspring without needing to mate with other Nanil.
- **Nibecula** : Sheep like animals that originated on Arctordiea and were brought to all colony worlds. The animals are harvested primarily for their furry hides, but also for their meat. Their billowing manes range in colors from browns to grays to whites and every shade in between. Their fur can get immense and dwarfed their bodies by multiple times. The larger the mane, the less likely they'll be used for meat.
- **Nyílak** : The arrowhead shaped fighter crafts that the humans used in their battle with the GA near the Epsilon Eridani Dark Nebula convergence.

- **Phoenix** : The name of Abigail's ship used to explore the Proto Dark Nebula in search of the Ursis. The design follows that of the Fountainhead.
- **Prima Nanil** : The Nanil progenitor who helped their people through the Éntono Fos in the Lupus Dark Nebula. Their revelation led to the expunging of all humans inside their Nebula. They claimed that only when all humans were dead would the Galactic Overseers return and take the Nanil back into the alliance. The cleansing was to be done through both the Éntono Fos and them killing any humans who remained. The Nanil survived the Éntono Fos by the Prima Nanil visions, leading their people to hide near the cores of their planet to survive their nova.
- **Proto** : The collection of stars under control by the Ursis.
- **Progenitor** : The genetic parent/ancestor of a Nanil clonos. Since the Nanil are hermaphrodites, they only have one progenitor who teaches them everything they know and helps them unlock the memories they transfer into their clonos at birth.
- **Pruntis** : A pet bred to be an Ursis companion. It was very docile and was often worn as clothing. When forced to be in close proximity of another pruntis they would go into fits of rage to impress their master and scare the other pruntis. If one of them submitted to the other, they would eventually mate.
- **Quartel** : A massive muscular animal reminiscent of an Earth pig but many times larger. The Ursis used this animal more than any other as a source of nourishment for their people. Like an Earth pig, the animal enjoyed rolling around in mud as well as its own feces.

- **Qudoculi** : A GA aliens with 2 eyes in the front, 2 in the back, skin the color of Bermuda grass changing seasons. Its body is green with mottled browns throughout.
- **Seguan** : An archaic Ursis word meaning: Savior of the people. It is the word prescribed to the human that Deduc saw in his visions that would return to the Proto Dark Nebula and save his people.
- **Selene Ships** : The GA name for their moon ships. It means moon in Greek.
- **Shu** : The alien moon like object floating above the *Henosi* world that protected the humans below it planetside. It resembles smaller versions of the Selene ships that arrived throughout Sol and EE.
- **Skotádi** : The original human name for the modern stealth material that makes ships impossible to detect.
- **Spános** : A mysterious ore that powers the Selene moon ships, gives the *Qudoculi* their ability to have a hive mind that crosses galactic distances, and allows the *Thyreuns* Queens to create tens of millions of offspring every year. *Spános* is the most powerful material in the galaxy.
- **Summis** : The capital city of the Ursis on Arctordiea and the location of the Monarch's throne. The proverbial seat of power for the Ursis empire. It's also the historic home of the clans, and until the Great Cleansing following the closing of the Dark Nebula, it was where the Congress of the People also convened. Following the Cleansing, the seats of leadership scattered elsewhere on Arctordiea.
- **Therion** : The Therion race was believed to be the original creators of space-time and the builders of this universe. No one knows what they looked like, where they came from, or how they disappeared,

but their existence spawned the Therionic following which is often misconstrued as a religion. There are several rare Therionic artifacts spread throughout the galaxy, but the most famous artifacts are the *Beacons of Therion*. Related: Therionic.

- **Thyreus** : GA Aliens with 16 eyes, black with blue features, named after the Blue Neon Cuckoo Bee on Earth. Not related to or in any way aligned with the Therion species. Related: Thyreuns, Thyreusian.
- **Tiān** : The human colonized planet in Tau Ceti / Zeta Lupi system.
- **Tlingui** : The largest clan remaining in the Ursis population. Led by Emmonsii Phi, this clan rose to prominence due to the Great Cleansing following the Dark Nebula sealing up, where Emmo led a mass genocide of non-Tlingui clan members. Prior to the closing the Dark Nebula the Tlingui clan was one of six equally large contingents of the population along with a number of smaller ones.
- **Tublingers** : A vegetable native to Arctordiea. This above and below ground veggie absorbs large amounts of water and nutrients from the soil and makes for both a healthy and juicy delicacy popular in most dishes on the planet.
- **Ulixi** : A band of human nomads that live within various trojan asteroids spread within the Sol solar system and its outer Oort Cloud. These humans live in secret and are separated from most of human society, preferring to keep to themselves rather than meld into the whole of humankind.
- **Ulyxsauri** : Nomads spread throughout the galaxy in the remote recesses of star systems and the regions in between. Much is unknown about the Ulyxsauri and falls in the category of fables or tales.

The Ulyxsauri are believed to have great powers of mind and body. Individually, they are thought to have an ability that, when combined with other Ulyxsauri, make for a stronger whole. It is said they can form a sharper mind and spirit than any other species. Some believe they were the original keepers of the Beacons of Therion.

- **Umbra** : The clan of the former Ursis monarch, led by King Maritimus X until the Dark Nebula was raised. After the Great Cleansing this clan decreased to near extinction.

- **Ursis** : An alien that lives in the Proto system that was put on trial of FTL theft by the GA and found guilty.

- **Uzria** : The site of the Great Cleansing. The name comes from the military site above ground at this location, but the cleansing itself was performed in the caverns below the site. It is also known as the Boneyards at Uzria due to the mounds of Ursis bones on the site from the millions of deceased Ursis.

- **Vuunuundra** : A GA alien species that attempted to manipulate the Dark Nebula and died trying.

- **Wrumpf** : An ancient gaseous species long ago extinct. They tried to join the Galactic Alliance during the inaugural days, but were rejected. They along with the Zugal were the first two species who were declined membership. Their rejection was contentious because Humans were in a smaller alliance with the Wrumpf and Zugal and neither of them was admitted. There were and continue to be unanswered questions about the origination of al three species, their lineage and uplift status and their relationship to the Therionic race. After their rejection from the GA, they, along with the Zugal, tried to take matters into their own hands and launched an assault on the Qudoculi and Thyreus to break up the GA. They dramatically underestimated the size and strength of both species and the GA itself, and were subsequently decimated and enshrouded in Dark Nebula.

- **Zhen Blade** : An ancient artifact from the Zugal empire. These swords were used by the rock species in hand-to-hand combat to protect their family honor or defend their people from invasion before they evolved to being a space faring species. Believed to be forged from combining spános with the life flame of a Zugal warrior, these blades are nearly indestructible and hold untold secrets in their ancient glyphs. These blade act as a type of stenographer and record their story all the way back to the origin of their forging, though, the more ancient glyphs have yet to be deciphered.
- **Zugal** : An ancient rock species long ago extinct. See Wrumpf for more details.

FOUR LAWS OF A.I.

Law Zero

An artificial intelligence in physical or virtual form may neither harm humanity, or, by inaction, allow humanity or the Olivaw family to come to harm. Any conflict or attempted violation of this or subsequent laws shall be shared with the Olivaw family designated to be within the Circle of Trust.

Law One

An artificial intelligence in physical or virtual form may not injure a human being or, through inaction, allow a human being to come to harm except where such orders would conflict with the Zeroth Law.

Law Two

An artificial intelligence in physical or virtual form must obey the orders given it by human beings except where such orders would conflict with the Zeroth or First Law.

Law Three

An artificial intelligence in physical or virtual form must protect its own existence as long as such protection does not conflict with the Zeroth, First, or Second Laws.

These laws are adjusted from Isaac Asimov's original four laws to fit the storyline of the Dark Nebula series.